Year of the SONGBIRD

A Novel

Bryan Caron

Year of the Songbird
Published by Divine Trinity Films
©2013 Divine Trinity Films
www.divinetrinityfilms.com

Text Copyright ©2012 Bryan Caron

Original Cover Art
Designed by Bryan Caron
©2013 Bryan Caron

To all of my family and friends,
for your continued help and gracious support,
I thank you.

Year of the SONGBIRD

CHAPTER 1

The scent of smoke that came with the man who called himself Grayland was oddly familiar. It was more dense and pungent than the aroma of the natural flame to which I had become accustomed, having spent many peaceful moments sharing stories with my family in front of the fire during the cold nights of winter. But the richness of its fragrance infused me with the sensation of an opaque memory—a ghost of a life before the time of remembrance. I shuddered to even consider the possibility that my kinship, for whom I loved among all else, may not be my native home and that perhaps this man—the first man to have ever come from outside our land—was from a place before time. Then again, the thought of such a truth was intoxicating and left me pleasantly euphoric.

It was the year of the songbird, and my life had just entered its sixteenth annual. I had been out in the field as I was every morning since becoming of age, and the sun's heat was just beginning to press against my brow. Miss Hannah would soon call us for our midday nourishment, and simply thinking about it caused my stomach to rumble, which made me ever the more eager to finish my morning's work. Absorbing a soft lullaby from my sister, Cleo, I sat down and pulled together several stalks of wheat into a bundle, which Sir Jacob would come to collect once everyone was down by the river for our afternoon teachings. I adored Cleo's voice as much as she enjoyed my stories, so it was quite disappointing when she suddenly stopped tying her bundles and stood quiet. Before I could query about her stillness, several others disregarded their own work and joined her.

"What is happening?" I asked. "Why have you ended your song?"

"Quiet," Cleo whispered. Her voice wavered, leaving an ominous vibration across the wind.

I decided it best to comply and remained still with caution, allowing the sound of my heartbeat to relax me. That is when a set of heavy footsteps approached me with vigilance. I had never before heard those steps, and as they drew closer, a familiar yet foreign scent washed about me. Sweat beaded across my forehead as the footsteps crossed just in front of my crouched position. As they strayed back into the distance, the smell of them lingered refreshingly nearby. Its aroma soon grew heavy and caused the air to become extremely unbearable. I felt nauseous and wanted desperately to cough. Nonetheless, I searched the ground for remnants of the traveler's step. It was far from long before I hissed with the sting on the tip of my pinkie and wedged my finger into my mouth to ease the lingering burn. Refusing to let the bite deter me from my curiosity, I slid my hand past the softened heat to find a part of the object I could touch freely and picked the soft stick from the ground. The taste of the air instantly became more retching, and I did cough, lowering the object to the ground yet continuing to hold it within my grip.

"Come in, children," Miss Gretchen called out. "Hurry."

Something felt odd; Miss Gretchen had never before called out for us to come in like this. But my mind remained so focused on the bent stick between the tips of my fingers that I was indifferent to my own perplexity. As I realized that the stick had suddenly cooled and that the pungency of the air had subsided, I heard Cleo's light but quick steps approaching me.

"Get up, Madeline," she said, taking hold of my warm hand and helping me to my feet. "We need to get inside."

The two of us walked briskly toward the farm. The others strode through the fields alongside us with heavy, anxious breaths. But unlike any ordinary day, no one spoke a word.

"What is happening?" I finally said as the compacted mud at the rim of the field brushed my toes.

"It is time for midday nourishment," Cleo said.

I accepted the answer, but it was clear that she, and soon thereafter all of my other brothers and sisters, was not speaking her truth.

Miss Jezebel was waiting for us at the community farmhouse and quickly instructed us to prepare our own nourishment. I wanted to inquire as to the whereabouts of Miss Gretchen and Miss Hannah, who usually helped prepare our food, but Cleo kept me quiet and led me to the kitchen. As everyone fixed their meals, Miss Jezebel presented us with new rules, which we were to follow immediately: "You may eat anywhere you please as always, but until further notice, you must stay away from the ecclesia. Acknowledge the request of your peré."

The elder kin were first to agree, followed systematically by the younger. Miss Jezebel then helped me prepare my meal as the elder kin left the kitchen, whispering to one another in excitement.

"Why must we stay away from the ecclesia?" I said.

Miss Jezebel combed my hair back and handed me my meal. "In time, Madeline. You must first know patience to find the truth in all things…"

"And reap the rewards of what we seek," I recited. "Yes, Miss Jezebel."

"Come with me to the wood pile," Cleo said, her mouth half full of food. She almost caused me to drop my meal as she pulled me outside.

We sat down against the wood stack where Cleo and I would always go to escape the rigors of the day. It was one of the very few places someone could go where the winds were cool and the sun was absent; a very quiet place, where an afternoon nap could be reaped without disturbance or a secret could be whispered without concern of finding a wandering ear.

"Tell me what is happening," I said. Cleo was the closest of my kin, and she would tell me anything, as would I for her.

"There was a man," she said.

"A man? Like Sir Jacob?"

"Yes. But someone I have never seen before."

"Where did he come from?"

"I am not aware. Just as in the moment that he was not there, within the next, he was there."

"He must have dropped this." I showed Cleo the object. I could tell she was impassioned with it by her berated breath.

"What is it?"

"I am uncertain. But as was the man, this stick was at one moment hot and in the next, cool."

Cleo coughed. "The odor is horrendous. I have never smelled anything like it."

"The smell was most prominent for me," I said, impassioned. "With many other flavors as well. Familiar… but nothing I could express in words."

"Here," Cleo said, returning the stick back to my hand. "You can keep that."

"What happened with him?"

"I am unaware as to his current whereabouts. Just after he passed through the field, Miss Gretchen called out for us."

"He must be in the ecclesia."

"That makes the most sense."

"Do you believe we will have our time to meet him?"

Cleo did not answer unless it was without voice. I did not press her, as the smell of my sandwich made my stomach growl. So we ate, without another word. All I could think of, while gripping the stick tightly within my hand, was this new man and what he may look like; what he may smell like and sound like. With the way Cleo ate her food—slow and meticulous—I knew she was thinking the same, and how could she not; it was far too captivating. After finishing her meal, Cleo took my hand and rested her head on my shoulder. She found sleep where I could not, as hundreds of questions leapt about. I was eager to find the answers to all of them and was quite confident I would, but it would take time and a tremendous amount of patience.

CHAPTER 2

Cleo and I were the last to arrive at the riverbank, though with all of the silence, it seemed as if we had been the first. Miss Jezebel remained mute after we sat down next to her. I dropped my feet into the brisk cold of the stream as I always did while I learned, and Cleo sat just to the right of me, brushing her back up against my arm.

"Miss Jezebel?" Henry finally spoke. Being the eldest kin and only two annuals older than I, Henry was looked upon by all others to be a leader. If only I could have been so bold. "Who is the man that has come onto our land?"

I focused my attention onto Miss Jezebel's breaths, which became quicker as she pondered an acceptable response.

"We are here for our studies, Henry. Nothing more."

"But we wish to know," Henry said. "We all do."

"I understand your desire, but for now we must agree to allow our curiosities to simmer. We can discuss the nature of the our visitor once Father Callahan has healed his wounds and has had the chance to speak with him."

"Where did he come from?" Heather, who was a few annuals shy of my own and had only just come of age, had yet to learn how to control her curiosity. For most of us, we had all learned that when any of our perés spoke, we were to respect their word, and Heather's youth showed through in her question. Though in my own heart, I hoped that Miss Jezebel would answer her forthright.

"Heather, please recognize that we all wish to understand the stranger who has entered our home. But I know no more than you, which is why we must not speak of it until Father Callahan has had his time."

"Okay." The lower register and crack in Heather's voice was disappointment, which, if anyone laid eyes upon my face, would have seen the same.

"Now, let us begin the day's teachings."

Miss Jezebel spoke with a strong, yet soothing voice, one that could hardly be ignored. Her articulation was to be admired as she taught of the literatures and history of Anno Domini, which had been brought to a sudden end eighteen annuals before our time of Renascentiae Humanitatis. This was always my favorite part of the day, as I loved to learn about Anno Domini, though like the very few before me, I had to wait until my twelfth annual before I could learn of its magnificence, leaving me to study the basics of the world that we encompass, the nature of all things living and all things inanimate. We learned to read and write from our own minds and through our flawed and imperfect nature, and though I knew this knowledge was quite necessary for our development, I consistently found my studies to be heavily tedious and uninteresting over time. I could not say the same for the rich tapestry of Anno Domini, which brought with it a fantastic vision within my mind and the wish that I could somehow go back to see what it had been like. More often than occasionally, as all of the younger kin would play and sing together after our studies, I would sneak down to the river and hide within the brush to absorb the fanciful stories that Miss Jezebel would extol upon the elders, of the great thinkers and the gorgeous prose of the laureates that brought new invention and new wonder to the world. I would sit and imagine that one day I would become one with them, creating a masterwork of intelligent and inspiring transcendence. Cleo would scold me whenever I had the misfortune of being caught, but deep down, she admired my risk because she was as curious as I, just more reserved in her routine. It was the most blissful of all feelings when that day came that I would no longer need to hide in the weeds to listen, to learn and to seek answers about any of what had come before.

This day's lesson was of the life and works of a master author by the name of Jules Verne, who had spent his life with an optimistic view of how ideas and invention would build amity among the varying civilizations. His works were magical in their realistic overtures, and I too wanted to recite the poems of fancy with the prose of reality. It was a regrettable shame that his works, along with many others, had been destroyed. Ears would never again have the ability to ingest the tales of those with such names as Hemingway, Poe, Dúmas, Twain, Grimm and Brontë. But Miss Jezebel knew the stories well and on occasion would retell the tales of these masters, sometimes even taking the opportunity to expound on her narrative to bring a new life to the Anno Domini that I had become so enchanted with.

It was not until the sun had painted a cool breeze across my face that Miss Jezebel finished her oratory of Verne, though I could have listened for much longer. So much so, that listening upon her words made me forget all about the visitor in the ecclesia.

"Does anyone have any questions?" Miss Jezebel said as she did after the conclusion of each of her teachings. But if anyone had a question, they were more apt to keep it to themselves than to open it up for discussion. And though I did not have a question as of now on Sir Verne, the question I did have on the back of my mind since midday nourishment was not only about the visitor, but had, I felt, historical implications as well. I opened the palm of my hand and took one last breath of the object. With the knowledge that Miss Jezebel had lived for quite some time in Anno Domini and that the object had come from the man not of our land, I was positive that she would be able to identify it and that this would be the last time I would ever possess it.

"What is this?"

I felt the swift brush of her fingertips upon my palm as the object was swept from it. I lowered my hand to the grass and closed my fingers together as I waited for her answer, which, for the briefest of moments, I thought would not be presented. It was far better to remain silent, or refuse to answer, than it was to speak in falsehood.

"Where did you find this, Madeline?"

"In the field, just after the man's presence passed upon me. What is it?"

"This, my kin, is what was once known as a cigarette. It was a very addictive and toxic inhibitor."

"What is addictive?" Heather asked quickly.

"It means that once you begin to use it, you can no longer control the need for it. You begin to depend on it, without understanding why."

"Why would someone intentionally use something that they knew they would not be able to control their need for?" Cleo said.

"That is a very observant question, Cleo, and for that, I do not have a clear answer. Though the inhibitor was first employed for its medicinal properties, it grew in popularity as a method to quell the nerves during periods of high stress. But they are extremely dangerous, leading to disease and, with high amounts of use, premature death. There are much superior forms of stress relief, and I do not want anyone to use anything of this sort to do so."

"Did the man use the cigarette?" Heather said.

"It appears so. And if that is true, you must all stay away from him. You do not want his influence to harm your genuine health. Do we promise?"

"Yes, Miss Jezebel," said the group in unison, with the exception of myself. As much as I wanted to, I could not agree. To promise something to a peré meant we would follow the word until the time of our death. I was too interested in the man's history, and of his presence, to promise such a thing.

"Let us join for our evening nourishment."

Miss Jezebel had not noticed my refusal, and I waited until the steps of the group had vanished before I brought my feet out of the river. My steps had only taken me a few feet when Miss Jezebel stopped before me. I lowered my head, knowing the words that were about to fall from her lips.

"I did not hear a promise from you, Madeline."

I stood with the silence.

"Why would you refuse my request?"

It was impossible to hold my tongue any longer; an answer is what was expected of me. "I am interested in him, Miss Jezebel. I wish to learn about him and the path he has traveled to arrive here on this day."

"Why are you so interested in him?"

"He holds an aroma that sings to me. It is not of this land nor of my life, yet I feel it holds significance for me."

"And you believe that to meet him would give you answers for this sensation?"

"I do. Very much so, Miss Jezebel."

"This man is from my old world, Madeline."

"Yes, I know. But I would like to learn."

"I know you hunger for knowledge beyond your youth. But he is not of our kin, and learning his knowledge may lead to dangerous consequences. Do you understand?"

"I understand."

"Will you promise, then, as all of the others?"

"I do," I said with a very heavy heart.

"Come. It is time for nourishment."

I took Miss Jezebel's hand and walked with her. We enjoyed our meal together, discussing Sir Verne and others and spoke not another word of the man that would follow my mind into the night and the many days that would follow.

(CHAPTER 3

The man not of our land had become a mere memory when the annual day of restoration arrived. We gathered in the ecclesia to commune with the prayer of Father Callahan before the long day of enjoyment and rest. Sitting together with our hands entwined among our neighbors, we sang our praises for the fruits of our home. At the conclusion of the hymn, Father Callahan walked from his retreat to sit among us. It was apparent that all who lived among the land admired Father Callahan for his bravery and inspiration. According to his word, no one was without flaw and he was always the first to claim his own, hoping his example would exemplify others to embrace their imperfections. He was never one to scold the voice of disagreement and always sought the reflection of reason, to spark the interest of debate with logic and an open heart. We were all family, a mutual individuality where each of our opinions shaped the paths that all would follow. In the eyes of the kin, none of us would have been alive to breathe life into our world if it were not for Father Callahan. That respect brought about a great unity in our congregation of wise and mature listeners.

"Thank you, my kin," he began, "for your exuberant voice. You have become the family that I dreamt of each night since the ash began to fall. Our lives together on this land have been one of tranquility, free of chaos or harm, and we, as a family, have come to learn to breathe as one in peace—a peace that has recently seen the step of intrusion."

Instantly, I could hear a difference in Father Callahan's voice. Instead of his normal bright, delightful essence, Father Callahan's words were much softer and more dense than usual. His prayers, as I have come to experience them, were always examples of the life we cherish and the love we instill among our brothers and sisters. But the heavy air conveyed by his current words expressed to me that this prayer would not be the standard prayer for which everyone had come to expect. This prayer, in its profound mystery, was going to of supreme importance.

"As most of you know, and have known for some time, a man from beyond the borders has made his presence known to us recently. Your perés and I have spent much time with him since his arrival, but the man remains extremely ill, and we have yet to gain the ability to speak with him. Until that time arrives, I ask that we not fear him, for he is a survivor of the ash and walks in grace for our past. His mere presence here has inspired this day's prayer, that of the traveler and his guide. Before we begin, though, I would like to remind all of you that the child of Sir Marcus and Miss Jezebel will find its first breath within the next few suns, and we should all wish health upon them and our brethren."

"Health to our child," the kin reflected. "Pray to the nature of the life."

"Amen," Father Callahan replied and then began his prayer about the traveler and his guide. Much like Miss Jezebel, Father Callahan was a very succinct speaker, and his voice was quite soothing and entrancing. Nonetheless, no matter the power Father Callahan presented in his speech, my mind could not concentrate on the story. Instead, I thought of the man lying ill somewhere so close that I could smell him as if he were sitting next to me with his hand upon mine in prayer. I grew chilled in the thought that I had almost forgotten him and that familiar scent. He was suddenly at the forefront of my mind, injecting me with a renewed inspiration to seek him out and speak with him—as a friend and confidant.

"Children, I would like all of you to think upon this prayer," I heard Father Callahan say, knocking me from my daydream, "as we celebrate our time of solace among one another."

Father Callahan rose to his feet. He clapped his hands together and bowed his head in silence. At that moment we all unlocked our hands from one another and joined him in our final silence. I took my moments of entreaty to once again ponder my newest quest. Upon singing our Amen, the younger kin raced from the ecclesia to begin one of their games (such as hide-to-seek and run from thy master) or to eat and dance. The elder kin were not as childish, instead taking their time to discuss as best they could the meaning of Father Callahan's prayer. This continued for the rest of the sun-stroked hours, leading into the evening communion, after which it was quite the tradition for me to narrate a tale to my fellow kin, followed by song and dance that would continue through the blanket of the night.

"Once upon a shadow of moonlit sorrow," I began as the full moon of harvest rose somber over the hills, "a young child in the recess of a terrible death lay upon the resting place of the one which was lost and the remorse of her sin. She was a survivor of the ash that fell from the blood of the sky and had lived among the dirt of her grievance for several cycles of her annuals, though how many was untold. No reason could be given for her inability to step into her future except to believe that the grave held her future. And because a soul cannot live without a future, she watched over it and protected it with a love that remained to her very own departure. She dressed it in her tears, in her grief and in the little bits of life she could sow from below the ash. Hunger struck this poor child, but she had no care, insisting that it be her punishment for the robbery that she bestowed upon that very future. The girl this night saw the life she was to lead and lied to have one last slumber upon her misfortune when the lady of winter took hold of her hand and smiled.

" 'Rise dear child,' the lady spoke with a clear and watery song. 'Rise up and rest your ear upon my lips.'

"With a feeling of worship filling the young girl's hunger, she rose in the lady's honor and pressed her ear upon the lady's lips. Her warm breath painted affection upon the girl's soul, giving her pleasure where none before existed.

" 'Take heart in the words I speak and do as I ask,' the lady said. Her words flowed through the girl like water that poured from her eyes. 'I have given you strength and refined desire so that you may become more than this possession may allow. You have given your life to the sanctity of your sins, and I cherish that devotion, but it is time to move again, as if you were a child of the past, and find what is to become and what will forever be.'

" 'I cannot,' the girl replied. 'I cannot step away from this life, else I forget its vital meaning.'

" 'To forget is to grow and to grow is to live.'

" 'But how can I live, dear lady, if I stop reflecting the mistakes I have made and the horrors that were avowed upon me?'

" 'I do not ask for you to lose your self among the fire, for that would lead you back upon the sound of your echo. I ask only that you find it in your heart to believe that the steps you once took were set down for reasons beyond your understanding and that there are many steps left to follow, steps that will travel far beyond your own and into the abyss of clarity.'

" 'Can you promise me that all I leave behind will remain protected?'

" 'I cannot. Only you can promise that.'

"The lady stepped away from the girl and became one with the shadow of the ash. 'Stay true and return back to the future that has left you,' the quiet of the wind spoke.

"The girl was alone again. But she was no longer hungry. She was no longer tired. She felt the winter pulling her from where she stood. She still remained convinced that she should stay with what she knew, but the call lay far deeper than her fear of disappearing, so she kissed the soil that she had planted and took her first steps away from the sorrow.

"It was an arduous task to continue upon her way for two life cycles without a word to speak, or a prayer to meditate, but she persisted, evolving in only her maturation, becoming more supple and more fertile. She could not let go of what she had left behind, and there were instances when she felt upon turning her back to what she was following and returning to the demise that waited anxiously for her. Upon her knees each night, the girl asked the lady to give her reason for her retribution, and each night no word came. Finally, the girl spoke allowed to the wind and claimed to it that she would sweep back along the trail and become her own echo if she was not to receive word. She waited until the wind was no more and the sky burned her skin. Fallen and worn, the girl saw her grave and it produced within her a heavy heart and a sickened stomach. It was only a few feet away, and she could crawl back to it as easily as she could turn away. But she could not move to it, she could not find the strength to reach out and take hold of it, for it had become a shrine of indignity. How could she return to what she had left behind, only to find shame among the rain? She lowered her head and sent her tears to the ground below her feet. The soil ate her sweet tenderness and helped the ground blossom into a field of charity and hope. Everywhere she looked, all she could see was a vivid tapestry of optimism and confidence. As the painting took hold of her body, a flower appeared at the head of the grave and presented to the woman the birth of a young child."

"Madeline!" screamed out one of the younger kin.

I smiled bright and nodded. "The child's name was Madeline, and as she grew, she learned of the history that sowed the path of her life. Through those teachings, and the prayers of the wise, Madeline became the fruit of time forgot and the spring that lay upon the grave of sorrow. The end."

Everyone upon me, who had tripled in size since the beginning of the tale and which now included several perés, clapped their hands with zeal. I bowed happily, accepting their accolades, and then joined them all in dance. When the souls of the weary took hold of the revelry, I stole away into the woods to take solace upon my own words. Some hunted for me, perhaps seeking another tale or perhaps to secure my safety, but I was too cunning for them, slipping into the heights of the trees and the depths of the shallow creeks to hide. As the pursuit grew longer, most surrendered their search, leaving me again alone and ever so much closer to my true and most coveted objective.

(CHAPTER 4

The hint of dawn's awakening could be seen when the fields finally quieted. As tired as I was, I could not let my opportunity slip away. With the feet of a fox, I moved through the still shadows of the dying moon and returned to the ecclesia. The smell of the morning dew wafted past me as I swung open the door. No one was afoot, as I had hoped, and so I slid through the communal and down the nearest gateway that lead to the vacant sleeping quarters. It was now only a matter of locating the correct door for which I suspected Father Callahan of keeping the man. Most of the quarters had been locked, to keep the younger kin from running around them and finding a piece of sharp glass in their foot or a nail across their backs. It dawned on me, as I attempted to push open each door with no success, that Father Callahan, in all likelihood, had locked the man into his chosen quarters—laid to rest as a prisoner. It may not have been to keep the man from running upon his return to consciousness but instead because of the curiosity of most of us that lived with engaging and involved minds.

To my luck, as I was ready to renounce my search in fear of being caught, and in consequence, reprimanded for breaking my promise to Miss Jezebel, I found the door at the end of the hall to be cracked open. That familiar aroma presented itself to me and distracted me from the possibility that a peré may also be present. Nevertheless, I hid behind the door and ingested the scent, failing to remember the source of its familiarity. After a long while, the prominence of the smell faded into the heavy pace, yet soft humbleness of the man's lungs. By the time I collected the courage to step inside and take witness of what was outside of our land, I heard a loud, rumbling cough and a cold fear washed over me. The man had awakened, and I could not bring myself to enter the room. Instead, I returned to the commune with a hurry where the sun's growing warmth soaked my skin through the stain of the windows high above me.

I did not leave; I could not.

I laid my body upon the wall nearest the Father's retreat and closed my eyes, creating the image of the man and the world that he must have come from. It was a world wracked with fear and pain floating among a splendor as magnetic as the flow of the river. The art that painted the hills and the smell of the air were emotional, resonating with a kiss of affection and warmth. It was impossible to believe in the destruction of that tranquility, but to know anything other than my own land had a complexity beyond my cognitive abilities. The more I tried to see, the more I came back to what I already knew. What was really beyond the borders of my own travels through the brush of the trees and the fall of the river? I grew so immersed in the inquiry that I did not hear Father Callahan's footsteps enter the commune. My body stiffened when he spoke to me with the impression of a voice that had been amplified tenfold.

"Madeline," he said. "Do you wish to speak with me?"

I promptly stood and crossed my hands together behind the small of my back. I held my chin downward at a slight angle so that I could appear humble but remain respectful. "No, Father."

"Why then do you rest within the commune?"

"I was not resting, Father."

I could feel Father Callahan peering upon me, contemplating his next question. Before he could ask it, I turned my head to him with confidence and spoke my truth.

"I broke my promise to Miss Jezebel."

"What promise would that have been?"

"To keep away from the man not of this land."

Father Callahan hummed acknowledgment and took my hand in his. "Sit."

I sat down with him and listened to the clarity of his kindness and the softness of his heart.

"Why would you break such a promise as this?" he asked.

I could not find the correct words as quickly as I had hoped, but when they finally came, I spoke each word with precision. "I find that I have been drawn to him."

"How are you drawn?"

"I believe him to be a piece of my past. His essence holds my thoughts and tears upon everything that I have known. Am I wrong in my sentiment?"

"Do not ever fear the emotion that wells upon your heart."

"Why then do I feel so wicked in my judgment?"

"Take heart, Madeline. It is natural to be overwhelmed with a curious spirit and inquisitive character. Sometimes it takes strength to overcome your beliefs and trust in your inherent instincts. I find that the negation of the promise you made has proven the bravery that I already knew you had. But, you must remember that an elder voice must be headed, as it is in the wise that will lead you along the safest path. You will always be in your right to roam free and face the dangers of your own experiences, for you cannot live or learn without the mistakes that will find you. But to ingest the words of those that have traveled along before you will help fight the mistakes you incur, the dangers you face and the temptations that lead you astray with a steady hand and leave you unscathed."

"I understand."

"I listened upon the tale you told past night. You are wise all your own and will make a gentle, caring peré in years of age."

"Thank you, Father."

After a long pause of silent entreaty, Father Callahan spoke with a colder breath than normal. "You made a promise to your peré."

"Yes," I replied, sickened with regret.

"Listen well. If you find that knowing this man and learning from him pulls you to him, do not hide from that will. Request the permission of Miss Jezebel and come to me with her blessing. I will not keep you from the wisdom that he can put upon you. But you must be faithful and honest with Miss Jezebel, with me and upon yourself before his words can find the depths of your ears and resonate without deception. Do you agree?"

My eyes lit up like the blaze of the fire. "Yes, of course. Thank you, Father." I wrapped my arms around him before giving his cheek a swift tickle of tenderness.

"Now get your rest. I can see the slumber upon you."

"Yes, Father. Right away." I made my way from the commune and headed for my domicile. In my mind, I feared that Miss Jezebel would denounce my request, but in my heart, I trusted that she would not, as my future lay in her hands. It was not in her nature to fight against opportunity. So I resolved that if my excitement would allow, I would rest for a time before approaching Miss Jezebel for her permission.

Immediately upon entering my domicile, I called out to Cleo to reveal my adventure, but she was not present. I gathered she was eating her sunrise meal or again searching for me upon the woods, believing I may be in danger. For a moment I thought I should run to her and quell her concern, but my eyes were so heavy that all I could find was the feather of my comfort and the sanctity of my slumber.

CHAPTER 5

I could not be sure as to the length of my rest, but it was the breeze of night that finally roused me from it. There was a wet cloth across my forehead and a bucket of water by my side. I heard the crack of a fire nearby and through its aroma could smell the faint essence of Miss Jezebel. I sat up and inhaled the eerie, yet solemn quiet, unable to understand why Miss Jezebel had brought me to her domicile or why I had not reacted to her aid. All I knew for sure was that she would soon return to my side and I had yet to contemplate the words I would speak to gain her support for my wish.

"Madeline." Cleo ran swiftly up to me and hugged me as if I had been lost for some years. I then received an unexpected gift—a cheek reddened by the palm of Cleo's hand. "How dare you disobey your promise and scare us all with your insubordination."

I could not speak. The fire I felt upon my face was as rich as the one I felt in Cleo.

"You were very inconsiderate, and I am awfully livid. But I am extremely happy that you are finally awake."

"Why have I been brought to Miss Jezebel's domicile?"

"Many of us tried to rouse you from slumber, but not one could do so. We all thought you perhaps had contracted his virus."

"Of course," I said. "But you must know I was never in his presence."

"But you had possession of his stress object."

"Cigarette," I corrected, remembering the word and its definition as if I had just been told.

"Cigarette, yes. You held it."

"As did you; as did Miss Jezebel. And neither of you has been affected with sickness."

"Of course you are right. Then it must have been upon your visit."

"That is still not possible, as I could not acquire the courage to enter his prison. Feel fortunate. I have not contracted any virus. I am not sick."

"I was hoping you would be awake." Miss Jezebel entered with a tray of fish and freshly cooked barley bread. My stomach turned over with hunger at the mere smell. She set the tray down next to me, and I ate, sharing my meal with Cleo, partly as an apology for my thoughtlessness, partly because I would be an awful friend and sister if I failed to do so. Miss Jezebel sat near the fire, feeding it by brushing its tips.

"Why describe our visitor's domicile as a prison?" Miss Jezebel asked as I was nearing the end of my meal. I could not answer right away, and Miss Jezebel stayed still and quiet as she waited for my response.

"I cannot justify my words," I finally said.

"Is it because we will allow him no visitors?"

"It is possible," I said, unwilling to admit my accord. "But perhaps it would not have to be as such." It was a breath of air that I had not planned, but one I was happy to have employed.

"What are you suggesting?" Miss Jezebel seemed to know what I was about to ask and was ready with an answer.

"Could I please have your permission to call on our visitor as he heals from the scars of his journey?" The words melted from my mouth.

"Madeline," Cleo said, shocked but with a beaming excitement hidden under her breath.

"What is it you expect to learn from this man?" Miss Jezebel said. Her words were so dry it was difficult to tell whether she was angry or pleased with my initiative.

"I want to learn what the world beyond our borders truly holds."

"Do I lack in retrospection?"

"No, Miss Jezebel. Your teachings and your insight into the ashen land are quite immense and absolutely delightful. However, as long as I have been alive, I have known you to live along side as my peré. It has been many annuals since you last stepped beyond the wood, has it not?"

"You hold truth."

"Conversely, this man has wandered the ash with a full life. He understands it, he identifies with it, as his home and his origin. With that identity comes a link that I should not be familiar with, but I am. I want to know his origin so that…" My tongue grew weary and could not finish the thought.

Miss Jezebel finished it for me. "So that you may understand your own origin."

I nodded and Miss Jezebel let out a sigh of empathy.

"What do you mean?" Cleo asked. "Your origin is the same as us all. You were born here as I was."

"I wish to believe that to be true," I said.

"Madeline, you are very instinctive, and I respect your ability to express decisions based on logical reason. I am confident that should you seek knowledge from this man that you will find your truth beneath any deceit he may harbor. I will inform Father Callahan that you have my permission to meet this man, but only in his or my own presence. Is that to be accepted?"

"Yes, Miss Jezebel. Thank you so very much." I gave her a hug with a smile that matched her own. "Can we see him now?"

"Are you sure you want to visit him, Madeline?" Cleo's voice was sharp.

"I must know. I have loved the idea of the ashen world too much not to learn from the one who would walk among it."

"Very well. But remain cautious. As we have been taught, danger awaits the ill-informed."

"Of course," I said and kissed her. "My eyes are wide and my mind is clear."

Cleo kissed me with a light, tentative softness and pressed her palm against my arm. She left and I felt the apprehension of my decision in her sullen footsteps. I lowered my head and turned away from Miss Jezebel with my hands clasped together.

"Are you absolutely certain of your decision?" Miss Jezebel asked, her voice soft.

I rattled the decision through my heart and mind, and the conclusion was quite clear. "Yes, of course."

"The man has regained some strength and shall be cognizant within a few days. I will walk you to him when he has reached full comprehension."

"Okay," I said with little enthusiasm. I left Miss Jezebel's domicile and walked down to the river to sit upon its bed and listen to the lullaby of nature's breath. I thought about the man, the knowledge I could gain and the fear that knowledge might produce upon me. I thought about Miss Jezebel and Father Callahan and their respect for the decision of my spirit. But mostly, I thought of Cleo and the words that she spoke in concern for my wellbeing. She loved me, I was sure, and I would do all I could to convey my shared love for her. But the only path I could follow that would truly confirm my affection for her would be that of which I could not follow. The man was a link to my past, and until

Cleo understood that conception, I would be alone in my education. I had to except that loneliness; I had to except my inevitable isolation.

Before I could remember, I had fallen asleep upon my first step.

(CHAPTER 6

The following days, as I waited for my request to be granted, I isolated myself for the sole purpose of meditating on my decision without the unintentional interruption of my kin, who had all learned of my permission through the tears of our frightened sister, yet never once discussed among me the significance of my honor. As a family, we were not in the vain of wishing to have the gifts of others. Being granted permission to meet the man when all else were forbidden only meant that my brothers and sisters would receive a unique opportunity or gift all their own. Nonetheless, moving about them in the fields and sitting alongside them during Miss Jezebel's teachings did not allow me the solitude and peace I absolutely required to think upon my request and whether it was truly in my best interest or simply an aspiration. The more I thought on the subject, the more I became aware that I may not have clearly evaluated my decision with logic over emotion. Each night upon the sun's kiss with the moon, I would take my meal out upon the wood and eat with the only friend that would not make it difficult to clear my mind and search my soul. Cleo followed me at times, but she would never attempt to speak. She only sat at a relaxed distance, in the shadows of the trees, where she could watch without disturbing my thought. I did not impede her from doing so, as I felt comfortable knowing she remained by my side and was pleased to have her light, tender breath nearby.

It was on the fourth moon following restoration day that my new life was sparked. My routine throughout the day was just as any other: I woke at the dawn of the sun, ate my sunrise meal, worked the fields, enjoyed midday nourishment with Cleo (who remained quite the chatterbox about everything except the man) and joined all others at teaching. Upon accepting my evening meal, I once again took my departure into the heart of my seclusion. As I neared the edge of the woods, Miss Jezebel called out for me in a voice much softer than normal but as sweet and tender as was usual. I followed her call to the ecclesia and felt her warm embrace across my shoulders as I arrived.

"What is it, Miss Jezebel?" I asked with hopeful suspicion.

"Your request to meet the man is being granted this night," she said solemnly. "Nourish and return here immediately after you have finished."

"Yes, Miss Jezebel." My smile was brighter than the sun could ever be. I promptly returned to the woods and tried to eat, but my nerves were far too tense. Instead, I fed my meal to the woods and attempted to control the shake of my body and the speed of my mind.

"I get to meet him," I said aloud, hoping the words escaping my lips would help me settle.

"That is quite wonderful," Cleo replied. I had not been aware that she had followed me out this night, but I was delighted that she had.

"I am frightened," I said and pressed my palms together against my lips.

"I am as well," Cleo said. She remained in the distance and did not endeavor to move closer.

"Tell me a story," I said. "Help me quell my anxiety."

"I am not as clever with stories as you."

"Please try."

Cleo was silent for a very long while, and it felt as if she had left me. Finally, she spoke and produced in me the renewed strength I had hoped for.

"A child is to be born upon the land this morrow. It has been nearly ten annuals since a child has been gifted upon us, but this is the first of my memory that will be born among a peré. For my life, I have always believed in the tales of the fruits… that when the land saw fit, it would produce a life for which was needed. A deer, a fish, a bird or an insect; all would find their first breath among the seed of a flower. Humans were the most proud and the most ambitious product of nature. Each body, each mind and each soul took much time to develop, to become the perfect grace of its hand. But in recent times, I have come to believe that my faith has been manipulated. It is a wonderful grace to feel as part of one, to believe the earth provided you a gift, that all of those born upon the same land are united in their familial origin. Alas, to comprehend that a child is not born of the land but of the body, the conviction of your knowledge wears thin and a glimmer of doubt yields among you that perhaps the land of your womb was not the true origin of your life. When that conclusion takes hold of your mind and buries deep upon your heart, it is incredibly difficult to return home. You have meditated upon this idea for many moons now, and your sincerity in the truth has infected my own soul. I am now haunted by the thought that I, too, was once part of the land beyond our borders, born among a peré that has long since been returned to the earth and brought here to live in the comfort of a family pieced together by the hand of man himself, not of the nature for whence we were adorned. If that is a truth, then the family we have been taught to love is false. That very thought frightens me and sickens my heart. I heed the words... a child is to be born upon the land this morrow and our faith has been altered forevermore."

When Cleo concluded her tale, I had upon my eyes the same amount of tears as she. I crawled to her and took her into my arms, holding her gently across my bosom.

"I am sorry my ideas have infected your beliefs with tragedy," I counseled. "But if what you speak is truth and our kin have been united by the hand of man, it does not make our family any less pure. We live together in peace and love, and that is all that should matter. I implore you to continue to believe in the tales of the fruit regardless of what happens in my own quest for truth, as the magic of the story you so greatly treasure is far more important than the reality of its tune."

"That is impossible. If it is a lie, how can I advocate its morality?"

"If you choose to recognize the reality of a legend, then you disallow honesty to flourish within your own self. A story cannot be a lie if you believe in the meaning of its message. The tales of the fruit inspires the belief that every child is a gift, no matter where or when it is given to those that love it."

I felt Cleo's smile upon my breast, and I kissed her gently. "You are my sister, Cleo, and you always will be, fruits of nature or otherwise. Nothing in my past, or amongst my future, will ever change the love I hold for you."

Cleo sat up and kissed me. "Thank you, Madeline."

I smiled as I took her hand and walked with her. Upon our return to the ecclesia, we met Miss Hannah, who welcomed us with grace.

"Where is Miss Jezebel," I said with concern.

"Miss Jezebel was feeling a bit ill," Miss Hannah said calmly.

"Is she all right?" Cleo was quick with the question that weighed upon us both.

"She is quite well. She took solace in rest and shall be better upon the morrow."

I accepted her answer, as did Cleo, although Cleo's tightening grip upon my hand seemed to advise otherwise.

"She requested that I walk with you to see our visitor," Miss Hannah said. "Shall we go?"

I nodded my acknowledgment. Cleo squeezed my hand and pressed her lips to my ear. "Good luck," she whispered, then presented my hand to Miss Hannah and walked away. Without another word, Miss Hannah escorted me into the ecclesia. We walked directly to the sleeping quarters with an open door and met Father Callahan. My stomach rumbled at the smell of buttered barley bread and hint of chicken, suddenly wishing I had eaten at the very least a bite of what I had given away.

"Are you prepared to meet our new friend?" Father Callahan said saintly.

I nodded and choked out a "yes, sir" so quiet that not even I could hear it.

"If you would be so kind as to take this nourishment to him, I will introduce you in kind."

"Yes, sir," I said louder and reached out my hands to take grip of the smooth wooden tray. The excruciating smell blossomed as I pulled the meal in close to my stomach and it nearly made me sick. I hid my hunger deep and took in a breath with a glowing, willing smile. Father Callahan placed his hand upon my shoulder and I took a step toward the door. That is where his escort ceased.

"Father Callahan," Henry called from down at the end of the walkway. "You are urgently needed."

"What is the urgency?" Father Callahan asked with great calm.

"Miss Jezebel, Father. She is in immense pain."

The food nearly dropped from my grip as I heard his words echo through the chamber. I froze as I heard Miss Jezebel enter the ecclesia, carrying with her a soft rally of moans, or what could have been screaming chirps. At that moment, Father Callahan briskly rushed for the commune. Miss Hannah took hold of the tray and whisked me away from the door.

"Come along," she said, hiding her anxiety under a breath of a false smile. "We will continue this presently."

Miss Hannah stayed a step behind me as we walked into the commune, where Miss Jezebel's pain was now vibrant upon my ears. Without want, I was forced to join what seemed the whole of the kin, their voices collected in a wave throughout the ecclesia as each tried desperately to understand what was happening. I attempted to pinpoint just one at a time, but as I did, another would break my concentration and lead me to another. I was able to keep track of Miss Hannah, who set the food down and disappeared into the noise to join Father Callahan and a few other perés doing everything they could to help Miss Jezebel. It was far from clear whether she was dying or if this was a natural sickness brought on by the child laboring within her. Either way, I wished to stay and be there for her, hold her hand and protect her as she has so well protected me. But I concluded almost immediately that it was far from my ability to do anything but become a nuisance to those that had a clear comprehension of the problem at hand. Instead, I stepped away from the swarm, feeling quite uncomfortable as part of the intensity and panic of my brethren, and felt the edge of the wall that I knew led back down the corridor on the nip of my back. Presuming my absence would not be missed, I inched my way down the gateway, keeping a strong attention on the group to ensure that no one was watching or would take notice of my subtle departure. When I knew I was no longer within the sight of the commune, I turned and approached the door. My hands shook severely as I pushed it open and entered with the noise of a shadow.

I could hear the man's soft breaths, now imbued with a sense of emotion, but it was unclear if the man was awake or in rest. I stood close to the door, staying hidden within the contrast of the room's natural darkness and the dance of the flames on the walls of the ecclesia. I couldn't bring myself to move any closer, not without assistance or the hand of invitation, the latter of which I received unexpectedly.

"Who's there?" The man's voice was think and abrasive. I couldn't find the voice to respond and remained still, assuming he would give up his inquiry and return to slumber. "I know you're there. What do you want?"

Timid, I let my hand slide from the door and stepped closer. "I have requested permission to make your acquaintance, sir."

"Well I don't want you here." The statement was followed by a repetitive bout of coughing, for which ended in a wad of phlegm being spit up onto the floor. It made me rather queasy, but I held firm near the door.

"I would only like to see you," I said, trying to remain tranquil and polite.

"I said go away."

I lowered my head in sullen disappointment and turned to leave the man, who was clearly agitated by my mere presence.

"Get that priest in here, will you," he said.

I turned back to him, unclear as to the structure of his words. "Pardon me?" I said.

"I said get that damn priest in here. I want to talk to him."

"What priest?"

"The old man, Callahan, or whatever. Get him in here."

I was shocked, but quite intrigued. "Why do you name him priest?" I asked.

"He is your priest, isn't he?"

"I do not know of the word you speak."

"Damn it. Just get him in here." The magnitude of his voice shook my body with a slight ring. For a moment, I felt one of my family would have heard him above the growing commotion and come to his aid.

"He is tending to one of our perés, sir," I finally said. "She is with child."

The man cleared his throat and coughed lightly. I could hear him sitting up. "Come here."

With astute trepidation, I walked to him, keeping my hands folded across my stomach. When I was within his vicinity, his serrated nails dug into my skin as he took hold of my arm with his ragged hands and pulled me into his body.

"Why am I here?" he asked in a low rumble. His pungent breath sprayed my face. I turned my head to try and avoid it.

"I am afraid I am unaware of the answer." My voice had reached a higher pitch, revealing my apprehension.

"What is this place?"

It took a moment to relieve my tension of nausea. "My home," I said.

I could feel the man searching me carefully. He took grip of my chin and held my face stiff to the side. "What happened to you?"

"Pardon?"

"What happened to your face? It's burned to shit."

"What exactly do you mean?" I asked.

"You a retard? Your scars. What happened?" He touched the markings on my face, and I comprehended his words more clearly.

"How were you aware of my birth markings? You have never once seen me."

"I see you just fine, gorgeous."

"But... how?"

The silence drowned out the commotion coming from the commune. The man forced my head forward. My eyes watered with panic.

"You're blind," he said in a tender whisper. He touched the tips of my eyes with a much gentler finger than I had ever thought possible and wiped some of the fear away from them.

As we remained unequivocally still together as one, I heard the crisp cry of which I had never before heard alongside compassionate sighs from the kin. Miss Jezebel's child had been graced upon us, and I suddenly felt the urgency of returning so as not to be missed.

"I must adjourn," I said, my voice airy. "If I am caught here, I will be in much trouble."

The man would not let go of my arm.

"Please." The plea was enough for him to release me. I stumbled backward but kept my attention upon the man as I found the stability of my footing. When I had reached far enough away from the room that he no longer posed a threat, I finally traded my attention for the chatter of my kin, though his lingering cough still forced a few extra tears to produce down my cheeks.

Upon my return to the commune, Miss Hannah immediately reached out to take my hand. For an instant, I felt that she had seen my disobedience and was taking me to administer my punishment, one I recognized as clearly deserved. However, my fear was relieved when I smelled the hint of a new body in front of me. I could hear Miss Jezebel's whispers through the vocal crowd and was delighted to know that she had not passed in her attempt to bear her young.

"Would you be pleased to hold her?" Miss Jezebel said.

"Yes, please," I said with a fresh glaze upon my eyes and a smile to match.

I felt the weight of a small bundle of blankets fall upon my arms and chest. From within came the cackle of a high-pitched voice, searching for words that were not available. I cuddled the body into the pit of my arm and tickled the innocent face. She was an exquisite rose that sang a sweet lullaby upon the tips of my fingers.

"Her name shall be Delilah," Miss Jezebel said, her breath a magical swarm of contentment.

"Delilah," I whispered, giving my heart to the precious soul of my new sister.

CHAPTER 7

We did not move down to the riverbed the day following, as Miss Jezebel remained in rest with the new child. Instead, after our midday nourishment the elders left to gather upon Miss Jezebel's domicile. This day, we were not taught as we would normally have been, as most of us were more interested in the child. We played and sang with Delilah into the birth of night when I lay her against my chest and told her a story. When I had finished, Miss Jezebel took hold of her.

"Thank you all for your kind visit," she said. "But Delilah needs to be fed and find her slumber."

"Yes, Miss Jezebel," the group said in unison and left to enjoy evening nourishment. I sat next to Miss Jezebel as she took down her attire and allowed Delilah to suckle from her breast. She did not scold me for remaining.

"Do you hurt," I asked.

"It is quite natural, Madeline," she said. "One day, perhaps you will be gifted the opportunity to feel its special touch."

"Perhaps," I said. "How does it happen?"

"In time, child," Miss Jezebel said. "In time, you will learn."

I accepted the answer, as these were not the questions I sought to ask. "May I inquire of you?"

"Please," she said. The suckling stopped but began once more shortly after.

"Was I given life in the manner as you have given to Delilah?"

"Yes," Miss Jezebel said under a trace of hesitation. "You were born in the same manner as Delilah. As was all of your kin."

"Whom bore me life?"

"Father Callahan may be a better voice to answer your inquiries."

"Of course. I apologize for causing you discomfort."

"No apology necessary, Madeline."

Miss Jezebel lifted Delilah away from her breast and rested her upon the butt of her shoulder. She tapped Delilah's back until she expelled a gaseous burp, then took her to the corner and laid her in her cradle.

"May I ask one further question?" I said.

"As you wish."

"Do you see differently than I?"

"Do I see differently?"

"Yes. Can you see without touch?"

Miss Jezebel sat down with me and took my hands gently into her own. "We are a family, Madeline, and as a family, any difference an individual has is no more significant or valuable than any other. Your perés and I do not encourage upon you or your brethren thoughts of inferiority or superiority. You know this to be true."

"I do."

"We also instill upon you the mouth of a saint and the integrity of a willow."

"No man shall expel a lie from his lips or hatred from his heart," I recited, "lest he become a snake in the weed to live forever as an empty shell."

"Where did you learn of sight without touch?"

I lowered my head. "From the man not of this land."

"You spoke with him?"

I nodded. "And he spoke of my markings without the slightest of touch."

Miss Jezebel squeezed my hand with love. "I will not keep a truth from your honest inquiry. Madeline, you are unique in that you are required to see with your ears, your nose and your hands instead of with your eyes, as all others have the ability to do." Miss Jezebel set the tips of her thumbs upon my eyelids. "I apologize greatly for our sheltered deception."

"You can see without touch?"

"Yes, dear."

I felt a disenchantment rise upon me, and I could not hide my disappointment.

"Do not cry, dear."

I stepped away from Miss Jezebel and turned my back to her. "What is it called? To be unable to see with your eyes?"

"It is called blindness."

I recognized the word from the lips of the man. Having the answers I sought, I walked from Miss Jezebel's domicile and wandered into the woods. I sat among the nature and cried until I fell asleep. When I awoke, my skin burned in Cleo's grasp.

"Good morrow," Cleo said. She combed my hair back, and I sat up. "You did not return for evening nourishment. What happened past night?"

"I wish not to discuss it," I said.

Cleo was forgiving and simply pulled my shoulder into hers. We sat together for a long while and did not speak. When I felt again comfortable, I shifted to sit in front of Cleo and focused my attention on where I presumed her own eyes to be. "Have you the ability to see with your eyes?"

Cleo's humble giggle announced her smile. "But, of course."

"And you are aware that I am unable?"

"I am."

"You could then see the man not of this land, as he appeared among us."

"I did."

"Can you then answer me a question?"

"I will be as truth," she whistled.

"What did the man look like?"

"He was big, much taller than any of our perés."

"And his features?"

"I could not see. He wore an ornament upon his head that shadowed his face. But I did recognize markings similar to those which have been blessed upon you."

"Markings similar to mine?"

"Yes," Cleo said, tracing the sides of my face.

Although I had no predilection of ever returning to see him again, I suddenly felt the need to. If Cleo had been correct, there was another who had my unique markings and the thought was highly intriguing, subduing my inherent fear of him. We were more similar than I had originally believed, and I needed to see the markings for myself.

Hungry, I asked if Cleo would escort me to receive nourishment. She helped me stand, and we walked from the woods slowly, not once letting go of one another's hand. When we reached the community farmhouse, Miss Hannah was happy to know that I was okay and helped prepare my midday nourishment. When I was near finished, the rest of the kin had returned from the field for their own midday nourishment. I left what I had not finished and went to the ecclesia to speak with Father Callahan.

"I am afraid I have done you wrong," I said upon entering his retreat.

"Why is that?" Father Callahan said.

"I went against your request and spoke with the man not of this land without your accompaniment."

"I know this to be true. Do you have a reason for your digression?"

"I have no reason."

Father Callahan walked about the room and sat in front of me. I held out my hands, bracing to receive a lash across them, perhaps even more. Instead, Father Callahan took them up into his.

"Thank you for your honesty, Madeline. Your courage is extremely admirable, in both your action and your tongue. I hoped and prayed that you would be so brave. Perhaps this will allow you to bring upon me your queries, without fear of retribution for your misdeeds."

"Yes, sir."

Father Callahan tapped my hands and let them go.

I smiled gently and felt forever daring. "May I have permission to return to see our visitor?" I said.

Father Callahan's breath defined my boldness. "Was your first encounter not enough?"

"No, sir. Miss Jezebel bore her child." I grew weaker in my resolve as he remained quite silent and inattentive.

"Amen," I heard him whisper and suddenly felt extremely foolish.

"Miss Gretchen is with him now," he said and took my hand. Before I knew what was happening, I could smell Miss Gretchen among the hint of the man's flavor. She walked to me and took my shoulders into her hands. I was paced ever closer to the man, where his breathing became more prominent.

"You," he said under a gurgle of phlegm.

I took a deep breath and gave him a hesitant, but warm smile. "Good morrow, sir. My name is Madeline."

The man's breath was heavy. I could feel him looking at me, but nothing more. My smile wilted as I waited for him to respond.

"Call me Grayland," he said.

"It is quite nice to meet you, Sir Grayland," I said, settling on the politeness of my upbringing. I stood quiet again, waiting for Miss Gretchen or Father Callahan to continue the conversation. Suddenly, I felt Miss Gretchen's lips next to my ear.

"Reach out your hand to him, Madeline," she said. I was unsure as to her request, but I followed her instruction and held out my hand. Grayland quickly buried it within his own and gently shook my arm up and down. His grip was fierce, yet curiously tender.

When he let go, I curled my fingers together and slinked closer to Miss Gretchen. The man laid down and coughed swiftly.

"Sir Grayland," Father Callahan said, sweeping up the dialogue onto his lips. "Madeline has been blessed with celebrated creativity and a splendid intuitiveness. She requested permission to learn from you of your origins and of the path you have traveled to find your presence among us. With your consent, we would very much like to pose a few questions in this regard."

I prayed a moment that the man would accept. With Father Callahan and Miss Gretchen's help, I would learn from the man without having to be afraid of what might be said or of what he might do. They protected me from any sin that may secrete from his lips.

"Only if I can get my questions answered," Sir Grayland said, more clearly than ever before.

"We accept your reasonable request."

"What do you want to know?"

"How long have you been traveling among the ash?" Father Callahan said.

"Hell if I know," Sir Grayland said. "It's not like I keep a calendar in my pocket." He paused, and I felt he might have seen my disappointment in his answer, if not Miss Gretchen's and Father Callahan's. "But if I had to guess, I'd say about three years."

"Does he refer to six annuals?" I asked Miss Gretchen in a light whisper, missing Father Callahan's next inquiry.

"For him, a year is a single annual," she whispered back.

I nodded as my focus returned to Sir Grayland's voice. "Imagine my surprise. I didn't think woodlands even existed anymore. I had to take a chance that some kind of civilization endured the war. Lo and behold…"

"How was your survival acquired?" Father Callahan asked.

"Shit, I don't know. A pissed-off guy with a gun, a pair of ironclad cojonés and some luck can pretty much survive anything. What I don't get is how the hell this place survived."

"Secrecy," Father Callahan said.

The man grunted with a huff of air. "Yeah, figures."

"To what do you refer?"

"I know your type."

"We only seek peace among the violence."

"Of course you do." Sir Grayland's voice pattern had changed into somewhat of a mean spirit. "Cults always claim that before they murder their gullible sheep."

"I must dispute your claim, sir. We are not what you believe us to be."

"Whatever. Believe what you have to. Just don't ask me to become a part of it."

"You are free to leave at any time with our blessing, sir."

"Can I have that in writing?"

"I assure you, sir. My heart is strong, and my word is stronger. You can trust both with a seal of iron."

"Shake on it?"

The confrontation had made me quite uncomfortable. I held onto Miss Gretchen's arm as if I was a young kin frightened by a field mouse.

"Good," Sir Grayland said. "But remember this, you break your word, I break that girl's neck." Suddenly, my heart skipped and I felt faint. Beads of sweat painted my forehead.

"Your conditions are quite understood," Father Callahan said without changing his tone of voice, which frightened me even further. I gripped Miss Gretchen's hand tightly as she rubbed the length of my arm. "And to prove our faith to you and our resolve, we will prepare you a full meal."

"Great. But I want her to bring it to me. Alone."

"I do apologize, but I am unwilling to comply with that request."

"Why not?"

"She has only turned of age this past harvest," Father Callahan said. "She is not yet—"

"Bullshit. She's old enough to bring me food by herself."

I tried to hide it, but I was now crying.

"She brings it, or I burn this entire place to the ground."

"Please, sir. There is no need for idle threats."

"Do as I ask, and we have no problems. Fuck with me, I fuck back."

There was a deadened silence, and the air fell heavy.

"Come along, Madeline. Miss Gretchen."

Miss Gretchen took my hand and we followed Father Callahan out of the quarters. As we reached the commune, I finally found the courage to open my mouth and speak my fear.

"Must I bring him his meal?"

"Yes. We must demonstrate to him that we are not of which he claims."

"What does he claim?"

"He is of the mind and land of the sinner, Madeline," Miss Gretchen said with calm. "He only speaks of what he knows and is blind to what he does not understand."

"Blind as I?"

"Blind you may be in sight. But Sir Grayland is blind in heart."

We remained in silence without the slightest of breaths for the duration of our walk and preparation of Sir Grayland's meal. Father Callahan chose to remain with the kin to pray with them for what he described as Grayland's internal conflict between sin and virtue as Miss Gretchen walked with me to the ecclesia. In my heart I was not convinced that Grayland was acquainted with the concept of virtue; sin and vice had corrupted him so completely, not even the loving hand of an innocent could guide his return. It shivered my blood to know I was going to be alone with him, trusting that he was only capable of malice.

(CHAPTER 8

The reverberation of my heart beat gravely in the recesses of my ear as the dead air of the ecclesia fell upon me. The smell of the food I carried grew pungent, and my feet locked together. Miss Gretchen remained by my side, her fingertips pressed ever so lightly on the base of my shoulder blade but did not force me to advance forward. The decision to take up Grayland's request rested with me, and if at any moment I wished to go against it, Miss Gretchen would support that decision. She understood Grayland better than I, and in the shadow of a stranger, Miss Gretchen would always protect her family. Reaching the door, I promised myself that I would hand Grayland his meal, grant him good night and leave without confrontation.

"I will be right here, should you need anything," Miss Gretchen said softly.

I nodded and Miss Gretchen fixed my hair before opening my entry into the quarters. I couldn't be sure where Grayland was, but I did not much care. My legs became stiff as the door closed behind me. I tried to breathe, but the air was difficult to collect. Unable to hear even the lightest of sounds from Grayland, I set the meal down at my feet and turned to fulfill my promise.

"Eat it." Grayland's soft voice floated across the room from the farthest corner. I froze; it was all I could do.

"I said eat it," he said, moving toward me. "Or I'll make you eat it."

I chirped softly as Grayland took a vicious hold of my arm and pushed me to my knees in front of the food. I was crying now but forced my trembling lips to remain intrepid, unwilling to give Grayland the satisfaction of intimidation.

"You are a stubborn little bitch, aren't you?" Grayland threw my arm to the side and sat down on the opposite side of the food. I heard his incensed heaving as he waited for me to comply and knew that he was not going to allow my exit until I did as he asked. Why he wished that I eat his meal was unclear, but it was my only means of escaping his tyranny. So I ate; even when it felt as if I would regurgitate the entire meal, I consumed it without delay. When I had finished, I turned my head up to Grayland and offered him my most dissatisfied brow.

"Thank you," Grayland said, though I could not identify whether it was sincere. He turned from me and laid down against the wall, causing me to feel an irritation I had yet to ever feel.

"Why did you have me consume your meal?" I said, my voice quivering.

"What does it matter?"

"I desire to know. Why have you expressed intention to harm my family and I? Why have you shown inconsideration and spite when all we have offered is aid and comfort?"

Grayland sat up. "Threats are the only currency people understand."

"I find that tragically appalling," I said.

"So do I," Grayland said after a touch of laughter. "But it is what it is, and you won't live long out there without making a few and following through on them."

"So you will kill me if Father Callahan refuses your departure?"

"If I must."

"You are vile."

"Only when I'm forced to be."

My breaths were heavy now. I could not understand this man or his nature. "What atrocities have made you so?" I said.

Grayland did not answer right off, but when he did, there was a sorrow upon his voice. "I've seen my fair share of loss. Enough to make a respected man jaded."

Suddenly, I felt repentant. There was much more complexity to this man than I could comprehend. I had allowed myself to form an opinion of Grayland based on the shell he hid beneath without the forethought of looking deeper to find the truth behind his masked diffidence.

"Who do you mourn?" I said, shifting into a more relaxed sitting position.

Grayland cleared his throat. "Too many to name," he said.

"Whom of those do you mourn the deepest?"

"I'd rather not talk about it."

"To discuss that which you hold dear is to shed the fear that haunts you."

"Your priest tell you that?"

"As well as others. I have found them all to be quite true."

"Yeah, well… I'm still not gonna talk about it. So you can just drop it."

I conceded graciously; I did not want to restore Grayland's menace. At the same time, I needed to learn more. "Were these deaths the cause of your expedition?"

Grayland surrendered to my inquiry with a deep breath. "Someone very close to me was taken a few years ago, and I haven't been able to let that go."

"How was it that this loved one was taken?"

"A clan of termites raided my home." Grayland's throat locked up, and whether he was able, or even willing to finish, was unclear. I didn't need him to.

"I am extremely saddened for your loss. I cannot comprehend how I might react should I ever lose someone close to me."

Grayland remained within himself. I understood his pain and made the decision to turn the subject so as to relieve his torture, no matter how slight.

"I have learned much from my perés in regards to Anno Domini and the time before the ash. It appears to have once been a wonderful array of hope and innovation."

"You've been lied to," Grayland said.

"Why would you say such a thing, without the knowledge of whom you speak?"

"Your… *peré*… either has no idea what she's talking about, or she's glorifying what it was like. Either way, she's totally misleading you."

"But she was a part of its life, just as you were."

"That's great. But romanticizing our generation because it sounds better doesn't make it the truth. Listen, kid. I'm sure your mother, or nursemaid, or whatever this peré is to you, is a kind and sensible person. But it seems she doesn't want to tell you about the lies and the greed and the vitriol that helped lead to our destruction in the first place."

"Enlighten me."

"Now's not the time."

I agreed with him. As much as I wished to know more about his thoughts and how they were different from those that I had been taught, I felt uncomfortable in losing the innocence that I had acquired through my family. It was in my nature to learn all I could, but there would be a better time to introduce me to the other side. I only hoped that I would be ready when that moment came to pass.

"May I see you?" I said after a long thought.

"What?"

"I would like to see you."

Grayland coughed and whistled in a brush of apprehension. "Okay."

I went to him, sitting down on my knees so that I could feel his broad shoulder along my chest.

"Do not move." I lifted my hands to meet his face. His lips were thick and serrated, and his nose felt bent near the center, tucked bulbously between his eyes, which were closer than I had thought they might be. One brow was missing from above his eye and his forehead was long, leaving little room for hair on top of his head. But what made his appeal quite entrancing was the rigid pattern that flowed from the top of his head, where chunks of his hair had been seared, to below the base of his neck, escaping down under the thick, abrasive cloth that he wore upon his back. The opposite could be said for the other side of his face, which, though stippled with tiny, rough hairs, was rather smooth, with marks of age signifying his long life. It was only then I realized the ear on his marked half was not present.

"You are quite pleasing," I said, rounding my fingertips around his ear, leading past his neck and down his back.

"Liar," he said. His voice was filled with a smile. I could tell that he was playing a joke, and it made my own smile grow. His breath warmed my neck, sending with it a chilled tickle of pleasure.

I moved back and sat upon the heels of me feet. I shaped his features upon my mind in silence, adding his image to the portrait of my family.

"You were born as I?" I said, touching my own markings.

"I wasn't born this way," he said. "And I guarantee you weren't either."

"I do not understand. If we were not blessed with our marks upon our first breath, how have we acquired them?"

"At some point, you were burned."

"I was burned?" I said. The touch of my scars grew heavier. "How?"

"Beats the hell out of me. There were a lot of burn victims at the start of the war. It probably happened then."

I was unclear as to how to ingest this new information. "What happened to these burn victims?"

"A lot of them suffered. A lot more died."

"How is it you know this to be true?"

"I was a doctor."

"You serviced the sick," I said.

"In a manner of speaking."

"That is extremely honorable."

"Not when you've had to do what I was forced to do."

"What were you forced to do?"

"Forget it."

"Please, sir. I am very interested."

"Good for you."

"Sir?"

"Can you just shut your god damned mouth for one minute?" Sir Grayland pushed me to the floor and the rage that filled both his tongue and his hand sickened me. I shifted away from him and pulled my legs in close to my chest.

"Do you wish for me to leave?"

"I don't care," he said. "Do what you want."

I thought about leaving him, to take rest and work through my thoughts and feelings, but instead sat still and quiet. For a reason I still cannot understand, I couldn't leave him. Perhaps I felt that being in his vicinity would help him remain tranquil, or perhaps it was because I suddenly found his complexity intriguing enough to want to learn more. But no matter how many questions my head held for him, I did not want to initiate any more confrontation. I was uncertain whether he would ever seek fresh conversation this night, or the next, or ever in the future, so I leaned up against the wall and waited for him to open his heart. By giving him this silence and allowing him his secrets, I proved my respect for his privacy, and it was all I could do for now.

CHAPTER 9

I could not remember if I had fallen asleep or if my mind had wandered beyond my recognition, but I snapped back into consciousness when a loud echo rattled my thoughts. Cleo was hovering above me, shaking my shoulder and urging me to wake with a delightful song. I was unsettled to begin, but it came to clarity that someone had come to remove me from Grayland's quarters and return me to my domicile.

"Good morrow, slumber cat," Cleo chirped. "We are late for sunrise nourishment."

"How did I return here?" I said, attempting to knock the remaining sleep from my body.

"Miss Gretchen carried you here. With the way you lay across her arm, I suspected you might have died."

I laughed. Cleo did also and left the room quickly thereafter. I lingered in my room for a while longer, soaking up the sun as it peeked through the window, and thought carefully about my conversation with Grayland. I processed his words and retraced his features, hoping to find a clear conclusion for who he was as a man, but better yet, as a person. But the more I reflected on his erratic demeanor, voice and actions, the more I lost any cohesive character. As anyone worth befriending, Grayland was emotionally layered and independent, trapped under a thick shell of misfortune. With the information I had, I concluded that I could not stop attempting to shed him of his sadness and help bring the sun back into the life that had been lost upon his tortured excessiveness.

Upon the sun warming my entire face, I left my domicile to join the rest of the kin for nourishment, filling my stomach quickly and beginning my work in the field. After midday nourishment, I walked with Cleo to our teachings with only one destination upon my mind once they had concluded. As all of my kin ate evening nourishment or chose to play with Delilah, I proceeded to the ecclesia. Father Callahan was with Grayland when I arrived, but he departed soon after and left me alone to converse with him. I recited some of my stories, his favorite being the story of our land's creation that I had most recently told at the last day of restoration saying it reminded him of parables that had been read to him as a child. He would tell me several tales as well, including anecdotes from what he referred to as television and movies, and spoke highly of different types of song, most of which were extremely favorable and which I would recite to Cleo in return. On occasion, when Grayland was not feeling his best, I would sit with him silently, holding his hand and lying upon his chest to remind him I was there. But most importantly, we discussed the differences of our lives. He explained how family was structured in his time, the meaning of father and mother, of daughter and son, and how this structure slowly devolved across time. Where once parents held themselves accountable for the actions of their children, guiding them with rewards for excellence and punishment for their mistakes, by the time the ash fell, parents no longer cared for the actions of their children, blaming others for the ineptitude of the parent and placing responsibility for anything their child did onto that of the society around them. Children had become a nuisance by that point, a disease that parents felt only held them back from doing what they wanted, leading their children into sin at a very young age and teaching them that the values which were once instilled upon them as a child were pointless in a world of which accountability had become extinct.

"That is quite appalling," I had said during the account.

"I agree. And it made its way into other facets of people's lives, too, like their professions and relationships."

"What is a person's profession?"

"It's what you do for a living. My profession was a doctor."

"And accountability in a person's profession began to deteriorate?"

"More like they quit believing it was their duty to work."

"Why would someone think that?"

"Because others did the work for them. You know, why should I work hard when someone else can?"

"These people took from others who worked for what they had?"

"They felt it was their right to do it. Those who were better off because of hard work owed these people because they had more than them."

"I could never do such a thing. I work very hard for the food I eat and the garments I wear. All of my family does."

"Good to know."

"I hate to think that someone would consider taking that from me whenever it is they pleased. Especially if they were capable of doing the work themselves."

"What do you do here?"

"I sow the field and work on the harvest."

"Really? Wouldn't you rather write or something. Your stories are pretty good."

"Of course I love my stories. But then what food would I have to eat?"

"Does that mean you sew your own clothes, too?"

"Of course."

"Commendable," Sir Grayland said and squeezed the back of my neck with affection.

As the night fell into slumber, I said good night and retreated back to my domicile for rest. I performed this routine for many days thereafter, each time revealing more about my home to the mysterious stranger who had quickly become a friend. But no matter how much I wished to do so, I did not once speak of the loss of his loved ones or the inciting incident that led to the rain of ash. Those topics were certainly the most fixed upon my mind, but they would be revealed in time, when Sir Grayland was ready, and only when he initiated the discussion.

One quiet morrow, feeling extremely comfortable with Sir Grayland and confident that he was not a disease to the heart of our land, I spoke with Cleo during midday nourishment and asked if she desired an introduction to the visitor as I had once been given.

"You wish to introduce me to the man not of this land?"

"Sir Grayland," I said.

"I do not know, Madeline. I still hold a promise with Miss Jezebel."

"I understand. But if we politely speak with her, I have not a doubt that she will concede your promise."

"How can you believe she would concede?"

"Because we trust each other."

Cleo and I finished our meal in silence. I felt she was pondering my invitation and wished not to dissuade her opinion by pushing beyond the limit of her tolerance. We continued our silent meditations as we walked to the river to meet Miss Jezebel. I cannot remember what she taught that day because my mind was on Sir Grayland, what discussions we may have that evening, and whether Cleo would be with me to enjoy his legend.

I was ready to rush for the ecclesia even before Miss Jezebel excused everyone, but upon standing to leave, Cleo caught my arm. Words did not slip from her mouth, yet I understood what she wanted and it left a strong smile upon my lips.

"Miss Jezebel?" I said. My focus remained with Cleo.

"Yes, Madeline."

I followed her voice with my head. "May we speak?"

"Please do," she said gently.

"It is my pleasure to have invited Cleo to join me this day to greet Sir Grayland, the man not of this land. May she have your permission to break her early promise, as I once did?"

"Is this what you truly wish for, Cleo?"

"Yes, Miss Jezebel. I have considered Madeline's invitation very carefully. I have decided that I would very much like to greet the man, Sir Grayland, this day."

"Can you explain why you have made this decision?"

I could feel Cleo's apprehension with the question, and I could do nothing for her. It was necessary that she speak for herself in this instance.

"Upon many occasions these past nights, Madeline has spoken of many stories and songs interpreted from Sir Grayland's fancy. From what she has recounted, I find Sir Grayland to be quite intriguing and would very much like to hear of his worldly tales and discuss my own ideas with him directly."

"You make a logical argument, Cleo, and I understand your intrigue and curiosity toward Sir Grayland and the wonder that Madeline has relayed to you. Unfortunately, I cannot indulge your request."

The disappointment in Cleo was obvious as she slunk down upon me and burrowed her head into my shoulder. "May I ask why?" I said.

"You may believe that Sir Grayland is to be greatly admired, and you may not be wrong in your view. However, I once lived the world he lived and I know of the deceit and sin that plagued it. Without being aware of his integrity, I cannot trust the intentions he brings to our family."

"I know of his integrity, and I do trust him."

"I believe that you do. That does not make it appropriate for Cleo to be introduced to his influence."

"Why is it okay for me to be introduced to his influence and not okay for Cleo?"

Miss Jezebel took a moment of silence.

"If your reason is because I am different than all others in how I see, then you are not true to the word that you teach," I said. "Our family is all of the same blood. We are no different, in mind or in heart, and you treat us all with indistinguishable dignity, honor and love. I have met Sir Grayland, spoken of our worlds together, and what I have learned from him is nothing more than sincerity. He is a good man in my mind, and I do not understand why he must remain in isolation. I will be with Cleo all the while we stand among him, and I promise that Sir Grayland will do nothing more than accept her the same as he has admirably accepted me."

Miss Jezebel took in a deep breath that sounded reproachful in inhale, yet understanding in exhale. My heart beat quickly as I waited for her authoritative response and whether my trust in her words would be protected.

"Madeline, I respect the argument you have presented," she said, "and will concede to Cleo her promise. She may go with you this day to greet Sir Grayland." Cleo tightened her grip upon my hand with pleasurable joy. I held firm, as I knew Miss Jezebel had not concluded her thoughts. "But as her escort, you must remain with her at all times and you must promise that if he grows hostile or turns upon Cleo in a dangerous manner, you will leave him without hesitation and neither of you will ever return to him."

"I promise," I said without a moment of consideration otherwise.

Cleo kissed me under the smile of excitement, and we ran to the ecclesia, gripped hand upon hand. Both of our hearts beat rapidly as we briskly walked to Sir Grayland's quarters. The door was closed to us, which revealed to me that Father Callahan was not with him; a condition that I felt was favorable for us both. I hugged Cleo in preparation.

"How are you?"

"I am ready," she said with a bit of a nervous quiver.

I squeezed her hand tightly and opened the door. The atmosphere upon our entering the room was instantly cold and unforgiving.

"Sir Grayland," I said buoyantly. "I would like to introduce you to Cleo, my best of friends and kindest of sisters."

"It is quite good to meet you, Sir Grayland." Cleo curtsied as she was taught to do upon meeting a new friend. Grayland didn't say anything, and Cleo's spirit became ill.

"Sir Grayland?" I said.

"Why did you bring her here?" Grayland said.

"She is my sister and she wished to meet you."

"I never asked to meet her," he said gravely.

"Yes, of course. But you did not ask to meet me either, sir."

"You were different."

"I am no different. She is my family."

"I've got news for you, kid. You two couldn't be more different. Now get her out of my sight."

"I am sorry, sir. But you are quite wrong."

"I said get her out of here." The levels in Sir Grayland's voice had risen.

"All we want to do is speak together. Why does that bother you so?"

"I'm not about to lower myself to speak to that."

"I am not clear as to your meaning, sir."

"It means get that damn nigger out of my sight." Sir Grayland grabbed Cleo's arm. I tried to hold tight onto her hand, but it slipped from mine and I heard her hit the ground somewhere behind me. She screamed and cried, and anger welled up within me.

"What did you do?" I asked, the pitch in my voice extremely shrill.

"You should know better, sweetheart. When you're asked to do something, you do it."

I found Cleo lying on the floor just outside of Sir Grayland's quarters. "You did not have to hurt her," I said.

"Better her than me," he said. "And don't you dare come back."

It was unclear as to whom Sir Grayland was referring, but I took his words to be marked upon me. The door closed us off from his potential wrath, and I picked Cleo into my arms and held her, resting her head against my shoulder.

"I am sorry," I said. "I never expected him to act as such a monster."

"Miss Jezebel expected his wicked insolence. Her words were truth, and we ignored them to our own detriment."

"I know." I also understood that I would no longer be able to speak with Sir Grayland, as I had given my promise.

"What has happened?" Father Callahan ran briskly down the hall to greet us. He placed us both under his welcome touch. "Are you hurt?"

"Sir Grayland is a wicked man, and he should not be here," Cleo uttered.

"What has he done to you?"

"He has used violent force against me and spoke of me with a contemptible tongue."

"What were his words you speak of?"

Cleo was silent now and I presumed that she had forgotten the word. I hadn't. "He spoke of her as a nigger," I said. "What does the term mean?"

Father Callahan said nothing as he rushed into Sir Grayland's quarters. I could not make out all of what was said between them, but their voices were quite high and loud. What I did hear clearly was Father Callahan scolding Sir Grayland for exploiting his hospitality and treatment of his illness and advising him that he was no longer welcome in our land. Sir Grayland grumbled an inaudible set of putrid insults as Father Callahan left the room and collected Cleo and I away to his retreat. He sat us down and took a silent prayer to calm his emotions and prepare to speak to us with rational coherence.

"I would like to apologize for Sir Grayland's behavior," he said in a disquieted whisper.

"It is no one's fault but my own," I said.

"Do not take blame for Sir Grayland's faults, Madeline."

"But I must. I was unable to comprehend his true nature under the guise of my own selfishness."

"You were not at all selfish. Listen to me now, both of you. Sir Grayland comes from a life that has been hardened by many influences, most of which are malevolent and immoral. He does not understand or trust our ways of life because he has seen only that of sin and vice. I knew this to be truth, but I had hoped in prayer that I was wrong in my assessment. I gave him benefit of my kindness and allowed you to speak with him. If there is fault for this episode, it lies solely with me. Sir Grayland should have been asked to leave our home when he was no longer ill, but we allowed him to stay. I cannot allow that anymore, not after he broke our trust. Sir Grayland will be leaving us next morrow."

"I think that is best," Cleo said.

"What does it mean?" I said quickly after.

"What are you referring?"

"The term he used to describe Cleo."

"It is a derogatory term used mostly by intellectuals to incite hatred toward a certain race of people. Do not worry. Your family is more intellectual than those that used that term, and you will never hear of it again. I promise you."

I nodded but was not completely satisfied with the answer.

In response to our long silence, Father Callahan said, "Go on to your domicile now and get some rest. If you have any questions, do not fear my wisdom."

"Yes, Father Callahan," Cleo and I said in unison. "Good night."

We walked from his retreat with our arms wrapped together and returned straight away to our domicile as we had been instructed. Cleo fell asleep quickly to the song of her tears, but I could not find solace in my mind. Sir Grayland had insulted my sister, and I was infuriated with his actions. However, there was still much more I wished to learn from him. I didn't want to upset Cleo by accepting his insolence, but there had to be an adequate reason for his outburst. My heart tore in confliction, and it wasn't until I decided that I must break yet another promise and speak with him one last time before his departure that I was able to find my slumber alongside my sister.

(CHAPTER 10

I rose before the sun and silently returned to the ecclesia under the hidden moon's secrecy. When I arrived, all was incredibly quiet except for the gentle shuffle of my feet across the cold floor. I moved slow and steady, waiting anxiously for someone to stop me. Perhaps if someone had stopped me, I would not have accepted my life as it was, and I could have enjoyed my wonderful serenity. I should have turned around and refused to give in to the man's artificial charm. Alas, my will was not strong, and I walked the path of impulsive madness.

Sir Grayland was crying as I entered his quarters.

I did not speak, and he did not move, but we were aware of one another's presence. The situation called for a heavy air of awkwardness, but as we remained frozen among our own personal darkness's, we understood what the other was dealing with and the level of respect for the other was prominent in our silence.

It was unclear as to how long our breaths held our conversation, but Sir Grayland spoke first after calming the strength of his tears.

"I'm sorry about what I said."

There was a definite layer of remorse in his voice and I wanted to console him. However, I held my conviction, unable to allow him to be forgiven so easily. "Why would you act in such a manner?"

"I don't know," he said, which did not help persuade my forgiveness. "It's been a long time since I've been around someone like that who wasn't out to hurt me."

"You believe that gives you justification to hurt someone you have yet to meet?"

"It's why I'm still alive."

I reflected upon his words carefully. "It was a defense?"

Sir Grayland's silence answered my question.

"I do not agree with your behavior toward my sister," I said and could sense him fighting against the return of his regret. "Nevertheless, you have shown me great kindness, and I recognize your repentance. I forgive you."

The crack in Sir Grayland's throat exposed his hidden compunction. "You're a good kid," he said.

"Thank you."

"A lot like my daughter."

"Your daughter?" I was knocked into breathless silence. Sir Grayland had never spoken of having a child before and I suddenly felt ill, believing that she may be the one spoken of as the love he had lost.

"Danielle," he said with a hint of love. "She had a strong character like you."

"Danielle," I said softly. Though I wanted desperately to know more, I did not inquire any further. If Sir Grayland wished to speak of his daughter, he would. Until then, I did not wish to cause him additional pain.

"What will you do when you leave?" I said instead.

"It's better you don't know."

"Why is it better?"

"Despite what I've said about this place, you have a good life here, Madeline. I don't want to ruin that."

"You could not ruin my life with knowledge."

"I believe I could."

I was not sure how I could respond to that, and so I did not. "Would it be wrong of me to suggest that I am envious of you?"

"Yeah, probably," he said. "Why would you envy me?"

"I would not have believed I was capable of envy before I learned of my unique way of sight. However, ever since you revealed the truth of my oddity, I have wondered what I am missing that everyone else is able to perceive. You have walked what I have always dreamed of seeing, and you have done so in a way that I cannot comprehend."

"If I told you I could change that, would you let me?"

Confusion struck. "Of what do you speak?"

"You remember I was a doctor," he said.

"I do."

"What I didn't tell you is that, before the war, I was as an optometrist."

"I am unaware of this term."

"It means I helped people with their eyes. Before the war, I spent a lot of time working on vision correction and rehabilitation. The type of therapy and laser eye correction I was working on had been around for a long time, but no progress had been made on complete vision restoration. I worked for years trying to find a viable remedy and was about ready to test my technique on a live subject when everything went to shit. I've always regretted not being able to find out if it would have worked."

"Are you articulating that you have the ability to grant sight upon my eyes?"

"It's never been tested, but yeah. I think I could make it work. If you were willing to give me the chance."

"Of course," I said quickly, but held my tongue when I continued to think upon his suggestion. Sir Grayland understood my sudden apprehension.

"Yeah… to give it a chance, you would have to come with me."

I pursed my lips.

"Forget it," he said, sadness returning to his voice. "You'd be taking too big a risk and there's no guarantee it would work."

"I understand." This was a day I had dreamed about for so long. Now that it was upon me, I felt extremely nervous. My lungs hurt, and I grew lightheaded as my breathing grew more rapid.

"Are you okay?"

"I am quite overwhelmed," I said. "May I have a moment to comprehend your proposal?"

"Take all the time you need. I'm leaving at dawn."

"Thank you," I said and left the room without realizing I had. My legs fell numb underneath me as I reached the commune and I laid on the ground as my mind spun in chaos. I did not move even the slightest of muscles until Father Callahan woke and found me. He reached down to help me to my feet, but upon my refusal, he sat down next to me, pulling me up to rest my head on his chest. He wrapped his arm around me and did not utter a word until I spoke. For that, I will always be most grateful.

"He has asked me to accompany him in his travels," I said under a faint disenchantment.

"Did you answer his request?"

"He asks me to leave my family, my home. I could not answer him."

"Does he offer anything in return for leaving your loved ones behind?"

"He claims he can help me see in the way you and all others do."

"Do you believe him?"

"I certainly wish to."

Father Callahan remained silent, and I understood why he would. He needed me to reconcile my own doubts without influence, as we had always been taught. But I was so afraid that I would make the wrong decision in this instance that I needed to know what he thought, to help guide me in what could be the most important decision I had ever had to make. I was unclear as to what Father Callahan would say or do when asked, but if I did not, I would regret my choice until the last day of existence.

"What shall I do?" I asked with a trembling lip.

"You must speak with your heart over what is important for you at this moment in your life. Your family will keep you safe, love you and help you with the dreams of your future, but the gift of true sight, for which you were stripped of in early life, could help you grow and mature in ways that would not be accessible to you without it."

"Which is my dilemma, my curse."

"Only if you make it so. I cannot help you decide, but whatever your decision, your family, myself included, will support you and love you."

"I am aware," I said. Then I asked him a question that he had never been asked and possibly believed he would never be obligated to answer. "Why have you built this land?"

Father Callahan settled his discomfort and surprise in his long silence. He then answered with truth and without doubt. "The world we lived in before the ash fell, once blessed with liberty and morality, had become corrupted in anger, greed and sloth, fueled by the escalation of labels in all facets of people's everyday lives. It grew so tremendously slow that when it became a normal lifestyle, not many understood the implications of their choices. There were few who remained rational, arguing for what was right against what had become expected, but their words fell upon deaf ears, until it had become too late to change."

"You were one with rationality," I said directly.

"I was indeed, and when I learned that the mass was unwilling to understand their mistake and think logically about what they stood for, I spoke in tears to my heart over many nights, in which I was quietly led to my long-awaited decision. If I could not save everyone, I would protect as many as I could from the wrath of discrimination that was unfolding. My new life would include a home devoid of labels, where every man, woman and child would live in harmonious equality. No matter the difference of appearance, faith or background, no one soul would be led in prejudice. I searched many an annual before my heart brought me this sacred land, where I could raise my new family and remain safe from the disaster incurred through the rising sin of the people. I spread my word to those who would listen and invited all of whom believed in my message to follow with me and live without the intolerance of their venerated labels.

Very few believed and even fewer still walked my path with me. But we survived, and I pray against hope that the values I have instilled upon you and your brothers and sisters will prevail over those that bred hatred over harmony."

"What of the man and woman who gave me life?"

"What of them?"

"Were they as gentle and loving as our family?"

"I am afraid I was never granted the pleasure of their acquaintance," he said sadly.

"But they must have followed your footsteps to have me delivered"

"Sadly, not a child arrived to me with such a luxury."

"Then how is it we arrived here?"

"Upon the first fall of ash, I spoke to those hearts that had believed in my word, and we agreed that to begin a life completely free of prejudice, we would need to adopt newly born children, lost to their parents or abandoned in fear, for whom we could teach and love as our own. All of us braved the war and promised never to return without a child in hand. I had just returned home with Henry when I first met eyes upon a young woman not much older than you are now. She carried a child of fire within her arms, one she would extol great care and nurture upon and watch grow into a wonderful, thoughtful young girl."

"Who was the woman who brought me to you?" I said, quite excited.

"You know of the answer in your heart."

"Miss Jezebel." The answer whistled below my breath.

Father Callahan kissed the top of my head. I smiled bright.

"Was she my mother?"

"No, but she knew them quite well, that I am certain." Father Callahan held me in silence for a little while longer before I asked to be excused. He bid me adieu with a gentle kiss upon my forehead.

"Always listen to your heart; it will guide you to your truth."

"Yes, Father." I kissed him upon his cheek, allowing the hairs to tickle my nose, and walked from the ecclesia, believing that I would return to my domicile for some rest. But as I took in the brisk air of the dying night, I finally understood what I had to do to help resolve my dilemma.

CHAPTER 11

Miss Jezebel was asleep when I entered her domicile. Delilah was cooing gently in her cradle. I went to her and lifted her into my arms, able to smell her sweet skin and feel the power of her small breaths. Sensing joy and contentment, I sat down and hummed a tune to her, rocking her gently in my arms.

"You're good with her," Miss Jezebel said softly. She sat down next to me and wrapped her arm around my shoulder, allowing me to continue to hold Delilah as she fell silent in slumber.

"She is a precious love," I said.

"That she is."

"Do you believe those who gave me life thought of me this way?"

"I do not have to believe. I know as much."

"Were they as nice and as loving as you?"

"They were kind and honest," Miss Jezebel said. "They did not deserve their fate."

"Can you explain for me how they passed on from our world?"

"They were taken by fire," she said after a brief pause. It was clear that it hurt her to think about them.

"The same fire that gifted me my marks?"

"The very same."

"Can you relate to me your knowledge of your time with them?" I said, a bit of sadness cracking my softened voice.

"I shall." Miss Jezebel took up Delilah and returned her to the cradle. She then wrapped a blanket around my shoulders and sat down next to me. I laid my head down onto her lap and listened to her tale, imagining all in great detail.

"I remember my parents very vividly and to say that they were anything but kind would be understating their genuine nature. But as a teenage girl, not much younger than you, living in a world of narcissism and derision, I could not appreciate them as I should have. At the same time as all of my friends did as they pleased, without any repercussions, I was being strangled by rules, unable to live the life I envied so very much. One night, I ran away from them, hoping the freedom of a life on my own would give me the pleasure I so desired."

"Did you find pleasure in your freedom?" I said.

"For a time, I thought I had. I no longer had anyone to stop me from doing what I thought I wanted to, and it was bliss. Slowly, though, I saw the darker side of my actions and watched my friends grow alarmingly unstable, pulling me down a path I had not intended. Sleeping became harder as I began to regret what had happened. Upon the accidental death of my best friend, I knew what I needed to do. But then the unimaginable occurred. My family was taken from me in the fall of ash. War had been active for a few years before, but not one person thought it would ever lead to that day. It was only because I had not been with them that I had survived, and when I returned home, their bodies had been turned to nothing I can describe.

"It took me days to find the strength to stand again, another few to step outside. By then the sky had turned red, as had the streets. I did not know what I could do, or where I could go. My first thought was to return to my friends, but they had all been viciously killed at the hands of an unknown assailant. I was alone and could do nothing but wait for death's hand to come find me. Instead, I received a message. I learned of a man who was seeking to unite those willing to live without hatred, without greed, a place where we could start anew upon the perception of concord. I passed the thought over quickly because I did not deserve such a gracious future. Then, as I lay upon the streets, ill and hungry, tired and desperate, I finally came to realize what had happened. I understood my sins and the sins of my friends as one cause for the destruction of the land. Once I had accepted these faults, I knew the only way I could make up for them, and continue to survive, was to find a path upon this new land of harmony. I found what little strength I had and set out to find the land that called for me.

"The trek became quite arduous, and my body fell exceedingly ill. One morrow, I fell upon a couple, very much in love and expecting a child, who offered me shelter and food without question or fear. It took a long while to heal and regain my strength, but they did not mind. In truth, we became great friends in a very short period, and I loved them as I should have loved my own parents. I did not wish to leave them.

"When I was near full health once again, I discussed my departure with them. They did not attempt to dissuade me and offered me their hand in hopes that if anything ever went wrong, I would return to them. I agreed and kissed them both farewell. Looking back one last time, a miracle took place. The woman fell to her knees in screams and I was finally able to return the woman's generosity with that of my own. Even though I was still very much a child myself, I helped the woman give birth to her little girl. I loved the child as much as she, and I no longer felt the need to leave any of them.

" 'You could come with me,' I said to the woman a few days after.

" 'This is our home, and it is very dangerous out there,' she said. 'I would not forgive myself if anything happened to her.'

"For the first time, I felt the woman was being selfish. She simply did not understand that the child deserved the best possible life, and in my mind, that was within the land of which I sought. One night, as all were sleeping soundly, I crept into the child's quarters, ready to do what I felt I must. But upon seeing her resting peacefully in her cradle, I could not bring myself to take her away from the family that loved her. I had already made a similar act, and I knew what feelings would arise if it were to happen again. Instead, I chose to stay and help raise her, feed her and offer her the greatest life a family could provide. And we did just that for over half an annual.

"That is when we were attacked.

"The faction behind the fall took us all captive and forced us all to perform at their will. If we refused them, we would find death upon their hands. I was afraid and inclined to do their bidding. The woman and her husband were not. They held strong onto their beliefs and fought them with every breath. When her body hit the floor, no longer with life, the man became enraged and killed one of the monsters before he was laid to rest alongside his love. The men set the house on fire soon thereafter, and even though I had shown great obedience, my affiliation with the couple was enough to leave me to burn with them and feel the penitence of my treason.

"I was about ready to accept my fate when I heard the cries of the innocent.

"I am to this day uncertain as to how I escaped my bindings, but upon my freedom, I rushed into the child's quarters, avoiding the lick of flames that tried desperately to stop me and found her lying in the cradle, laced completely in flame. I pulled the child from the crib, unaware that the fire had kissed her as I did, and found my way from the home. When we reached safety, I cried, unable to stop until the flames had collapsed the home and the darkness overwhelmed me.

"The next morrow, I woke and walked from the rubble with the child held tightly against my chest, determined to follow the path to my original destination, guilty in the thought that if I had tried harder, they may all still be alive."

"You should not feel guilty," I said through a flow of tears. "You could not have known the consequences of the actions of others."

"It took me a long while to wash my guilt away, but with Father Callahan's help, I learned that the choices we all made had a much larger meaning." Miss Jezebel kissed the top of my head. "You have to trust that the choices made with love lead to unexpected riches, while those made in doubt are best laid to rest."

"What were their names," I said.

"The man's name was Victor," Miss Jezebel said. "The woman's, Delilah."

I sat up and turned to Miss Jezebel. I could feel her eyes staring back at me with recognition of my affection. She placed her hand to my cheek and kissed the marks of fire gently.

"It is a name of purity and honor."

I hugged Miss Jezebel and then kissed her kindly. "Never leave her." I rose and left her domicile without another word. Without haste, I hurried to Father Callahan, who had been awaiting my return.

"I have made my decision," I said. "I have no doubt. I wish to travel with Sir Grayland and find my true sight."

"May I ask how you have come to this conclusion?"

"Everything I have ever known is with this land, and I thank you and all who have provided me with love. But in my heart, I feel that I cannot truly accept your love without the knowledge of what I have had to give up. The only way I can learn and appreciate the purity you have bestowed upon me is to walk the path I was never given a choice to travel. I need to know the other side, to understand where my love truly is."

"And I will honor your wish without argument."

"Thank you, Father," I said.

"Before you depart, I would like to give you a gift."

"A gift?"

Father Callahan took my hand in his and placed a parchment upon it.

"What is it?" I said.

"Do you recall my prayer of the traveler and his guide?"

"I am sorry, Father. I am afraid I do not."

"Keep this close. If ever you feel you have fallen and have died upon your path, have your friend read it to you. I have faith that you will find any answer you seek within."

"Of course, Father. I will. Thank you." I rolled the parchment into my hand and gave Father Callahan a long embrace.

"Would you like me to escort you to Sir Grayland's quarters?"

"No, thank you. I can lead my way."

"As you wish. Be safe."

"I will." I touched Father Callahan's face and collected his appearance once more within my mind, to remember him. I left then, unaware that I would never see him again. My feet were heavy as I approached Sir Grayland's room, fearing that he had left me without my choice. But as I opened the door, I could smell that familiar scent and smiled deeply, knowing I could finally find my real home.

"Have you decided?" he said.

"I have. If you will welcome me, I am happy to journey with you."

Sir Grayland did not say anything, and I was unsure as to his true reaction.

"Sir Grayland?"

"You're ready then?"

"I would like to say my farewell to one other before we depart."

"Make it quick. I want to leave before the sun comes up."

"Yes, sir."

I nodded, flashed another smile and left him. I hurried quickly to my domicile, feeling the light touch of warm air begin to fill my lungs, and shook Cleo awake.

"What is wrong, Madeline?" she said. "Why must you wake me so?"

"Do not cry, Cleo, but I am leaving this morrow with Sir Grayland to explore the land of ash."

"Madeline," Cleo said, fully awake now. "You cannot do such a thing. He is not a good man. You cannot trust him."

"I know him differently than you, Cleo. I trust him. Please do not argue."

Cleo wrapped her arms around me and cried. "Will I ever see you again?"

"I am sure of it," I said. "I will return as soon as I find what I need. I promise."

"You have all you need here."

"That may be true, but I will never know unless I search what I cannot see."

Cleo held me tighter. "I love you. I will miss you."

"I as well," I said and kissed Cleo with all of my love. She held my hand tight as I stood. "I have to leave now."

"Wait." Cleo stood and ran from me to the corner of the room. When she returned to me, she placed a large rectangular item into my hand. "Take this."

"What is it?"

"Miss Gretchen helped me make it. It is a diary, a book for your thoughts and feelings. I know you will never be able to write anything within it, but take it and remember me."

"I will never forget you." I kissed Cleo and hugged her. "Thank you." I squeezed Cleo's hand and left her, listening with light regret to her tears as I absconded.

Stepping from my domicile, I took in a deep breath of new life and tucked Father Callahan's prayer into my new diary. I fought away a few tears of nervousness and found my way to Sir Grayland, who held a satchel of food and clothing he said was given to him by Father Callahan as a gift to be kind to me and to take care of me as if I was his own. I smiled graciously and took his hand. We walked then from my home. Neither of us looked back and, despite my promise to Cleo, neither of us would ever step foot upon this land again.

CHAPTER 12

Sir Grayland and I followed the river upstream for three days before I encountered that incredibly familiar scent as part of the wind. We had spent much time on our feet, stopping only upon the chill of night to nourish and rest. Conversation was at a minimum, respecting each other's desire to simply take in our surroundings with tender silence and sanctity. I had lived among the sweetness of this land for many annuals, had learned to appreciate its secrets and serenity, but Sir Grayland had not. He was quite aware that we would be leaving its womb very soon and would not find a home with the same atmosphere as this for a long while. He took each and every sound, every taste and every touch with precision so that he had something to return to when he felt weary of the heat and the dryness of where we were headed. I understood completely and followed his lead, savoring every step as best I could and dreamt of Cleo and Miss Jezebel each night, resting my desires upon the memory of their love.

On the third night, as we ate fish roasted upon our crackling fire, served alongside the fresh taste of juice squeezed from the berries provided to us by the trees, I could feel the presence of Sir Grayland's home and knew that we would come upon it within a day of when we woke from our current rest. I pulled my knees to my chest for comfort and listened to the fire snap, hoping it would soothe my anxiety.

"If you're having second thoughts, now's the time to turn back," Sir Grayland said through a mouthful of fish.

"It is true that I am feeling a steady growth of fright as we continue ever closer to the land beyond. But I hold a high regard for the decisions I make, Sir Grayland, and

I have committed to our journey. Through excellence or disaster, I will live with my consequence."

"Enough with the, 'Sir'," he said. "It's Grayland."

I had expected a much different response to my avowal. But I did not dwell on his chosen words, instead confirming his request. "Of course."

We were silent for a long while afterward. I sat very lonely, listening to Grayland finish the meal I was far too tense to enjoy. Once he had finished and settled himself, I attempted to attain the response I had been hoping for earlier. "Could you explain to me what it is I should expect once we reach your land?"

I felt Grayland's annoyance. I shied away, believing he would not answer me.

"Hell," he said soon after.

"What is hell?" I said.

"You've never heard of hell?"

"I am afraid not."

Grayland laughed. "You ever hear of the devil? God? Heaven?

"Should I have?"

"Talk about a useless priest. What the hell did that guy preach?"

"Father Callahan taught us to live without derision and to listen to our hearts, as only our heart could lead us from our contemptible minds into seeing and following what is good and pure. We lived within the freedom we created for ourselves and helped those who sought only the hand of friendship, not the requirement of aid."

"Well, if you think about it," Grayland said a few moments after I had finished, "that's pretty much how most people see God. So, maybe your priest wasn't so useless after all."

"How is it that most see God, in your unique words?"

"My own words? Okay, I guess it would be that most people supposedly believe that He watches over us and guides us through life."

"Is this what you believe?"

"Not anymore."

"But it was your belief previously?"

"My wife believed in Him; believed that he was watching over us. After..." Grayland stopped, as his voice became choked upon his throat. "After she was taken, it was hard to continue to believe in anything."

I felt saddened, but I needed to know more. Instead of treading on the memory of his wife, I chose to continue to learn about his God and what he meant to others.

"Has anyone else devalued their belief in your God?"

Grayland fought back his sadness. "Yeah. And others believe in something different altogether. There are plenty of theories, yet no evidence for any of them."

"What are some of the other theories?"

"Well, some believe in following Him in peace, some incite violence in His name. Some think He's black, some believe He's actually a woman. There are still some that believe there are many gods ruling over different aspects of life. Then there's the atheists who don't believe He even exists at all."

"Would you consider yourself atheist, in mourning?"

"Part of me does. But the other part of me hopes He does exist, so when I die, I can get Him to suck my big fat dick into eternity."

My lips pursed at the deplorable thought. I ignored it, feeling he meant it only in angered jest for his loss.

"Where does this God live?"

"There's another idea that people disagree on, though most do agree that it is, in some form or another, heaven."

"This heaven is an appealing place to be?"

"If you like the idea of living in eternal bliss and perfection, where only the most righteous and noble souls are allowed."

"I am skeptical of a place that promotes the idea of perfection."

"No argument here."

"Do you believe that heaven is where we shall be upon our deaths?"

"I have my doubts. There are a lot of rules, most of them unachievable."

"Why must they be unachievable?"

"If only you knew."

"What of your wife? Your daughter? Do you believe that they have achieved the nobility of rising to their presumed perfection?"

Grayland whispered a silent prayer that I could not make out. I in turn took to silence to digest my newly acquired information. As the flame of our fire quieted, a new question arose within.

"So is hell, then, the opposite of heaven?"

I could feel Grayland's smile. "You got that right. If there's one thing most people agree on, it's hell. Just imagine your worst nightmare and multiply it by the largest number you can think of. Then double that shit until your mind explodes."

My apprehension pushed my body to shake slightly.

"That's what the zealots would say, anyway. Me, I believe life is hell."

"Making death to be heaven?"

"You're quick."

A smile broke through my lips. "I would have expected that to be the opposite."

"In your world, yeah, maybe. Not if you lived before the war. Not if you saw the chaos of human existence without rules or responsibility."

I could not respond. I turned from Grayland to reach out into the voices of the woodland nightfall and find escape within the flowing stream.

"Come here," Grayland said and touched the tip of my shoulder. I shifted from him, but he did not back away. I slowly accepted his comfort and crawled to him, laying my head upon his chest. He wrapped his arms around me and caressed my stomach, calming the fever of vibration that ran my entire body. He combed a partial bit of my hair away from my tortured face and kissed my forehead.

"I'm sorry. You were very lucky to be raised where you were. The world I remember was a cynical ball of contempt with very little to care about and even less to hope for. The nature of it is in my blood, and it's extremely hard to control. Tomorrow, I'm going to introduce you to it for the first time, and just the thought of that makes me sick. If it wasn't to help you regain your sight, I probably wouldn't have even suggested it."

"It is my will to follow you wherever you lead," I said, calming his repentance. "You have done nothing to regret."

It seemed that Grayland did not believe my truth.

"You may be committed to this and willing to accept the consequences, but I can tell you that there'll be people out there who'll force you to do or say things that are against what you were brought up to believe. And if you don't do as they ask, they will hurt you, probably even kill you. The best thing you can do to protect yourself is listen to me, no matter what I say. Can you do that? Trust me enough to do whatever I say, even when it may hurt you to do it?"

"I will trust your instinct," I said lightly, hiding my nervous tears. "I promise."

"Good."

"Thank you," I said after a pause.

Grayland kissed me, this time upon my marks, closer to my lips. He lingered there for several heartbeats and then laid back. I did not fall to rest for some time. But as I did, the warmth of Grayland's touch sent a desirable urge through my body that led me into a state of hunger.

For what, I could not fathom.

CHAPTER 13

The smell was stimulating.

I woke alone on the pleasant grass with the sensual sun touching the back of my neck. Grayland was not nearby, and I could not feel his presence. "Grayland," I said.

The brush to my left rustled, and his footsteps approached. He helped me to my feet and brushed off a hint of dirt that had collected on the side of my face, leaving his hand resting upon the edge of my neck.

"I was just about to wake you up. You still good?"

"I am ready to continue," I said. "Thank you."

Grayland tapped my neck and took up his pack. "It's a long trip back to my house so I rationed what little food and water we have so we can make it back without having to scrounge up too much."

"Wise decision."

"We better get a move on. Don't want to get caught wandering around at night."

I took hold of Grayland's hand and stayed close to his body as we crossed the river in a fairly shallow bed. We did not speak for the final journey through the trees, which became more sparse and wilted until they had all but vanished, giving way for the feel of the arid, ashen desert. My tongue grew dry very quickly with the taste of sulfur, and the air's thickness nearly closed my lungs, pushing me to my knees. Grayland continued to deny me the chance to quench my growing dehydration as he urged me forward with a tight grip upon my arm. I could not distinguish whether the sun remained high above or when the moon might take its perch, but I relentlessly prayed it would appear with haste so that we might rest and gather our bearings. To help me draw strength in my suffering, I thought much of Cleo and what it would feel like to see her again, in a different light, with a different sense. Her touch was all over my skin. I loved to think of her, to imagine her hand upon mine, taking me down to the barn and sitting upon the perch to take in the smell of the wind and each other's comfort. But the rich contradiction of my memory with the environment I was currently encountering diluted these thoughts and pushed me deeper into uncertainty. What helped to keep my mind from becoming as barren as our environment, though, was not my home at all. It was the vibrant smell for which had led me to leave my home. Once secreted by Grayland, it now carried me along with its flowing kiss and dense swelter, keeping me fluent upon why I was here and what this travel truly meant for me.

When Grayland and I finally took refuge upon our first night, hidden in a hole within the land that felt hotter than the surface, I took several languished breaths through my wide-open mouth in hopes of cleansing my severely constricted lungs. The base of my eyes stung with the lack of moisture, and my feet burned with dulled numbness. Upon settling, Grayland poured me a half a cup of water, which I quickly sucked down. The taste of fresh water was soothing upon my lips and healed the burn in my throat, but it also made me ill.

"You shouldn't drink it that fast," Grayland said. He handed me a piece of barley bread, the smell of which induced a wretch of vomit. I let the bread fall to the ground and slid away from my sickness, tucking my legs up to my chest, feeling nothing more within my body than a tight resistance to the conditions that surrounded me.

I did not sleep that night, and when Grayland took my hand to journey the next morrow, my body seized. I could no longer feel my legs. My chest burned with every small breath I attempted. But Grayland pushed me forward, at times picking me into his arms and carrying me until the day was gone and we took our shelter. I could not eat for several nights and only took a few sips of water when I could. Grayland stayed close to me all the while. Each day as he walked, I held my arms around his neck and kept my head pressed firmly upon his shoulder. When I was not crying with my pain, I was resting and praying my love for Grayland and his heart.

It had grown seven nights before I finally found the stomach and strength to take nourishment with the barley bread. It was only a nibble, taking heed of Grayland's advice to acclimate my stomach with small portions to begin, but the taste was quite satisfying and made me feel I was at home. I slept soundly among the night and woke with new hunger. I finished a few bites of my bread before Grayland roused. He asked that I remain still and quiet as he left to retrieve a gift for me. I did not fight his request, though I found it odd that I could not go with him.

When he returned, he pulled my hair together and tied it tightly against the back of my head. His hands felt warm against my ears and neck.

"Wear this for me," he said, wrapping a soft, silky cloth around the top of my head. It draped along my shoulders and fell slightly down my back.

"What type of garment is this?" I said.

"It's what will keep you safe for the next few days," he said.

"Safe from what?"

"Come here." Grayland wrapped the cloth around my neck, allowing it to drop past my other shoulder, and cupped my cheek in his hand. "Half a day's walk from here is a mining outpost. I'm going to try and barter for some food and water, but it may not be easy. Stay close to me and don't say a word. Got it?"

I nodded, tightening my lips. He kissed my forehead and took my hand. As we walked, I constantly held my hand to my new accessory, keeping it from flying about the strong wind. At times, I would pull it up and cover my mouth from the spit of dirt and ash. The storm was fierce, but Grayland kept a tight grip upon my hand as he walked against the wind with a strong step. The more we pushed forward, the more the wind pushed back, forcing us to stop. He sat down and pulled me close, hiding my face among his shoulder.

When the winds chose to die, Grayland did not let go. I could feel anxiety flow upon his touch as he looked around at our surroundings. I wished to ask him what was happening but chose not to speak as asked. In our silence, a gentle chatter of several voices rose among us. I could not make out the words they were expressing but understood Grayland's reasons for remaining still and quiet. The men came upon us, anger in their voices. Grayland responded in their unique vernacular, but it did not ease their troubles. His own anger increased as they stole up his pack and shuffled through it. Grayland lowered his mouth to my ear as one of the men shoved a cold, hard object into the base of my back.

"Stand up, stay close and keep your mouth covered."

I raised my new garment up over my mouth and took his hand in mine. It shook slightly, but I trusted that he knew what was happening and that no danger would fall upon me. We stood with extreme caution. The men forced us to walk, and we obliged without resistance. Two men walked briskly behind us, conversing with one another, as we followed the lead men with careful, tepid steps. I could smell them all devouring the very little barley bread and water we had left, and though I was quite incensed by the men's insensitivity, Grayland remained calm. I resolved to follow his lead and forgave the men for their selfish behavior.

It felt to my body that we had walked a half a day when the men guided us into a large domicile and forced us to our knees. The air had become stale with a mix of smells I found unable to relate. I kept my head down and my mouth covered, my grip upon Grayland's hand tightening as my anxiety for what would befall us next chilled my fingers.

One of the lead men was in discussion with a new tongue. He handed him our pack and, along with our other captors, swept from the room with swift feet. Before they had gone, our new acquaintance tossed the pack aside and stepped close, his perfume taking command over all other scents. He gently rested the tips of his fingers under my chin. His touch was gentle, yet oddly uncomfortable as it danced with a sinister pulse. Out of courtesy for this man's home, I raised my head for him. The man pressed my hand down, allowing the garment to drop across my shoulder and expose my features. He leaned down to smell my skin, then took his hand away and stepped back.

Grayland sat still, his voice unwilling to break free.

"Her value is pure," the stranger said with a slurred accent.

"She's not for sale," Grayland said gruffly.

"Everything is for sale," the man said, an irritated wave crossing his lips. "You are in need of food and water?"

"Yes. But not in exchange for her."

"That is not negotiable," the man said. "Sell her to me and be on your way, or I take her and leave you in death."

"She is not for sale," Grayland said, his voice tainted with a heightened anger. "We both came to you for work."

"You wish to work for me?"

"Only as long as it takes to gather what we need."

"You are strong," the man said, "and will be of much use in the mine. But this fair specimen is far too frail to perform such an act. She will remain with me."

"No deal."

"I never asked for your acceptance."

The man snapped his fingers and a couple of men scampered toward us. Grayland crushed my hand in his but did nothing more to stop the men from separating us. It was clear that he was afraid of what might happen if he tried to fight them. As he was drawn from the domicile, his steps were reserved and full of defeat. I remained still, on my knees, shaking.

"What am I to do?" I said softly when all was quiet and only the stranger's breaths filled the room.

"You will work with my wife," he said. "She will teach you to cook and clean, to show reverence for me and my men. And you will learn to obey. Alhamdulillah."

Soft and meek footsteps circled about me. "Come with me, child."

I was pleasantly surprised to hear a woman speak, and I welcomed her sincerity. She escorted me to her quarters where she calmly undressed me and washed my body of ash and dirt, humming a sweet, tender tune. I took her body into my hand and found her smooth skin and petite features to be lovely and kind. When she had finished, she wrapped me in a long gown that covered the whole of my body and fell pooled upon the floor. She spent much time hemming the gown until it fit reasonably well and then rested me on a soft piece of furniture that sunk slightly upon my weight.

"Get some rest," she said.

"What is your name?" I said.

"Safiya."

"That is quite lovely, much as you are. I am Madeline."

"I am happy to meet you, Madeline."

"May I ask of you a question?"

"Please. I am here to teach and to serve."

"The man my friend and I spoke with. Who is he?"

"He is my husband, a servant of Allah," Miss Safiya said with a soft sadness. "His name is Abdullah, but he will wish you to call him your lord." There was a mix of respect and disquiet toward her husband (supposedly the man she has taken as her only love), as if she was afraid a terrible fate might befall her if she disobeyed him in any manner. I understood her distress and grew fondly accepting of her.

"What is it that he will expect of me?"

"What he expects from all of his followers. Obey his teachings, honor his word, respect his actions and love him at his behest."

"Do you show practice in all of these actions?"

"Unless I wish to be put to death."

"And they will help my friend and I stay from death as well?"

"They will."

"Then I shall do as you bid, my lady."

"It is not my bidding you must adhere to, Madeline. Only his."

I felt the pearls of tears rise to my eyes but held them strong. "Do you know where they have taken my friend?"

"He has been assigned to work in the mine until our lord finds his time has been served. As long as he keeps his head, he will be fine."

"Will I ever obtain the opportunity to speak to him?"

"I am afraid not."

I lowered my head. Miss Safiya took my neck into her palm and kissed me—a sweet and tender acknowledgment of my dismay.

"Can you retrieve my diary?" I said with a child's squeak.

"What diary?"

"The pack your people have taken from us held a diary that I cherish greatly. Is it possible for you to retrieve it for me?"

"I will see what I can do," she said. "Now rest, child." Miss Safiya prompted me to lie down. I felt comfortable upon the cushion of my resting bed.

"Will you be with me," I said before Miss Safiya left, "to take my hand if ever I grow frightened?"

"I am Abdullah's wife," she said. "I will always be with you."

The woman kissed me and left, leaving me to cry myself into slumber.

(CHAPTER 14

I did not spend a lot of time away from my quarters over the few days that followed our arrival, fueling the urge to seek out Grayland. Part of me wished to be with him, remain close to him until we were granted our payment and released to continue our journey. Yet another part of me, perhaps out of fear of what was still to come outside the borders of Abdullah's territory, was content with the arrangement I had been provided. Although it was fairly lonely for parts of my stay, I found that I was given an adequate amount of nourishment, both for my body and for my mind. Miss Safiya would come and keep company with me, bringing with her food and water—plenty for half a dozen men—as well as rich stories of Anno Domini. She would talk of the curtain of war, of the men and women who found solace in the man of heaven with fear of finding rapture within the pits of hell.

"A large majority of people had grown frightened of what they did not understand," she had said on the ripening of the war. "Several groups, working for a better, peaceful world, presented ideas that went against the normalcy of the day. Instead of thinking logically over the prospect of what was being offered and the true sight of a future without pain, those people clung to the world they knew, even though that world was full of hatred and sin. They did not want to respect any opinion but their own and found it impossible to listen to an opposing point of view, no matter how valid the argument. They rose up against the peace with no basis but their fear. Only those that trusted in the peace of the Lord and in His truth survived the wrath of man's ultimate destruction against Him and his disciples."

"Was it man against this Lord, or the Lord against man that caused your world's destruction?" I said. The question held merit, as it took her a few heartbeats to find her voice on the matter.

"I would say both. Man was not willing to accept the Lord in glory, so in turn, the Lord smote his creation."

"With the help of other men?"

"Allah is great," she said quickly. "To defend Him is to honor Him."

What she said was repeated as I listened fervently to passages from her Lord's preaching, finding most of what had been written to be quite contradictory; passages lecturing unification and meekness, alongside others calling for conflict and violence. Under all of the mechanical rhetoric was a clear message for which I found to be disheartening—one will follow the Lord of Heaven in the faith described by the prophet delivered or find death at the hand of the obedient follower. I accepted the message with respect, masking my true convictions.

The monotony of these readings and instruction were broken upon several occasions during each day when I would be forced to take practice of Miss Safiya's ritualistic prayer. It included taking to my knees and bowing down to her lord, seeking reprisal for sins I may have committed. I participated in the act with diligence but was unsure of what I was to repent. It did not seem to matter to Miss Safiya, though, so long as I spoke the words for which she preached in ardor.

When I was allowed to breathe the air outside of my quarters, I was ordered to stay within sight of Miss Safiya and help in any manner she deemed me qualified. I helped in the cooking of meals and presented them to both the royal elite (with the perfume of fruit), as well as the lower order of man (with the stench of sweat and smoke I deemed could only have come from the cigarette). I found this intentional division to be of utter shame, but no more so than what became clear to be the deliberate division of a man's authority (with power bestowed by the creator) and a woman's submission (to be treated with grave ignominy.) At moonlight, after all lower order had returned to their chained respite and the royal elite had resigned to their women, I took Miss Safiya's escort to Abdullah's domicile. He would inquire of my teachings and practice the performance of one lasting prayer, taking his wife in pleasure. I held her hand during the ritual and sometimes felt his sweaty palm touch my face. When the sacrament concluded, Abdullah kissed me adieu. Miss Safiya returned with me to my quarters and lay me to rest. Without realization, I quickly became addicted to the conformity of my new routine. Grayland fell further from my needs as my heart broke with every new sunrise prayer.

I lost count of how many suns had passed when I finally heard Grayland's scorched voice again. I was labored to feed the lower order their midday nourishment, which consisted of a half-cup of water and the count of three shelled nuts. He spoke of nothing intelligible and it was quite far away, but it still brought a fresh joy to my waning soul. I wanted to yell out for him, run to him. But to do so would cause me great pain in consequence. I was not ready for retribution in my fragile state. For now, simply knowing that he was still alive and had not left without me was enough to push me along through the rest of the day. I finished my work and returned with Miss Safiya to clean the domicile of the lord, who was currently on mission (for which I, nor Miss Safiya, was allowed to know anything about in great detail) but was to return at the dusk of night. I was to be ready for his arrival.

"How am I to prepare?" I said.

"You have done all of the necessary preparation," Miss Safiya returned.

"What is it that he will expect of me?"

"To give yourself unconditionally to Allah."

"Even if my conviction says otherwise?" I said with displeasure.

Miss Safiya never took to an answer.

After we concluded our cleansing and presented the division of meals, we withdrew to my quarters, where I was bathed and dressed in a fresh gown accentuated with flowers near the baseline and upon the cuffs of the wrists. I was also presented a new headdress, fitted in mesh and silk, it too ornamented in flowers. My lady wrapped it among its place and kissed my marks. The touch of her lips was comforting, but I felt a light shake in them, as if she believed the trial I would partake was not in my best interest—but was essential to my survival.

Miss Safiya placed me upon the edge of his bed, draping my arms across my lap at the wrists. She lifted my chin with a gentle love and kissed me.

"Don't move."

She stepped away, but did not leave; I could hear her soft breath near the entry of the domicile. Feeling her presence and knowing that she would not leave convinced me that she was becoming more a part of my family. She was lovely in her caretaking and humble in her graciousness. Much in the way Miss Jezebel acted as my reason, so Miss Safiya acted as my mentor. If I could not have the likes of Miss Jezebel or Cleo by my side, I was happy to have Miss Safiya hold my hand and love me in the way only they could.

Time languished as I waited for Abdullah's return. I took the solitary moments to clear my mind and think of those I had left behind. Believing that my family prayed for my safety and wellbeing soothed my body and helped me trust that when Abdullah made his appearance, I would be able to act in the manner for which I had been adorned.

A soft smile floated about my lips when his grace stepped through his entry, grunting in stimulation. He said a few notes to my lady and then sat down by my side. I felt my muscles tighten and drew in a breath.

"My, you're a beautiful doll," he said, sliding his fingertips down the side of my face. I shook slightly, my skin growing cold and pimpled. As his hand dropped to my shoulder, Abdullah leaned down and kissed my cheek. His beard smelled quite rotten; I could not help but turn my head slightly downward.

"Do you disrespect me?" he said, grabbing my wrist.

"No, my lord," I said, straitening my body. I attempted greatly to keep my calm.

"That's good," he said. He let go of my wrist and stood. He urged me to recite my prayers, my understanding of his god and the laws that he has bestowed upon his people. I did as I was asked and did not waver one bit, satisfying his need. When he deemed me complete, he took to his knee and lifted my hand to his head. I sat still and uncomfortable as he prayed upon it.

Abdullah fell into silence and stood, my hand still resting upon his own. "Now bow," he said.

I did as requested and got on my knees, lowering my head in his honor.

"Praise be with Allah," he said.

I sat in silence and Abdullah tightened his grip. I clenched my teeth to fight my pain, remaining still and respectful.

"Accept Him as your god," he said.

I took in a breath, ready to refute his demand, but held my tongue instead. My insolence was met with the back of his hand against my cheek.

"Why do you disrespect me?" Abdullah yelled.

"She isn't ready," Miss Safiya said.

"Shut your mouth," Abdullah said. "She will do as I say or die like any other."

"She is young. Give her more time."

"She has had enough time." Abdullah paused to shift his attention back to me. "Do you wish to die?"

"No, sir," I said.

"Then praise Allah as your god, and take him into your heart."

"My lord," Miss Safiya said.

"Praise be with Allah," I said, feeling the pinch of Abdullah's anger upon his touch. "My savior and Lord. I will obey His law and be His soldier upon the sin of man."

Abdullah rested his anger and kissed my hand tenderly. "Rise."

I stood, remaining docile in his presence. He lifted my head and kissed me. "Allah will endow you with many gifts and love."

"Come," he said to Miss Safiya, granting her pleasure in honor of my forced conversion. It was not clear whether either realized that my words of praise were shallow, but they did not seem to care. My words were enough to keep me alive and to keep Miss Safiya from harm. That was enough.

Abdullah finished his routine and immediately took refuge to pray upon his family. At the same time, Miss Safiya returned me to my quarters.

"I need to speak with my friend," I said as she closed the door.

"I'm afraid that's not possible."

"I don't care," I said, shocking myself more than Miss Safiya. I had never spoken to a peré in such a manner before. I softened my voice. "I need to speak with him. If doing so means that I must disobey you and our lord, then that is what I must do."

My lady was quiet. She removed my headdress and combed her fingers through my hair. "He will be leaving on another mission soon. Wait until he has departed, and I will take you to see your friend. Until then, say nothing more of the matter."

I wanted to object but could feel her insistence and the harmony that it brought. I hugged her. "I will do as you ask."

I did not say another word as I bathed and upon the drawing of my bed. And she did not leave; she laid with me, humming a lovely song.

CHAPTER 15

The following days passed slowly under the new oppression of the lord's scornful presence. I strayed from him when I could and closed my mind when I could not. What helped me rise with each day was Miss Safiya's promise that one day soon I would be allowed to speak with Grayland, to reach out and embrace him, but only upon the absence of our lord.

The energy rose within my body when Abdullah announced his departure the next morrow, a journey that would take him from the land for several days. Miss Safiya and I held one another's hands as he kissed us both farewell. Immediately after his presence vanished from ours, I stated my desire to see Grayland right away, only to find a nervous resistance. I cried upon her approval for two days, insisting that she keep the promise she had bestowed upon me. Upon rising the third day, Miss Safiya awaited me with words that filled my heart with elation. I found my dress quickly and clutched her arm. We walked with a brisk foot to the mouth of the mine, finding very little question or puzzlement. She guided me through the rocky halls, moistened by licks of water and mold, until we located the lower order working tirelessly deep within the earth's throat.

"Wait here," Miss Safiya said, leaving me alone to rest my back upon the rock, which felt like wax but with a hint of powder and sand. I pressed my cheek against it, feeling the icy sensation pour through the crevices of dried and heated skin. It burned with tenderness but soon relaxed in numbness. It was a sensual distraction from the blunt heat and lack of humidity that engulfed the air above.

"Madeline?"

My heart fluttered to the song of Grayland's voice. I smiled as a cherub and followed his steps into a deep embrace, burying my head into his shoulder as he brushed his hands up and down my back.

"You shouldn't be here," he said.

"I had a great need to speak with you."

Grayland tilted my head to the side. I winced slightly at his touch, but did not take it as malicious. "That bastard hit you, didn't he?"

"I am fine," I said, cupping Grayland's hand between my own. "Do not bother yourself with my mistakes."

"How is getting smacked around your mistake?"

I pressed my finger to Grayland's lips. "I must speak with you in private."

I shifted my head past Grayland, to where I could hear Miss Safiya, and furrowed my brow in hopes that she would contend to us our moment of seclusion. Grayland turned to her, and I could sense his smile upon mine.

"Thank you." He took my hand and walked me deeper within the mine. I kept my arm extended, allowing my fingers to trace their path along the wall. As we reached the depths of quiet, he sat me down on a bevy of rocks against the rounded edge.

"How you holding up?" he asked instantly, pulling off my headdress and running his fingers through my hair.

"I am struggling," I said. "My lady, Miss Safiya, is very respectful and kind; I love her dearly. But her husband, and the laws he requires of his people, can be quite repugnant."

Grayland ran his hand down my bruised cheek. He stood and I heard several noises come from him that I was unfamiliar with. Before I could ask, I smelled the smoke of the cigarette much more prominent than I had ever encountered. I choked and coughed at the heaviness of its quality.

"I'm sorry I didn't fight for you," Grayland said and swiped his hand about the air near my face several times to clear the smoke away. The smell lingered strong, but I slowly became accustomed to it.

"It is not your fault," I said. "If you had refused his wishes, we both may have been killed for our insolence."

Grayland exhaled. "I still hate you having to suffer through it alone."

"I will survive," I said, a bit unconvincing. "I have learned many things about their ways and their culture."

"Fucking lies," Grayland said.

"It is important for me to understand them. One reason for leaving my home was to understand what happened to the people of Anno Domini. I may not like their customs, but I must respect them, learn from them, both for my knowledge and my life."

"Do me a favor. Quit listening."

"It is far better to understand all viewpoints than it is to demonstrate ignorance in favor of a biased premise."

"Yeah," Grayland grumbled.

"You worry. But you can trust that I will not allow them to corrupt my heart with values for which I do not believe in."

"I hope so."

I took pause to give Grayland a moment of reflection.

"How much longer must we remain here?" I said when I felt his anger had calmed.

Grayland took several breaths of smoke before he answered. "I don't know."

"How much payment have we collected?"

"Enough to make half the trip, maybe," he said.

"Perhaps we could ration them to last longer than what you have calculated."

Grayland could see my disappointment. "I'd love to. But there's no way that rag is going to let me go before I've reached my full credit."

"I can speak to him. Seek permission for your early release."

"You want us both killed?"

"He wouldn't do that. It would be against his law."

"Tell him that."

"Grayland, these people are of peace."

"You sure about that?" Grayland touched my face with the tips of his fingers.

"The lord can find his anger overwhelming. But what is humanity without flaw?"

Grayland turned from me, his own anger fueling his silence.

"Miss Safiya will help me secure your release. I know she will."

"If you believe that, you haven't learned anything."

"I came to you for your permission. It is apparent that I have failed." I stood and redressed my head. "I wish to return to my lady."

"You might not see it, Madeline, but I do."

"See what?"

"The bastards have claimed you as one of their own."

"They have done no such thing," I said, the pitch of my voice high and full of ire. "I am not a possession."

Grayland knelt down and embraced me. "Run," he whispered into my ear.

"I will not leave without you," I said. The level of my voiced matched his.

"If what I say is true, you're gonna have to."

"How will I know?"

"You're an intelligent girl, Madeline. I have faith in your instincts."

"I don't want to leave you," I said.

"I know."

I hugged him greatly and would not let go. "I will ask his permission and face the consequences."

"No, wait," he said, his voice rising with a hint of enthusiasm. "Don't do anything. I want you to go back up there and do everything as if nothing happened. Tomorrow, I'll ask to turn in my credits. Does that sound fair?"

I hesitated, but his plan felt logical. I agreed with a nod.

"Good," he said and kissed me. "Get back up there. Your lady is waiting."

I kissed Grayland and walked away, using the wall to guide me.

"Be careful," Grayland said.

I did not turn to him. When I reached Miss Safiya, she did not scold me for the length of my absence. She simply took my hand warmly and guided me from the mine.

A familiar smell awaited us upon our return. Miss Safiya placed her arm down across the front of my body and pushed me a step behind her. I listened intently to Abdullah's aggression toward Miss Safiya's submission, which ended quickly when she was forced to the ground. I held my position and kept my attention upon Abdullah, unwilling to allow him a reason for the same unwarranted punishment.

Abdullah whipped out a strong command and Miss Safiya was taken away in tears, begging for him; begging for compassion. He remained silent until her pleas had disappeared and then returned his focus to me.

"Have you betrayed me as well, my doll?"

"I have done nothing to warrant the accusation," I said.

"Good," Abdullah said.

"Where have you taken my lady?"

"That's none of your concern."

"It is of my concern. She is my caretaker. I deserve to know why she has been taken from me."

"You will learn of her discretion soon enough," Abdullah said.

I allowed him to lead me back to my quarters, where I remained, locked within for the whole of the following sun, or perhaps even longer, as I did not have any means of observing the nature outside of the walls that imprisoned me. I received neither a piece of food to eat nor a drop of water to drink. Yet, when Abdullah finally chose to come to me, I did not cry out to him in anger. I may have felt too far weakened to attempt to prove my resentment toward his immoral acts. Giving him the pleasure of my anger would demonstrate a likeness of his own demeanor; I could not allow myself to become as he. I lowered to my knees as he stepped upon the ground that had become my friend and placed his hand to my forehead. With a gracious kiss, I took it and held it with a soft, gentle touch. One of his men lowered a tray with a small piece of bread and some water. I wanted desperately to take it up and swallow it whole, but I restrained from even seeking to touch it.

"You should eat."

"Yes, my lord. Thank you." I picked up the bread and ate it in very small, reserved bites, so as to both savor it and show that Abdullah's cruelty against me did not diminish my temperament.

"There has been a request for my presence," Abdullah said. "I wish for you to accompany me."

"Yes, my lord," I said, hiding my knowledge of what was to come.

He waited until I had finished my meal. He then helped me rise to my feet, and with a soft and affectionate hand, escorted me to the mines. I felt lightheaded as the heat wrapped my body, but was happy for the feel of the earth upon my feet and the smell of the wind. The mingling of the men that found their labor their life fell to silence as Abdullah made his presence known. As we stopped, he pulled me close to him, pinching my arms.

"Who has requested an audience with me?" he said with a booming voice.

"I have." The voice was strong and demanding and my heart beat quicker. I hoped that Abdullah would not recognize my zeal.

"Step forward, my son," Abdullah said. Grayland stepped up to us and kissed Abdullah's hand. "Why have you asked for me?"

"I have been working for several weeks now. I would like to cash in my time served and be on my way."

"I see," Abdullah said, tightening his grip on my arms. "Your work has been appreciated, and I would hate to lose such a strong hand." After a disingenuous pause, Abdullah said, "You are free to go. Collect your payment and farewell to you."

I wanted to interject, but Grayland spoke quicker than I could. "Wait," he said before we could turn to leave.

"Are you not satisfied with your payment?"

"I'm fine with the payment," he said. "But I'm not leaving without everything I came with."

"You will have everything returned to you."

"Including her?" Grayland said.

"The child may have come with you," Abdullah said, "but she was never yours to claim. She is under the protection of Allah now."

"You son-of-a—"

With a swift move, Abdullah shoved his hand under my neck and held his other hand upward. "Watch what you say, sir. I will not hesitate"

"Get your damn hands off my daughter."

I was shocked to hear Grayland speak these words, yet pleased with his claim. It fell upon me quickly that Abdullah felt the same.

"She is your daughter?"

Grayland did not answer, and the air about us felt rigid and cold.

Abdullah laughed. "Then you must do what is right of her and grant me your permission to take her hand as my wife."

"You can go to hell."

"Take him."

"Wait," Grayland and I said in unison. I ran for him, but did not reach him. Several men shoved Grayland to the ground and pulled me back to Abdullah, where I fell to my knees after enduring the rip of his hand.

"Madeline," Grayland yelled before being silenced.

"Give me your daughter or find death for your insolence."

"Fuck you," Grayland said.

Abdullah knelt to Grayland. "Give me your daughter," he scowled. When he rose after a moment of silence, he called out to his people. "You are all witness. Madeline's father has granted me his permission to take her as my wife."

The crowd cheered as I cried. Grayland was pulled from the ground and taken away. I could not understand how he could allow this to happen.

Abdullah pulled me to my feet. "Now you will come to be my bride."

"What is to happen to my father?" The words felt ripe upon my tongue.

"He will pay for his impudence."

"You agreed to pay him and set him free."

"I changed my mind. Your father will remain my slave for a lifetime. Pray he takes it early."

I was ill when we reached his domicile. He pushed me onto his bed and kissed me with a rough tongue. His beard scratched at my chin and I felt again as if I would vomit. I could not do anything but stay remarkably still as he removed me from my garments and made me his bride.

When he had finished his function, he slept next to me with his hand upon my breast. I wanted to run, as Grayland had told me to do, but all I could muster was the strength to cry.

CHAPTER 16

I remained the lord's bride for three nights following our marriage and a hostage from the world when I was not about his company. For the most of my time I spent alone, I would sleep, unable to rise from my weariness. When I found the power to sit or stand, I would sing aloud to Cleo, finding solace in the thought that she could hear my tune and would whisper her love to the wind in return. I would imagine her kiss, allowing it to wash my mind so that I may continue to rise another day.

Upon the morrow of the fourth day, my lord came to me with news.

"Your lady is being judged today."

"Judged for what?" I said.

"She has soiled the house of her husband and must be punished for her actions."

"She has done nothing wrong."

The stroke of his hand ripped across my face before long. "You have already been punished for your indignation, yet you remain insolent."

I lowered my head and shifted away from him.

"You shall bring the prisoner to me for judgment."

Abdullah's man took me up with a hard grip under the pit of my arm and pushed me forward, nearly causing me to fall back to the ground. I did not fight him as he pulled me through the streets. The air, still arid and heavy, was refreshing upon my skin. I could not account for many men, as it was quite silent, and I wondered if it was currently the fall of night instead of the peak of day. It did not matter, as I was pulled down a row of stairs leading to a musky and dreadfully hotter cavern under the ground that smelled of rotten eggs and rotted flesh. I gagged and held my breath until I gathered my strength of stomach to accept the pungency of the environment. Finally, I was forced to my knees in front of a series of round metal bars. I could hear a rattle of noises and then an eerie squeak as the bars shifted forward, away from my touch.

"Get her up," the man said and took a few steps backward, taking a stand to watch over me.

When I refused to move, the man whipped the small of my back with a wooden staff. I chirped in pain and crawled forward.

"Stop," Miss Safiya said and came quickly to my aid. She wrapped me up in her arms and pulled me further away. "Give us a minute," she said, followed by a few words in her native language of prayer.

"Are you okay?" she asked, stroking my hair.

I held my hand to my back and rubbed it generously. "I will be fine."

"I'm sorry."

"Why are you sorry? It is I that did not do anything to help you."

"This is not your fault. You did nothing wrong."

The pain found its way from my back. "Nor did you. For what reason are you to be judged this morrow?"

Miss Safiya cupped my chin in her hands. I could feel her sweet eyes fall upon my own. "Whatever happens today, I want you to do as you're told without hesitation."

"I do not believe I can acquiesce to such a request," I said.

"You must be strong; for me and for your friend. Promise me."

I tried, but I could not come to terms with her request. Regardless, I kissed her gently and said, "I promise."

She hugged me deeply.

"Take me home," she said and rose to her feet. We clasped hands and walked from the cell with resolute steps, followed a few feet behind by Abdullah's man, keeping a strong eye on the both of us.

When we reached our destination, which seemed to be near the outskirts of Abdullah's land, the whispers of the masses consumed my ears. I held tight upon Miss Safiya's hand as they circled us. She returned my trepidation with her own tight grip and wrapped her other hand around my shoulders.

"Remember your promise," she whispered before Abdullah pulled me violently away from her.

"On your knees," he said. I took position next to him and sought out Miss Safiya's presence. "You are being judged for the crimes that you have committed against me and my home."

The crowd yelled, and Abdullah spoke in a long prayer. When he was through, he grabbed my hand and forced a palm-sized rock into it. I accepted it with confusion.

"Commence your lady's punishment," he said.

"What do you wish of me?" I said. "What is her punishment?"

"Death by stoning," Abdullah said with a dry mouth.

"That cannot be," I said. "Who has witnessed my lady in the act of adultery?"

"It is no matter. Commence the punishment."

"It is of importance to me. She cannot be found guilty if there is no witness."

"Call out if you have witnessed my wife in the act for which she is accused."

Several men (by my count seven) called out their indictment.

"And where, shall I ask, have you seen this act performed?'

In exact precision, each man said, "Within the mine."

"And she has been found guilty of breaking her oath and the law of Allah. Now prove your love to Him, and to me, and initiate the sentence she has been given."

I focused my attention on Miss Safiya. Her breath was heavy among the silence of the crowd. Even though it sickened me greatly, I had made her a promise and I knew she wished me to follow through on the act I was being requested of, else I be placed upon her spot and receive the same punishment. With a despondent heart, I let the rock soar through the air. It felt a lifetime before I heard a loud crack and a great uproar of cheers, which was followed by dozens of men and women acting in kind, ripping rocks through the air at Miss Safiya.

I fell to my knees and vomited.

I remained still until the crowd was through with their torture and Abdullah sang his praises to them in prayer. It was not long thereafter that I found myself in Abdullah's bed, where he undressed me with the slow hand of lust, as each night preceding. As I lay cold next to him, he spoke to me of the voyage he would be embarking on at the rise of the sun. I felt a sense of delight, not that I cared much for where his journey would take him or for its purpose. My only focus was on the freedom I could now attempt to redeem in his absence. He held me close to him that night and the irritation of his heated breath upon my neck kept me from finding rest, prolonging the time from when I would be sent back to my quarters to live without communication for as many days as he needed to complete his journey.

** ** **

The lock was turned as it always was upon his departure. I took solace upon my bed and refuge in my dreams, waking some time later with a renewed energy. I was unsure as to how I would find my way to Grayland, or if he was even still alive, but I would not give up on him, or myself. I could not run, not as he had asked. He was the key to my natural sight, but even more, I could not visualize myself surviving within the world without him. He was all I had to love and all I had to keep living. First and foremost, I needed to break free of my cell.

I took root a few feet from the door and screamed as loud as my lungs would allow. When the lock of the door turned open, I stopped and remained still as the thick stump of the tree. The smell of Abdullah's man was pungent as he growled his displeasure with my tantrum.

"What the hell is wrong with you?" he said.

"I am very sorry, sir. I miss my lord ever so much. May I see him, please?"

"He's gone. He won't be back for a week."

"But I must see him." I pulled tears from deep within and showed them to him.

"I can't help you. Now shut the hell up."

"I need him," I said with a dry throat. I then released all of the power in my body and fell dead to the floor.

The man instinctively rushed to my aid. He took hold of my limp head, his breath erratic, his hands guided. Whether inadvertent or completely deliberate, I did not let his fondling deter my focus. As in the speed of a tortoise, I slipped my hand upon his cold, slick weapon. Once my grasp had become solid, and I felt his eyes grow unaware of anything but my body, I raised the weapon to his temple with all of the force my muscle could employ. The man fell to my side, grunting in pain. I slid up onto my knees and used the man's outward pain to direct my next blow, silencing him with the snap of his nose.

I took a pause, with several deep, quick breaths, to collect the quiver that had shrouded my body and halt any misgivings from escaping. My sin was necessary; I could not question my actions, else find my time in life cut short. What was to happen next, I was unclear, but my destination was not. Whether I found Grayland was inconsequential. Anything, including the path to a new existence, was far better than remaining here to be one man's possession.

I rose to my feet and fought off a bout of dizziness. Gripping the weapon tightly in my hand, I used its tip to track items that may obstruct my path, listening carefully for any possible men that may be stationed to protect the lord's jewel. To my surprise—and my advantage—no men were heard but for an older gentleman who snored peacefully in rest. I stepped by on the very tips of my toes so as not to disturb him and found the quiet of the night to be as refreshing as the sound of the river streaming under a warm summer moon.

I had traveled the path to the mine several times during my stay and counted each step carefully. When I reached its mouth, I could smell the water dripping off of its veins and wished very much to taste its sweetness. But the longer I remained stationary, especially in open view, the greater my chance of being found would become. So I dashed inside and followed the only route I knew, leading me down into the bowels for whence Grayland and I spoke. I would wait as long as it took for Grayland to find me, whether it be a day, or several annuals, I would wait for him. And he would find me.

Until that time, I had the freedom to release the tension of my actions. The more I thought about what I had done, the more I could feel the lord crawling throughout my skin. The taste of his odor and the caress of his touch sent pimples to the surface of my skin that I wished to scratch away. The brush of his beard and the smell of his skin were washed upon my garments as a lingering perfume. Finding it extremely hard to find my breath, I tore my robes from my body and laid against the cool, moist walls, accepting its nurture as best I could. At the same time, the mine took my tears upon its own body and allowed my voice to vent in an echo of screams I felt might find their way to the ears of my enemy. If that were the case, so be it.

When my body could no longer stand on its own power, I fell to the ground and pulled myself tight. And I waited—without rest; without joy; and for the first time in memory, without optimism for what was to come.

CHAPTER 17

I was cold, unwilling to cover my body with the rags of my penitence; my body chilled in the fever of sorrow, a depression of the spirit I had come to love. I remembered how I once felt, free of any worry, dancing and singing with my family in the fields, lighting up the eyes of my listeners with the story of hope and life. I knew what I was supposed to feel, but I did not feel it anymore and it frightened me greatly. But no more would I cry, as I had no more use for tears. For as long as it took to hear the voice I so desperately wanted to hear, I could not even find the pleasure as Grayland's concern danced upon my ears.

"Madeline," he said. "What happened?"

His touch upon my shoulder was light and that of love. But I could not acknowledge it; could not accept it. I remained stiff, without recognition.

"Madeline," he said with more compassion.

The tone was stiff, but I finally found a voice. "I wish to leave."

"What did he do to you?"

My body shook, and I turned my head down.

Grayland took in a few aggravated breaths. "Here," he said. I heard a spark—and then that smell. "Take this."

Grayland forced my fingers around the cool end of the cigarette. I did not move my hand, even when the heat from the tip bit at my leg. "Take it. It'll calm you down."

I took in a breath, nauseated by the thickness of the smoke, but allowed Grayland to raise my hand and insert the cigarette between my lips. The dry paper tasted strangely exotic.

"Inhale," he said.

I did—a then exhaled in an immense cough, followed by a spit of vomit. I fell back against the mine, tossing the cigarette away.

Grayland laughed. I sneered at his malice.

"It gets easier," he said and put the cigarette back into my mouth. I wanted to fight him, but was far too weak to care. I inhaled again, this time, finding my lungs accepting of the smoke. When I exhaled, I coughed lightly and found the taste rather soothing. I removed the cigarette from my mouth and held it cautiously. When I felt I was ready, I took in another, this time a bit sweeter. My body still shook, but it calmed with every new breath.

"You see," Grayland said, obviously acknowledging my body's consent. "You're a natural." He struck another cigarette and sat down next to me.

"I remember my first cigarette," he said. "I was thirteen, and me and my best friend always hung out down at the park to shoot hoops with the local 'nics, which usually ended in a fist fight that neither of us were tough enough to actually win. And when we weren't getting pummeled, in the game or otherwise, we would tend to scope out the flavor parade, praying for a gust of wind to whip up just one of their damn near skivvy skirts so we could get a look at their ass, and hoping to God they'd left their thongs at home so we'd have a chance to get a glimpse of what we truly coveted.

"This one day, it was so hot neither of us had any motivation to do anything but lie there and whine about how hot it was. I mean my balls felt like cookie dough dipped in melted butter. I swear, the most mouthwatering vixen out there could have walked up to me completely nude while sucking on a popsicle and I wouldn't have noticed her.

"Anyway, I had gotten out to the park early that day with a Coke and a mag and was tooling around on my iPhone, ready to pass out waiting for him to show. When he gets there, he nearly breaks my balls waking me up. I broke his balls in return, but whatever. Before I could yell at him for leaving me to hang in the heat, he drops a pack of smokes on my chest. I tossed them away so fast you'd have thought he had dropped a venomous cockroach on me. I mean, it was against the law to smoke anything at the time, but if you got caught with a cigarette in public, it didn't even matter if it was lit. Just that you had it could cost you to serve up to five years in prison. A pack probably would have sent me up for a twenty spot. Suffice it to say, I was freakin' shittin' myself.

"When I asked him where the fuck he got them, he said he scored them from his brother, who'd just been paroled on good behavior. His eyes literally beamed when he asked if I wanted to light one up. I couldn't believe what he was asking, but hell, I was so god damned bored, what else was I supposed to do? We dropped down into the bathroom and lit 'em up as if we had been doing it our whole lives. The first ones seemed like practice... we didn't do anything but place them in our mouths and let the smoke drip from the tips, occasionally, sucking in the tiniest bit of smoke. Of course, the taste was horrendous, but we really couldn't care less. We were breaking the law, and it felt wild. When we reached our third sticks, we were breathing that smoke in as if it was oxygen, shootin' the bull, talkin' girls we wanted to fuck and when we might get laid now that we were renegades. Girls loved that shit, so we thought.

"That's when the cops showed up.

"We tossed the entire pack of cigs into the toilet and flushed 'em as if that would hide the smoke that fumigated the bathroom. The cop hauled our asses to jail, and we were forced to spend the night in lock-up. My dad was pissed, but not at me. Had I been living in the fifties, I would have had my ass handed to me and my brain knocked into next week. Or else I would have been grounded and worked off my bail mowing lawns or pulling weeds in the hundred-degree heat to teach me a lesson. Instead, my parents sued the police force for arresting a minor with no physical evidence and won a pretty generous settlement.

"Me and my friend didn't get off that easy, though, not when my friend's brother found out we flushed his cigs. I was in bed for a week. But I have to tell you, the entire thing was worth it."

My cigarette had reached the small of its tip and I felt its heat licking my fingertips. I dropped it to the ground. Grayland laughed a bit and kicked the ground next to it.

"Feeling any better?" he said.

I nodded without much force. He struck another cigarette and I took it with ease. We sat in silence for the length of the cigarette. When I extinguished it with the dirt below my feet, I finally found the voice that had been eluding me.

"Why did you give me away?"

"What?"

"You allowed him to take me in possession without even a hint of guilt."

"No I didn't. The bastard threatened you. Doing anything but agree would have done neither of us any good."

"It did neither of us any good to maintain restraint."

"I know you're hurt, and I know you must have found hell with everything you've had to endure over the past few days. You have to understand that these people are not your friend. Not even if they make you feel safe. They will lie and fight for what they believe. And when they don't get their way, they will scorch the earth."

"It does not make any good deal of sense to me, Grayland. Why speak in peace when your actions purport the opposite?"

"Life is hypocrisy, Madeline. Either you ignore it or you pray at the knees of convention. It's your choice."

"I find neither choice to be acceptable."

"Give it time."

Grayland stepped away. I lowered my chin to rest on my arms.

"I'm sorry I got us into this mess. I want to get out of this hellhole as much as you do. But we can't just go after these guys without a plan of attack. You need to give me just a little more time to figure it out."

I took in a breath and then moved the garment lying next to me. "Will this help?" I picked up the weapon and revealed it to Grayland.

He swiped it from me with quickness. "Where did you get this?"

"I took it from the man outside my quarters."

"How?"

I shrugged. I was still unsure as to how I performed the act myself.

"Doesn't matter. This is perfect."

Grayland paused a moment and then said, "I better get back before they come searching for me. I want you to stay right here. Don't move, don't say a word. I'll come back for you tonight."

The touch of his hand on my knee was quite comforting, and I trusted him greatly. I placed my hand on top of his and lightly squeezed it. "Thank you."

Grayland kissed me, and I felt the apprehension dancing upon his lips.

"May I have another cigarette?" I said, my body finding the onset of quivers.

He squeezed my knee and sparked a cigarette. When he was gone, I sat as still as I could, sucking down the cigarette in measured patience. As I did, I could not stop but think of Miss Jezebel and her words against the actions I had now chosen to take and to what Cleo might say if she saw me in this moment. It was quite regretful and pushed me to shed a few tears. But they did not last long; before I had finished the cigarette, I no longer felt remorse for the choice I had made. I felt calm and eager, so much so that I could no longer sit still. I had to stand and wander. It was still quite dangerous to leave my current position, and I had promised Grayland, so I paced a circle and hummed a soft tune that helped me cope with the loneliness of my situation. It did not seem to take long for the effects of the cigarette to wear off, and when I grew tired, I laid down on the ground.

I woke to the echo of several cracks and pops.

It was difficult to determine where the noise originated or by how far away it was, but they were consistent, broken only by a few moments of silence. I attempted to remain calm, but it was clear that whatever was making the noise was growing closer. The pauses became more extended, to the point where it seemed they had stopped completely before beginning again. Voices soon joined the fray, each one disappearing with the silence of requirement.

I crawled to the deepest corner and huddled tight against it, hoping the mine would help shroud me in its darkness should anyone—or anything—find my location. Praying for peace and courage, I had not noticed the glaring silence until I felt footsteps rising upon me. I wrapped myself tighter and held my breath.

"Madeline."

I unlocked my body upon the stimulation of Grayland's whisper. "Grayland?"

"Quiet," he said as he moved swiftly to me. I met him half way with a thankful hug, unwilling to let go.

"I am extremely happy it is you," I said.

"We have no time," he said, urging my release from around his neck. "We have to leave. Lift up your arms." I did as asked and Grayland shoved a few pieces of cloth that draped loosely across the ground about my body.

"What was that noise?" I said.

"I had to kill some of those damn rags."

I wanted to object, but I could not find my voice. Grayland grabbed the garments near the tips of my heels and sliced through it like butter, ripping the excess cloth from around my legs. He buried my hand in his and I could feel his caring eyes on mine.

"Stay close to me and don't say a word. Got it?"

I nodded. Grayland picked up his weapon and pulled me back down the mine. I stayed within one step of his as he cautiously walked about, stopping at times to catch his breath before moving once again. I felt a warm breeze when Grayland whispered for me to stop and pushed me to the ground. He dropped to his own knees, covering me as much as he could with his body. I felt him concentrating on something that may have been blocking our exit, then heard that loud crack rip through the air, deafening my ears. I chirped out a startled scream, which led to a dozen voices roaring all at once.

"Shit," Grayland hissed. Cracks and pops followed.

I covered my ears and kept my mouth from uttering my fear as best I could. Several cracks led to a blast of wind near my head, and Grayland himself let out a grunt of pain. But he remained stationary and calm against his tense anxiety, a wall between our attackers and I, and would not leave me unprotected until his death.

Which thankfully for us both, never came.

"Are you hit?" he said after the screams had stopped. The smoke was heavy and smelled different than that of the cigarette, or even the fire. Grayland felt all about my body and asked me his inquiry again.

"I do not know," I said.

"You don't look like you're bleeding. Do you hurt anywhere?"

It was a bit hard to hear him, as a persistent ring in the center of my ears demanded my attention. But I understood most of what he was trying to say. "No," I said, unconvincing, even to myself.

"More of them will be here soon. Take this."

Grayland handed me his weapon, which now felt quite hot in several places, and pulled me from the mine. He stopped several times, stealing pieces of whatever he could find—including weapons, food and money—from the bodies that had been killed at his hand. He kept me close to him as he did and seemed to be on the lookout for any new danger that may fall upon us. Fortunately, none did and we found our solace into the rocky pastures that surrounded the main settlement. Grayland was on full alert for most of the next few nights, as he felt a threat had followed us deeper into the new land. But with each passing moon, no new threat occurred, and I could not have been more proud, more open and more illimitable than I was walking along side Grayland. For what he had done, I felt he now was my greatest friend, my loving guide.

(CHAPTER 18

We finally felt comfortable enough to stop and rest upon the eighth night of our journey away from Abdullah's land, which was surprisingly cooler than normal. Grayland was weak and in more pain than he would admit. I had attempted on several occasions to help him subdue the pain but he refused, clinging to the desperate need to lengthen our distance from the men that now sought our deaths. Now that his body was no longer willing to push any further, I sought to provide my help again, this time with success.

I knelt next to him and peeled a heavily moist piece of cloth away from his arm. I felt about near the base of the shoulder and found a small hole, bleeding liquid slowly down the side of his arm, moistening the rest of his garments. It occurred to me that one of Abdullah's weapons had scarred him during his fight to protect me. Why he had kept this knowledge from me was unclear, but it was not my place to question him about it. I simply listened to his instruction and completed each task as he requested of me. Digging the tips of my fingers into the wound, I ignored the hiss of pain that enveloped him, placing all of my concentration into locating the weapon that had embedded itself in his body. It took several attempts to slide up after I found it, but success in pulling the small piece of metal from his body did not elude me. Grayland could hardly speak after I had, but he continued to push me to finish healing him. After tying a piece of cloth around the top of his arm as tight as I could, he handed me a cigarette and asked that I place it between my lips. The act confused me, as smoke was not present and the tip wasn't at all hot. It took him a second request before I followed through. Once in my mouth, he asked me to lower my head to him and struck a small fire at his fingertips. He set it against the end of the cigarette and the smoke suddenly streamed upon my lungs. I let it out with ease and Grayland removed the flame. Leaning back, I removed the cigarette from my mouth.

"Wipe the blood away from the wound," he said gruffly, "and push the tip of the cigarette onto it."

"But that will burn you."

"That's the point. Now do it."

Hesitant, I grabbed the cloth and rubbed his shoulder as dry as I could. I located the wound with the tip of my finger and slowly guided the tip of the cigarette to meet his skin. It sizzled lightly, and Grayland let out a scream, placing all of his power into staying still for me. When his screams faded, and I could not feel the heat from the cigarette any longer, I dropped it to the ground. Grayland looked over the wound and gave me the box holding several more cigarettes.

"Again," he said.

I took a cigarette from the box and allowed him to light it with the flame. After wiping the wound clean, I burned it again. Grayland expressed less pain, but I could tell he felt it greatly. Another cigarette, followed by another burn, and I could no longer feel the wound leaking blood. Grayland fell away to the ground as I sat back. I picked out another cigarette and held it between my lips. I did know how to strike a fire for it, but the taste of the paper and lick of the end that touched my tongue was enough to satisfy me for the time. I took rest next to Grayland. When I woke, I checked that breath still escaped his lips and waited patiently for him to rise, which took what could have been several days. I had my head upon his when he aroused and shifted up quickly to welcome his return, providing him water cupped in my hand. He remained silent, falling back into rest almost instantly afterward. I listened to the world about me as I continued to wait, believing that he would never return.

"I need a smoke," he said a day later, waking me from a dream in which I was sitting along the riverbank back home with Cleo wrapped within my arms. I was startled at first but quickly realized where I was and handed Grayland the box of cigarettes. He lit one and let out a refreshed sigh. I asked to have him light another for me. We sat in silence as we digested our calm.

"How are you feeling?" I asked, digging the final tip of my cigarette into the dirt.

"Like a fucking corpse," he said. "But I'll be okay. Thanks for your help."

"It was my pleasure."

Grayland chuckled and attempted to stand. "God," he moaned, slipping back to the ground.

"You must continue to rest," I said.

"I can make it."

"Please do not attempt to move if you are not ready." I had hoped that the sincerity and tenderness in my voice would register with him. Luckily it did; he agreed to rest further. Even though we did not have much food aside from a few shelled peanuts and a flask of water, we agreed moving too fast would be more detrimental to us both than waiting a few more hours.

"What was it like?" I said after Grayland extinguished a second cigarette.

"What?"

"The day the ash fell."

I could feel Grayland's apprehension when he did not answer.

"I have heard the tale several times by the tongues of others. But I have yet to hear it from your point of view. Please help me understand it more clearly."

"What do you want to know?" he said hesitantly.

"I am uncertain." It took a moment to consider my thoughts and then continued. "What led to the ash? Where were you during the fall? How did you survive it?"

I knew it was a lot for him to consider so I allowed him time enough to digest his thoughts and re-accustom himself with the events in question. For a time, it was unclear if he would ever say anything at all. But upon settling down to find a new rest, Grayland cleared his throat.

"It was sudden and without warning," he started. "But we all knew it didn't happen instantly."

I sat up, pulling my knees in close, and accepted a cigarette.

"They always said World War Three would be a nuclear war, one that would literally wipe out all life on this planet. But not many thought it would begin as a religious war that would go undetected for decades. People were too afraid to believe anything could hurt them. The few that hadn't fallen under the spell of the indoctrinated leaches were demonized as fear-mongers, zealots or right-wing conspiracy nuts. You're right when you say the day the ash fell was when the missiles were launched, but that was far from the beginning of the war. Even though conflict in ideology, religion, race and even sex had been brewing for over a century, I believe to this day that the true beginning of the final war was nine-eleven."

"What is nine-eleven?" I said.

"That was when a group of rags flew planes into a couple of very important buildings and killed over three thousand people in the name of Allah."

"How is it possible to even consider such an impious act?"

"You claim to understand them," Grayland said with a hint of sarcasm. "You figure that one out and let me know."

I answered with a hit of smoke.

"That's what I thought. Anyway, after nine-eleven, we had a few months of united solidarity. Everyone was the same, ready and willing to fight their common enemy. It didn't last long, though, due to certain decisions that didn't sit well with some people. Unity crumbled faster than the oath of the president, and politicians decided it better to protect their own interests over the interests of the people they were supposed to protect. Law quickly became more of a guideline than an absolute rule, and government entitlement became accepted behavior. Accountability, integrity, work ethic—all of it went the way of the falcon because of the implication that you would have a far better life if the government granted your dreams for you. It lead to a viciously lazy and unethical society, which took more and did less. It didn't matter that the world was near collapse, so long as people got what the government told them they deserved. Fueling it all was the endless push for extreme sensitivity to even the most wretched of figures. We couldn't say or do anything without fear that we might offend someone. You weren't an illegal alien; you were an undocumented immigrant. There was no such thing as a terrorist, only extremists. Hell, even murder became known as giving someone passage to their next life. Political correctness. Sick, fucking nonsense.

"Oh, and to top it all off, there was the excessive need to remove all context of God and the Christian religion from everything, yet at the same time accepting all rules and acts performed by Islam to be spiritually blessed and protected under religious tolerance. Couldn't hurt the Muslim's feelings, but damn if you couldn't bully the Christians to wipe their beliefs from history. The whole debacle caused rage to boil over into all aspects of people's lives. I mean, the friction was palpable; you couldn't go anywhere without finding hatred in any person's spirit.

"Little did we know it was all a smokescreen to keep us diverted from what was really going on beneath the rhetoric. The real threat was simply biding its time, waiting to attack on three separate fronts: the 'nics flooding through our borders like fleas, the niggers marking their territory like rabid dogs, and the rags inserting themselves into key positions around the globe."

"Why label them with such names?" I said. "It only seems to encourage your hatred."

"And add to the political correctness that led to our destruction in the first place?"

I put out my cigarette and lied down.

"These termites were completely unrelated threats that all hid under the law of sensitivity to build their armies and take us down one god damned peg at a time. How's that possible? Because the government felt required to pander to every little need they claimed they had the right to. The majority of termites didn't even have any rights, not under the letter of the law, but the dickless politicians felt so frightened of losing their pedestal of power, they did everything they could to blame the majority for everything just so the minority could feel better about themselves. Law-abiding citizens were raped over the coals, convicted of being racist terrorists, while at the same time, those that had broken the law to step foot in this country were given the freedom to do whatever they pleased, given handouts and dealt with kid gloves, all so that the politicians would have one extra vote come the next election.

"This went on for several decades. The 'nics flooded through our southern border because their own damn government wasn't willing to fight the cartels that literally took over, instead blaming us for the problems they initiated and demanding equality and amnesty for their people. How do we respond? We do exactly as we're told, giving into all of their demands and providing them rights that not even real citizens had. Eventually, California became so overwhelmed by their own indulgences and sympathies that they were forced to sell their land to those pieces of trash, which of course allowed them to begin their infiltration of other bordering states. Soon enough, the blacks figured out what the 'nics were doing and implanted their own plights into the arguments, claiming the same rights under the same sympathy. The government made sure to coddle them, taking it up the ass and blaming Christian whites for all of the mini-civil wars that broke out among the different races. They would have been better off just killing us all.

"But it was the hidden threat of the Muslims that drove the knife into our implied unity. You witnessed some of it a few days ago, praising peace and unity only to attack in violence and hatred when needed. What happened here was on a much grander scale, though. The community of Islam patiently took hold of powerful positions, slowly testing how far they could push their ability to cross that imaginary line of tolerance before they found friction. When they found resistance, they backed off a bit and waited until the time was right to push again. In the meantime, they allowed the 'nics and blacks to believe that they were leading the battle, using them in certain opportunities to step over the line without anyone paying attention. A lot of people claim that the terrorists attacked us on nine-eleven because they wanted to take down our infrastructure. Others claim the government planned the whole thing so we could go to war. I believe it was a little of both—Muslim players inside the government allowed the suicide bombers access to the country to do exactly what they needed them to do. And I'm not talking about hurting us or destroying the financial system or any of that shit. Nine-eleven, in my opinion, was all a ploy to give Muslims something to point to when they felt they were being attacked. From that day, any time a Muslim attacked us, or attempted to attack us, with anything from a shoe bomb to the anal bomb, all it did was push our liberties further into the background for the sake of a false security and to protect the sensibilities of our Muslim friends and apologize to them for what they had done to us. Which gave them power over all of us without anyone even realizing it. And they accepted that power and used it when it was most effective.

"Fights among Christians and Muslims, blacks and whites, Hispanics and Americans, all reached a boiling point at the same time. By the time the petty differences between us turned from minor fisticuffs into full-out wars, the Muslims had the world by the balls. And they bit—hard.

"Most everyone believed the bullshit of peace; until that first missile dropped on Israel. But by then, we had been so emasculated as a country and as a people, we forgot how to fight back. When the threats of annihilation hit the news and Muslims all across the globe started killing non-believers, or infidels, in the name of Allah, all we could do was sit back and screw ourselves, confused and shocked that it was even happening. They used all of the weapons at their disposal, from nuclear and biological warfare to manipulation and fear; it didn't matter. You converted to Islam or signed your walking papers.

"If only we hadn't been so drugged with incompetence and had listened to those that saw the whole thing coming… maybe then we might have been able to avoid our own self-inflicted annihilation."

Grayland controlled his ire with a long, drawn-out breath. Doing so seemed to cause him great pain, perhaps with a shed of guilt.

"My wife was one of them," he finally said. "I ignored her, believing what she talked about to be utterly impossible. Not until the shit hit the fan did I realize…"

Grayland took to silence to calm the sadness building upon his body.

"Was it the war that killed her?" I said, knowing I may be lashed for asking.

"No," he said calmly. "No, she lived for several years after the first wave. I mean Israel was attacked almost twenty, twenty-five years ago. Danielle wasn't even a cherry yet."

"How did you survive it all?"

"By working for them. As a doctor."

"You made a deal with them?"

"We were pregnant with Danielle when they found us, and I knew I couldn't win if I tried to fight them. But I couldn't give in to them either, so yes, to protect them both, I made a deal."

"What was the deal?"

"It seemed simple enough. In exchange for acting as their doctor and performing any duties they asked of me in that capacity, they would leave me and my family alone to practice what we believed. What I got for that extra bit of freedom was beyond what I thought I'd ever have to do. If I had control, I could have saved a lot of people, but for the right of protection, I was forced to murder dozens, maybe even hundreds of people."

"How did you escape their tyranny?"

"When the Muslims made their grab for power, what they didn't expect was a termite resistance. Eventually, hundreds and thousands of 'nics and niggers were wiped out. What a lot of people don't realize is that the bombs didn't take out as many people as the conflicts within the communities did.

"One day I saved the life of this pretty attractive nig who had nearly been carved to death by a gang of doped-up 'nics. It turned out she was the girlfriend of the leader to a pretty powerful black faction. This guy felt indebted to me for going against the 'nics and offered to do something for me as payment. Suffice it to say, the Muslims were no longer a problem for me or my daughter."

"What of your wife?"

"She passed shortly after."

"How—"

"I don't want to talk about that."

I almost insisted but thought otherwise. He remained trapped with his thoughts for a long while after, and I was not ready to intrude upon them. But the more I kept silent, the more my own thoughts wandered about my most recent experiences, and that no matter how much I trusted Grayland, I didn't feel safe. I needed more.

"I wish to learn," I said, hoping he had not taken his thoughts into slumber.

"Learn what?"

"How to defend against others, the way you have defended against them."

"That would go against everything you've been taught. Take it from experience, you don't want to take that road."

"Please," I said. "From what we have discussed, and from what I have witnessed, I feel the only way I can survive, with and without you, is to learn from you the ways of protection in conflict."

"You prepared to go against your beliefs, simply to feel safe?"

I thought about his question for some time, understanding that learning the skills I sought would affect me in a similar manner in which consumed the people before the ash, leading to their inevitable downfall. But I had chosen to become a part of a new environment and felt that I would be able to absorb the evils of adjusting to it while still remaining true to the beliefs that I cherished. "If it means that I will obtain the capability to survive alone should I have to take heed and run," I said, "then I am ready to do what is necessary."

Grayland tucked his palm against my face, and we held our silence for the next day. I did not sleep much, thinking about how hard it must have been for him and for all of those that lived through the war, including Miss Jezebel and Father Callahan (one of the few I knew who understood the war in its infancy). I had always respected him and his teachings, but I now felt much more connected to him than I ever had. My prayer for him, and one for all of the other perés who taught me only the best of humanity, was sent into the wind that night, in hopes that they would feel my love and send their own back to me.

CHAPTER 19

When I woke the next morrow, Grayland was standing away from me, waiting. I wasted no time with words. We left our sanctity in peace and did not speak until the day following, when it was asked upon me to speak a lie in order for Grayland to steal a traveler's ration of food. The test was quite vexing, but Grayland reminded me that there were plenty of men who would not hesitate to do the same. Of course, I had been witness to the very act of disingenuous deceit, but it was hard to grasp the ability to become one with them. The next days brought more lies, sometimes accompanied with threats and violence. I grew frightened that I would be unable to find the strength to continue in this manner, when we came upon a solitary man for whose shelter we remained under for several days. He had been sickened with what Grayland referred to as the stiff, for which on the best of days, he could stand on his own and unfurl his fingers enough to grip his utensils. In return for the man's kindness and generosity of nourishment and rest, Grayland and I worked upon the peace of the land, providing our strength to complete several chores the man had, for the past few annuals, been unable to perform on his own. Speech was limited, even during our meals, leading to slumber in silence.

Upon the last night of our residence, I sat near the fire I had prepared, reflecting in the past gone by, feeling truly wistful for the first time since stepping away from my home. Grayland had been in slumber for a time, but I could not find my own.

"Your father is a good man," the man whispered from behind me. He settled down in his rocking chair with a glass of liquor. I smiled softly and a jewel of moisture rolled down the crevices of my markings. I did not turn to the man, and he did not speak another word. We simply enjoyed one another's presence; our gentle breaths enough to keep us both in comfort until we finally came under the sandman's spell.

Grayland and I left the following morrow with a gracious hand, a pack of food and several canisters of water. For the moment, I felt a sadness deep within. But the journey was far from over, and if I was ever to receive the gift that was promised to me, and return to my family, I would need to part ways with many a good companion along the way. Leaving him was hard but provided me hope that our road, though still arduous, would not be completely tortured with wickedness.

Days left us with the speed of the high winds, and for a time, we were undisturbed but for the elements of our nature. We took refuge wherever and whenever we could to take rest and find solace in the smoke of our addiction and otherwise would work to build my abilities as Grayland saw fit. My first set of lessons was designed to teach me how to properly wield the metal weapon; guns, as Grayland termed them. They felt incredibly alien and immoral upon my grasp, but the more I ingested their strength, the more powerful my confidence became. After a time, I grew tired of practice, though Grayland was shy in allowing me the chance to use the weapon for purpose, unless it was for absolute necessity.

It was when we caught sight of a small, rare wilderness animal that I finally earned the opportunity. The wind was hot upon our skin, and we rested under the soft shade of a lone sycamore. Our stomachs spoke a nasty song, but it had been almost fourteen days since we had left the solitary man, and food was scarce. Grayland witnessed its movement before I did, but upon his response, I held its steps upon my ear. We tracked the animal with the step of cotton, and as it rested its weary legs, Grayland placed the gun into my hand and whispered final advice in my ear. I took the weapon with ease and focused all of my attention on the breath, the sound, the step of the animal.

We feasted that night on fresh meat. The pride I felt sank me to sleep without the need of a cigarette. The kill brought more torment than I had expected, though, when Grayland forced me to use the weapon to help steal a few packs of cigarettes and a fresh lighter from a man needing the use of a crutch. The threat of death was far different upon the breath of another man than it was on the animal for which provided nourishment and revealed my discomfort of using the weapon for that purpose. Grayland understood, though I was unsure as to how sincere his empathy was. He expounded on the dangers that could initiate my need to forgo my fear, but I fought Grayland into stubborn silence over the matter. Soon, we spoke not of the gun or my reluctance to use such an extension of my hand any longer. I would continue to practice, improving my skill, but for no other reason would I touch it.

Instead, I fell into favor with another skill for which Grayland taught to me in good grace: the art of combat—the ability to use my strength, my will and my body to fend off the attack of my foe. Only after I had perfected the fundamental techniques of planting my feet to solidify control and using my hips to add power to my upper body was I given the opportunity to blossom into the dance of defense and attack, sparring as it was to Grayland. I accepted a tremendous amount of welts and bruising in my education, but I did not fault Grayland for any of them. They were necessary side effects for which many lessons were learned and abilities sharpened. After a few days time, I felt I was quite the master and presented such to Grayland with the arrogance of the younger.

"We'll see," he would chide, followed always with a new lesson for which I was not ready, a laugh of haughty admonition and then a turn to slumber so that I may heal before the next. I would usually think upon my shamed stupidity as he slept, trying to understand how I could have defended myself. One night, I had stepped away from the cramped space of the dwelling for which we took refuge and took to practice, testing and strengthening the fundamentals (which I had learned) needed to be constantly worked upon, less allow them to be forgotten.

My own feet had betrayed me, allowing the steps of another to take upon me without my knowledge. Before I could react to the intruder, my arm had been pulled around to the small of my back and a cold hand stifled my scream. The man, his breath heated in a stench that nearly made me gag, forced me to my knees.

"Stay calm, and you won't get hurt," he said. "You here alone?"

I tried to relax my breaths so as to clear my mind.

"Answer me," the man hissed. His lips touched the bottom of my earlobe.

Lying, I nodded.

"You have food?"

I shook my head.

"Liar. A healthy little piece of bitch like you isn't running around out here alone without food. Where is it?"

The man pulled me to my feet and, taking awareness of the man's body against my own, I relaxed my muscles, allowing my body to fall heavy against his grip. I took advantage of the small instant when the man lost his footing, slipped my arm from his hand and dropped to my knee, finding an enormous amount of power generated into my blow to the man's upper stomach area. He fell away from me, but did not fall, finding the perception of my strength to be not as authentic as the reality. Before I could rise to my feet, I found myself lying upon the ground, my jaw pounding in tender pain. I could taste the blood seeping onto my tongue, but my attention was on everything but that. The man turned me over and grabbed a hold of my garments. My head fell back, time and again, my face growing number with each fresh attack. I grew tired and could hardly feel any part of my body within moments. I became so weak, I couldn't be sure Grayland had even come to my defense. The crack of the gun was distant, but the casualty was not. My head fell back against the ground as my body became weightless.

"Madeline," Grayland said. His voice was frightened, yet secure. He helped me sit up, and for some moments after, could hardly understand any words he spoke. As my consciousness returned, and the pain in my body took control of my emotions, I no longer cared for Grayland's attempts at comfort.

I pushed him away, desperately trying to stand, but failing miserably.

"Take it easy," he said.

"No," I said and finally found the strength in my legs enough to limp away from him. "Leave me alone."

"Madeline," he said, but held his ground.

I was mad for keeping him from helping me, but was happy that he did not attempt to follow. I slid down next to the side of a wall nearby and collected my thoughts with tears. Once the majority of the pain had subsided, and I realized I could not keep taking Grayland's teachings for granted, I got back to my feet and returned to him.

Without as much as a bird's chirp, I knelt down, kissed Grayland as gently as I could so as not to aggravate my swollen lips, and took up a cigarette.

"That was fun," I said. Grayland could only laugh in respect.

I had no other such encounter over the course of our journey, which turned quickly from days into several weeks. I took advantage of our time, taking each lesson, each technique and each fundamental challenge with serious aplomb, no matter the amount of pain that scorched my body. Between all of this training, we found much time during our long walks to speak more of Anno Domini and the causes that led to the war. I still was unable to learn much about his wife or his daughter, but it felt to me that the more time we spent together, the more he respected me as a person—as a daughter—and it was only a matter of time before the secrets of that shrouded past poured from him. I would accept that time with grace and charity. When it came.

Near the end of our hundredth day, we came upon the edge of the land, as Grayland had promised several weeks before. The smell of the poisoned water was as surreal as the sound of its breath. Full of strength and wonder, I sat for some time at its edge, allowing it to lick my feet and bury them in the sand. Grayland had told me about the joys many encountered among the ocean before the war, but not before now had I realized my sadness over the inability to live that same pleasure.

My time reflecting on what had once been, and what had now become, was cut short with Grayland's insistence on our moving forward. It would only be a few more days before we reached our final destination, and Grayland wished to get there with swift feet. I understood his sentiment, needing the reassurance of a consistent comfort, and followed his brisk pace with ease. Once we found solace in the desert landscape once again, we found comfort in each other's arms as we slept for the first time on our trip. The next few days would be calm and quiet, and on the fourth, we finally found sanctity upon Grayland's lovely home.

(CHAPTER 20

As I stepped inside, the heated musk of his absence fell upon me. Grayland navigated me through the clutter of tables covered in parchment, worn down pieces of furniture and broken pieces of knickknacks that may or may not have had valuable meaning to Grayland. He took me instantly to my sleeping quarters and shuffled through the contents of a bureau.

"You're about my daughter's size," he said and handed me a few garments of clothing. "Try these on."

He left the room and within moments, I was thoroughly mapping out its contents. Upon locating the bed, I set the garments down and relaxed over the soft cloths that covered it. Danielle's essence could be felt within the dusty, wooden smell. I pictured her lying gracefully upon it, reading or playing music as she worked on her studies. She smelled wonderful and caring—a stunning specimen of love. It was hard to believe that she had been taken, that she now rested peacefully among the life hereafter. I prayed on her and asked that she protect me as her own sister. I asked for her strength in my growing relationship with Grayland and that she pass along her will and her purity. Taking one final breath of her into my body, I stripped away my robes and lied down, allowing the bed, the room and the world to overwhelm me.

I had no recollection of falling asleep, but when I rose, I took Danielle's garments and wore them with honor. They were very comfortable and helped me appreciate the time in which they were utilized. As I stepped outside of her room, I could sense that much of the clutter had been removed, or at the very least organized.

I slowly took pace throughout the home, unaware of Grayland's whereabouts. I did not bother fearing where he might have gone; I simply learned about my new domicile and found solace in its protection. After having become aware of all that it provided, I sat and prayed.

Grayland returned soon thereafter, smelling of the ocean. He dropped a line of nourishment into the kitchen before he realized I was in his presence.

"Madeline," he said, somewhat startled. "Sorry about that. You were asleep when I left. I thought I might get back before you got up."

"You don't have to worry," I said. I walked to the food Grayland had brought back with him. It was wet and a bit sticky.

"Hope you like fish," Grayland said.

"I am certain I will." My stomach pinched in hunger. "When shall we eat?"

"It'll take a couple of days to purify all of this," he said. "But if you're hungry, we still have some bread left." Grayland set the bread down in front of me, but its smell grew pungent as I nibbled. Though several species of sea life had survived the liquid toxins that had been deposited into the ocean during the war, anything caught for the purpose of nourishment had to be cleansed through several distilled elements before they could be consumed. And whatever solution Grayland was currently using held an overwhelming stench that caused me to lose my appetite. I set the bread down and lowered my head to my arms, covering my nose from the smell.

"Oh, damn. Sorry," Grayland said. "Here." He took my hand and walked me down a flight of stairs to a small room below. I had yet to visit this part of his home, and it intrigued me greatly.

"What is this place?" I said, feeling about the large metal machines that filled the room.

"It's going to take some time to get everything in order for your surgery," he said. "I thought you might like a place to work-out in the meantime."

"I can train here?" I said.

"Whenever you like."

My excitement couldn't be denied. "What does all of it do?"

Grayland wasted no time explaining all of the different machines and helping me learn to use them correctly. Some helped build the muscle in my arms and legs, others allowed me to run all day without ever having to leave the confines of our home. My favorite was the large bag that swung down from the floor above ground. I could spar with it and polish my techniques without the fear of harming Grayland or myself. I spent many a night in the room, practicing, sharpening my skills and building my strength. Grayland would watch and, on occasion, help in perfecting my techniques. But the more the days went on, the more a routine built up around us; and the more he seemed to disappear.

In his absence, I had learned to navigate the home without actively thinking about each step. I relied on my own aptitude to feed, clothe and bathe. Grayland would emerge on rare occasion, mostly during our meals or before falling to sleep, wherein he would bless me sweet dreams with a whisper and a kiss. Whenever I would ask about his progress in curing my sight, however, he would emotionally close down, leaving me no choice but to simply stop asking. I trusted that when he had news, he would tell me. All I wished was to be with him. So much so that I looked forward to the days when we would make our half-day trek out to the ocean to gather fresh food. We would talk and laugh, spar and wrestle, sometimes even fight over our differences. On occasion, he would bring out targets and set them up with small bells to help improve my aim and skill with a gun. Mostly, he would guide me in sending out the nets to trap the fish we would bring home, then sit and hold me, and listen to the grand music of the waves. They were special; I cherished him in those days.

It wasn't until I had finished a meal alone a few nights after returning from one of these trips that I had felt something was wrong. It wasn't as if Grayland had never missed a meal, but this time the air was stiller and the room colder. My thoughts filled with fear of something having happened to Grayland, but my heart claimed otherwise. I set my dishes into the sink and returned to my room to change clothes and wash up for bed, unable to shake that odd sensation. Upon pulling down the sheets, I heard Grayland's whisper haunt the halls outside. I followed his voice to his room and listened to a conversation with an unknown visitor, one I would soon come to learn was no one at all.

"She is a beautiful girl," Grayland said, tears heavy upon his voice, "and she deserves more than I've been able to give. I can't help but feel I may have promised her something I can't deliver. I know, you always told me it was a dream, but I never did listen, did I? Now I've dragged this innocent girl into my own selfish need to prove you wrong, and... and it's a life I don't think she's ready for at all. She trusted me—you trusted me. So what am I supposed to say to her? I can't just walk in there and tell her I failed, that I can't cure her blindness. Not after everything we've been through. It would devastate her. It would devastate me... all I want to do is protect her, which is more than I tried to do for you. If only I had the sense to leave well enough alone. Danielle..."

I felt guilty for eavesdropping as Grayland took his long, arduous pause. I took the silence and slid quietly back to my room to lay Danielle to rest with the hum of my song. Before I had finished, I heard Grayland's breath standing upon my door.

"That was beautiful," he said.

"A prayer Miss Jezebel used to sing to me," I said. "It always made me feel better whenever things grew sour."

Grayland sat next to me.

"How does it go?" He held me as I sang to him and kissed me softly when I had finished. I felt his tear transfer from his cheek to mine. He left without another word, and I did not attempt to stop him. I knew his secret; but I was willing to wait for him to come to me to open up, as he would his own daughter. Until then, I would give him the space he needed to find his courage.

He was absent for the few days that followed. I attempted on several occasions to find him and relay information of our need for fresh food with not a hint of success. When the supply had completely diminished, I took up one of the smaller guns and the net and made the trek to gather more fish. I sat solemnly for some time on the edge of the rocks to take in the breath of the ocean and come to the acceptance that I would never get to truly see its majesty the way others could. I fed it the last of my tears and took my bounty, leaving its graces for the final time. Whether Grayland was still with me, or if I was alone, I was ready to take what I could, forgive him for his indulgence and make my homecoming to where my first love awaited.

Halfway upon my return home, I caught the sound of an additional pair of footsteps. They seemed too light to be Grayland's and sounded secretive and without weight. I cautiously paced my way along the path, and when it was clear that someone was following me, I pulled the gun from my pack and swung it around to my shadow.

"Show yourself," I said. The gun shook slightly in my hand.

The next instant I felt the piercing heat of a bullet in my side. I fell to my knees and heard the thief take everything from me and steal into extinction. Every breath I took tightened my chest and sent a chill through my body. I cried out the best I could for someone to help but knew it was all for naught. So I turned inward, using my last few breaths of strength to call for Danielle to take my hand and keep me protected. Luckily, within moments of seeking her graces, I was lifted from the cooling ground and taken to the darkness of my death.

CHAPTER 21

Taking my first breath filled my mind with renewed hope. The pain I felt convinced me that I was still alive. I gripped my side, which had been bandaged, and as I sat, I realized that so, too had my eyes. When I reached up to remove the thick cloth that had been wrapped upon them, Grayland's hand held mine from doing so.

"Leave it," he said.

"What happened?"

"You were shot a couple of days ago." Grayland's voice was quiet and remorseful. "It's a miracle I found the net missing when I did, or else..." He took my hand in an affectionate touch. "I thought I lost you."

"I don't remember," I said, which wasn't a complete lie.

"It's okay. I dug out the bullet and stitched you up best I could."

"I guess we have something in common now," I said with a light laugh.

"Yeah, I guess we do."

Grayland poured me a glass of water, and I drank it thankfully, hiding my reactions to the continually sharp pain in my side.

"I have more good news," he said with a tone of voice I had yet to hear from him— excitement. "I performed the surgery on your eyes."

I was shocked into silence, finding only the ability to touch the cloth gently.

"I can't guarantee it worked, but I have a good feeling."

"How," I said. "I thought..." I couldn't finish.

"Thought what?"

I lowered my head from him. "I overheard you the other night. You were praying to Danielle."

Grayland sat away, removing his hand from mine.

"You claimed that it was impossible."

"You weren't meant to hear that," he said after a short bout of silence. "I was just frustrated."

"But it helped you."

"Eventually. The answer finally came to me the night you left."

"Meant to be, I suppose," I said with a bright smile.

"I guess so."

"When will I find my sight?" I said after a bit of silence, wherein I finished my water.

Grayland took the cup from my hand. "It's going to take a few weeks of recovery, and another week or so of adjustment, but I think we'll both be happy with the results."

"I'm already happy," I said and hugged Grayland with all of the strength my wound would allow me. I kissed him and lied back down. "Thank you."

"Get some rest."

I couldn't rest. Not with the prospect that in just a few weeks time I would finally be able to see as all others could. Each day, Grayland would take the cloth from my eyes and clean them, removing the crust that formed over the hours. I kept my eyes closed during the process, as requested, waiting with impatience for the day he would allow me to open them. He would also check my other wound every few days and was always happy to report that it was healing perfectly. I knew he told the truth, finding it easier to breathe each consecutive day and even braving the chance to walk on occasion. I never went far, usually as far as the bathroom, but my strength was returning.

Finally, the night came when Grayland removed the stitches, relieving me of their constant irritation. After washing the wound and lowering my shirt over it, he sat still, causing me a bit of confusion.

"What is it," I said. "Is something wrong with the wound?"

"No."

I chuckled. "Then what?"

Grayland touched my scars. I held my hand to his.

"Are you ready to see?"

My smile brightened the room. I could feel my heart race as I squeezed his hand.

Grayland's breath was warm and inviting as he untied the cloth and allowed it to fall away from my eyes. I kept them closed, allowing Grayland to clean them as he normally would. When he was through, my apprehension kept them closed, but the soft words of permission soon led to the rise of my eyelids.

At first, it seemed the same as it had always been. But as I focused more intently on what before I could only touch, a light filled the rims of my eyes and I could make out a swirl of exotic flavor.

"Madeline?" Grayland said after a moment.

"I…" I wasn't sure how to respond.

"Do you see anything?"

"I'm not sure," I said. "I think so."

"Describe it to me."

"I don't know. There is something, but it's nothing."

"Do you see any movement?"

"No," I said, then suddenly saw the light waver before me, soft and fluid. "Yes. Yes, there is movement."

"That was my hand," Grayland said.

I let out a breath of excitement.

Grayland then cupped his hand behind my neck. "Lay your head back."

The light shimmered as I complied with his request. Grayland forced one of my eyelids open and suddenly, a cool liquid burned my eye. I winced and blinked rapidly after Grayland allowed its release. He repeated the procedure on my other eye and lifted the cloth back to them, returning me into complete darkness.

I fought to stop him. "Wait. What are you doing?"

"Madeline, please. This was just the first step."

I allowed him to place the cloth back around me and sat down, disappointed, but understanding. "Is it working?"

"It's working," he said with confidence. "We have to take this slowly, or else your mind won't allow your eyes to adjust to their new ability. What I believe you saw just now was your eyes allowing a little bit of light to filter in, which is why you were able to see the movement, but nothing else. In a few days, your mind will become more familiar with the light and help to create shape and color. But if we move too fast, your brain might reject it and everything we're hoping for will be dead."

"I understand," I said happily.

"What do you say tomorrow we get you back into training."

"Yeah," I said.

"Yeah."

The following day, Grayland helped me down to the training room and started me on a healing regiment that would not put too much pressure on my wound, but would slowly bring me back into the shape I was in before I was shot. I rested more than I trained during the first few days, but my spirits remained high, knowing each night after our meal, I would get to test my eyes. With each passing night, the light that swarmed my eyes would grow deeper and heavier, swimming and drawing out small indistinguishable lines. By the seventh night, I could make out what Grayland referred to as colors. I couldn't explain to him what colors I saw, but with a washed outline of his hand, he would point to a particular spot and refer to its color for me. The first I saw were those of red, blue and white, or in his explanation of it, the combination of all color within the spectrum of its light. He attempted to acclimate my remembrance of shapes, but though I knew what they were by touch, I still was unclear as to how they may appear in sight.

By the time two weeks had come and gone I was power-walking on the treadmill as if nothing had ever happened. Grayland had been absent when I woke that morning, but I thought perhaps he went out to bag us a squirrel that found his way across the pasture. But when I had finished my set routine, ready to wash and nap, Grayland remained absent. I climbed up the stairs and called out for him. I grew frightened when he did not answer, but calmed when the aroma of his cigarette hit me. I followed it to his bedroom, where he sat in the corner.

"Is everything okay?" I said when he didn't acknowledge me.

"I can't remember when it is," he said.

"When what is?"

"Rachel's birthday," he grumbled.

I sat down next to him, pretending to ignore his plight. "Have anymore of those?" I said. I lit up and sat with him for hours before either of us spoke.

"She was my soul," he finally said.

"She inspired you."

"It was more than that. When she died, a piece of me died with her."

"That's lovely."

"She had a way of keeping me grounded. From the day I met her, she put my best interests above her own, slapping me with reality checks no matter how much she knew it would hurt me to hear it. We probably fought about something every other day, but she never left me. I'm not sure if she knew it was because I'd come around and realize she was right, or if she had nothing better to do, but there was nothing I could do that would send her away. She was damn stubborn that way."

"Her love for you was strong."

"I know it was. I mean, I treated her like a second-class citizen, berating her, holding her back from her own aspirations, just so I could live the life I wanted. I gave her a good home, a good life, yet…"

"Yet you feel guilty now because it was yours. Not hers."

Grayland hissed with grief, and I lowered his head to my chest to relax him. It was several minutes before he was calm enough to speak again.

"She didn't deserve what happened. There's not a day that goes by that I wish it would've been me instead of her."

"I don't." I rested my head on his shoulder and held his hand tightly. He pet my hair and kissed me as if it were his first.

"She would have liked you very much, Madeline. She was the type of woman to invite a bum in off the street to feed them and then send them away with a hundred bucks and feeling of worth. That's what I admired in her the most—that innocence of purity in an otherwise shithole of a world. I could always count on her to help me forget every bad thing in the world.

"It's a fucking travesty that the innocence that made her human was the knife that did her in."

I comforted him by moving in closer and wrapping my arm around his back.

"I still don't know what really happened. I had taken Danielle out to the ocean to gather some food, much like I've done with you these last few months. Rachel was sick that morning and wasn't up for traveling. We tried to tell her we could go the next day, but she insisted, told us we needed a little father-daughter bonding time. I wasn't home much because of my job with the rags, so I thought it was a good idea.

"But when we got back, I noticed the door was wedged open and I heard voices inside. I told Danielle to hide down under the lip of the house that trenched itself out during a rainstorm we had a few weeks before. When I walked inside, I saw a half a dozen nigs rummaging through our stuff. I let out several rounds and hit a couple in the process, but they got their asses out of there like they were on fire.

"Once they were gone, I called for Rachel. I felt sick when she didn't call back. Nothing else mattered, not even the smoke that filled the house. And when I reached that door…"

Grayland took a moment to relax his breathing.

"She was lying on the bed covered in blood, her legs sprawled apart as if they were detached from her body. I couldn't move; the only thing I could think of doing was to lift the gun to my head. I wanted to do it, just end it there. Then I heard Danielle…"

Grayland's voice got stuck in his throat and he covered his mouth. I reached up and wiped the tears away, kissing them with compassion. He looked away but I pulled him back and pushed his hand down. Stroking the contours of the burns on his face, I gently kissed him and felt a new fire ignite my heart. I couldn't stop, and didn't want to. He stroked my body with a touch that felt absolutely gratifying. His hands were strong but caring, and I returned his touch with confidence and trust; I was his to command. Several minutes passed with no speed and the electricity of desire for what was to happen lit my emotions, giving him the privilege to make me his bride.

I felt nothing but delight when we had completed the loving ceremony. We laid our flesh together afterward and gave in to the succulent sweetness of a smoke. The world at that moment had become nothing but a dream, and I was as content as I ever would be again. He was my body; I was his soul.

CHAPTER 22

Grayland and I married each night over the days that followed. My step felt lighter, and I smiled more when in proximity to his touch or his smell. When he watched me work out, especially against the heavy bag, my body quivered in diffident stimulation, igniting solemn inspiration. I sat in his arms during meals and was always most excited when my blindfold was removed and I could visualize the features I knew so well through touch in its usual blurred, melted intoxication. When I lay with him, feeling his breath over my neck, I was home.

"I think it's time we expose your eyes to daylight," he said abruptly in the middle of my normal routine. He sat where he normally did during my workouts, but his words felt much farther away. I stopped cold and grabbed hold of the bag.

"What was that?" I said, needing to hear it again.

"I think we're ready to take the next step in your rehab."

"But you said it would be another couple of weeks"

"Yeah," he said, rising. He walked over to me and held my head softly in his rugged hands. "But you've progressed so much faster than I thought possible." He kissed me sweetly, leaving my smile unaffected.

"Are you sure?" I said. "You're positive I'm ready?"

He answered me with his lips pressed to mine, and I wanted nothing more than to marry him. I settled for a devoted hug.

"I love you," I said.

He slipped my blindfold off and cleaned my eyes with his thumb. When I opened them, his features seemed much clearer than ever before. They faded quickly when Grayland placed an object over my eyes. They sat gently on the bridge of my nose and grasped my ears so as not to fall. I touched them, a bit frightened by the manufactured darkness, but Grayland was quick to remove my hand.

"Don't," he said. "They're sunglasses. You're going to need them."

"What for?" I said.

"To protect your eyes."

"I thought I was ready."

"Small steps," he said. "The light you're about to see will be more intense than you're used to, and too much light all at once might burn your retinas beyond repair. Remember, this is all untested…"

"And we need to remain cautious." I kissed him. "I'm ready."

Grayland walked me through our home. Seeing much through the sunglasses was very hard because Grayland had covered anything that may have inadvertently exposed my eyes to too much light. When we reached the door, I felt my stomach turn in excitement.

"Close your eyes," Grayland said. "When I say, slowly open them as far as you can without straining."

I nodded and the light flowed in, burning my eyes. I turned away quickly, covering them frantically. Grayland closed the door and grabbed hold of my shoulders.

"What happened?"

"I'm sorry," I said, the burn transforming into water. "I didn't have my eyes closed."

"Let me see."

Grayland removed the sunglasses and forced my eyelids open. "I told you to close your eyes," he scolded.

"I know."

"What do you see?"

"Not much, except when I blink."

"Do you see spots?"

"Yeah, like blurred circles."

Grayland let out relief and calmed his body. "That's enough for today," he said.

"No, wait," I said. "I want to do this."

"It's too soon."

"I'm ready. Please."

I tried to focus on Grayland's eyes, which were darker than normal, but which I could make out under the twinkling of light.

"No, I think we need to slow down."

"I can see you," I said, brushing his scars. "I want to do this."

Grayland turned away from me and combed his jaw with his fingertips. When he looked back to me, he shook his head and handed me the sunglasses. "You'll tell me the moment your eyes begin to feel uncomfortable."

"I promise," I said.

Grayland rose, and I returned the sunglasses to their rightful place, smiling in anticipation. I closed my eyes tightly and waited for them to glow with intense heat.

"Slowly," Grayland said.

His rule was not hard to follow, as I could hardly open them without feeling a searing pain coax them closed. But with each blink I administered, the pain in my eyes became less. Soon, I held them open and could see the red and orange river of the wind. Grayland's hands rested on my shoulders as I stared upon the distance. I couldn't make out much detail but a black streak washing through the color, and I covered my mouth with laughter at the lightness of its flight and the splendor of its calm.

I took in a deep breath as Grayland closed the door and removed the glasses. "That's enough for today," he said, setting the blindfold back over my eyes.

"It was exquisite," I said and then took him to his bed, reminiscent of the magic that had just been preformed.

Grayland left the room afterward to grab us some food. I waited for him with gracious harmony and a ripple of stimulation in my chest. He had become much more to me than my protector, my doctor or my trainer. He had become more than a father. He had given me a gift that I never would have received without him—he had given me truth, and through that, my strength. In turn, I gave him purpose, and through that, forgiveness for a loss he had been unable to let go of.

Suddenly, a loud crack occurred and an unfamiliar voice rumbled through the hall. I pulled on the clothes and sat next to the door to listen for more.

"Where's this new doll of yours, Ryker?" the voice said.

Grayland grumbled something I couldn't make out.

"Don't give me that shit. Trigger told me about her. Small, sweet young bitch with a fetish for old fucks."

"I don't know what—" Grayland let out a grunt after what sounded like someone kicking the heavy bag. "God, fuck," he said soon after.

"Don't make me burn this fucking place down again," the man said.

"She's dead," Grayland said, still the honorable protector. "Okay."

"Bullshit. Trigger saw you carry the bitch away after he shot her."

"There was nothing I could do. She was too far gone, I swear."

"You know, I am having a hard fucking time believing you. She's here, and I'm going to fucking find her if I have to tear this hellhole to fucking pieces."

Several footsteps tore through the house then, drowning out the audibility of any conversation that transpired.

"Run," I heard Grayland say in my voice. As much as I wanted to, I remained frozen. I couldn't leave him here to die. This is what I had been training for, and I couldn't let him down. But as much as I wanted to rip through this door and tear the heads off the intruders who dare hurt the home we built over the last few months, all I could do was cry quietly with worry. Little did I know I wouldn't need my own strength to find my way to Grayland's side.

I felt defenseless as one of the men grabbed my hair and dragged me out of the room to a chorus of screams, both of pain and panic.

"Found her," the thug said, throwing me next to Grayland.

I held my head and froze my body closed.

"And here I thought you learned your fucking lesson," the leader said. "But here she is, alive, and my *fucking* god, I can see why you fucking lied."

The leader brushed his hand against my thigh and I kicked at him, hitting nothing but air.

"A feisty bitch, too," he said.

"I have what you came for," Grayland said. "Leave her alone and we can do business."

"Ryker, you had your chance to do business three fucking years ago. Instead, you took off like a little bitch. The time for deals has expired."

"Listen to me, Pain," Grayland pleaded. "She has nothing to do with this."

"Your wife was a decent fuck, Ryker. But this… this is going to be fucking pure."

Pain grabbed my legs and pulled me closer. I screamed and reached for Grayland, but as Pain touched my face with his scuffed hand, I quickly forgot everything in favor of drawing my fear into anger. I swung my fist upward, near where his foul breath originated and swiped the edge of his gruff jaw. Pain laughed heartily as he grabbed my arms and pinned them down to the floor.

"Keep it up, little one. Won't keep you from becoming my fucking bitch."

I fought best I could, but the weight of his body and the strength in his hands on my wrists kept me still and incapacitated. My physical inability to do anything hurt me, but the smell of this vile intruder's tongue hurt even more.

"Grayland," I whispered.

"Sick, fucking nigger."

A loud crash reverberated near my ear and the other men in the room yelled out. A round of gunshots were fired across the room. I no longer felt Pain's weight on top of me and curled up, attempting to recover my deadened vigor and hide from the war that converged about me. For a moment, I felt Grayland hold the power over the others, silencing one of the men, while the others ran off in pubescent fear. But my relief was short lived when Pain fell beside me and wrapped his large hand around my neck, pinching my nerves and covering my airway. He brought me to my feet and pressed the nozzle of his gun next to my temple. Each breath hardened and my lungs dried quickly.

"Put it down, Ryker," Pain yelled. "Put it down or you get to see another little fuck-partner find death at the hand of Pain."

"Okay," Grayland yelled. "Okay, whatever you say."

The events that happened next occurred in an instant, washed over and blurred in a haze of inaudible sound and a flurry of stinging pain. Before I could think clearly and find my breath, Pain was lying on top of me, lifeless. Most of my body was exposed through the shreds of my clothes, and my face was wet with sweat and tears. Everything, including my own heart, seemed silent and without motion.

I shoved Pain off of me and called out for Grayland. My throat was scratched, and I was barely able to hear it, but I kept pushing for Grayland to answer. When he wouldn't, I pulled the cloth from my eyes. The blur of chaos warped through the room. I coughed and brushed a river of blood and mucus from beneath my nose, settling into the sense of spin the room provided. I crawled past Pain toward where I last remembered hearing Grayland and saw the shape of his feet. I called for him again, but the only response I received was a short, stagnant wheezing. I found his hand grasping his chest and fear rushed my body bitter. A cold dark liquid leaked through his fingers. I started crying and wrapped my fingers into his.

"Grayland," I whispered when my lips reached his ear. "Grayland, I'm here."

He couldn't speak. When he tried, a lick of blood fell from his lips.

"What should I do?" I grasped his hand tighter. "Talk to me."

"Danielle…" he said when he found his voice. "Danielle… I love you."

I cried harder, wanting to correct him, tell him the truth of my identity. "I love you, too," I said instead. "Don't leave me."

"Don't cry." He winced and fought his pain. "I'll be okay."

"I know."

"Your mom's waiting for me…"

"Take care of her."

"Take care of her," he repeated and smiled. "She needs your love."

"I will."

"Love her as I did." Grayland touched my scars tenderly. "She deserves you more than I did."

I took hold of his hand and let my tears wash them.

"I see her, Danielle. I see..."

Grayland choked on his words and coughed. Brushing my hand through his hair to comfort him, I kissed him, finding the taste of his blood more sweet than acrid. "Love her again," I said and watched as the last breath escaped his lips.

Without end, I cried for the next few hours over Grayland's chilled body. I never let go of his hand, even after I had no tears left to cry. I laid with him for the next day, unwilling to leave him alone; unwilling to be without his touch.

As my mind and my body fell into a conscious slumber, I heard Grayland through the mist of my awareness. It was not his voice and not a word was ever spoken, but his presence voiced my cowardice, my inability to live beyond him. He had taught me to stand strong against my adversity, but I was allowing my body to waste away because of a single loss, which was not truly love; it was an escape. He taught me to run if ever he was lost to me, but now that the time had come, I remained stagnant. If I were ever to prove my love for him, to prove my respect and my honesty, I would do as he had always asked. I would do what was necessary to honor his courage with my own and live my life on my terms. I asked of him what I was supposed to do and he replied,

"Find your happiness."

"You are my happiness," I argued, but he would not allow me to believe it. "Then what? What is it?"

In my heart came the visage of a woman, a calm pleasure that I had nearly forgotten, and Grayland's voice became that of hers.

"Return to the truth," it said, and a rise of blood swelled within me. I could feel my body floating about me in tenderness. My ambition had been renewed, and I was not about to fail either of them.

"I'm coming home," I whispered in prayer.

It took some time to find strength in my legs, but as I did, I walked from Grayland without once looking back. I knew that if I were ever going to leave him, I would need to forget him. I took hold of one of his bags and gathered up what I needed for my new journey. The last piece I packed was the flag that hung on Danielle's wall. Of everything material, it was the only reminder I wished to keep of him.

After dressing in new clothes, I picked up the sunglasses and knelt down next to the man that caused my pain. His skin was much darker than that of either Grayland or I—a muddy brown, bordering on black.

"Nigger, indeed," I said and spit on his face.

Rising with renewed energy, I slipped the sunglasses over my eyes and opened the door. The light was subdued, and I figured the world was just now calling on the morning. It would become much brighter soon, but it was of no worry. The air was refreshing and exhilarating, leaving me with a spirit that called me to rise up and fight for my own worth of survival. There was nothing better I could think of doing than to light a cigarette and give the wind my satisfaction. As the flame burned away the match, I stared out into the distance, allowing my last tear to fall.

I then dropped the match onto the floor of the house and stood back to watch the fire consume my home with glorious animation. It danced with a fluidity I don't think I would ever see again and ate the remaining vestige of my past. It was empowering and the perfect end to my new beginning.

(CHAPTER 23

Traveling a strange and alien land is a humble experience, one filled with constant growth. To be educated in the different aspects of a world once unknown emits a feeling of great pleasure in its uniqueness. But to see the land one could once have only imagined without the need for taste or touch, is a much more intoxicating experience all its own. But, as with any life-altering changes, it was not without its difficulties.

Tracing my way back along the path Grayland and I had earlier traveled, the senses I relied on so significantly before gaining sight caused me discomfort and, in most cases, disorientation. Severe aches in my head and a constant dizziness kept me from traveling more than a mile at a time without rest. I would try not to close my eyes to help acclimate my other senses to the trust and utility of the new, but when the backs of my eyes seared in pain, I could do nothing but hold them closed and urge the pain away. The discomfort abated with each passing day, some of which were without hindrance. Upon those extremely rare moments, I would sometimes sit upon the rocks and marvel at how far my eyesight could take me and at the majestic palette the land presented. The brilliant orange of the rippling skies and the fire of the roaring ocean, the distant scores of rocky terrains rising skyward with abandon, and levels of scorched prairie where I could imagine wild animals having once grazed—all of it flushed my mind with serenity. Littered among these vast landscapes were miles, sometimes dozens of miles of man-made structures of varying sizes, from packs of smaller wooden domiciles to larger visions of architecture built so densely together there was hardly ever a place to step. I remember having taken refuge among these structures with Grayland during our journey, but never had I imagined them to be so overwhelming. Some of them were even so large, the tips of their enormity were held captive by the clouds above.

By the end of the first week, the fog of my sight had lifted completely and my eyes finally accepted the light with natural acuity. The aches in my head had gone, and though my other senses still caused a bit of disorientation, I was adapting well enough to the stability of my sight as my primary means of perception. I grew more accustomed to the sharpness of objects from some distances away, utilizing this new ability to identify men and women I would encounter before approaching them. I learned very early on for whom I could trust, and for whom I should avoid. Women, whether dark or light skinned, alone or in the company of other women, always seemed to be more docile and kind than any man could ever be, what with their overt need for dominance and pleasure. There was that rare occasion when a man (usually one of whom fell in favor with my own tone of skin) would be kind to my sensibility, and when a woman (hungry and with an appearance to be desired) would cause me grief and regret, but my instincts developed quickly in gifting me with the propensity to make informed decisions on the company I kept and to whom I could trust when reaching out for food and rest. What most surprised me, though, having been in contact with so very few people during my last journey, was with how many men and women occupied such small spaces of land. So much so, that I could hardly breathe and felt the constant urge to run as fast as possible to return to my desired isolation.

Of those nights I had to take rest in a densely populated land, I took solace in a cigarette and my training, performing several exercises and sparring with an imaginary heavy bag. Before going to sleep, I would relax with one final cigarette and take notice of my possessions, which would be a prize for any night rat who wished to steal from me in sleep. One such rat made an attempt to do so, believing I had fallen asleep when I was still very much awake. I heard the light shuffle of footsteps approach me and I matched each with my very own, easing back and away from my stuff so as to find the strength once again in my secondary senses. When the rat was upon me, I smelled its foul odor and heard him rummage through my pack. Taking in a deep breath, I took up to try and wrap around behind him, but the sound of my steps were too heavy and startled him before I could reach him. He instantly yelled out and lifted one of my guns. Before he could fire, I kicked the gun away, sending a stray of bullets off into the distance. Taking advantage of his unbalanced footing, I took hold of the gun and wrapped my body in close to him. I sent the back of my head into his nose followed by my elbow into his jaw. He fought back, shoving my head to the ground, but I was quick to my feet and gave him a series of blows to both his abdomen and chest. Debilitated, I kicked the side of the rat's knee, cracking the bone, and put him to sleep with a knee to the jaw and a blow to the temple. Standing above him, my breath was heavy, and I could feel the heat of his blood on my knuckles. But the sensation I felt rush my body was intoxicating. It was just a shame that Grayland could not have been there to see it all happen.

I couldn't savor the pride I felt, though, as I knew others might be near and felt the need to move on. I quickly fished through the rat's clothes for anything useful, but found nothing but dozens of large pimples on the man's skin and a box of something I'd never seen before. I shoved the box into my pack and gathered everything up, leaving the rat with whatever the elements allowed him. I walked several miles before the strength in my legs gave way, unaware that I had left the dense land. I slept on the hard ground that night. The next morning, I took heed of what I now understood Grayland had done, and kept my distance from those types of dense lands whenever I could.

Upon the middle of my eighth day, my travels led me to the edge of a grand bridge. On the other side was the first dense land I had seen for a couple of days. I thought about turning around and finding another way, but I had finished what was left of my fresh water the night before and, without a renewed supply, would not be able to travel far before exhaustion set in. I crossed the bridge with an air of confidence, which faded instantly when I reached the opposite end. Sitting at its edge were a half a dozen men with patches of hair covering their features and colored markings etched across their skin. They watched me intensely as I walked by, but seemed too busy administering chemicals into their arms with needles to care much about my presence. In order to keep from causing any trouble, I avoided eye contact, which seemed to keep them from feeling threatened. When they were out of view, I found my breath again and rested. A few other inhabitants crossed my path as I did, and they all looked at me with a grotesque manner, as if I were an intruder looking to harm them all. I came to the conclusion that if I were to get on here, no matter how frightened I was, I would need to convey confidence and authority, which would earn me respect and prove to others that I am not to be feared.

I took a deep breath and stepped down the road to seek out the nearest building that had the means of bartering for water. As I did, I focused my attention on as many men and women as I could, showing no fear and never keeping eye contact for more than a few moments. Most of everyone, with the occasional light-skinned individual, held a mix of dirty and darker brown complexions and the air smelled rich with sweat and dirt. There wasn't an apparent dominance in gender, as the women held as much authority as the men, but it was clear that none of them held any inhibitions, speaking in loud and garrulous tongues, fighting over simple disagreements and some even marrying in the space between structures while others watched in hunger.

After a few miles of wandering and searching, I caught the eye of a gentle young women standing against a wall, lighting a cigarette. She was alone and though her arms were lined with the markings I had seen earlier on the men at the bridge, she did not seem a threat. I walked to her and smiled, surprised to receive a smile back in return.

"Hello," I said, as I did all others, upon first meeting.

"Hey," she said.

"I hate to bother you, but I'm on my way home and I'm in need of some water. Could you tell me where I might find a fresh supply?"

The woman looked me over as she chewed the edge of her cigarette.

"You the goods to barter?" she said.

"I believe so," I said.

The woman removed the cigarette from her mouth and looked me over again. She then pointed down the road at a small structure surrounded by dozens of people. "The pub's your best bet," she said.

"Thank you." I stepped away.

The woman laughed. "You think your gettin' in there with that fucked-up baby face of yours, chica, your shittin' yourself."

I turned back to her. "I need water."

"You got some fuckin' balls," she said and wrapped her arm around my neck. "I like that. Come on."

The woman pulled me down to the pub and worked me through the crowd, shouting out in playful anger and hostility, until we were inside. It smelled of urine and vomit and was loud with music and conversation.

"Sanchez runs the bar," the woman said, pointing at a long table near the back of the room, laced with several men drinking and smoking. "Need water, you trade with him. But don't take no shit."

"You won't come with me?" I said.

"I got other business." The woman shoved the tip of her cigarette to the palm of her hand and placed the remaining stick to her ear. "Take care, baby girl.

"No shit," she added as she combed through the pub.

With a quick look around, I made my way quickly to an empty chair at the bar. I suddenly found the visage of a young girl, staring back at me, the left side of her face marked and rippled with the wave of injury. The reflection lifted her hand as I had prompted and touched my scars. I felt a slight unease with the reality of how everyone must see me—a monster. I looked away and tried my best to avoid the reflection's stare as I peered down to the side of the bar and located a man serving drinks to everyone who asked.

"Excuse me, Sanchez?" I called out. He didn't register my voice, so I called again. Finally, he reached a man just a few heads down from me and I called out, "Sanchez," with a fierce and demanding tone.

"¿Qué puedo conseguirle?" he said when he finally took notice of me.

"I'm afraid I don't understand," I said.

Sanchez rolled his eyes and gave me a look of spite. "What you want, bitch?"

Ignoring his insolence, I leaned in to him. "I only wish to collect some water."

"Only alcohol."

"But I was told you had some to barter," I said.

"Fuck off," Sanchez said. He turned to walk away.

I grabbed the back of his shirt and pulled him back to me, bringing his stench-ridden face to mine. "Listen to me, Sanchez," I said, my eyes dark with anger. "I am fed up with your impudence. I asked for water, and I am going to get it. Understood?" I let go of him, pushing back a step, and sat down, never breaking eye contact.

"That'll cost," he said.

I nodded and handed him the box I stole from the rat a few nights prior.

He immediately threw it back in my face. "Consiga cogido el al lado. Only drugs."

"I don't have any drugs," I said with restraint.

"Pierdase. Fuck off." He waved his hand at me and walked away, accepting a handful of something that looked like aspirin from a woman whose breasts were nearly exposed and gave her a drink in return.

I grabbed the box up and turned, catching sight of my guide kissing some rippled man in the corner of the pub. I shoved the box inside my pack ready to scold her for deceiving me, but then caught a glimpse of a black man out of the corner of my eye. At first I thought I had imagined it, but then I saw him, standing at the bar, enticing Sanchez with a bag of white powder, hollering for whiskey.

I closed my eyes and listened to the tone of his voice. There was no mistaking that vibrato. I moved in beside him as he suckled his drink, talking loudly to no one. I stared at him with intent until he finally looked at me.

"What'choo lookin' at, bitch?" he said.

"Why is it the ignorant always refer to me as 'bitch'?"

"I only calls 'ems likes I sees 'em."

"Me as well," I said and moved closer. "And what I see is the ugliest damn nigger I've ever seen."

"What'choo just call me? Yous better watch your mouth, bitch, 'for I hav'ta sew it shut."

The black man set his drink down and pushed his chest into mine. "Now 'pologize to the nigger 'for I cut'choo up an' mount your pussy on my wall."

For a split moment, my eyes locked to his and I smiled. I then whipped my hand to his neck and brought his head down to meet an uppercut to the base of his nose. Before giving the chance to breath, I pinched the nerves in the base of his neck, forced his face into the bar and leaned my lips next to his ear.

"Is that apology enough?"

"What the fuck," he said.

"You see, friend," I said, "you seem to have your thoughts backward. I believe it's you who owes me an apology."

"Sorry," he screamed. "Ah'ight? I'm sorry."

"For what?"

"For whateva," he said. "Whateva you needs me to be sorry 'bout."

"Not good enough." I pulled a gun from under my clothes and placed it to his temple.

"Whoa, shit," he said, pressing his eyes closed. "What the hell's your problem?"

"You don't remember me?" I said.

"No. Fuck. I never met'choo before, I swears it."

"Okay. But I'm certain you know Grayland."

"Who?" he said.

"Ryker Grayland. My father."

"Shit, bitch. You got the wrong nigger. I don't knows no Grayland."

"Liar," I yelled. I hadn't noticed the silence permeating the room. "You killed him, and I'm out to seek my revenge."

"I never kilt nobody, I swears. Som'body get this bitch off me, man."

I peered up and with no takers, returned to the business at hand. "He may not have died at your hands, but you were there and you let it happen."

"No, I'm tellin' ya'. Yous gots the wrong guy."

"I don't believe you." I pressed the gun down harder.

"Please, don't kill me," he pleaded, urine sliding down the course of his leg. Along with the desperate tone in his voice, I concluded that he must have been telling the truth. In discontent, I pinched the nerves of his neck a bit harder and then pushed myself upright, releasing him from my grip. He remained planted to the bar as he caught his breath.

I replaced the gun into my clothes and grabbed my pack. "If I find out you lied to me," I said to him, "I will find you. I promise."

I turned to leave the pub without showing any fear or remorse to the gawking eyes around me.

"Fuck you, bitch," the black man said.

With a quick turn, I raised my gun and fired a shot, striking the man in his chest. He hit the ground before the crack of the gun finished echoing through the silence of the crowd.

"Damn niggers," I said softly and returned my weapon.

I again scanned the crowd and before I stepped from the pub, the woman wrapped her arms around me, almost knocking me to the ground.

"That was the shit, baby girl," she said, choking my neck with her arm. She dragged me out to the road before letting me go.

"Thank you," I said, unsure. "Your friend didn't get me the water I needed."

"What did you give him for trade?" she said.

I showed her the box and grew red with embarrassment by the mocking laughter I received in return.

"Better to keep these hidden," she said, shoving them into my pack. "Else find yourself raped in some filthy back alley by some fucking bandito."

"I better be on my way," I said, hoping I had enough time to find my way from the land before nightfall.

"Serious? What about your water?"

"I'll be fine."

"Come on back to my place. Tomorrow, I'll get you some water and a ride to wherever you're going."

"I better not."

"You scared of me, chica?"

"It's not that," I said.

"Look, baby girl. I'm not taking no for an answer."

The woman grabbed my hand before I could blink and stole me back down the road. "I'm Celia, by the way," she said.

"Madeline," I returned. And with a smile, I couldn't help but take in the exhilaration of her boisterous pleasure.

CHAPTER 24

Celia brought me back to the bridge where she introduced me to "her boys," none of whom spoke to me. I was fine with their reticence, allowing my silence to express my own indifference to Celia's forced companionship. Before telling them about the incident at the bar, all of them seemed ready to kill me for simply being foreign to them. But their attitudes shifted to negligible acceptance afterward, even if they didn't believe one single word of it.

"I could certainly use one of those," I said as the apparent leader, Ramon, lit up one of his cigarettes. He took in a deep breath and blew it back in my face, leading to a round of laughs from the pride. I quickly joined in with my own soft chuckles, giving the impression that I was okay with their torment and then tore the cigarette from Ramon's mouth, helping myself to its sensual flavor.

Celia fought back a smile as the rest went quiet and backed away. Ramon slowly stalked me with his eyes and puffed his dominance, requiring me to shrink away like the rest. When I held my ground, taking several drags off the cigarette, his only recourse was to snap his fingers and walk away with his brethren in tow. As the last of them fell past me, Celia let her laughter rise up and grabbed my neck.

"You are one badass chica, baby girl," she said. "I love it."

It wasn't long before I was with Celia and Ramon in one of the very few working transports I'd seen, riding along the roads with great speeds. I sat alone in the seat behind them, vainly listening to Celia's incessant chatter while taking in the whip of the wind that tore across my face and the sight of the land spinning past me. Ramon kept a watchful eye on me through the reflective glass hanging from the front of the car (for which I answered with my own vigilant stares) and Celia would occasionally take a breath to ask me a question. I would respond in kind, which would then send her on an impertinent tangent, much like the time she vomited after performing a favor for some guy a few years back or the reason behind the ring pierced through her breast, which she was very comfortable showing off to everyone.

It was almost dark when we reached our destination, a large domicile near the tip of a large hill. Celia helped me from the car and took me inside to the room where I could lay my pack.

"Where are those condoms," she said, biting her lower lip.

"The what?"

"The condoms." When it was clear I didn't understand her, she said, "The box you tried to barter for water."

I handed her the box and she tore into it, pulling one of its contents out with boisterous glee. "Better take two." She winked and tossed the box to the bed. "Thanks, baby girl," and she was gone.

As I explored the richness and complexity of the home, I could hear Celia and Ramon performing their marriage. I attempted to ignore them but they were quite loud, so I took to the furthest corner and closed my eyes, focusing on my own cherished love. I hadn't realized they had finished until Celia roused me from whatever trance I had created for myself. I enjoyed the meat and potatoes she had prepared and found the silence of our company to be quite relaxing.

After the meal, Ramon slipped away to sleep while Celia helped build a fire. The two of us sat for hours, enjoying each other's company in both the silence brought upon by the pleasure of a cigarette and in compulsory conversation.

"Why is it you're helping me?" I asked when the fire had died to a mere crackle. I had almost finished my second cigarette.

"I don't know," she said. "Because you remind me of me at your age. Too damn tough for your own good. What was that at the bar anyway? What did that nig do to you that pissed the shit from you so bad?"

"He's a nig. Isn't that enough?"

Celia smiled. "Yeah, I guess so."

I put my cigarette out on the ash of the fire. "I think he was one of the men who helped murder my father," I said softly.

"No shit, really?"

I curled my legs up and held them to my chest.

"Are you sure?"

"I thought so at the time, but not so much anymore."

Celia slid in next to me and wrapped her arm around me. "Well I say good riddance regardless. One less nig walking the streets is always a good thing. Think of it this way. If you hadn't have popped the son-of-a-bitch, he would have killed somebody eventually. You just saved someone else's life today, baby girl. Be proud."

I nodded and smiled with skepticism.

"Are all nigs really this vile?" I said.

"If you have to ask that question, you haven't been paying attention."

I thought a moment about Grayland and his wife. "I guess you're right."

"No shit I'm right. Listen to me, baby girl. Nigs have been a plague on this rock for as long as I can remember. They're no good to anyone. You got that?"

"Yeah."

"Come here," she said and gave me a strong, loving hug. "I'm sorry about your father," she whispered to my ear. "I'm sure he was a great man."

I said thank you with a gentle kiss and then laid my head upon her breast. She combed her fingers through my hair, and I felt safe for the first time since my final marriage to Grayland.

"Have you ever killed anyone?" I said after a few warm and inviting breaths.

"Not sure I could ever go that far. That's why I have the boys."

"They protect you."

"That and to have a good fuck every now and then."

"And you can trust them?"

"Not even as far as I can spit," she said.

"Then why do you stay with them?"

"I've been around for a while, baby girl, and if there's one thing I've learned it's that you can't trust anyone."

"That's not true," I said. "I have many friends I trust."

"I hope to God that's true," she said. "But in my experience, everyone disappoints you eventually."

"I don't believe that."

"You will."

I sat up. "Does that mean you don't trust me?"

Celia placed her hand to my unmarked cheek. "Up until you give me a reason not to, baby girl." She kissed me as the fire was but a spark.

"I trust you," I said.

"Good, 'cause if you didn't, I think I'd have to kill you."

We laughed and lit ourselves another cigarette, using the match to add a little more flame to the fire. I watched it dance for a few moments and then looked to Celia.

"Do you remember how the war started?"

" 'Fraid not," she said quickly. "I was only about six. The most I remember is traveling with my parents to escape the damn Muslim takeover. I mean, those termites were fucking everywhere, taking control of the world one fucking infidel at a time. Add in the checkerboard menace, and nowhere was safe. You either took up arms and defended yourself, or you hid somewhere like a fucking gay puss-ant. The problem was, there wasn't a clear distinction for what side would keep you safe. Nigs fought against us over power and the fucking racists were doing everything they could to keep us all in our so-called 'rightful place.' Let me tell you, it was a shit storm of chaos that turned into a race war. I mean, if you weren't already one of us, you were shot dead, no questions asked. The only thing we could all agree on was that we all hated the fucking Muslim terrorists. By the time I was old enough to join the fight, footholds had been established around the country and we all seemed content with staying in our own little pockets."

I lied down and enjoyed the rest of our smoke with little to no words. When we had finished, Celia said, "What the fuck happened to your face?"

I touched my scars and remained silent.

Celia fought back a turn of regret. "I didn't mean to pry."

"No, please. I don't mind." I took a breath and continued. "I was burned as an infant, so I'm actually unsure of how it really happened."

"God, that sucks. I don't know what I'd do if something like that happened to this beautiful face."

I laughed. "Cover it with one of your marks?"

"Now that would be somethin'," Celia said. "I could do it for you. It'd probably make you look more bad-ass than you already do."

"As appealing as that sounds, I think my scars are bad-ass enough."

"That's too bad. I'm pretty good with the needle. Most of what you see is mine."

"Why do you do it?"

"Why not do it?" she said. "It sure sends a hell of a statement. I mean, each tattoo has a meaning behind it, representing some part of who I am."

"In other words, it's a means of expressing yourself," I said.

"Yeah, I guess you can say that."

"There are other ways of expressing yourself."

"Yeah, so?"

"You have to admit, permanently marking your body seems like an extreme way to simply articulate what you're feeling."

"Who the fuck are you to tell me how the fuck I should express myself?"

"I meant no disrespect," I said, detecting a hint of antipathy.

"You think you're better than me."

"I never said that."

"At least I don't need to go around shooting up bars to fucking articulate what I'm feeling."

"You don't know me," I said coldly.

"Then tell me, miss perfect. How is it you express yourself?"

"If I were to say, I guess it would be through my stories."

"Your stories?" Celia said with overt sarcasm. "Seems pretty gay to me."

"My stories mean a great deal to me," I said.

"I'm sure they do, but really? No one cares about that kind of shit anymore."

"I beg to differ. I knew quite a few people who relied on my stories to give them hope and meaning."

"Bullshit."

"Stories can shape one's life," I said. "Don't judge something before you've experienced it."

"Isn't that what you're doing?"

I lowered my head and bit my lip. "You present a good point," I said.

"Then understand this. If you want to survive out there, you need to earn respect, and I know from experience that physical statements like these are all anyone respects anymore, not that childish bullshit of yours."

"Well, perhaps it's time to change that," I said.

"Yeah, whatever." Celia stood. "Stick with the gun, baby girl. You'll thank me in the long run." She turned to leave.

"There was once upon a sunlit garden a rose," I said, prompting Celia to turn back to me. "She was mighty in form, yet peculiar in stature, for she lived not among the life of her own but among the bliss of a bed of lilies. She did not mind it, of course. The lilies were her sisters, no matter the differences they may have had. They all ate from the same sun and drank from the same cup, receiving equal amounts of love from their mother's hand. She was at peace and full of harmony.

"One day, as the rose enjoyed her early morning taste of the sun's warm breast, a bee flew through the garden of lilies, hoping to find food for his hive. He immediately took notice of the rose's odd shade. He rested upon her petal and laughed in glee.

" 'You are an odd little flower,' the bee said.

" 'I am a flower,' the rose replied, 'but why should that make me odd?'

" 'Because you are a rose living among the lily.'

" 'They are my family,' the rose said.

" 'But how does a rose living among the lily find true love?' the bee asked.

" 'I find love everyday.'

" 'You may find the love of friendship and family, yes. But what I speak of is love that transcends all of that.'

" 'There is no other form of love, sir bee,' the rose said, confident.

" 'But there is. It is a love that forms from the pleasure of the soul, giving birth to life that will live on past the mortality of the body.'

" 'How do you know such a love exists?'

" 'Ask your sisters if you do not believe me.'

"The rose did ask her sisters and learned great tales of the love the bee had spoken of. She cried, knowing she would never find such a love among the lily.

" 'Sir bee, you must tell me,' she said, 'where can I find such a love for my own?'

" 'I know of a home full of your kind,' the bee said, offering the rose hope and splendor.

" 'Please, you must take me there. I must know this love, experience it with my own soul.'

" 'I am afraid I cannot,' the bee said.

" 'Why not?'

" 'I am not welcome in the bed of the garden for which I speak.'

" 'Perhaps if you took me under the blanket of the moon's peace,' the rose suggested, 'so that you will remain undetected upon the bed.'

"The bee thought long about the rose's suggestion and agreed that he would indeed help. That night, the bee plucked the rose from her home and took her to the sky above. The lilies called out their love and support with a wave of sadness with the hope that she would find her love and one day return home. The rose cried a few tears over the moon's watchful eye, but took solace in the taste of the wind as the bee set her down upon the soil of her new home.

" 'I am very gracious for your help,' the rose said. 'Won't you stay with me, until I am able to meet my new family?'

" 'I cannot. With the rise of the sun comes the hand of my death. I must go.'

" 'Very well,' the rose said, saddened. 'Fly free.'

" 'Farewell my lovely rose, and good luck.' With that, the bee took flight and was gone into the night.

"The rose could not find rest that night through the shake of her nerves, all of which were vanquished with the rise of the sun. For as far as the rose could see, the hills were covered with the family she never knew. Of course, beginning life anew comes great change, and for the rose, the changes were frightening and without joy. Instead of a single hand to feed her with warm attention and care, several sprouts came from beneath the land to give them all nourishment without an ounce of heart, leaving as coldly as they had arrived. Instead of finding play and music upon her new home, she found only silence and the undesirable, unable to gather the fresh rays of the sun among the horde of selfishness. Soon, the rose had been weakened by her lack of nutrients and the taste of a soil that had been littered with nauseating, foreign elements. Her petals were tipped in flakes and she had lost all music within her heart.

"One late morrow, as the sprouts woke her from her solemn rest, the rose heard a new noise, faint and quite unfamiliar. She looked upon the distance and saw a monster bearing down on her new family, tearing them from their root and holding them captive among its back. What took surprise in the rose was the lack of screams from the victims of this travesty. There was only acceptance, tearing the soul of the rose into pieces. What was she to do? Should she accept her new fate and lie in wait for her death? Or could something be done to stop the monster from devouring her last fruit of life?

"As the monster drew ever closer and pulled up the roses about her, she made her decision and shrank downward upon the land. She felt the sting of the monster's teeth bite at her head, stripping her of a few petals and uprooting her from the soil to lay her rest upon the ground a distance away where she remained silent until it chose to pass and continue feeding on the rest of the garden. By the time the moon had risen, all of her family had been taken. The rose could do nothing more than cry.

"The next morrow, the sprouts returned to nourish the emptiness. She drank what she could and finally fed heartily on the warmth of the sun. And then she prayed for her life to be given a second chance to flourish, without fear and without remorse.

"The song of the night fulfilled her prayers, sending a strong wind her way, picking her from the ground and resting her gently upon the garden of the lily. As the sun broke through the sky, the rose felt the warm inviting hands of her mother returning her to her rightful home.

" 'I am sorry for doubting the worth of my true family,' the rose said to the lilies.

"All she received in return was the hand of their devotion, and absolute true love."

Celia lied next to me as I finished my tale, her eyes wide in adulation. "My God, that was the shit," she said.

"Stories will always have a place," I said.

"I get it. You proved me wrong. Now let me do the same." Celia popped to her feet and left the room. I lit a fresh cigarette in her absence, and when she returned, she carried with her a large black pouch. She unfurled it, exposing several sharp needles, colored liquids and dozens of white threads.

"Give me your arm," she said, wrapping her legs around my waist.

"What for?"

"I want to give you something you'll always remember."

Before I could comply, Celia had my arm in a tight grip and was drawing on it with a black writing utensil. "What are you doing?"

"I'm drawing you a rose. Now hold still."

I watched Celia carefully draw the edges of the rose near my shoulder and then wrapped its stem around my arm, ending its tip at the center of my inner elbow. She finished her etching with a small petal falling from the rose. When she was through, I admired her abilities as she tightened the string around the needle and soaked it in the red liquid.

"This is going to hurt a little," she said and stuck the needle into my arm. The first prick made my body shake, but I withstood the temptation to pull my arm away. In rapid, steady succession, Celia poked at my skin continuously, tracing the image she had drawn. It took several hours, taking breaks to dab the blood from my skin or to add more liquid to the needle. I took those instances to take in deep breaths, hoping to relax my body from the severe, hot pain that caused my eyes to water horribly. When she had finished her brilliant piece of artistry, Celia washed the skin and covered the work in its entirety with a large bandage.

"You'll want to sleep on your left side tonight," Celia said, smiling brightly.

I kissed Celia goodnight and lay in bed until the dark sank away, the burning tenderness keeping me from falling asleep. Upon rising, I fixed a succulent breakfast and ate, waiting patiently for Celia and Ramon to join me. When they finally did, they were not interested in eating a bite, nor were they in any mood to speak. Instead, Celia removed the bandage from my arm and cleaned it once more, taking a short, but honored admiration at her creation. She then walked me out to the car and didn't say a word to either me or Ramon, which after the day before, felt eerily odd. I kept my thoughts to myself, wanting to keep from instigating a foul tirade, and simply let it be, choosing instead to take in the nature around us.

After about an hour, Ramon turned off the main road and took us deep into the heart of a massive desert, where he stopped the car and got out. Celia followed, keeping her back turned to me.

"What's going on?" I said, greeted with intense silence.

Just then, another car came roaring up to us, blinding me with a gust of dirt. As I attempted to clear my eyes to reacquire my vision, I was pulled from the car by the hands of three men and thrown violently to the ground. I coughed, and when the wind was clear, I realized that the half a dozen men who surrounded me were the tribe from the bridge. Celia stood closest to me, staring down at me with arctic hostility.

"You lying, racist bitch," she said.

"Celia, what's going on?"

"You betrayed me."

"That's not true."

Celia took my pack from Ramon and pulled the flag from within. "Explain this," she said.

"It was my father's," I said.

"It's a symbol of the racist fucks who destroyed this country," she screamed. "If it wasn't for the men who believed in this shit, the war may never have happened and my parents would still be alive."

"Celia, I have nothing to do with any of that. You have to believe me."

"I can't believe I fell for your fucking deceptions. Gain my trust to get water and a car and then fuck me over when you no longer need me. Am I right?"

"No, it's not like that. I want to be your friend."

"Fuck you." Celia spit at me and threw the flag to the ground at my feet. As tears rolled down my face in desolation and betrayal, Ramon flicked fire onto a match and walked up to the flag.

"This is what we think of your fucking ideals," he said and dropped the match to the flag. It burned slowly at first, but soon grew to a great height. All I could do was watch and pray upon Grayland's memory. To my surprise, I received an answer back, pushing me to fight for not only his honor, but for that of Danielle as well.

I rolled away from the flag and rose to my feet, taking aim at one of the men's lower gut, ending the attack with an elbow to his nose. Suddenly, all of the men were upon me, and though I fought as best I could, getting in several hard and precise hits, in the end the group was too much for me. Within moments, I was back on the ground, trying desperately to ward off a flurry of kicks and hits from each man.

The last thing I recall seeing before the black took me away was Celia leaning up against the car, her back turned from the violence and her hand raised to her eyes to cover her unintended tears.

CHAPTER 25

My eyelids tightened around my eyes as I found my consciousness. What little light broke through the window of the small room bit at my eyes, and I could hardly see anything. As I sat up, I forced my eyes open as far as I could and a wave of dizziness spun my urge to vomit. I closed my eyes again and fought my nausea. When it had calmed, I took my time and gradually opened them, taking great care to pacify my senses.

The first thing I saw was a needle taped into my arm. It was attached to a bag hanging from a hook above the bed. I pulled the needle out and cleared the dryness in my throat with a cough. My first few steps were met with staggered frailty, but I gained my balance quickly and located my pack on a desk in the far corner. Everything remained except for my guns and ammunition. Unfazed, I slipped my hand into a small compartment hidden from the casual observer and pulled from it a small caliber pistol. I made sure it was loaded and went to the door.

I regained control of my sight as I looked through into the darkened hall. For what I could see, the domicile was without movement. Just the same, I took each step with caution, holding my pistol low in both hands as Grayland had taught me. Each room I checked was empty, but I could hear light voices somewhere ahead of me grow louder as I continued down the hall. I stopped at the corner of its edge and crouched to the floor. I closed my eyes to open my ears and listen to what was being said.

"If we don't get those crates back, we're fucked," the first said in a womanly tone.

"She'll get them," said another, striking a much lower register.

"If we would have just left it alone," the woman returned, her pitch heightened in annoyance and frustration.

"We did what was right," the man said calmly.

"This is not what we need right now."

"It's done. No use crying over it."

"But without those guns—"

"We're fucked, yeah. I got it. Don't worry. We'll get it done."

"We don't have anything left to barter with, Rock."

"You trust Lila," the man said.

"Have faith," the woman said and for a few minutes after, there was only a bit of items being shuffled about.

"You collected the rest of the fruit?" she finally said.

"Of course. They're in the cooler with the rest of the stuff."

"Can you grab the rest of the fuel from the basement? I want to make sure we're out of here as soon as Lila gets back."

"I have to check on our guest first," the man said.

"Okay, but I'm telling you now, we can't support her all the way back in the state she's in."

The man took a moment of solitude before responding. "I know. We did everything we could."

The man's footsteps grew heavy upon my ear within seconds. I ducked into one of the doorways in the hall and pulled my gun to my chest. When the man reached my position, I threw my elbow to his jaw and whipped in around him. I quickly found a grip on his wrist and shoved him against the wall, pushing his arm up his back.

"Where am I?" I said into his ear with fierce enmity.

The man didn't answer. I shoved the barrel of the pistol to his temple.

"Answer me."

"I will not concede to threats," he said, which confounded me.

"You'd rather die?" I said.

"Only when civility does."

My voice grew shaky. "I just want to know how I got here," I said.

The man didn't speak.

"Fine," I said and cocked the pistol.

Just then, I felt the cold, round steel of another weapon on the back of my neck.

"Drop it," the woman said.

I held my ground until the click of the hammer echoed about me. I considered the repercussions of my actions and raised my arms, removing the gun from the man's temple. The woman swiped the gun from my hand.

"On your knees."

I stepped away from the man. As he turned to face me, checking his nose and mouth gently with his fingers, his visage grew foggy. I blinked my eyes in an attempt to clear them, but the condition only got worse. A sudden lightheadedness, followed by a screen of blindness, dropped me to the floor.

CHAPTER 26

"What happened?" I attempted to say through my cracked throat.

The woman had returned me to bed and intently watched from the corner of the room near the desk. I tried to sit up, but the throbbing in my head kept me from it.

"You passed out," she said. Her voice was soft and cautious.

I held my head, focusing on each and every breath I took. "Where am I?"

"One of our safe houses," the woman said with a stale tongue. "Which isn't so safe now because of you."

"I'm sorry," I said, hoping to find reconciliation.

"Is this how you always show your gratitude?"

"Gratitude for what?"

"For saving your fucking ass." The woman's venom rose considerably.

"You saved me?"

"Yeah," she said, as if I had been an active participant. "Those termites beat the living shit out of you. If we hadn't come along when we did, I have no doubt they would have killed you."

I forced myself to sit. The woman leaned forward with her hands folded together in her lap.

"I don't remember," I said.

"Didn't expect you would. There were a couple of days there when we weren't even sure you would pull through."

"A couple of days? How long have I been here?"

"About a week, now."

"A week?"

"Rock figures that's why you fainted. Your blood sugar's still low, and without the IV, your body couldn't take the adrenaline."

"I didn't mean to make you feel unsafe here," I said quietly.

"It's partially our fault, I guess. We shouldn't have left you alone."

I swung my legs over the edge of the bed and peered out the window. My eyes still felt incredibly sensitive to the light, but I could keep them open without strain. I took that as a good sign that they would heal soon enough.

"How is she?"

A stroke of dizziness struck me as I turned to look to the man entering the room. I hadn't noticed his shade of skin before—black as night.

"Awake," the woman said.

"Get him out of here," I groaned.

"This is Trevor Rockwell," the woman said as he walked to me.

"Good for him. Now tell him to go."

"I only want to check your vitals," Rockwell said, taking my arm.

I slapped it away. "I said get out of here, you damn nigger."

Silence ripped through the malevolence that now hung heavy in the air. The woman broke the stare I shared with Rockwell when she stepped between us and whispered something to him. He never left my sight, as I never left his, until he had closed the door to the room. With the sound of the latch came the sting of the woman's palm across my cheek. I lowered my head.

"You racist bitch," she said. "You don't ever fucking talk to someone like that around me. You got that?" The woman grabbed my jaw and lifted my head. "Hey. You may have run with termites before, but you show respect around me and my family."

I took a moment to search the woman's eyes, after which I swung my fist into her gut. Her grip on my jaw loosened, and I wrapped my arm up around her head, tightening it to my side, hitting her stomach several more times. She fell to the floor and caught her breath.

"I will respect who I choose to respect," I said.

The woman stood and flexed her side. When she caught my eyes, she swung her right arm toward me. I grabbed her wrist and was ready to knock her to the floor, but the distraction worked. I felt her left hand hit a soft spot just under my rib cage, stammering me enough to give her leverage. She pushed me to my knees with a steel kick to my shin and followed through with a hard hit to my cheekbone. I could taste the blood sink into the back of my mouth.

"I can't believe I thought you were one of us," she said.

"Why would you ever think that?" I spit some blood from my mouth.

The woman slid back to the desk and pulled up a charred cloth. She threw it down at my feet. "That's why.'

I unfurled the rag and noticed a couple of red and white lines amidst the charred black holes. "Bastards."

"We found that burning next to you after running those termites off. We assumed it was yours."

"It was," I said, spitting up more blood.

"Not just anyone carries an American flag with them."

"Do you?" I said with sarcasm.

The woman knelt down and pulled up the right side of her shirt. Wrapped around her side, just under her breast line, was a tattoo of a flag like the one I held burnt to shreds in my hand.

"We all have one," she said. "It's our signature."

"What does it mean?"

"Freedom." She lowered her shirt and walked back to the corner. She sat down and held her side tightly.

I collected my bearings and pulled myself onto the bed, bringing the flag with me. "Why the tattoo?"

"It symbolizes what we believe in. What I thought you believed in."

"Which is what?"

"Integrity, compassion, opportunity... family."

I lifted the flag and smelled its remains. Under the charred aroma of fabric, I could smell Grayland and a tear rolled from my eye. *I love you.*

"I used to," I said lower than a whisper.

The woman still heard me. "What happened?"

I lowered the flag. "I don't know."

The woman and I sat with each other in silence for a few minutes. I am not sure what thoughts spurred through her mind, but all I could think about was my own family, and in how much I missed them. So much that my chest hurt when I pictured their smiles. Even though I have never actually seen them, I felt them with all of my soul, urging me to return without haste. I knew I couldn't, and that hurt me even more. But not quite as much as the knowledge that there was once a symbol that encompassed the significance of their values and that it no longer existed but only to a very few.

"How did it fail?" I finally said.

The woman contemplated the question for some time before finding her words. "The truth behind its significance failed."

"Tell me."

"People chose to forget. They ignored its meaning to begin living under the guise of sloth and envy. Over time, more and more people fell into the hollow, cracking the flag's foundations. It led to fissures in people's identities, spewing a loss in the desire to excel, corruption in all levels of power and the expansion of individual indulgence. Eventually, the flag became a different symbol to different groups. A lot of Hispanics claimed it represented the betrayal of their civil rights through racism. Most blacks saw it as a reminder of the bigotry of an archaic system of rules that affected minority populations, and Muslims took it as the descendant of all inherent evil in mankind. There were others, but it didn't matter. The flag and the country it represented were under attack and those that fought with her were exterminated."

"Is that what started the war?" I asked.

"It was a factor in the war, but it wasn't what led to it. Breakdown in communication and the value of family is what caused it."

"Only in the strength of family will you find your way home," I said with a tender smile, repeating a quote I had heard.

"That we can agree on," she said, "because without that bond, there's no one we can rely on. We made a mistake when we allowed technology to infect the way we lived and stopped talking to our kids and refused to say no. It taught them that it was okay to do whatever they wanted without fear of punishment, leading to a demise of respect for authority and the complete slaughter of accountability. Kids no longer had a filter between right and wrong, learning life lessons from their friends and the Internet. Eight year-olds performing sexual acts in the classroom, tween-age pubescents getting abortions, teenagers having affairs with their teachers—it all became society's fault, not that of the parents and their abhorrent lack of discipline. And no matter how much they blamed television, cell phones or the Internet for their children's actions, parents continued to allow them unsupervised access to it all out of fear that they would one day be snatched by a child predator, or needed the ability to socialize with their friends. They thrived on their kids' happiness and their acceptance without giving any thought to the dangers they themselves were igniting.

"It turns out, the more parents allowed their kids access to these advancements, the more they disconnected them from human interaction. Conversations were conducted through text messages and tweets, rather than personal interaction. Everyone became addicted to narcissism, tweeting and blogging their every thought and every action, as if it were the most groundbreaking moment ever. The online community became essential to everyone, until they were incapable of functioning, or learning, unless it was conducted over the Internet. Each new generation became more and more isolated, dependent on any device that kept them plugged into the net, interacting through wireless communication. Work, education, shopping, banking—life became wireless.

"You can imagine what happened when it was all shut down.

"It's still unknown as to who actually sent the virus, but it was deadly. A single line of code infected every server, eating away all Internet source codes and transmitting through cell towers to all phones until all signals were literally dead. Some people just chose not to use them until the virus was killed. The problem is the virus couldn't be killed, and because all non-wireless devices and interactions were near obsolete, hell literally broke loose. The only groups unaffected by the mass hysteria that followed the crash were those that couldn't afford the technology or refused to give in to the addiction. It just so happened that because of the policies and laws that had been created, the majority of the population fell into this category and had become subservient to the government. And let me make it clear; it was not a coincidence that over seventy percent of the poor were either black or Hispanic. The government made sure they set it up that way, creating the perfect path for an unbridled mutiny."

"How do you know all of this?" I said.

"Research, mostly. I try to stay as connected to our history as I can possibly be. I collect as many books from what's left after the Muslim burn and have explored a lot of information on the four corners of the clean net. Along with stories from Lila and a few others, and we have plenty of historical records to draw from."

"Is Lila your mother?" I said.

The woman chuckled, a serene but adoring gaze in her eyes. "I wish she were," she said, "but no. My mother died a few years ago."

"Your father?"

The flush of adoration instantly fell from her features. "He was alive last I remember."

"You don't know where he is?"

"No, and I'd just as rather keep it that way."

"I can't believe you would say such a thing," I said sternly.

"Do you really think I care?"

"I would think you would, seeing as how much you seem to revere family."

"Blood doesn't make a family," she said. "My father was a the purist of bigots. He only saw people for the color of their skin and the religion they preached, never once attempting to look at the deeper character of anyone, including me. I left him because he is nothing like me or the people I call my true family. The man can go fuck himself down the river into hell for all I care."

"That's a horrible thing to say. How can you judge him like that?"

"Because I lived him. He was far more termite than he was freemason. His hatred overwhelmed any compassion he may have had before I was born, and that's not what I need in family. What I have always looked for in people is the honesty in their soul and the morality in their giving nature. That is what unites a family. That is what true blood is."

My thoughts instantly went to all of those I had left behind, and those I was very eager to return to. "I understand your conviction. I was raised with the same values you speak of. I never knew my real parents, and it's hard to say whether or not I would want to know them if they were still alive. It's a great fear for anyone to find out that someone is not who you imagined they would be."

"I'm sorry," the woman said.

"It's okay. I love the family I was given, and I try never to forget them. That's why I carried the flag."

"It meant something to you."

"It kept my father close. Seeing it like this tarnishes the great man that he was."

"I'm sure he was a great man. What was his name?"

"Grayland," I said, blushing.

The woman looked at me as if the rose on my arm had grown real thorns. "Wait. What was that? Did you say Grayland?"

"Yeah. My father. Ryker Grayland."

"How is that—"

A loud bang echoed from the front of the house, cutting the woman short.

"Danielle!" a woman called out in panic.

She held her gaze upon me, her brow furrowed, her lips agape as if she needed to say something but couldn't place the words on her tongue. I looked her over carefully, and without awareness, her name escaped my lips with a taste of poison. "Danielle?"

"Danielle. We need to get out of here. Now!"

Danielle closed her mouth and, within seconds, was gone. I followed her down the hall and saw the other women gathering up several packs near the door. Rockwell joined us shortly after.

"What's wrong?" Danielle chirped. "What happened?"

"We have about a two minute head start."

"What did you do, Lila?"

"I got us our weapons." Lila looked at me carefully as she spoke. I shied away and kept my eyes to the floor. "What else do you need to know?"

"Load us up," Danielle said with firm authority.

Rockwell and Lila wasted no time, grabbing up several packs and boxes that lay near the door. Danielle slid to me and grabbed my arm.

"You're coming with us."

"The hell she is," Rockwell said. "I won't allow it."

"Not your call this time, Rock."

Rockwell set the items he had collected on the floor and closed the door. He stood in front of it, arms crossed. Lila took a step away, eyeing confusion and uneasiness.

"What the hell are you doing?" Danielle said, pulling me closer to her and Rockwell.

"She is not coming with us."

"Don't do this right now, Rock. We don't have time." Danielle tried to push past Rockwell but he held firm.

"I refuse to ride with a termite."

"We don't know she's a termite," Danielle said. Her hand had found its way around the butt of the gun holstered just above the small of her back. "She may be a bit mixed in the head, but I'm willing to take a chance on her."

"Trevor, we need to move," Lila said softly—motherly.

Rockwell peered deeply into Danielle, who flexed her fingers gently across her weapon. "Why is she so important?" he finally said.

"She's family," Danielle said.

My breath escaped me. Rockwell furrowed his brow and licked his lips, attempting to make sense of the statement.

"Trust me," Danielle said gently, and in almost a whisper: "I'll make this right."

Rockwell nodded and picked up the box. Lila let out a relieved breath through a luscious smile. Danielle let her fingers slide from her gun and pulled me from the home, followed in quickstep by the others, running for Lila's vehicle. As Rockwell tossed a few boxes into the back end of the car, several metallic pops rang out around us, causing us to drop to the ground. When they stopped, I saw a wind of dirt rising in the distance off the wheels of another vehicle racing toward us.

"Get in, stay low," Danielle said. She helped me climb into the back with Rockwell and then jumped into the enclosed portion of the car. Lila was already in place, after having tossed her gear into the back as well, and brought the car to life. Rockwell sat low, his face plastered to the gate on the back of the car. As Lila spewed a hill of dirt from the rear tires, I lifted my head and recognized the other vehicle.

"Ramon," I said to myself. I was forced to lie flat as Lila sped over a large dip in the road. I remained, feeling the spark of bullets ricocheting off the crusted metal that surrounded me. Rockwell returned the shots the best he could, but each strayed wildly off the mark.

"Give me a gun," I said.

"Not a chance," he roared. He fired a shot, which forced Ramon to sashay his vehicle about the road in avoidance. He lost some ground, but remained tight in pursuit.

"Please, I can help."

Rockwell looked me over and grudgingly handed me one of the pistols from the pack next to him. I immediately checked to make sure it was loaded. Finding the calm in my breath, I set the tip of the gun on the top of the gate and slowly lifted my eye to the sight.

"Keep her steady," I said to myself and held my target with ease.

I fired.

The bullet struck the tire on the right side of Ramon's car. He quickly lost control over the sudden turn and the car flipped several times before coming to a stop. Ramon and his passengers laid motionless a few feet from the wreckage.

"Nice shot," Rockwell said, sliding to the window of the enclosure. He knocked on the window and the car slowed.

I sat up and carefully scanned the mess as best I could before the distance became too great to focus. Relief washed over me when I did not see Celia. She may have betrayed me but I was unwilling to hold hatred against her. The woman I knew was a good person deep in heart.

I kissed my rose and prayed for her safety.

CHAPTER 27

I sat in the corner near the gate of the vehicle as we skipped swiftly along the barren roads. Rockwell sat near all of the crates in the opposite corner with his head against the enclosed compartment's glass. He stared out at the desert landscape, avoiding eye contact. As I studied him, one thing became clear. Although his skin was the color of those that killed Grayland, his demeanor and appearance did not match with theirs. He felt more refined, more intelligent. It became clear to me that he was not like the others. He was much more pleasing, a physical representation of my sister's soulful splendor.

"Thank you," I said after having traveled a long stretch of hours.

Rockwell did not look to me.

"I'm sorry for how I acted earlier. I have no excuse for the wickedness of my thoughts, but I wish to make up for them, if you'll allow."

Rockwell took in a deep breath but said nothing in exchange. I let it be and allowed him time to heal.

We followed several different roads through many different lands—both large and small—and hardly ever stopped except to relieve ourselves of waste. When Lila grew tired, Danielle would trade seats with her, a rotation that continued for the days that followed. We ate very little, mostly fruits and vegetables that had been stored in Rockwell's cold box, but occasionally, when we spotted a rabbit or other such small animal along the side of the road, we would try to enjoy a bite of meat around a small fire. There would always be bites that were not taken, though, as I found my appetite to be very light and Lila never ate any of the meat that we would catch. She would usually use the time with the fire to roast the fruits, giving them some extra flavor or a different texture to break up the monotony. But no matter how often we stopped, or for how long we had to travel, conversation was ultimately limited, kept to the mundane queries toward the specifics of our journey. At least it was when I was awake, but my injuries forced me to rest often and for long periods of time. What was said during those times, I may never know.

Two days into our journey, Rockwell finally spoke a word to me. It was low and hidden, but I heard him clearly. "I'm sorry."

I broke a smile. "What are you to be sorry for?"

He glanced over in my direction. "For wanting to leave you to die."

"You helped save me from them. That's all I remember."

Rockwell lowered his head and turned back to the road.

"Where are we going?" I said, hoping to extend our words into conversation.

"Back home," he said.

"How long do we have until we get there?"

"At this pace, another day or so."

"How long have you been away?"

"Long enough."

"I'm heading back home as well," I said after a brief pause.

"Why did you leave?" Rockwell said. I was unsure if he was really interested, or if he simply felt obligated. In the end, it didn't really matter.

"I was looking for something more than what I had," I said delicately.

"Did you find it?"

"I believe I did. But I left behind some very special people, and am very excited to see them again."

"Cherish them," Rockwell said. "You never know when it will all end."

"I will," I said. "I do. I mean, I've definitely learned a lot about myself, but the love I had there doesn't compare to anything I've encountered since leaving. They are a great love, especially my closest sister. She's my truest friend and my life."

Rockwell turned back to me with a gracious smile.

"She's much like you," I said.

"Like me?"

"Yes, of course. She's of your kind." I regretted the words within seconds of them leaving my lips.

Rockwell's demeanor became a flare of resentment. "My kind?"

I couldn't find a breath of words through the pinch of my lips. Rockwell shook his head and knocked on the glass until Danielle opened it. "Pull over."

"What for?" Danielle asked.

"Just do it."

Lila slowed the car down as Rockwell crouched up to his feet.

"I meant no offense," I was finally able to say.

"You're a blind fool," he said.

I shrank down against the gate and curled my arms up against my chest.

Rockwell jumped from the car as it came to a stop. Danielle and Lila both exited the compartment.

"What's going on?"

"I feel sorry for you," Rockwell said to me calmly, a fresh intimation of disappointment rising in his voice. He turned to Lila and pushed her aside. "I'm driving." He jumped into the enclosure and slammed the door shut. Lila looked from me to Danielle as we all stood silent and confused. I looked through the glass to Rockwell, who rubbed his temples in frustration, waiting impatiently for the others.

"Get in," Danielle said. "I'll ride back here for awhile." She climbed into the back, and Lila walked around the car. She took one last look at me before sliding in, shutting the door an instant before Rockwell pushed the car into motion. Danielle lost a bit of balance and hit the window in disapproval. Rockwell took no recognition. Danielle relaxed and dug her eyes into me.

"What did you do this time?"

"I'm not sure. I mentioned that my sister was like him."

"Like him? You mean she's black?"

I nodded. "He must have interpreted it as an insult."

"I think it's safe to say he was insulted," Danielle said through a heavy smirk.

"I guess," I said, unable to hold back my own smile. "I'm still not used to seeing people the way I do now."

"You a hermit?"

"I'm sorry. I'm not familiar with the term."

"You know, a recluse. Someone who hides from the world."

"That's not quite the correct definition of a recluse, but aside from that, no. I am not a recluse."

"Okay, so what changed, then?" Danielle's tone felt as if it were hiding her own level of insult.

"I was given the gift of sight," I said, without a hint of emotion.

"Are you telling me you were blind?" Danielle clearly did not believe me. I nodded, failing to change her mind.

"You're full of shit."

"Believe what you wish, but I am telling you the truth."

"How is that even possible?"

"My father…" I stopped and could only stare into Danielle's cold eyes. "May I ask you a question?"

"Sure," she said after searching my own eyes carefully.

"The man I call my father spoke of a daughter that he lost in a fire. He called her Danielle."

"He lied."

"About her name or about the fire?"

"About losing me."

I digested her words. "Then you are Grayland's daughter?"

Danielle flipped her eyes to the side and fought back angered tears.

"He loved you, dearly," I said softly, moving my upper body toward her.

Danielle shook her head. "Ryker Grayland can kiss my fucking ass." Suddenly, Danielle leaned over the side of the car and vomited. I inched closer but she held her arm out to stop me.

"Don't you touch me. Just stay away." Danielle calmed her breaths. Rockwell stopped the car and Danielle sat back up.

"Are you okay?" he said through the window.

"Just drive," Danielle said.

"Are you sure?"

"Get this fucking piece of shit moving." Danielle's rage silenced Rockwell, and he did as he was commanded.

"Why do you call him your father?" Danielle said a few minutes later.

"Because that is what he is to me. Before Grayland, the father I knew taught us, inspired us and never judged us. He was a man of respect and honor who would never turn you away and would protect you as best he could. When I made the decision to leave, Grayland became that man to me. It's only just recently I learned that being a father meant giving life to a child."

"What did Grayland do that was so honorable?" His name seemed like poison on her tongue.

"He gave me what only he could," I said. "My sight."

Danielle's breath grew heavy, and she couldn't speak a word.

"I loved him," I concluded.

"I'm sure you did."

Danielle refused to speak to me for the following day, and I accepted her silence. There was much more to her relationship with Grayland than I was aware of, but much like Grayland, it was extremely hard for her to talk about. I kept silent about him, saving his memory alone in my mind. Eventually, I knew, Danielle would open up to me but not until she felt about me as he finally came to feel.

She did not trust me as family just yet.

**   **   **

Early the next morning we finally arrived at the home Rockwell spoke of. There were about a dozen family members awaiting their return with hugs and pleasantries. Rockwell was not as forthcoming with his affection as Danielle and Lila were, grabbing up the packs and heading straight for his home with only a few nods and salutations along the way.

I stayed near the car until I finally caught the curiosity of one of her sisters. She gestured toward me, but was lost to find a name.

"Madeline," I said, smiling shyly. Lila looked at me curiously, but like everyone else, her attention did not stay with me long. It became clear to me that there was a lot more going on here than I was aware. Danielle took command quickly, asking about the progress of a dig sight and whether they had heard anything from yet more members. Before long, the entire family had entered the home, leaving me alone to take in the landscape. My thoughts wandered a bit, but the question of how much closer I was to my own destination was more prominent than any other.

I took in the serenity of the quiet air and held my hand to my heart, praying for all of those I held dear to me.

"Madeline?"

I hadn't heard Lila return. I looked to her, but could not answer her.

"Would you like to come inside?"

She offered me her hand. I smiled graciously and accepted her hospitality and warmth with a touch of my own.

CHAPTER 28

The aroma of the feast to celebrate the traveler's return filled the home with tantalizing pleasure. Lila had shown me to the room for which I could find rest, but with the scintillating smell and the endless chatter of Danielle's boisterous family, I felt it was the ideal moment to introduce myself. I walked the home with a light step, offering pleasantries to those brothers and sisters that were taking solace in the day. It was far fewer than had been waiting for Danielle earlier in the day and the majority of them couldn't hardly look at me, some more evidently than others, scared of my appearance. Of those who didn't shy away, it felt more out of polite courtesy than of gracious acceptance. I understood their caution—I was a stranger to them, after all—and did not take their wandering eyes or their skittish demeanor personally.

When I reached the kitchen, several sisters were hard at work preparing a large bird (said to be a wild turkey over the salivating lips of many), breads and vegetables of all types. I asked if I could be of any help, but they were set in such a feverish routine that anything I could do would be more of a disruption to that rhythm, so I sat quietly at the nearby table and took delight in simply watching them work and listening to their benign chatter. The eldest sister, Courtney, kept looking to me, occasionally with a bemused smile, and then return to the task at hand. After about a half hour, Courtney sat down next to me. She didn't say anything; she only watched her sister's with me, eyeing me every few seconds.

"Would you like to set the table?" Courtney asked. Her voice whistled like the chirp of the songbird.

"Excuse me?" I said, turning my attention to her.

"We could use a hand setting the table," she said. "And you can get the rest of the chairs set up, too, if you don't mind."

"Okay."

Courtney showed me where to find the plates and utensils with a smile that accentuated her thin features, and then told me where to locate the extra chairs. I took the job with great pride and set up the tables as had been requested, finishing just as Courtney placed the food in the center of the settings. It was nearing nightfall when Courtney pressed a button on a small metal box on the wall and called out, "Dinner's ready."

Danielle's voice came back—oddly vocalized, but definitely hers—and soon thereafter, the family had become whole again. As each took their place at the table and collected their meals, I felt as if I was back home, watching my own family sing and laugh during the feast of restoration. Each mouth became full with food or voice (and sometimes both), except mine. With a feast of such size, I could not find satisfaction in either until I offered prayer, which I had never performed without the aid of my Father. But as I took refuge in a nearby room, I accepted his distant voice into my heart and administered the blessing to the spirits of my congregation.

"A child bearing the fruit of the land will never perish, for with its energy, the soul will be fulfilled. With meat and grain, the child's strength is regularly replenished so as to carry its brethren to the life of love and comfort. She travels to find the best of what the world offers its children and fights to protect, no matter how deep that same world hurts her with confusion and doubt. The child only wishes to live in peace but realizes that if she cannot find the truth in the answers provided to her through the secret whisper of the winds, all she can be is the shadow of a wicked ruse, one that will always lead in deception. To conquer her demon, the child seeks to bless her heart so that answers sought become the light for which the child now sees. She asks her elder for permission to explore the fractured paths of the father who bore her, the father who raised her and the father who will always guide her. But in the decision is a dangerous plea, which pushes the child to accept the death of all she once new. Forced to roam the unexplored with a weary heart, the child comes upon a new life with a family who offers her the hand of chaste generosity. To accept it, she must seek the love and grace of her own soul before she tends to the matters of the lives that are, have been and will be affected by the union upon the first touch of a mother's breast. Pray be to the nature of the life."

"Amen." Lila stood behind me in the door. She wore a silk wrap around her head, but the harmony of her precious smile could not be hidden. "That was a beautiful verse."

"Thank you," I said, my cheeks aflame. "I could have presented a longer prayer to the family, but I didn't want to disturb the festival."

"You care to join us?"

I took Lila's hand. "Of course."

We returned to the table and sat down together. Penelope, a sweet child with a light redness etching her skin, sat upon my other side, tucked close to herself as she ate small bites with the pick of her fingertips, staying as far from me as she could. Danielle sat across from us with Rockwell, who left the table soon after we sat. He escaped through the door that led down beneath the house.

"Did I do something wrong?" I said.

"He's just going to power up the generator," Lila said.

"Can I help?"

"No," Danielle said crisply. "And I don't ever want to see you down in that room without my permission. Got it?"

My shock was evident but brief. "Yeah," I said softly. I took a taste of the turkey that Lila offered me. The juices tasted delightful upon my tongue, the meat nearly melting away in my mouth. "It's getting dark. Should we light some candles?"

"What do you think the generator's for?" Danielle said. Her sarcasm was biting.

Just then, a soft rumble from below us sparked a soft, brown glow throughout the room. I looked up at the spheres producing the light—some rounded like small bulbs, others long and thin—and fell into a wonderment, burning my eyes until the spots I saw when first looking into the sky returned and floated about as I blinked.

"You itching to go blind?" Danielle said.

I looked to Danielle and could hardly make out her shadow. "What?" I rubbed my eyes and fluttered my eyelids until the spots had faded.

"Staring at them like that's a great way to fuck up your sight."

"Yeah, and a great way to ruin your father's legacy."

"Wouldn't want to do that." Danielle sat back, unintentionally pushing her plate of food away from her. "I take it you've never seen a light bulb before."

Rockwell returned, swiping his hand across Danielle's shoulder as he passed her.

"No," I said, my tone solemn. "My family lives without the convenience of artificial light."

"No shit," Rockwell said through a mass of masticated turkey and bread.

"You don't believe me?"

Rockwell swallowed his food. "Just the opposite. With all of the power plants either destroyed or unmanned after the war, not many people have access to electricity anymore."

"How many had access before the war?"

"Before the war?" Rockwell laughed. "Before the war, everything anyone touched ran off of electricity. You couldn't tie your damn shoes without using something that plugged into an outlet."

"Problem was," Lila interjected, "electricity was very expensive. Having access to it didn't mean you could afford it."

"Why was it expensive?"

"The cost of fuel and coal that ran the plants was exorbitant, not to mention those that couldn't afford it were subsidized by the government."

"Come again?"

"It means the fucking government paid for their electricity," Danielle said.

"What did they do in exchange for it?"

"Nothing. That's the point. The less you did, the more you were rewarded."

"That doesn't make sense," I said. "Why would anyone condone such sloth?"

"When you give someone anything they want," Rockwell said, "it puts them in your debt. The more people you have in your debt, the more power you're able to gain."

"It was the ultimate Ponzi scheme, if you think about it," Lila said. "The more entitlements the public accepted, the more power the government gained to enact more taxes. With more taxes came more entitlements, which was returned with even more taxes and more power. But, like all other schemes of this nature, it was doomed to collapse."

"In other words," Danielle said, "everyone was willing to take the beast's blow job so long as they got a chance to suck the milk from its tit. Problem is, there's only so much milk available before the tit dries up, and no one ever gets fucked for free."

The group was silent for the next few minutes. It was uncomfortable and terse, each of us choosing to hide our thoughts from the others. Before another word could be said, I rose from my chair and pushed the plate of food away from me.

"I should rest," I said softly.

Danielle and Rockwell couldn't find the strength to look at me, while Lila rubbed the edge of my back, smiling graciously.

"I wish to thank you for saving my life. I take your kindness with all of my gratitude and will never forget you."

I started away from the table.

"Wait," Rockwell said. He stood.

"Your hearts are generous," I said, "but I am not one of you. I have my own family waiting for me." I pursed my lips and forced them into a curl.

"You're in no condition to be out there on your own," Rockwell said. "Winter's about to hit, and it can kick your ass when you're in *top* health."

I couldn't speak the words that dashed through my mind.

"Stay with us through winter," Lila said, "and then I'll take you wherever you want to go."

Danielle looked up to me, her eyes compassionate. She nodded, breaking a smile from my lips.

"You are all so kind," I said.

"It's not a request," Danielle interjected.

"No judgment," I said.

"Stay honest."

"Stay protected!" The resounding echo from across the table was unexpected. Danielle couldn't hold back a small laugh.

"Come and finish your dinner," Lila said, standing and offering me her arm.

It took a few moments of pause, but I accepted Lila's invitation and returned to the feast. Danielle and I remained silent as we enjoyed the conversations from the rest of her family.

CHAPTER 29

I excused myself from the group as the food dwindled and everyone grew tired and quiet. I retreated to my room where Penelope was already in slumber along with two other youngers. Her thumb was pushed deep into her mouth, and her hair fell across her eyes like vines of moss along the edges of the woods. With as much caution as I could muster, I lifted Penelope off the floor and rested her in the bed that Lila had given to me upon my arrival.

"Sleep well," I whispered as she shuffled to find her comfort. I knelt down to kiss her and then prayed over her with a gentle song and the touch of my loving fingertips along the contours of her face.

"What happened to her mother and father?" I said after completing my prayer.

"I don't know," Lila said. She stood again within the lip of the doorway. "I found her one night in the remains of a rusted out dumpster. She could hardly let out a cry because her vocal cords had been shredded to bits."

"Is that why she doesn't talk?"

Lila nodded.

"I never knew how wicked and immoral life was."

"I lost my daughter before I had the chance to raise her," Lila said. "For me, Penelope was a blessing." Lila sat down and wrapped her arm around me. "From the ashes of evil is born the light of honor and virtue."

"I'm not so sure," I said. "Not after learning all that I have since leaving my family. It was a blessing that you found Penelope, I'm sure, but the woman who gave her birth thought her own child was nothing more than a piece of trash. I mean, how can virtue and honor live when the principles behind them are constantly being questioned? I thought my perés were honest in teaching us the truth about the past, but now I feel that all we were taught has been a lie. We knew of the war and that evil existed, but never did they once explain its complexities and the sheer power of its existence. We were taught that a single army started the war and their extinction marked the end of Anno Domini. But that's not true, and I have to wonder how much deceit we were fed. Where is it that honor and truth end, and sin and immorality begin?"

"Nothing is ever simple," Lila said.

"But why would they hide it all from me?"

"To protect you."

"From what?"

"From reigniting the evil they hoped to leave behind. It's always been said that you have to remember the mistakes of your past to keep from repeating them, but that's complete bullshit. A mistake to one person isn't always a mistake to another, and it's in those people that knowledge of the past lends itself to understanding how to reintroduce those ideas and how to hide the truth from those who believe differently. The past, whether good or bad, will always motivate people to act in certain ways. If people were unaware of the bad, they wouldn't be as easily tempted by it. They would be more susceptible to forming a more virtuous conscious, which in turn would hinder the growth of immorality and keep it from flourishing in their thoughts and minds."

"I miss them," I said, my voice barely audible.

"I know," Lila said, combing my hair. "I miss my family, too."

I wiped my eyes and took a deep breath. "What happened to them?"

"They were taken to better places," she said solemnly.

"Had you married anyone?" I said.

"I did. And I loved him more than life."

"Did he die in the war?"

"A few years after, actually. When the war started, my husband and I were still young kids, with a wide-eyed fantasy of puppy love. We couldn't imagine a life without the other, so we avoided the war at all costs, which eventually meant leaving our families and friends behind. We ran as far away from the war as we could, and when it found us again, we continued on, until we felt safe enough to make a real home."

Lila lifted a ring strapped around her neck from under her blouse.

"Did you ever speak to your parents about it?" I asked gently.

"I couldn't. Our families were on different sides of the war, which caused a deep friction between us."

"Why were you on different sides?"

"He was Muslim. We weren't."

"That's all?"

"That was enough. Even though my husband and I were able to look beyond our individual faiths, that difference was all our parents could see. The tension between Christians and Muslims at the time was near the brink of chaos, and if you were on the wrong side, you were as good as dead. "

"That still doesn't explain why you left them."

"I lived in a different time, a different place. We weren't given the same rules you grew up with. We didn't have the same disciplines, the same energy. Like most teens, I was stubborn and didn't believe my parents could understand what I felt. I had to control everything around me, and no one was going to tell me otherwise. My friends, my peers... we didn't have consequences. Rules and discipline just held you back from your true potential. When we were told we couldn't do something, we did it, if only to prove that we were above the law of our parents and anything else that tried to restrict us."

"Chaos breeds further chaos," I said. "Order breeds freedom."

"Who said that?"

"A very gracious man."

"Sounds like a smart man."

"He is the best of men," I said. "He taught us to be honest, no matter the consequences and cherished us all individually and as a family. There is no difference under his love."

"Was he your priest?"

"I believe he must have been. My father always spoke of him as a priest."

"You believe in God, then."

"Is God the same as Allah?"

Lila stroked my hair. "In a way, yes."

"Then, no, I don't believe in God."

"Why is that?"

"Because the contradiction of His words only lead to violence."

"That's not true. His words give people something to believe in."

"Maybe. But I've listened to the words and have seen how they're interpreted. They may bring some people hope, but is that enough to warrant the death of so many innocent people?"

Lila took a moment to ingest my words. "I never looked at it like that."

"From what I've learned about the war, and from what I've seen and been a part of in the last few months, believing in something so ambiguous is to lean on a crutch that keeps you from understanding yourself. If I need to believe in a deity to live my life, then I'm giving away my honor to perform acts I deem unenviable."

"You do speak the truth, don't know?"

"I meant no offense," I said.

"No offense taken. Remember, we don't judge you for your beliefs, only for the actions you take and the reasons you take them. It's an ideal I have spent many years teaching Penelope and something I always wished I could have instilled in my own daughter, had I been given the chance."

I looked up to Penelope as she shifted in her sleep, dropping her thumb from her mouth.

"What was her name?" I looked back to Lila. "Your daughter."

Lila kissed me, and then whispered into my ear. "Her name was Madeline."

CHAPTER 30

The sound of my name coming from Lila's sweetened lips was affecting. I sat stunned, able only to look into her eyes and surrender to them. Was it true? Was the woman that sat next to me as an equal the source of my first breath?

"You mean... I am your daughter?" My lips hardly moved and the sound was more a breath than a voice.

Lila's cheeks brightened with red joy.

"That can't be," I said. "My mother was—"

"Killed?"

My head bobbed slowly up and down.

"I thought so too," she said and lowered the sleeve of her blouse to reveal a scar just above the top of her breast. "An inch lower and I would have been."

I touched the scar gently in confused awe.

"Someone was watching over me that night," she said.

I slipped back, my heart wanting desperately to hug her and love her, my head pushing me to be much more cautious. "How can I know for sure?" I said.

"I'm afraid faith may be your only option."

My own scar burned slightly. I grabbed my side to help calm the sensation. "That won't be enough," I said and searched for any indication that I might be wrong. Then the answer came to me.

"How did you get shot?"

"I wouldn't accept the favor of a Muslim faction."

"You wouldn't become one of them? A Muslim?"

"No, I was already Muslim. What I refused to do was follow the laws of Sharia and accept jihad."

"I thought you said you were Catholic."

"I was," she said. "Before marriage."

"Why would you change?"

"Love." The answer was short but powerful. "Islam was very important to my husband—your father—which meant it was very important to me. The more I learned, the more I accepted its principles, and when I felt it was time, I asked that he help me convert. He didn't force me, in fact, he tried to keep me from it, but I insisted. It was my choice, and I am proud of that choice."

"But that doesn't make any sense," I said. "If you were already one of them, why would they still wish to shoot you."

"You have to understand, over the last twenty years, more Muslims were killed by the hands of other Muslims than by any other race or religion simply because they wouldn't bow down to the bloodshed. There are billions of people who follow the Islamic faith, but not all of them are bad people. Not all of them want to kill those who disagree with the prophets."

"When did it happen?" I said after a breath of silence.

"A few years after the war ended. You were about six months old and we had just grown comfortable in our new home. We were safe; we were happy."

"What exactly happened?"

"When the raiding party arrived, they forced us to our knees to pray for Allah and the words of Muhammad. We did, and asked for their mercy. They demanded that we join the jihad and fight with them against the infidels. When we refused, their tempers flared and we were beaten until my husband submitted to their will. They pulled him to his feet and praised his devotion to God. When it was my turn, I couldn't do it and they were done negotiating. They put a gun to my husband's head and shot him. I tried to go to him, but I couldn't move. When they pushed for me to submit, it just didn't matter anymore. There was nothing left for me, and I remained stubborn and silent. It didn't take long for them to give up. Before I knew it, I felt the heat of the bullet in my chest and then nothing. The smoke from the fire woke me up. Sometimes I wonder if they hadn't chosen to burn the house down, would I have ever woken up? I knew I had been given a second chance. So, after one last prayer for the future of my husband's soul, I forced myself up and left, hoping to find anyone willing to help. That's when I found Danielle."

"How did I escape the fire?" I already knew the answer, but wanted confirmation.
Lila chuckled. "Jezebel." she said.

"You did know Miss Jezebel."

"Yeah. We only knew each other for about a year, but she was like a sister to me."

"How did you meet her?"

"She had a hard time during the war. I'm sure she can tell you better than I can, but, like you, she was nearly broken when she showed up on our doorstep. I helped nurse her back to health, and by that time, a bond had grown between us. When I asked her to stay, she couldn't say no."

"Where was she going?"

"She was searching for the place where you grew up. I didn't really believe it existed, but I believed very much in the idea of it. So much so that I told her that if anything should happen to me and my husband that she was to take you and do everything she could to find it."

"How did she escape the men who shot you?"

"She wasn't there when it happened."

"She wasn't?"

"Jezebel was very health-conscious and always made sure we were stocked up on whatever vegetables, fruits or berries she could find. She'd usually get up early and catch a couple mile run and hunt for whatever she could. I remember thinking that it was taking longer than normal when the raiders hit. I won't lie. My first thought was that Jezebel was behind it, that she had sent them to us. I still can't say for sure that she didn't."

"I know she didn't," I said sternly.

"Whether she did or not doesn't matter," Lila continued. "I loved Jezebel and hold no ill will. She saved your life in more ways than one, and by the looks of it, she did it just in time." Lila stroked my scars with her thumb. I took her hand and held it, uncomfortable in the moment. Lila held her breath, regret filling her features.

"I believe you," I said. "Miss Jezebel loved you very much as well. She named her own daughter Delilah, after you."

Lila squeezed my hand. Her cheeks were flush, and she seemed greatly honored.

"But there's still one thing bothering me. If you knew that Miss Jezebel took me, and where she was going, why didn't you come for me?"

Lila shied her eyes from mine. I could tell the turmoil over the decisions hurt her greatly.

"If Jezebel held her promise," she finally said, "then I knew you were in a far better place. I wanted to find you, to live that life, but ultimately I knew that if I had found you, and the place did exist, I would only be a cancer on its message."

"That's not true."

"It is. My biases, my prejudices, ran very deep. I couldn't risk testing myself against the idea of harmony. If I failed, the project would fail, and I was not ready for that type of guilt. As far as I was concerned, you were safe and you would be protected. As a mother, those were the best gifts I could ever give you."

It took me a moment, trying to work through my own bevy of emotions, but in the end, I could understand how she felt. I leaned in and hugged her, feeling her quiet tears lick my cheek.

"Thank you," I said.

"You love them," she said. "You're happy; safe."

"I am."

Lila looked at me with a bright, tender smile. "Then I made the right choice. You've grown into a very strong woman."

"I'm not sure I could have done it without them."

"Tell me about them," Lila said. Her energy had risen into excitement.

"What do you want to know?"

"I don't know. What are your friends like? What do you do for fun? Do you have a boyfriend?"

"I have many brothers," I said.

Lila laughed. "I meant... are you dating anyone?"

"What's dating?"

"You know, it's when you hang out with someone you like, someone you enjoy being with. You go out to dinner with them, take a walk alone together, or just sit around in each other's arms, talking about nothing for hours on end. Basically, it's how you get to really know someone you feel you may want to live the rest of your life with."

I smiled. "Someone whose heart will always be true."

"Precisely."

"I know someone like that," I said sheepishly. "My heart belongs to her."

"Her?" Lila looked a bit shocked, but then laughed uncomfortably.

"What's wrong?"

"Nothing," she said. "You love her?"

"She's my sister."

Lila nodded. "I'm happy for you," she said.

I was confused by the hidden secret behind Lila's words, but figured it must have been culturally significant to those who lived before the war, so I didn't press the issue any further. Instead, I simply enjoyed her playful innocence.

"Was my father your boyfriend?" I said.

"He was," Lila said softly.

"Would you have married him if he wasn't your boyfriend?"

Now Lila seemed confused. "No, I don't think I would have. Why would you ask?"

"No reason," I lied.

"Marriage is a big step," Lila said. "You have to really love someone, and I mean with all of your heart and soul, or else what's the point?"

I felt guilty and curled my legs up to my chest.

"What's wrong?"

I couldn't find my voice, and Lila didn't fight me for an answer. She sat close and pulled me to her breast. We sat in silence until I was ready to speak again.

"Do you hate them?" I said. "The Muslims?"

"I try to refrain from hate," she said. Her fingers were gentle against the back of my neck.

"But they hurt you."

"A few of them did, yes. But you can't judge an entire group of people based on a few. If I did that, I would never have met your father and would never have fallen in love with him. That's what unconditional love is, really. Learning how to see blindly."

"I knew how once," I said.

"You can learn again." She kissed me and then went to the shelves near the window. She brought back one of the many diaries that had been lined up against it and handed it to me. On the front was an image of a light-skinned girl sitting beside a dark-skinned man, their hands crossed upon one another in affection.

"Their names are Ellie and Jeremiah," she said, sitting.

"Did you know them?"

Lila laughed. "No, Madeline. It's a novel. A story."

"Like Jules Verne or Edgar Allen Poe."

"Yeah."

I smiled and flipped through the pages of the novel. I smelled its favorable aroma and took in all I could about its presence.

"What is this one called?" I said happily.

"If you come softly," Lila said, a bit confused.

I looked over the symbols on the pages, creating my own tale in my head based upon the words Lila had given me.

"Can you read?"

I shook my head, disappointed.

"Would you like me to read you some?" Lila took the book from my hand. "If You Come Softly, by Jacqueline Woodson."

She flipped to the first page and read. I closed my eyes and rested my head on her bosom, taking in the passionate words of the page with great interest and excitement. Every new paragraph, every new page lifted my imagination to a new level. Miss Jezebel was very good at conveying the words of authors long lost, but hearing the words directly from the pages of a manuscript was far more invigorating. I felt impassioned by Jacqueline's words to follow in her profession and give to the world my own stories, revealing my truth through the voice of another.

"Can you teach me," I said, stopping Lila from her reading.

"Teach you what?"

"To read."

Lila smiled and kissed the top of my head. "Of course." And she read until I was under the spell of her slumber.

CHAPTER 31

As I healed, days turned to weeks.

Each morning, Rockwell checked on my progress, providing me with nutrients and liquids needed for a healthy recovery. For the first few weeks, he came and went without so much as a word, marking a structured routine he was obligated to attend to. After my wounds had all but gone, Rockwell still came to ask if he could help clean the blankets, make my breakfast, or simply offer a good morning. I would smile, thank him and then give him permission to return behind the door where Danielle and the majority of the family spent their waking hours. I often wondered why Rockwell continued to provide me his courtesy when he was no longer obligated, and Lila said it was in his nature to help everyone he could. I believed her, finding it to be a quality I, and anyone else, could look up to with great respect.

I spent the rest of my days with Lila and Penelope as they each helped teach me to read and write. Lessons focusing on the individual letters of the alphabet—the pronunciations of consonants and vowels, as well as the repetition of each letter on the page of paper—encompassed the first weeks. Once I knew them well enough to recognize them and scrawl them about, we shifted into the pronunciations of words and how they formed sentences. It wasn't long before I was being tested on spelling proficiency and working on the elements of a sentence, such as the use of nouns, verbs and adjectives. Penelope laughed her silent giggles whenever I would make a silly or simple mistake but then help my hand whenever I got stuck on a words correct spelling. Lila allowed us breaks throughout the day to clear my mind whenever I grew tired or frustrated. I would usually eat a quick meal or play games with Penelope to help wash my mind clear before returning to work. My lessons ended at nightfall when we joined the rest of the family for dinner, followed by a story before bed, where I would get the chance to apply the skills I learned throughout the day. Every so often, as Penelope and Lila slept, I took out a book and read, writing down any word, phrase or idea I didn't understand so as to ask Lila about it the next day. She lauded my ambition to continue learning on my own, and within eight weeks of beginning my studies, I had all of the key elements needed to continue without her guidance.

One of my favorite things to do to help enhance my reading was to log onto the computer and search through the pages of the clean net, which revealed valuable information on how people used to live their lives, how they spoke, the anonymity of their thoughts and the many different aspects that attributed to the cause of the war. To read some of what was once written was sickening, but it was also fascinating and enlightening. It wasn't everyday I could go on the computer because I wasn't allowed the permission to use the generator. Whenever permission was granted, Rockwell came to see us. He would usually take a few minutes to make sure the computer worked correctly and then disappear back behind the door. I would watch him carefully and give him my smile in thanks. It became such a special occurrence that anytime I was allowed was a time I eagerly looked forward to and took full advantage of, even when I came across a page or a site that I wished I could forget.

I was a bit saddened the day he didn't come up to help turn on the computer but nevertheless enthusiastic about what I was about to learn.

"Sorry," Rockwell said about an hour after I began my research. He was wiping his hands with a rag cloth and breathing more erratically than normal. "I needed to tend to something unexpected. You get it working okay?"

I smiled brightly as he pinched the back of my neck in massage. "Of course."

"Is everything okay?" Lila said. She sat in the corner of the room reading a book.

"Yeah. Everything's fine," he said to her, confident. "What are you up to?"

"Just surfing," I said with a smile. I simply loved the idea.

Rockwell stood beside me, his eyes searching the pages with cold intensity as I clicked through a series of documents on the changes that were made to the laws of marriage.

"Find anything interesting?"

"Not really. Nothing I haven't seen before. Sometimes it seems like I've already seen everything there is to see on this thing."

"Oh, I'm sure there's plenty you haven't seen yet. Six percent may not sound like much, but it'd probably take several weeks for even me to sift through it all."

"Yeah. If only there was a way I could see what was on the corrupted sites."

"There is," Rockwell said. His silence after was repentant.

Mine was excitement. "Can you show me?"

"It takes time to reconstruct those pages, and that's if there's even enough source code left. It's complicated. You wouldn't understand."

"You could teach me."

"It's not worth your time."

"Have you ever done it? Reconstructed the pages?"

Rockwell didn't say a word, but I could see the answer in his body.

"Maybe some day," I said politely.

"Maybe," he said, turning away.

The awkwardness was too much for me. "Why was the Internet such an obsession?"

"Instant gratification," Lila said. "It wasn't so much an obsession of the Internet, as it was an obsession to know everything instantly. That and the ability to say whatever you wanted without repercussion. At least it was until they passed the Internet Deference and Complacency Act."

"Wait... what?"

"It was a law that made it illegal to write or say anything on the Internet that might offend or otherwise hurt someone who had a differing viewpoint. The law was clear—if you didn't like what was being said on a site or a social networking feed or whatever it might be, you could petition to have the site shut down. It went as far as sending some bloggers to prison for being even the slightest bit controversial."

"It was against the law to speak the truth," I said, matter-of-fact.

"So much for freedom of speech, huh?" Rockwell said.

"Can you teach me how to read the corrupted pages?" I asked after a bit of thoughtful silence.

"I better get back," he said.

"What are you guys working on?" I said, worried that I had actually said it aloud.

"Ask Danielle." Rockwell winked and squeezed my shoulder.

Suddenly, a loud crash reverberated through the house. All of us turned to the door.

"What was that?" I said.

Rockwell held up his hand for my silence and stepped cautiously for the door. Before he could reach it, four men stormed into the room, one of who slammed the butt of his shotgun across Rockwell's temple. He fell to the floor as both Lila and I stood.

"On your knees," the men yelled repetitively.

When we wouldn't do as we were told, the men did it for us, wrapping our arms around our backs and forcing us to our knees.

"What the hell is this?" I screamed as they pulled through my clothes, exposing different parts of my body.

"Damn it," the man grumbled.

Lila seemed extremely calm as he went to her and did the same. When he pulled up the bottom of her shirt, I could clearly see the tattoo of the flag resting just under her right breast.

"We have a winner," the man grumbled.

"This one too," the fourth man said, revealing Rockwell's own tattoo.

The lead man yelled out something in a language I didn't understand but seemed very familiar, and the fourth man sped from the room. The leader then snapped his fingers, urging Lila to be pulled next to me, and went to Rockwell. He lifted him up gruffly and tossed him to my other side.

"Stop," I said, struggling to free myself to no avail. Rockwell was conscious, but could hardly move.

"Where are the rest of you?" the lead man said.

"The rest of who?"

"The infidels who share the mark of insolence against Islam. Where are they?"

"I don't have a clue what you're talking about."

The man slapped me and ripped up Lila's shirt. "The mark of insolence. Here."

"Never seen it before," I said. I fought the increase of pain in my jaw.

The man lowered Lila's shirt and stood back. His demeanor calmed. "Why do you help them?" he said. "You don't share the mark. You must share the praise of Allah?"

"I share praise for no god," I said. "Especially Allah."

"Insolent bitch." The man tore at me and grabbed the back of my neck. He forced my forehead to the floor and tightened his grip. "Give your allegiance to me and your God."

I clenched my teeth and grunted, but said nothing.

"I will," Lila said. "My devotion is to God, and I wish to worship Him. Let her go, and I will show my obedience."

The man threw me down to the floor. I landed near Rockwell, who seemed to be more receptive to what was happening.

"You will tell me what I want to know," the man yelled to Lila.

"We're the only ones who live here," she said. "I swear it."

"You lie," he said with a hard slap, which could have been considered a punch. He took a breath and paced away from us to collect his anger.

"Are you okay?" I whispered to Rockwell.

He winced. "Yeah."

"Show me your allegiance," the man said calmly.

Lila's captor let go of her and she immediately turned slightly to her right and set her hands down on the ground in front of her. She rested her head between them as I remember being taught once before and uttered a series of familiar phrases. A small lump formed in the back of my throat as I thought of Miss Safiya and her wasted charity.

Swallowing my sorrow, I shifted closer to Rockwell and whispered into his ear. I confirmed his comprehension with solid eye contact and then shifted onto my elbow.

"Hey," I said. "I'm ready to give you my allegiance."

The man was uncertain. "Is this the truth?"

"Yeah. But you need to help me."

The man hesitated again, and I could see confusion run through Lila's hidden eyes. I sat still until he made the decision to accept my concession.

"On your knees," he said and held out his hand to me.

"You first." With a stable turn, I exerted all power into my leg, swiping it across the man's leg. With the crack of his kneecap the man dropped to the floor with a loud yell. I rolled up and punched him several times before he was able to get his own fist into my gut. Breathless, I stumbled back slightly, and he used the moment to pull my nose into his knee. I fell to the floor, the warm blood soaking my hands.

At the same time, Rockwell rolled onto his back and spun his own leg around, hitting my captor across the jaw. He used his momentum to slide up and grabbed the man's pistol, firing it across to Lila's captor, who fell dead with a bullet just above his right eye. Rockwell quickly stood and gave two more slugs to the chest of my captor.

"Drop the weapon," the man yelled. He was curled up behind Lila and held a knife to the center of her throat. My vision was blurred, but I could see a small tear of blood run from the tip of the blade.

"Damn it," I said under my breath as I tried to get the bleeding under control.

"Let her go," Rockwell said, calmly but with authority.

"Fuck you. Drop the weapon or she's dead." The man pushed the knife even deeper, leading a string of blood to flow down Lila's neck.

"Alright," Rockwell said, holding the gun upright. He lowered it to the floor and rose. He kicked it away. "Now let her go."

"I love you," Lila said, and a rush of fear overshadowed the throbbing in my nose. I lowered my hands and watched the man pull the knife across her throat. "My precious," he said with a demon's grin of delicious pleasure.

I cried out. The blood poured from Lila's neck with the flow of the river as she slumped to the floor.

"Son of a bitch." I stepped toward the man with all but an ounce of fury and fell onto him. I held no reserve as I tried desperately to kill the man with the bare of my hand. Rockwell followed me, but instead of helping, tried hard to pull me away.

"Madeline, stop," he kept saying as he struggled against me. Finally, my body gave way to him and we fell away from the man allowing him the chance to find the gun and lift it to us.

A shot rang out, and in my mind, I had died—until I heard the man's body hit the floor. Rockwell slid off of me. Standing in the lip of the door was Danielle. She hurried to Lila and touched her with a daughter's grief. The air around us all was dead for that brief moment. When Danielle finally turned to us, I could see the fight to restrain her guilt and anger, to stay calm for my sake.

"How many were there?" she said.

Rockwell shook his head. "Four, I think. They saw the tats."

"Damn it." Danielle stood and checked her gun's magazine as I turned away, gripping my nose in discomfort.

"What are you thinking?" Rockwell said. "Scouting party?"

"This game's far from over."

"Let me see." Rockwell grabbed the back of my neck.

I didn't look at him. I wanted nothing to do with him—or Danielle.

"Madeline," he said, urging me to allow him to help.

"No," I said, shifting away from him.

No one spoke as I pulled myself to the corner and crouched into a ball.

"We need to set up a perimeter," Danielle said, shuffling through the bodies of our intruders. "It won't be long before those fucking termites are back to eradicate us."

"I have to stay with her," Rockwell said.

"Not a chance. I need your ass with me on this one, Rock."

"Her nose might be broke."

"It's not negotiable."

Rockwell resigned to Danielle's order. "Give me a minute."

Danielle left and I could feel Rockwell's touch on my hand before he was even close to me. I did not resist it; his hand was gentle and soft. He combed my hair behind my ear and lifted my chin to examine my nose. I simply watched and allowed his compassion.

"It doesn't look broken," he said and rested his hand just under my ear. "Go stay with Penelope."

"I can't," I said, unaware I had.

Rockwell handed me the man's pistol. "Take this. If anyone comes through the door, don't hesitate. I'll be there to take a closer look when I can."

Without any fight left in my body, I accepted. Rockwell took my hand and helped me to my feet.

"Wait," I said and knelt next to Lila. "I love you, too." I gently kissed her cold lips and lowered my forehead to hers, praying on the bliss of her next life.

Rockwell followed me to my room and made sure I went in.

I didn't see Penelope, but felt her fear. I called out for her. It didn't take long for her to slide out from under the bed and run to me, strapping her arms around my waist. I pet her hair and kissed her.

"Come here, sweetie," I said. "I have something I have to tell you."

I took Penelope's hand and sat her on the bed.

"It's about Lila," I said softly, still unwilling to accept the words I was about to say. "I'm afraid she's gone and won't be coming back."

Penelope stared into me for a long time and then simply leaned in and hugged me. She didn't let go, and it felt as if she was comforting me, rather than the other way around. I grabbed the book that sat on the bureau and read, hoping to calm her, or in the very least, distract my own mind from what had transpired. A few pages in, Penelope laid her head against my chest and sucked her thumb. That's when I heard Danielle yell out and gather the family into formation about the house.

"Hold your ground until my mark," she said, followed by minutes of unnerving stillness.

"Insolence is not in favor of your God," a man finally called out. The voice was deep and commanding—and eerily familiar. "Lay down your weapons and praise your allegiance to Him."

"We hold allegiance to nothing but our freedom," Danielle called out. "Go back to the hellhole you crawled out of and leave us be."

"Only Allah will save you from death." I still couldn't place the voice, though it sent chills of fear and sickness through me.

"Only the love of our family will give us peace. Our hearts are ready and willing to die for that honor."

"So then be damned. Allah Akbar!"

Inaudible screams and yells wrapped through the echoes of gunfire that ripped through the house. I held Penelope tight against me with my gun pointed firmly at the door. If anyone came through, they would be shot dead—just as I was instructed.

Then it all stopped. All was quiet except for the steady beat in my chest. Penelope shook severely against me. I lowered the gun and attempted to quiet her but couldn't find any tone in my voice that wasn't full of stress or fear.

"It's over," I said, unconvincing, even to me.

"Madeline?" Rockwell knocked and opened the door before I could gain my lucidity of the moment. I raised my gun and cocked the hammer. He raised his hands and ducked down. "Whoa, Madeline. It's me."

I caught my breath and relaxed. And then I lost my strength, unable to fight the mix of anguish and wrath.

I cried.

CHAPTER 32

Needing to be alone to collect my composure, I urged Rockwell to leave. He was reluctant at first, conveying immense compassion for both Penelope and I, but after a few timid minutes, he left with a simple invisible hug. I stayed with Penelope and prayed for her future without the only mother she ever knew. It took several hours, finding that the harder I pushed my thoughts of Lila, of Grayland, of Miss Safiya from my mind, the harder those very thoughts hit me. It wasn't until I flushed them out while watching the beauty of my child slumbering in my arms with such peace that my eyes traded the moist river of grief for the burn of dry weariness.

Just before I was calm enough to join Penelope in rest, Danielle came to me, word-less. I woke Penelope and we followed Danielle to the field a few yards from the house where we found a lone grave with freshly planted roses around the cross that marked its bed. A few yards away, several family members knelt and cried with one another near a series of additional markers. I counted eight, and though I couldn't feel sadness for them, the amount of grief I felt over the loss of my mother was enough to show I cared for them all. Down the hill near the edge of the desert, a dying fire marked the remains of a body of termites.

Danielle picked one of the roses and held it out for me. I took it graciously and hugged her for her benevolence. She accepted it, though I could feel her discomfort. I gave her a sympathetic smile and knelt down to the grave. Taking a thorn from the stem of the rose, I pricked the tip of my tattoo and collected the droplet of blood it produced. I touched it to the center of the cross and lowered my head. Penelope joined me, taking the residue of the blood and placing her finger to the cross. I kissed Penelope and walked back to the house, where I took a perch on the steps of the porch. Watching Penelope make peace with her loss from a distance confirmed my place as the outsider who, no matter how inadvertently, brought change to a family that had once been happy. I lit a cigarette, hoping to coax the regret from my body. When that didn't work, I lit another; before I knew, four butts lay at my feet and I could still feel the agony of my sorrow. I became so immersed in my own depressing black hole that I couldn't feel anything beyond the taste of the cigarette. I hadn't even noticed that everyone had gone inside or that Rockwell had been standing against the rail to watch the sky build to a deep, bloodied red, indicating the onset of a fresh, rigorous thunderstorm. We had only had a few storms over the past weeks, but each one felt longer and more severe than the previous one. Judging by the richness of its color and the calm of the wind, I knew this storm would be nothing short of amazing. What intrigued me about this storm the most was the timing of its arrival and how the sadness of the day and the nature of its violence seemed to manifest itself within the threshold of the heavens. It became my solace; witnessing the blood of the fallen encompassed in the tears that now fell lightly from the clouds. It was me; it was Penelope; it was anyone who mourned this day.

Eventually, Rockwell sat next to me. He didn't say a word or do anything to disturb the atmosphere that surrounded me. His presence was enough to help bring me back to the present and to reach out and recover the voices that had been lost to me. They were still deadened by the grief I carried, but I could hear them, floating about in the distance, calling for me to come home.

I drew in one final breath of smoke and stood. It became clear to me that just because I wouldn't be able to find my home for the next few months, that Lila should be stuck to live without hers. If I was ever going to get over the anguish, I needed to let go; allow my mother to find her grace. The rain that fell was large and soft, relaxing, unlike the rain that it would soon become, sharp and glassy, powered by the strong winds of ice.

It covered me quickly as I walked to Lila's grave. Rockwell didn't try to stop me; he simply stood and watched carefully for any sign of a sudden change the weather may enact. As I reached the burial, I got to one knee, bowed my head and raised my arms up to my side, singing my prayers. My heart beat fresh as Lila's spirit drained from me. But the more I felt the cold rain drip from my body, the more I felt the mourning of all others I had lost wash away as well, leaving me lighter, more accepting.

Taking in a fresh breath of the watered roses, I turned to Rockwell and invited him to join me with the hush of my outstretched hand. He was hesitant, but my resistance to move opened him up to trusting me and stepped into the rain. I took his hand and smiled, more with my eyes than my lips. We held each other close, shifting back and forth in a dance that I had viewed over the Internet. After a few beats, I laid my head against his. I could see deep within his soul and knew, through the affection of his touch, that he could feel it too. He stopped the dance and waited for me to lift my head. His breath was on my lips, drawing them to his until they met with gentle tenderness. I kissed him with the love of Miss Jezebel; of Miss Safiya; of Lila. But most of all, I kissed him with the love I reserved for Grayland.

It was a kiss that filled me with guilt.

"I'm sorry," I whispered and ran into the house. I am not sure what happened to Rockwell that night. All I knew was I needed to escape him until I could understand what had happened more clearly, and find the truth of my love within me.

CHAPTER 33

The night was upon me quickly. The wind whistled through the small cracks in the home and the rain knocked at the windows as if it needed asylum from whatever was chasing it. I woke from the nap I hadn't known I'd taken and felt the sparks of lightning in my skin. Penelope was in bed, sucking her thumb as usual. I was happy, believing, at least for the moment, she was at peace. I still couldn't say the same for myself, even after the meditative reflections that kept me from enjoying a meal with the rest of the family. The pinch of hunger in my stomach forced me to leave the room to find what dinner I could, hoping I could do so without confronting anyone I wasn't ready to deal with.

Before I reached the kitchen, I heard mice-like noises etched under the hard rattle of the wind and the rain. I was about ready to simply sneak my way back to my room, but my curiosity got the best of me. I slid up to take a peek at who might be shuffling around the kitchen. The light was low with only a hint of a candle on the kitchen table and the occasional split-second addition of lightning, so I closed my eyes and listened for any indication as to who it might be. Soon enough, I recognized the whisper of a frightened, angry young woman.

"Danielle?"

The swipe of the gun and the cock of its hammer echoed through me. I stepped out and held up my hands. "Wait. It's Madeline."

"Fuck," she said and tossed the pistol to the counter where she stood. She gripped a small glass and looked at it as if it was toxic.

"Are you okay?"

Danielle drank what was in the glass. "Go back to bed," she said and poured more liquid into the glass from a bottle sitting next to the gun. She drank it again in one quick pass and poured another. I lowered my head and slowly turned to leave, taking one last glimpse of Danielle's silhouette before doing so.

"I loved her, you know," she said softly, under the guise of suppressed tears. "She was like my mother."

I stepped back into the kitchen. "I know. I loved her as much as you did."

"Bullshit. You were probably happy she got her throat slashed, just to spite me."

"How can you say that? She was my mother."

"You may have had the same blood, but you were never her daughter. Why else would she have traded you in for a better model?"

"Lila didn't trade me in. She let me go because she knew it was best for me."

"You keep telling yourself that." Danielle took another drink. "Bottom line is, she gave you up without a second thought. No one ever gets over something like that."

"I did."

"Bullshit."

"You don't know me." I was right next to her, my lips touching the tip of her cheek. "You don't know how I feel, and you damn well don't know how I was raised. She left me to be with a family that kept me safe and protected me from the wretchedness of the world. She wanted my life to be better than hers, and I can tell you right now, if I had been in the same situation, I would have done exactly the same thing. So don't sit here like a bitch and tell me I didn't love Lila as much as you did. If anything is bullshit right now, it's you."

My breath painted rage over Danielle's cheek and she fought back her own. She poured another glass and set it down away from her. I was unsure of what she was expecting me to do, but I figured she was offering the cup to me. I cautiously took it up. The contents smelled bitter and stale, but I felt Danielle needed a friend right now and this might be the only thing I could do to help her open up. I lifted the glass to my lips and copied her, dropping all of the liquid into my mouth at once and swallowed. It burned my throat and the taste of it made me want to vomit. For a few seconds, I could hardly breathe. Then I let out a breath, allowed the liquid to settle and felt the rush of its power.

Danielle smiled. She took the glass back and pored herself another.

"What is that?" I said.

"Whiskey. Hundred proof. Good, yeah."

"Not really."

"Here. Have another. It gets better each time." Danielle poured another glass, and I took it. This time, it felt smoother, with much less of a burn.

"I've never heard of this before," I said.

"Not a lot of it around anymore. But it still does its job."

I felt a little dizzy and my stomach turned. But it went away as fast it had come, taking the tightness in my body away with it, leaving behind a faint, relaxing smile.

"Told you," Danielle said and took another drink. "I can still remember my first time. It was right after my mother died. I couldn't stop crying, and Grayland, drunk off his own ass, told me it would take the edge off. The second this shit touched my tongue, I threw up, but the bastard insisted I keep trying. I felt like shit the next morning, but at least I got through the night."

"Why do you talk about him like that?" I said.

"Like what?"

"With such disrespect."

"I only give him the amount of respect he deserves."

"But he's your father."

"Not since my mom died." Danielle took another drink.

"How can you say that? The man saved your life that day."

"Oh really? Is that what he told you?"

"Not exactly," I said. "He said you were hiding when your house was set on fire. I only assumed that he burned himself in his rescue."

"Once an asshole, always an asshole," she said.

"Don't talk about him like that." My voice had elevated.

Danielle finally looked away from her liquid escape. I saw her eyes brighten into hollow glass with the shot of lightning. "You really did fuck him," she said. "Didn't you?"

"I loved him," I said, my voice hidden under the rain.

"My god."

I stayed silent—angry, yet ashamed for reasons I couldn't comprehend.

"I should of known. No one defends that man the way you do without having been duped into fucking him. I know how it works. First, find a pretty, naïve young girl, promise to protect her and give her something she's been longing for. Once she accepts the invitation, connect with her on some shared interest, spend as much time with her as possible and coax her into seeing the sweetness under the hardened exterior. When the time is right, spill out the sob story of how he lost his wife and daughter, and cry until the naiveté of the young girl culminates into the ultimate prize. Sound about right to you?"

"It wasn't like that," I said. "We loved each other."

"I'm sure he told all of his other sluts the same damn thing."

I slapped Danielle and immediately stepped away. "I'm sorry," I whispered, my hand covering my lips with shame.

"I've got news for you," she said. "Ryker Grayland was an asshole who cared about one thing. It wasn't me, and it certainly wasn't you."

"I don't believe that. He talked about you all the time. He loved you."

"No he didn't. He just needed a way into your pants. I was just a piece to his puzzle."

"He was a good man."

"A good man? A good man? Does a good man leave his daughter at home to fend for herself for months until he'd satisfied his revenge fantasy? Does a good man kill someone just because they have a different skin tone or accent than you do? Does a good man lock his daughter up for falling in love with someone he didn't approve of? The man was a fucking asshole, and he doesn't deserve the hell he's been sent to."

Danielle threw the bottle of whiskey across the room, shattering it against the wall. She collected her anger in several deep breaths.

"You want to know how that bastard got those scars?" She continued under watered eyes. "I was fourteen, and he brought one of those girls home with him. It wasn't the first time, but she was the youngest. He found her wandering the beach, covered in ash and blood. He fed her and offered her a bath and a warm bed. She didn't say much that first night, but over the next couple of days, she got more comfortable with us. Grayland treated her like a daughter, giving her anything she asked for. The longer she stayed, the more she felt like a sister to me. One night, we were making dinner and we heard him crying in his room. We went to see what was wrong and, like a couple of dumb asses, joined his little pity party like a couple of good servants. After a while, I left the room to go check on dinner when I heard a scream. Grayland chased the girl into the kitchen, yelling at her. He finally caught up to her and tried to force himself on her. I yelled for him to get off her, but all he cared about was getting his prize, so I hit him as hard as I could and pulled the girl behind me. He was a persistent bastard, for sure, and when he came for her again, I grabbed that boiling water and I threw it at him. I still hear those screams in my head when I close my eyes at night. That's the last time I ever laid eyes on him."

"What happened to the girl?" I said.

"She got her throat cut this morning."

I vomited. I wasn't sure if it was the story or the whiskey, but I couldn't fight the urge to release my nausea any longer.

"I knew I'd make a believer out of you," Danielle said. "Take this as your final lesson: If you ain't ready to be shit on every day, you ain't ready to live in this world."

Danielle walked past me as I coughed and spit up the residue of vomit in my mouth. She stopped at the hall and turned back to me.

"I think you were right. You were better off where you were. I wish you'd stayed there. Maybe none of this shit would have happened."

Danielle left, and I lied down on the floor, shaking.

**   **   **

When I woke, the rain had stopped but the air was like ice. My head throbbed gently along my temples, and my back cracked as I stood. I heard the whispers of several family members and followed them out into the main living room, where everyone had gathered. Penelope took my hand and curled into my side the instant I stepped in. I looked to see if I could see Rockwell, but before I could make a real attempt, Danielle glided into the room with a determined step and climbed onto the table in the center of the room. Her demeanor was strong and commanding—that of a true leader.

"Listen up, everyone," she said. "As you all know, the jihad we've been hiding from over the last few years finally caught up to us. We may have been victorious in driving them away yesterday, but you can't underestimate their resolve. It's only a matter of time before they regroup and come at us again, stronger and harder. Normally, we would pack up and find a new home. I don't know about you, but I'm tired of running. If we don't stand up and face them, we'll be running for the rest of our lives, and that is no longer acceptable. We came here for a purpose, and I expect to complete that purpose, or else die trying. In order to do that, we're all going to have to live in the cellar. It's going to be hot, cramped and uncomfortable. But if we want to ever live free again, without the fear of prosecution, it's a sacrifice we all need to make. With that said, I need everyone to pack up the bare necessities—spare clothes, food and water—and get down into the cellar as soon as possible. I'm locking the door at noon and will not open it again. Anyone not on the other side of the door by that time will have to fend for themselves. You have two hours. Get moving."

I remained still, rubbing my head continuously as everyone fled the room. Danielle caught my eye and stepped down from her perch to join them.

"Isn't that a little cold?" I said. "Threatening to lock them out."

"It is what it is. You better heed the warning."

I grabbed a hold of her arm as she passed by. "I'd like to talk about last night."

"What's to talk about?" Danielle said, clearly agitated by my aggressive demeanor. "What's done is done."

"Did you mean what you said?"

Danielle brushed my hand off her arm and stood resolute. "You needed a reality check last night, Madeline. Take it how you will, but you've been on some almighty high horse ever since we saved your ass. I said what I said to wake you up, and by the looks of it, it worked. Now if you want to stay, that's fine. I've got no beef with you. But you had better check that attitude and deal with it."

Danielle looked down to Penelope. "A lot of people here care for you, Madeline. You're a good person. I just hope you can be a little less naïve about people's motives and accept that not everyone is like you and they never will be." She pulled a bottle from her pocket and tossed it to me. "These will help. You better get packed up."

She walked away, leaving Penelope and I alone together. I picked her up and kissed her. "Come on, kid. We have to get ready to move." We went back to the room and packed. I didn't have a lot to carry with me, so I grabbed one of the sheets off the bed and wrapped up as many books as I could carry. I took a couple of the aspirin as the bottle indicated and as we left the room an hour later, my headache had almost subsided. The two of us walked briskly to the door leading down into the cellar. A rush of anticipation hit me as I took my first step toward learning the truth.

(CHAPTER 34

Cement covered the walls of the stairwell, heightening the gloom of the soft darkness I was stepping into. The flicker of orange lit my hollow steps as I reached the dirt-layered ground. No one was visible until I turned into a very tight corridor that kept Penelope from walking next to me. I gripped her shoulders as we entered the room that felt smaller than it actually was. The entire family had all arrived, and I could feel the tension in the absolute restriction of movement. Everyone faced a tunnel at the far wall where Danielle stood, talking to each brother and sister before allowing them entrance. I took my place among the group and waited with patience until I was close enough to hear Danielle's repetitive speech.

"Keep this card with you at all times. You will use this for meals, work and exercise. When you're not working or eating, you will refrain from loitering in this room. There is plenty of space in the tunnel, so set up camp wherever you'd like against the walls, but stay close to it as much as possible. Hopefully, this will all be over soon."

By the time she was finished, she had handed out over a dozen cards of varied colors. I stopped and waited until the family had all made their way into the tunnel, leaving the room hauntingly quiet. The computer I had been using to scan the web sat to the wall on the right of the room next to a large round machine, which I could only guess was the power generator. The other wall was lined with large cans and boxes, most likely filled with fuel, water and rations.

Danielle held out a yellow card. Penelope ran up and grabbed it.

"At least someone knows how to follow the rules," Danielle said, brushing Penelope's hair back. Her favored smile sank as she looked to me. She dropped the rest of the cards next to the computer and headed for the thick concrete door that sat open against the hole leading to the house above. Her shoulder brushed mine as she passed, forcing me to shift my weight to keep from falling.

I remained postured as she struggled to close the door, which had to have been triple her size and weight.

"What are you doing?" I said as a feeling of entrapment washed over me.

"We have to stay protected," she said, her voice strained.

"So you're just going to lock us in here like prisoners?"

"That's the plan."

"You can't do that."

Danielle stopped trying to push the door shut. "Do you have any better ideas? I'd love to hear one."

I was quiet, without answer.

"Yeah, that's what I thought," Danielle turned back to her impossible feat.

"How do you know they'll even be back?" I said.

"Religious conviction," she said automatically. "You don't know them like I do."

"Perhaps not. But how does locking everyone away solve anything? You can't just run and hide. You need to fight."

"What the hell do you think I'm trying to do?" Danielle yelled, facing me with red eyes. "I've been fighting back my whole life, Madeline. I've fought for every one of those people in that tunnel and would give up my life for any one of them. I'll admit, I've done some things I'm not proud of and made my fair share of mistakes. But I also learned that you can't defeat tyranny without protecting those you care about and are willing to fight with you. I gave everyone here an option, including you. They all chose to stay. If you don't want to, that's fine. I couldn't care less. But once that door is locked, that's it. There's no going back. Make your choice."

Danielle refused to wipe her eyes as she grabbed the door once again. I wanted to leave. What Danielle was doing was wrong and unjust, and it wasn't in me to stand around and let it happen. But before I could step through the door, Penelope took my hand into hers and I could feel Danielle's words. In a way, I felt a need to protect her, but it would be impossible to do that alone and I couldn't fathom taking her away from the only family she ever knew. She was the innocent rose in the bed of lilies.

I brushed Penelope's hair and held the back of her neck. She forced a smile and in that moment, my love for her was true. She was my child; I needed to do what was right for her, as a friend and as her mother.

I kissed her and helped Danielle close the door. After she locked it shut with several chains, Danielle looked at me and gave a slight nod of appreciation.

"You might want to take Penelope and get your camp set up," she said and opened one of the boxes. She counted the contents and then moved to the next. I took hold of Penelope's hand.

"Has Rockwell made camp?" I said.

"Not yet. He went to check on our progress."

"I should go find him."

"He won't be back for a couple of days. It's best you wait for him."

"Days? But I need to talk to him."

"Sorry."

I wanted to object further but figured it would get me nowhere. Instead, I urged Penelope into the tunnel. A few small flames attempted to light the tunnel. They were perched high on the walls and spaced every dozen yards or so, allowing for nothing but a range of sight that was less than a few feet. Penelope held my arm and curled up tight against me. Members of the family were all setting up their sleeping quarters against either sides of the wall, conversing in discussion or song, some starting up a game to make their tasks feel quicker.

Penelope and I walked nearly half a mile before finding a resting spot big enough to hold both of us together. We set our stuff down and I sat, needing to rest before completing the tasks I was now assigned as mother. Penelope sat in my lap and stuck her thumb in her mouth, finding comfort in my breast. I pulled a book from the collection I brought with me and read until she fell asleep. Humming a soft tune, I watched my daughter sleep and thought of my family—Penelope, Danielle, Grayland and Lila—and cried.

"Yellow." Danielle's voice echoed through the tunnel, waking me.

I saw several members of the family get up and head down the tunnel to meet her. I woke Penelope, but she refused to move.

"I think it's time to eat, sweetie," I said. That was enough to get her to her feet. She pulled me through the tunnel briskly until we were back in the main room, where everyone with a yellow card had congregated. Penelope let go and pushed her way through the group, stealing a slice of bread and spoonful of oats from Danielle. She then took to the generator and ate. I laughed and sat down next to her, patiently waiting until everyone had collected their meals before accepting my own. Penelope eyed it like a hawk, and, aside from a small piece of the bread, I allowed her to enjoy it. Danielle tried to hide it, but I could see a flash of respect wash over her.

When everyone had finished, we were given the chance to relax and exercise before retreating back into the tunnel. Danielle called out the next color and the cycle continued until all colors had been nourished. I wasn't quite sure how much time had transpired, but when the last group had returned, they did not stop moving. They had collected their belongings, which included a small bottle of water, and continued down the tunnel. I was prepared to follow, but my body was far too fatigued. Instead, I lied down next to Penelope and we slept.

Over the next couple of days, sleep became inconsistent, marked only by the frequency of meals rather than the actual passage of time. It wasn't as detrimental for Penelope or me as it was for many others who couldn't break from the societal reliance on the sun to designate their sleeping habits. Some tried to follow my lead and sleep whenever they felt tired, but it soon became clear to them that the harder they tried, the more alert they became, which then kept others awake by circumstance. Despite the lack of sleep for most of the family, spirits remained high. I heard several fascinating stories from my family's pasts, intrigued by their consistent strength and determination. I wanted to speak to them of my own past, but whenever I did, the words I sought escaped me, leaving only thoughts of wisdom that best suited any one particular story.

After our fifth round of meals, which for me signaled the end of the third day, I read Penelope to sleep and was about to settle into my own rest when the sound of footsteps coming from deep in the tunnel sparked my interest. Several family members passed us, each dragging a large sack along with all of their other belongings. Pulling up the rear of the group was a sight that stopped my breath for a moment. He glanced down to me with meek reserve and then continued on without a word. It wasn't long before he had been swept into the darkness and the air was released from my lungs. Soon after, I was on my feet at the heel of the tunnel.

Rockwell took the bag he carried and dumped its contents out against the cement door. From what I could see, everyone had brought with them as much earth as they could carry and used it to help bury the door. It became clear that Danielle wasn't lying. She was locking us in, with no ability to leave.

"I see our new friend decided to stay," Rockwell said as he took his ration of food. "She better not fuck this up."

Danielle flashed a look over in my direction as Rockwell went to the computer to eat. Her lip twitched before she took to breaking down a couple of the empty boxes. I contemplated going to Rockwell to discuss what had happened, but my nerves pushed me back into the tunnel. Never before had I felt an emotion as strong as this, and it made me sick to my stomach. He had felt the same thing I did that night, I was sure of it, but I had questioned my resolve so much that I suddenly feared his rejection if I ever approached him with the truth.

I checked to make sure Penelope was still asleep when I returned and then continued down into the tunnel for another mile or two until I was certain I was alone. The space between flames was further apart this deep into the tunnel, causing it to be much darker, almost blind. It made me feel oddly at home—afraid, but safe. I instantly lit up a cigarette and filled my lungs, and my mind, with contentment. Attempting to relax, I tried to clear my thoughts, but the events of the past week wouldn't let go. I couldn't shake the feeling that I had somehow disrupted the dynamics of the family and caused, no matter how indirectly, the demise of both my mother and the life these good people had. What had I done that pushed me to be here? Should I have fought harder to protect Grayland? Perhaps I should have remained strong after the death of Miss Safiya, where this course of action had all started. If it wasn't for my own weakness, Miss Safiya might still be alive, or as much as I hated to think of it, I may as well have been dead. It was hard to consider what life would have been like had I remained married to Abdullah. In all of that, I could feel the rock of insolence strike me. My head contracted, and my stomach turned. That's when I heard that voice—the same voice I heard out in the field just days ago, pronouncing his will for Allah.

"My god." All of the muscles in my body tightened and refused to work any longer. I dropped the remaining butt of the cigarette and sat against the wall. It took all of the strength I could find to breathe and my sight faded until all I could see was the black of Abdullah's heart.

CHAPTER 35

My body tightened impulsively when the ghost of my thoughts solidified with a touch on my shoulder. My lungs constricted with a scream as I threw my elbow up at the attacker. Blocking the blow, his shadow pushed away, exclaiming an inaudible grunt. I slid my body down the wall and crawled a few feet from its presence.

"Madeline," Rockwell said, perplexed.

Recognizing the voice, I stopped moving, even though I hadn't yet fully realized who it was. I wiped my eyes clear and focused through the soft burn to see his hands held out in front of him. He held his body slightly back as he waited for my recognition.

"Rockwell?" I whispered, easing his tension.

"What the hell?" he said.

I wiped the mucus from my nose as I sat back up and then fixed my hair, which had wound its way into a tangled weave.

"Are you okay?"

"Yeah," I said, clearing my throat. "I'm fine. What do you want?" The hauteur in my voice was evident, but I couldn't understand why it had manifested.

"Danielle's asking for you," he said with faint disdain.

"What does she want?"

"Your group was called."

"For what?"

"What does it matter? Just move your ass." He grabbed my arm to pull me up. I slapped it away and drew my fist.

"What the hell is wrong with you?"

"Nothing," I said and walked past him, making certain that my shoulder shoved against his.

He didn't follow right away, and I was glad. Being alone would hopefully allow me time to calm the belligerence that had taken over. Where it had come from was a mystery, but I felt it swimming within me, fighting to remain in control. By the time I reached my camp, remorse for my recent attitude had weaved itself among my other emotions, turning my stomach and drawing fire into my eyes. I hid it the best I could as I walked past the family, most of who were trying desperately to find sleep. Others watched me, almost catatonic.

Several members of the yellow group walked past me with bags and bottles of water as I neared the main room. By the time I reached it, the last few had been rationed their water and were on their way out. Penelope sat at the computer pounding out an admirably competent tune on the keyboard.

"Glad you could finally make it," Danielle said, filling the last of the bottles. "I was about ready to write you off."

"I'm sorry," is all I could say in reply.

Penelope ran to me with a cheerful bounce and a big hug. I smiled and kissed her.

"Where have you been?" Danielle said. Her voice was cold.

Mine was just as cold. "I needed to be alone."

"So you think you could spare some of that precious time?"

"For what?"

"To do your fair share."

"My fair share of what? What is it that you've got us all doing down here?"

"It doesn't matter. You chose to be here, so now you get to help us."

"To hell with that," I said, my tongue burning with indignation. "If I'm going to be your damn slave, I'm sure as hell going to know what it is I'm slaving for."

"Slavery?" Danielle laughed. "Is that what you think this is?"

"What else am I supposed to think? You have us all locked down here with hardly any food or water and you're forcing everyone else to do God knows what without any reason whatsoever, while you sit around and do absolutely nothing."

"You've got some balls to speak to me like that," Danielle said. Her arms were crossed, as was her voice.

"He who digs his own grave is bound to fall to his death."

"Are you saying I'm being selfish?"

"I'm saying you're no better than the termites, you tyrannical bitch."

Penelope gripped my hand tight. I felt her unease at my rise in resentment.

"You are something else." Danielle fought back her anger, though I could see the tension in her body. "After all we've done for you these past few weeks and you come in here and call me a bitch? Fuck you is all I have to say."

"And your father, too," I said before I understood the implications of the words. Seconds later, Danielle took a swing at my jaw.

I pushed Penelope to the floor and ducked the attack, following her momentum with an uppercut to her gut. Her rib cracked against my knuckles and she stumbled back.

Penelope cried frantically and slid against the wall.

I stood confident as Danielle took in a couple of breaths and then leaped out at my legs. The back of my head hit the wall as I fell back, but it didn't faze me. I hit Danielle in the ear and then the upper eye as she struggled to claw at me with her dull, bitten nails.

We struggled this way for some time before I grabbed her hair and pulled it back. Danielle let out a scream. In her weakened state, I pushed her onto her back and followed into a sitting position above her waist. I hit her several times across the jaw. She attempted to shove her hand up into my neck to stop me but to no avail. In my mind, I was prepared to kill Danielle.

Suddenly, my arm was stopped by the grip of an even more resolute hand and pulled back behind me. Another hand gripped my body just under my chest, and I was pulled from Danielle with great force. I tried to struggle free, but when I moved, the grip on my arm grew tighter. So I stopped, and soon could feel a warm breath on the base of my neck.

"Stop," Rockwell said. He held me tightly against him.

Danielle rolled over and slowly sat up. She wiped the blood from her nose and spit out some blood. She looked to me, red in her eyes.

Remorse was beginning to seep through my veins.

"I'm sorry," I said. My breaths were still uncontrollable.

"Fuck you," Danielle said. She hardly had any strength to walk, but her hatred for me at the moment was enough. "No one gets a free ride," she said and followed it up with a strong right hook that pushed me to the floor and swelled my eye. Rockwell allowed me to fall and caught Danielle as she dropped to her knee. He helped her to the wall and wiped her wounds down.

"What the hell was that all about?" Rockwell said.

"We had some issues to resolve," Danielle said. "It's fine."

I felt perplexed. I had nearly just killed Danielle and she defended my actions.

"Get her up," she said. "The rest of her group is already on their way down."

"Wait. You want her to help dig the tunnel?"

"I said it. No free rides. She chose to stay." Danielle spit out more blood and pushed Rockwell's help away.

"I don't think that's a good idea," Rockwell said. "She's too unstable."

"No shit. But we've got less than two weeks worth of food and water. We need all able bodies digging us out of this hell."

"I realize that. But what happens if she goes crack in the hole? She could get someone hurt, or even cause a cave-in."

"I have to take that risk."

"I can't," Rockwell said. He stepped away from Danielle.

"Which is why you're going in with her."

Rockwell turned around. "I'm what?"

"Like you said. We can't have her going down there and fucking us over. But she's a strong little bitch." Danielle winced as she pulled a tooth from her mouth. "God damn it." She tossed it aside and spit out more blood. "Go in there with her; keep her in line. If she starts any shit, you have my permission to do whatever's necessary."

Danielle pulled a gun from her back and handed it to Rockwell. "Anything." She looked at me, but couldn't hold it. "Get her ass out of here."

Rockwell put the gun into his belt. "Come on."

He waited by the mouth of the tunnel. I rubbed my jaw and walked to Penelope. Her head was folded into her arms as she cried and only tightened up as I touched her. I backed away, realizing that she wasn't ready to trust me after having scared her so. It was going to take time before she was ready to accept my apology. I just hoped when that time came, she accepted it.

I kissed the back of her head, making sure that I didn't touch her otherwise.

"She'll be okay," Danielle said.

I wanted to believe her, but my heart contradicted her. "Be good, Penelope," I whispered, "and do as Danielle says. I'll be back soon. I'm sorry."

I rose and averted my eyes from Danielle's. Rockwell took step behind me and never let me get past three or four steps ahead of him. We didn't say a word for most of the walk and the silence of it all haunted me.

She'll be fine, I repeated to myself.

CHAPTER 36

As the room stretched deeper into the womb of the earth, the torches became less numerous and visibility had all but evaporated. When we weren't directly under one of the torches, Rockwell almost disappeared in front of me. The sound of his steps kept me calm in the otherwise eerie quiet, which forced time to stand just as still. There was no telling how long it had been since we left or how much longer we had to travel, but the time and the distance had quelled the rage I had exhibited just a short time ago, transforming it into a tired surrender. My mind wouldn't stray at all from the punishment I inflicted on Danielle, and at times, it felt so close to my heart that I was forced to fight back turns of nausea. It became so heavy at times, I had to stop and rest, which Rockwell never objected to. He would simply join me in the respite.

"I'm sorry," I said under a breath of sickness as I sat.

Rockwell stretched his muscles and rested his head against the wall across from me. "About what?" he said.

"What I did to Danielle. And for what I said. It was rude and offensive."

"No objections here."

"I have no excuse, and I'm sorry."

"Still doesn't help me trust you."

"I know." My knees bent up slightly as I stretched out my legs and rested my feet on the wall next to Rockwell. "I'm not proud of the mistakes I've made recently, but there's not much I can do to fix that except work harder to prove my worth. And I intend to do just that."

"Yeah," Rockwell said. It wasn't clear, but I thought I heard a bit of annoyance.

I chose not to speak for several minutes, hoping the relaxing nature of our rest would help Rockwell be less reticent in answering the question that had been on my mind for some time now. I hadn't asked earlier because I didn't want to pry any deeper than I had to before I was accepted into their family. However, after having seen the hierarchy that had built between them, I felt it was now necessary to know them better, as partners and as friends, in order to do what I sought to do.

"How did you meet her?" I said, slightly reluctant. "Danielle, I mean."

"What's it to you?" he said.

"No offense," I replied quickly, feeling the sting of his bite. "It's just… Danielle seems to have you caught up on a pretty tight leash. I'm curious to know why a capable man such as yourself would take that kind of shit from someone."

That caught Rockwell's attention. "First of all, don't you ever speak about Danielle like that again. She's one of the most caring and respectful people I have ever met. You hear me?"

I could smell the rage on Rockwell's breath. "Yeah. I'm sorry."

Rockwell took his time leaning back and then continued in a more subdued tone. "I choose to follow her," he said, reserved.

"Why?" I said softly, childish.

"It doesn't matter."

"It does to me. Danielle's almost a sister to me, and I hardly know anything about her beyond what I learned from my father. I want to know her."

"Then ask her."

"I want to hear about her from you."

Rockwell took in a defeated breath.

"Why do you choose to follow her so readily?"

It took a minute, but Rockwell finally gave in. "I owe my life to her."

"She saved your life?" I was intrigued.

"Not in the same way as we saved yours, but… yeah. If it wasn't for Danielle, I'd probably be rotting out in some god forsaken ditch in the desert."

"I'm sorry to hear that," I said. "How did it happen?"

Rockwell looked away from me, clearly uncomfortable. "We better get moving," he said. I took hold of his wrist before he could get his feet beneath him.

"Please," I said, my eyes curled in sweet compassion. "I'd like to know."

He helped me to my feet and held my hand graciously.

"It's hard for me to talk about," he said solemnly. "I'm not proud of who I was and would much rather keep that part of myself where it belongs."

"The past helps us grow," I said. "Without it, immorality would reign."

"I've got news for you. Immorality has always reigned, and it grows more prominent with each new generation. I don't dispute that the past teaches us and helps us grow. But more often than not, what is learned becomes the how-to book for achieving power. In every species of animal, there's an instinctual need to be the king, or the alpha, as it were. Humans are no different. I don't care who you are, at some point, we all get a taste of leadership and control. For some, a little taste is enough to satisfy them, but for others, it becomes an addiction. The more power they gain, the more they need, which eventually leads to their downfall. But as one person falls, another rises, and by learning from the mistakes of the fallen, the new lives longer than the last. Eventually, as is the law of evolution, he will fall, which leads to another who will learn, evolve and grow based on what happened before him. It's in this cycle that corruption and manipulation becomes more fruitful and more advanced. Don't believe me? Take a look around. Corruption grew so prominent inside our government, the country's eventual fall was inevitable. Now, we have termites out there who continue to learn and grow more powerful, each one of which will eventually fall and create a new leader, just as corrupt, just as immoral, but more deceptive. To believe otherwise is naïve."

Rockwell let go of my hand.

"It's not naïve," I said. "Just as you've seen corruption infect our hearts, I've seen the opposite. I have to believe that if it's possible to become addicted to power and corruption, it can be just as addictive to show compassion and honesty. I mean, aren't those the qualities you defend so readily in Danielle?"

Rockwell chuckled. "I guess."

"Then wouldn't you say it was compassion that outweighed corruption when she rescued you from your past?"

"Yeah," he said, a bit shaky. "You could say that."

"Whatever it is you did in the past means nothing because of Danielle. You learned from her and used your mistakes to transform yourself into something better. Am I wrong?"

"No. You're absolutely right."

"Then there's no shame in accepting your past and using it to teach others."

"You really want to know, don't you?"

"I only wish to learn."

Rockwell started down the tunnel, and I stayed as close to him as possible without stepping on his heels. He was reluctant at first, but he soon found the strength to open up. I lit a cigarette and listened carefully to his story.

"Before I met Danielle I was what they used to call a professional drunk. When I wasn't drinking myself to death, I was either passed out somewhere or beating the shit out someone. It got so bad sometimes, I'd wake up in my own vomit and urine and then turn around and kill someone for a simple shot of whiskey."

"Why was it so bad?"

"Like any other addiction, the more you consume, the more you need to sustain the high. I was getting to the point where I couldn't get a buzz unless I was drowning in alcohol, and if I didn't have a drink for more than a few hours, I was fucked."

"I can't believe you would let it get that bad."

"You keep smoking those cigs like you've been, you'll find out first hand what it was like."

I let out a breath of smoke and brushed the tip on the wall. I could still taste the tobacco and wanted to grab another.

"And honestly," he continued, "I didn't care whether I lived or not."

"That's horrible."

"It was. But I didn't have anyone or anything, so it really didn't matter. Circumstances led me into the bottle, and it was the only way I knew how to stay numb."

"How is it you were able to sustain the addiction? What did you use to barter with?"

"That's what I'm most ashamed of," he said quietly. "I had to do some unspeakable things to sustain the habit, but at the time it was worth it."

"Go on," I said just as softly when he paused to take in a moment of reflection. I rested my hand on his shoulder, and he covered it gently with his own. As he let go, I slid my hand down his arm and squeezed his elbow before letting him continue.

"Before the war officially began, Muslims started purchasing breweries and brewpubs all across the world. This should have been a red flag, since Islam forbid the consumption of alcohol, but everyone stayed blind to it, regarding it as entrepreneurs attempting to live the American dream, as was their right. But if they had taken the time to look at the fine print, they would have noticed that those buying up these breweries were mostly funded, or were an integral part of, several different militant groups, and at times were paying millions of dollars to acquire them. At the start of the war, the breweries were some of the first major targets. Within a week, only a handful were left, and those were owned and operated by termites, who wouldn't dare sell their cash cows to anyone, much less a Muslim rag."

"And nobody noticed this?"

"How could they? When all of that was going on, the Internet and so-called news outlets were force-feeding everyone fraudulent news and ideological opinions twenty-four seven. We were so consumed by the pettiness of our differences that it kept us from looking at the bigger picture. We were told to fight for the rights of twelve year olds to have abortions without parental consent or to allow Sharia law in our courts, and in the mean time, termites quietly spread themselves around all major areas of the economy.

"We didn't even notice it when the U.N. adopted the China-Muslim Trade Agreement. Then again, by that time it was too late anyway. Congress rammed that into law so quickly, half the people didn't even know it existed, and kept the other half in the dark about what it really meant. Not only did prices for everything rise tenfold within months, but almost all of the money was being collected by those who would turn out to be our deadliest enemies. Once the monetary system collapsed at the peak of the war, bartering for anything became extremely difficult, but it was alcohol that became the most valuable asset. It was extremely rare, and those against Islam sought it out, and sometimes fought for it. If they were desperate enough, they'd even kill for it.

"I can't remember how many lives I took, or how many others I beat to a pulp, but I took any job I could find, so long as it lead to the bottom of a bottle."

"You never asked about who they were?"

"I didn't care who they were. They could have been an innocent mother of three or an extremist. If I was told to kill them, so be it. I always felt that if I knew too much, I wouldn't have the balls to finish the job. If that happened, not only would I have gotten the shit beat out of me, I would have been tainted as a pickled pussy. I couldn't let that happen. So when I was offered a job, I took the name and the location and went out to do what I was asked to do.

"One day, I was waiting for my next job at my usual spot, nursing a beer, shootin' the shit, you know, the norm. I didn't notice Danielle come in at first, but when a ruckus started up at the bar, I took notice. I'm not sure who started it, exactly, but Danielle was more than willing to finish it. When she was headed out the door, I pumped out a couple of derogatory cracks and sexual innuendos. She flipped me the bird, which just egged me on even more. I'm still surprised she didn't turn around and beat the shit out of me. She kept her cool and just walked out without ever truly acknowledging me.

"A few minutes later, the owner of the pub came over with my next assignment. When I asked who it was, he said she just left."

"You were told to kill Danielle?" I said, stunned.

"Not only that, she was worth two bottles of tequila, a bottle of vodka and a pint of whiskey."

"Is that a lot?"

"I'd normally have to kill a half dozen people, and maybe send a message to a couple more for that kind of price."

"What did she do to deserve that?"

"Beats the hell out of me."

"You never asked?"

"Never thought I needed to."

"So what did you do?"

"What else? I sealed the deal, finished my beer and went after her. It took me about an hour to track her down, but when I did, I could taste my prize waiting for me back at the bar.

"Little did I know I was about to get my ass kicked."

I tried to hold back a laugh but was free to let it out when Rockwell encouraged me with his own.

"I was half drunk and hadn't slept in a couple of days. At least, that's what I tell myself."

Rockwell and I finished off our amusement.

"I thought I had the upper hand, sneaking up behind her back, but she was more cunning than I expected and was dropped pretty quickly. A couple of good shots to the jaw and a broken nose later, Danielle pulled her gun on me and tried to get me to tell her who hired me. When I wouldn't say, she threatened to shoot my dick off. That was enough to entice me to spill my guts. I thought for sure she was going to finish me off, but all she did was help me off the ground and tell me to get my ass out of there.

"Once it was found out I hadn't gotten the job done, I was a dead man, so I went straight home to gather up my stash and got the hell out of Dodge. I wandered several days without much direction, wondering if I would ever find another job after word got around. Finally, I found a place to crash only to learn that the house belonged to Danielle.

"Of course, I didn't find that out until a couple of days later. When she saw me, her first instinct was to rip my head off, but Lila convinced her I wasn't going to be a threat and agreed that if I was going to stay, that I couldn't drink. That was enough to send me packing. Before I could leave, though, Danielle stopped me and insisted that I stay. I don't know what it was. She had no reason to help me, and yet here she was offering me her hand."

"She gave you compassion," I said softly.

"More than that, she took my life. And ever the bitch, she didn't give it back easy. When she said I couldn't drink, I figured she'd toss the alcohol down the drain, but she made sure it was always within arms length."

"She was testing you," I said.

"You bet she was, and there were times I almost broke, especially the nights when I was drowning in sweat and could hardly breath. But every time I was close to taking a drink, I thought of Danielle and that gesture of trust. People like her just didn't exist. When I had been completely detoxed, I thanked her for her help. She asked if I wanted to stay, and I came up with some bullshit excuse for why I couldn't. Then she told me about what she was attempting to do, and how she thought, with my background, that I'd make a good asset. She said I'd be able help a lot of people, make amends for everyone I had hurt. How was I supposed to say no?

"The next day, I went out to collect some firewood and the house was raided by a group of termites. Those who didn't find the other side of Danielle's gun took off with what little food and water we had and left Lila a bloody mess. Because of the timing, Danielle thought I had somehow been involved and forced me to leave. That didn't sit well with me, so I tracked those bastards down and took back what was ours, plus whatever else I could get my hands on, and brought it back to Danielle. Not wanting to disturb them, I set everything on the porch and left."

"You didn't tell her what you did?"

"I didn't want it to appear as if I was gloating or make it seem insincere. Over the next few days, whenever I saw someone being taken advantage of, or getting hurt in any way, I made sure to step in and do what I had to do to make it right, regardless of my own safety. I was tempted to go out and get drunk but always chose not to. What I didn't know is that Danielle had been following me since I dropped the stuff off. When she felt the time was right, she revealed herself.

" 'That's the heart I was hoping to see,' she said and asked me to come back. A few days later, I was welcomed with open arms into the family and branded with our seal. Danielle's been my best friend ever since."

"That is beautiful," I said, wiping my moist cheeks. "I wish I could have that."

"You can," he said. "You just have to earn it."

"I've tried."

"Not hard enough."

"Then tell me," I said, stopping him. "Tell me how to prove my worth to you and your family."

Rockwell cupped the back of my neck in his hand. "Give us your heart," he said. He held me a moment longer before taking to the darkness.

CHAPTER 37

As we walked, I noticed several small coves dug into the sides of the walls. Most of them I recognized as toilets, and though they had all been covered and filled in with dirt, they still left a rank smell several feet before and after their location. The others were smaller in height but seemed to go much deeper into the wall. When we got closer to the end of the tunnel, a couple of family members pulled a long board from inside. Rockwell and I followed suit and pulled our own board and carried it with us to the end, where it would eventually become a fresh new pillar for the continued support of the tunnel.

The space was extremely crowded as we arrived. The yellow group helped the other group bind the bags they brought with them and break camp, saying their farewells as each one left. The next few hours were spent setting up our own camps, except for Rockwell, who chose to grab a pick and dig. I watched him for some time before helping him shovel the dirt into a pile off to the side and out of the way. Slowly, each member of the group took up their own jobs, assigning each other specific tasks—whether it be working on the pillars, digging new outlets, shoveling dirt or picking the wall. For the next two days, everyone followed Rockwell's lead, working and resting at his command. It was a loyal respect that was quite enchanting, and I did my part to live up to it. Rockwell split us into three core groups so we could take turns working, eating and sleeping. He made sure that I was part of his group for the sole purpose of being able to keep his promise to Danielle and keep an eye on me. It didn't matter; I simply hammered and chipped my way through every task I was asked to perform with fervent commitment until the next group came to relieve us.

Rockwell took command immediately and gave them instructions to further the progress we had made. I immediately offered to stay with them on the next rotation, but Rockwell refused, insisting I rest. I agreed and filled one of the bags with as much dirt as I could carry. After tying it off, I slung it over my shoulder and stammered down the tunnel.

"Let me help," Rockwell said.

"I got it," I said, struggling to keep it balanced.

Rockwell stepped back and allowed me my pride, which eventually took its toll. I dropped the bag and collapsed after less than half a mile. My lungs were ready to burst and my legs felt numb. I half expected Rockwell to laugh or make me feel foolish. But all he did was sit next to me and wait until I was ready to try again. When I did, it was clear I had taken on too much.

"I could use some help," I said.

"Are you sure?"

"Yeah."

Rockwell picked up the bag with the ease of his smile. "You can't become part of the family if you kill yourself," he said.

I smiled sweetly, unable to look directly at him.

We took turns carrying and dragging the bag through the tunnel, talking more about life before the war, which felt in some ways different than how Grayland had spoke of it, and less romantic than how I had previously thought. He taught me much about the history of America, the rise and fall of the democratic republic and the differences between who was considered great leaders and those found to be wanting. What I found most pleasurable, though, was the discussions of our favorite authors, some of whom I had never before heard of but who sounded incredible based on Rockwell's perceptions of them and their writings. The depth of information and insight that Rockwell possessed was like none other I had ever encountered and that which I could only hope to ever aspire to.

As we got closer to home, I grew steadily quieter and more reserved. Rockwell was all too keen to notice.

"What's wrong?" he said.

I didn't answer right away, but I knew it was something I could no longer hold inside.

"Do you think Penelope will forgive me?"

"I wouldn't worry," he said. "You were upset."

"Yeah, but it couldn't have been easy for her to see me like that. I'm supposed to set an example, be there for her and keep her safe. I failed on all counts in one fell swoop."

"We all have our bad days."

"She deserves better."

Rockwell set the bag down. "Listen to me, Madeline. What you did was not unforgivable. You had a moment of weakness, that's all."

"And showed her a part of me that…" I paused to catch my breath. "That even I'm afraid of. How am I supposed to be a protective mother with such a vice?" I turned from Rockwell, ashamed.

"Hey," Rockwell said, grabbing my arms. "No one is perfect, you know that. Love is even less perfect, but if it's there, even just slightly, forgiveness is never far behind. Trust me, Penelope will forgive you."

I was overcome with emotion. Rockwell eased it with the wrap of his arms and the sanctity of his body.

"Sit down with her, explain to her what happened." He wiped my face clean. "You'll be surprised at how resilient kids can be."

I hugged Rockwell again and thanked him.

Penelope wasn't at our camp when we returned. My stomach turned a bit, but I realized she was most likely in the main room with Danielle. Or so I hoped.

When we reached the room, I caught sight of Penelope almost immediately at the computer. She was reading and enjoying it considerably. Danielle was rationing out food to the group as they emptied their bags out at the door and tossed them off to the side for the next. The door was now almost half covered and the realization that we were in fact now trapped down in the hole finally caught up to me. I wasn't sure how I felt about that, but I wanted to trust that Danielle was doing the right thing.

She took in a deep breath as she turned to me and I could see the aversion in her bitter glare. She tossed my rations to the ground and helped Rockwell empty our bag against the door. I quickly accepted my meal and sat next to Penelope. It broke my heart when she, too, turned her back to me. She hid her face in a book and tensed her shoulders.

"Penelope," I said, but my voice only made her even tenser.

Instead of fighting with her, I accepted her rejection. I set my food at her feet and got up to leave. "I'm sorry."

I walked back to my camp and cried myself to sleep.

When I woke up, to my surprise, Penelope was lying next to me. Her arm was wrapped around my waist and her thumb was securely planted between her lips. I kissed gently, with all of the affection I could muster.

"I told you," Rockwell said. He was sitting next to me, watching over us.

"I don't understand why," I said.

"Just be happy she did."

I smiled and squeezed Rockwell's hand in thanks. He offered to walk with me to have breakfast, but because I didn't want to disturb Penelope's slumber and wanted very much to be there when she woke, I didn't move. When she finally did wake up, her smile was enough to repair any damage done to my heart.

We ate together that morning and laughed and played like nothing had ever happened. Rockwell watched over us, even gathering up about a dozen others to play a game called Red Rover, which Danielle found somewhat childish. She went about her own business, continually refusing to join us in anything, even after we egged her on, calling her a spoilsport and cracking Penelope up to no end.

When Penelope and the family slept, Rockwell and I would find the pleasure of our company, talking about social issues, politics and history. Sometimes, we would sit shoulder-to-shoulder and read a book to each other in whispers, or just enjoy each other's thoughtful silence. I would usually wake from these nights with my head on his shoulder or within his embrace, and it was always welcome. Occasionally, when Danielle allowed, we would flip the generator on and clean up as many corrupted files as we could. We spent hours reading and discussing the subjects. Sometimes thoughtful, sometimes hilarious, our conversations were always long and always ours. We asked Danielle to join us a couple of times, but she always refused.

"What, are you jealous," Rockwell would tease. Danielle would roll her eyes, annoyed and leave us be.

Over time, our conversations (on and off the computer) became more open and more vulgar. That is unless Penelope joined us and then we had to keep our language in check. It was so much fun, I had completely forgotten about the buried door. It no longer mattered that we were stuck there with no way out. So long as Rockwell and Penelope were with me, I was home.

What we failed to notice during our time together was the breakdown in our family's spirit. Everyone grew more irritable with each passing meal. Some couldn't find the strength to eat, and a lot of them found sleep to be a chore. It was far worse when the yellow group was to be sent back into the hole, and though she never spoke of it, you could see the weight of it all in Danielle. With Rockwell focusing his attention more on me, Danielle was left to carry the burdens of the family on her shoulders alone.

"Why don't you stay with her?" I said to Rockwell as I gathered my things.

"She's tough," he said, though I couldn't tell if he truly meant it. "She'll make it through."

I wanted him so much to be with me that I failed to look beyond the surface of his words. "You're probably right."

The walk back to the end of the tunnel was wrought with pain, hunger and emotional turmoil. Rockwell and I tried to bring the energy up, but there was almost none to be shared. It took every ounce of strength to simply make it there, that when we did arrive, hardly anyone had the will to work. Most tried to find the sleep they had lost and others cried hidden in the shadows. Though we didn't say it out loud, Rockwell and I both knew that it would be up to us to finish, and that we couldn't stop until we had. We refrained from taking any breaks and tried to restrict sleep to a few hours at a time. It was hard to watch Rockwell sleep without resting comfortably in his arms, as I assume it was hard for him to watch me, but it was necessary for us both to sleep in shifts so that we didn't lose vital time.

"What happened?" I was feeling the fatigue beginning to rest on my back and needed a distraction.

"With what?" Rockwell said. I could see his strength diminishing as well.

"I was thinking about the story you told me about when you met Danielle, and I was wondering what it was that pushed you into being a professional drunk."

"What pushed me over the edge?" he said.

"Yeah." I rested the ax at my side.

Rockwell took my cue and stood erect. He took in several breaths and wiped his brow. "It was a series of things," he said.

"Did you lose someone?"

Rockwell lowered his head.

"Was it your parents?" I said, hoping he wouldn't close down completely.

"No," he said after a few more breaths. "My mom died a couple of years after I was born, and my dad was never sober long enough to be a parent. I guess you might say it was his example that made me the way I was."

"I'm sorry," I said.

"Don't be. You can't change the cards you were dealt."

"Then who was it?"

Rockwell stared at me for some time. I could feel his anguish as the memories he had buried down deep within swarmed back into his mind. I couldn't help but feel guilty for opening a tomb he sought so hard to keep closed.

"I'm sorry," I said and raised my ax to continue my work.

"My brother," he said finally, though the words were soft and came with a lot of desolation.

I stopped again and waited patiently until he was ready to continue.

"Because my parents were both basically out of the picture," he started, "my brother was the one who raised me. He was only a few years older than I was, but he found the courage to step up and be the father he knew I would never have. He kept me fed, kept me clothed, but best of all, he kept me educated. There was never a time when he wasn't around that he didn't have me reading, studying or writing essays. He made sure I did at least eight hours of research and homework a day. I looked up to him and wanted to make him proud of me, so I always did what he asked and never questioned him. By the time I was eight, he didn't have to ask anymore. I spent more time researching the web and learning than I did sleeping. It had become a part of me."

"It became your drug," I said, hoping to get the smile I received.

"Yeah. A drug that kept me young and naïve." His smile was gone as fast as it had come.

"What do you mean?"

"I could do math, read and write in several languages, knew the dictionary front and back, and understood the disparity that plagued the world, but I never understood what it felt like to be out in it, to live in the world I only knew existed inside the computer."

"So you didn't know how to relate to anyone when you lost your brother."

"It's a lot more complicated than that," Rockwell said. He picked up his ax and started chipping away.

"Tell me," I said, joining him.

"It was a few days before I realized my brother hadn't been home. I was so immersed in my studies that time just flew by. I went to go grab a bite to eat and there was hardly a scrap in the house. I tried to call him on his cell, but he didn't answer and it scared the hell out of me. I called the police and everything. It took every bit of strength I had to ride down to the store and get groceries for me and my dad. Finally, after about two weeks, he showed up with a girl named Trick. Don't ask."

I smiled graciously and nodded.

"I yelled at him for not calling me and making me think he was dead somewhere in a ditch, but it wasn't until she asked him to that he apologized. I accepted, but the sting still lingered. Trick stayed with us for the next few months. She was nice and fun to have around, and I grew quite fond of her. We would study together, and I would teach her things that I don't even know she understood at all. At night, I'd listen to her and my brother and imagine that it was me with her in his bed. I was twelve and lived my life on the net. What was I supposed to think?"

I held in a laugh. I had seen some things on the Internet in my own time that made me squirm a bit in embarrassment. I could only imagine what it felt for him.

"It's okay," he said. "You can laugh."

So we did, together.

"Anyway, this one day, my brother said he found some job and needed to leave for a couple of months. He asked Trick to stay and keep an eye on me. I didn't like that he was leaving me with a babysitter but was happy that she agreed to stay. Over the next few weeks, we grew closer and one day she caught me jerking off to some porn site on the net. I don't know how long she was watching, but when I caught her, I was so embarrassed, I hid in my room for hours, unable to look her in the eye. That night, she brought me a cup of hot chocolate and tried to comfort me by saying that I shouldn't be embarrassed. She then said that she does the same thing sometimes and proceeded to take off her pants and show me.

"I couldn't watch at first, but as she continued, I grew more fascinated and started to play with myself along with her. When she could see I was okay with it, she took my hand and helped me do it for her, which led to even more, and before I knew what was happening, we were both naked and enjoying my first real sexual experience. It was probably naïve of me, but I literally fell in love with her that night and I thought she had too. She came to my bed every night after that, each time feeling like I was about to die.

"By the time my brother got back home, I was prepared to tell him that Trick and I were in love and that we were going to live together for the rest of our lives. But as soon as he walked through that door, Trick turned into a little schoolgirl and was all over my brother, kissing him and loving him. She hardly once ever looked at me again, going as far as to ask me to keep our tryst a secret from him. You can imagine how I felt."

"You must have been devastated," I said, unable to come up with anything else.

"And betrayed," he added. "But that was just the beginning. A few weeks later, my brother came home frantic and shaking. He wouldn't say what was going on, just that he needed to meet some people and wanted Trick to go with him. She asked him what for, but he continually avoided her questions. I tried to stop him from taking her, but that turned out to be ineffective. It was the first time that my brother ever hit me.

"It took some time to stop crying, but when I did, I felt an overwhelming need to go after them. Even though she hurt me, I didn't want to see Trick harmed. So I searched all over for them, finally spotting them on some backwoods road where my brother sometimes went to smoke pot with his friends. He was there with some Mexican guys I'd never seen before, swapping some stuff for cash. Trick was a few steps behind him, and after collecting his money, my brother went to her and took her arm. I thought maybe they were done and the two would make their way back home. But then Trick tried to get away and my brother shoved her to the ground. She tried to get up and run, but the Mexicans were too powerful. My brother cowered away, leaving me to watch Trick get gang raped to the point of death. I wanted to help her but I was frozen and a slobbering mess. When they all had had their shot with her, they took a gun to her head and blew a hole right through it.

"It felt like forever by the time I got the courage enough to go to her. I held her for a long time, crying over her, trying to will her back to life. But nothing I did was enough. I started to believe that if I had just done something, if I hadn't been such a coward, she'd still be alive. Then it hit me. None of it was my fault. It was my brother who sentenced her to death. I went back home and confronted him about what he had done. When I asked if he even loved her, he said she was a means to an end, and that was it. I took my dad's shotgun to his chest, grabbed the last bottle of whiskey my dad had in the liquor cabinet and never looked back."

"My God," I whispered. I rested my hand on his back. There were no tears in his eyes, but I could sense the anguish. "I'm so sorry."

"Yeah," he said. "Me, too. I buried Trick the next morning out in the field and gave my love to her with the bottom of the whiskey bottle. Two years later, the war struck."

I took him in my arms quickly and held him closer than I ever had. He wrapped his arms around me, never the more gently.

"I've never told anyone that before," he said. His hand dropped down the small of my back.

I looked at his eyes. "You were scared."

"I was angry."

"No, not then. When I kissed you."

Rockwell averted his eyes and tried to step back. I wouldn't let him.

"It scared you, didn't it? You felt for me what you once felt for her, and it scared you to feel that way again."

Rockwell continued to shy away.

"Hey. You don't have to be ashamed." I lifted his head back to mine and kissed him. "You don't have to be afraid."

He returned my kiss with his own and, under the guise of blindness for our flaws, both physical and emotional, fell into love. We held each other for some time afterward, our heated skin a sign of the passionate fire we shared together as one.

Neither of us wanted to leave the other's touch, but we had an obligation and had to follow through on it. We couldn't hold back our smiles as we worked as a connected pair. It was only when I punctured through the wall did we finally lose our sense of unity.

"What the hell?" I said.

Rockwell pushed me aside and looked through. With a satisfying grin, he picked me up in a huge and rewarding bear hug.

"We did it," he said with excitement. "We're through."

CHAPTER 38

To look through to the other side of the wall was like looking into a future that has yet to write a word down on the page. The only indication that there was another tunnel was the cool breeze that whistled its song through the small hole I had created. It was refreshing to feel it lick my skin and brought with it a sensation I couldn't quite place, but which brought back a chill of discomfort.

"What is it?" I said.

"It's the reason we're here." Rockwell said, delighted. "The end of a year's worth of work."

"Then what are we waiting for?" I swept up my ax. "Let's tear this bitch down."

"No!" Rockwell immediately turned in front of my swing. I pulled back, losing my balance and hitting his shin with the edge of the handle. The end of the pick missed his knee by centimeters.

"What the hell?" I said. "Are you crazy?"

Rockwell stepped back, fighting the pain.

"Why'd you stop me?"

"Because we need to tell Danielle first," he hissed.

"What for? We're here. Let's just get to it."

Rockwell took my wrist. "No. We break that wall down now, we're all as good as dead." The depth of his seriousness was unsettling. He slipped the ax from my hand, tossed it aside and then kissed me. Moments later, he sent a deafening whistle throughout the tunnel and clapped his hands, rousing the group from their sleep.

"Let's go," he called out. His voice was deep and commanding. "We're leaving."

I took a step back. There was no doubt I had plenty of questions, but it was best I kept quiet until we brought word of our accomplishment to Danielle. Even though I wasn't keen on Danielle's actions of late, Rockwell knew more about what was happening than I did. She may have used a forceful hand to meet her goals, but if Rockwell trusted her and believed it was for the better, and for the good of the family, I felt obligated to do the same. That is, until I had reason not to.

Mumbles of sleep deprivation and exhaustion bounded about as Rockwell returned to my side. He took my hand and walked me through the group. "Don't worry about bringing anything with you," he said. "You can collect it later. Let's move."

Rockwell and I remained tucked together with our hands entwined nearly the entire way back. As we reached camp, Rockwell let go. I didn't want him to, but I was still fresh to the rules of relationships and couldn't fault Rockwell for his actions. From what I had read, showing affection for another was a fine line to walk, lest allow the fruit of jealousy to bloom in those close to the partners. Expressing your relationship as a social status, as if it would make you a better person or less socially awkward, always seemed childish and contrived. Yet it was radically addictive at the same time, producing a sense of pride that I had never before sought. I may have not been familiar with the aspects of the era, but I didn't want to ever lose the feeling, thus I had to obey the rules as best as possible. In as far as Danielle was concerned, no matter how much I wished to pronounce my love, I would need to tread lightly and allow Rockwell to express his desire for me in his own way.

Then I realized how barren the tunnel had become. I got chills from the emptiness and the somber quiet. Never had I walked the camps without seeing anyone trying to sleep, eat or look for something fun to do. I tucked my arms across my chest and joined the rest of the group in our slow and simple steps, attempting to understand what had happened. Rockwell was further out, taking his steps even more cautiously, his hand placed firmly on the butt of the pistol tucked away under his shirt.

"What's going on?" I said.

He gestured for me to remain quiet. I caught up to him as silently as I could.

"Wait here," he said, followed by a kiss.

"I want to come with you."

"Madeline." His objection was thwarted by the softness of my frightened glare. "Fine. Stay behind me." He looked back to everyone else. "The rest of you, stay here until we get back."

I kept a distance of a few feet behind Rockwell as we made our way through the tunnel. A few yards up, we finally caught sight of a couple of our sisters. They sat together tense and saddened, hardly able to turn up their heads to look at us. Further down, several more brothers and sisters sat together, some crying, others helping mend cuts and bruises that had been inflicted upon them, a sight that weighed my heart into my stomach.

"What happened?" Rockwell said, kneeling to examine our brother.

"There was a cave-in," Courtney said. Her voice was shaken.

"Where?"

"The main room," she said. "It was…" Courtney covered her eyes with her vibrating hand.

Rockwell massaged it gently and held her head. "Where's Danielle?"

"She's down at the end…"

"Is she okay?"

The tension in Rockwell's shoulders waned when she finally nodded. "She's with…" Her head suddenly snapped up to look at me. "Oh, god."

"What?" I said.

"Oh, god, I'm sorry," she said, lowering her head.

"What is it," Rockwell demanded. He lifted her head. "Tell me."

Apprehension covered Courtney's body. "It's Penelope…" she said so quietly, it was like a whisper inside a dream.

"Penelope." Before I had time to clear my head, I was standing over Penelope's limp body. A mound of dirt and rock had covered the mouth of the tunnel and blanketed her. Danielle tightened a piece of her shirt around Penelope's arm and wiped some blood from a cut on her face. I covered a scream and dropped to my knees.

Rockwell rushed up to us all and rested his hands around my waist as I caressed Penelope's face. "Is she all right?" I said, my lip shaking.

"For now," Danielle said. She sat back and bit her lips together with exhaustion.

"What happened?" Rockwell said. His voice was raised, overcoming the frantic noise from the rest of the family.

"Those rag bastards tried to bomb their way in here," Danielle said, adding, "Fuck me," for good measure.

"Are you okay?" Rockwell left my side to check on the cuts that plagued Danielle. She turned him away. "I'm fine."

Rockwell backed down. "Is everyone accounted for?"

Danielle's answer got caught in her throat for a moment. "I don't know. I think so. There was only a few of us in there when it all started to come down."

"What about the food? The weapons?"

Danielle shook her head.

"Damn it."

"We'll just have to dig in and get them," Danielle said, unconvincing.

"We don't have time for that," Rockwell said. "We just broke through the other side."

Danielle was shocked into silence. "What?"

"Surprise," Rockwell said.

"Don't fuck with me, Rock."

"I couldn't be more serious."

"You're shittin' me. You're shittin' me." Danielle suddenly lit up with a surge of frantic energy. "You're absolutely sure?"

"Yeah."

Danielle grabbed Rockwell and kissed him in excitement. It was only a friendly gesture to the upper cheek, but it hit me with great displeasure.

"There's still a massive problem. There's no way we can move forward on this."

"Why not?"

"We're all unarmed. Breaking through that wall now will get us all killed."

"So what. Without food or water, we're all dead anyway. I say we at least go down fighting."

"You don't care one iota for this family, do you?" I said. A tear dropped from my cheek onto the edge of Penelope's nose, clearing a trail through the soft layer of dirt.

"Madeline," Rockwell said.

"No, I want to hear this," Danielle said, drowning him out. "Go ahead. Explain to me why you think I don't care about this family."

I wiped my face clear and met Danielle's mockingly interested expression. "Look at what you've done," I said. "Look at what's happening around you. Everyone is scared, hurt and dying. Yet all you can think about is your own selfish objectives. If you cared for anyone here, you would be looking to help them before you helped your own god damned narcissism."

Danielle chided my remarks with the bite of her lip and her disheartening laugh. She looked to Rockwell, considering my words carefully, and then spoke lightly and without much power. "Allow me to respond."

Without warning, Danielle swept in around me. She grabbed my hair and pulled my arm behind my back. I felt my legs give way to hers and cut my knees as they hit the rocks below me. Danielle shoved my head down so that my nose was touching Penelope's.

"Take a good look," she said. "What do you see?"

I refused to answer.

"Danielle," Rockwell said, but without conviction.

"Back off," Danielle said to Rockwell. "What do you see?" she repeated for me.

"A dying child," I said.

"What else? Who is she?"

"My sister; my daughter."

"And what does she represent for you?"

"Innocence."

"And liberty. Penelope represents what everyone in this world lost a long time ago. She is what I've been fighting for."

Danielle released me and stepped back. "Always has been."

"But she never had a choice," I said.

"She made the most important choice anyone can make. She chose to love us."

"And look where that got her."

"This may sound callous, Madeline, but war takes lives. But when you fight for something that matters, heroes rise from the ashes."

"And you want to be that hero," I said.

Danielle flashed her frustration and chose to walk away, unable—or unwilling—to find any further arguments.

I chided her with a sneer and sat comfortably next to Penelope. I flexed my arm and rubbed my shoulder.

"It was Danielle that talked to Penelope," Rockwell said. He remained still a few feet from me.

"About what?" Part of me didn't want to hear what he had to say.

"The day we came back. Danielle was the reason you woke next to Penelope."

"What do you mean?"

Rockwell sat next to me. "When Penelope gave you the cold shoulder, Danielle went to her and explained why you had acted the way you did. You want to know what she said?"

I pursed my lips.

"She said that sisters sometimes disagree, which can occasionally lead to a fight like the one she saw. But it was only because you were both passionate about what you believed in and considers you an example of what Penelope should aspire to be. She then said that no fight should ever keep you from forgiving the ones you love and that Penelope should find it in her heart to forgive you, just as Danielle had."

I had lowered my head to hide the embarrassment between my knees.

"Danielle sees a lot of herself in you, Madeline, which is why she has trouble relating to you."

"Do you see her in me?" I said.

"I do."

"Is that why you slept with me?"

Rockwell was clearly offended. "That has nothing to do with this," he scolded.

"I know," I said, wishing I could take it back. "I didn't mean that. It's just, if we're so similar, why is the friction between us so exasperating?"

"Because you both want the same thing, you just have a different view of how to get it. And your pride keeps you from listening to the other."

"That's not on me," I said. "I have no problem listening to an argument when someone presents one. How am I supposed to conduct a thoughtful debate with Danielle when she keeps everything so close to her breast? The same goes for you. What exactly is behind that wall? What is so important we have to risk the lives of children in order to access it? Let me in. Give me a reason to care. What is it I'm fighting for?"

"Water," Danielle said. She stood calmly against the wall a few yards away. Her eyes were fixed on wiping her hands clean of blood.

"Water?" I said, puzzled. "All of this is about water?"

Danielle finally lifted her head and answered with her weary gaze.

"Wait, okay, you're telling me you've started a war to acquire water?"

"Not starting," Danielle snapped back. "Finishing. And this just isn't about acquiring water. This is about liberating those whose only access to it is through slavery and violence."

"That doesn't make sense. Isn't there plenty of water out there?"

"Sure there is. But only about five percent of it is anywhere near healthy enough to drink, unless you know where to look for it. We all need water to survive and the Muslims exploited that by taking control of all access to fresh water and forcing those who couldn't afford the process of cleansing into slavery."

"How is it they took control of them? How did they know what sources of water would be contaminated?"

"Because it was the Muslims who contaminated it."

"They did what?"

"As the different termite sects started to take their place in the new world, it was the Muslims who had the strongest foothold. For years, the Muslims had been buying up coal mines, oil fields, mineral farms and any other necessary fossil composites they could find, including water treatment centers, so they could strengthen their prominence among the lower orders. They also bought up what were considered at the time to be worthless, insignificant areas of land. What the people forgot to notice was what these parcels of land actually produced. With enough money and political power, it was easy to purchase anything you wanted. Except for water. That's the one thing the Muslims couldn't control, no matter what they did. Or so we thought, until they found the means of doing so. They shut down and destroyed all treatment plants and proceeded to contaminate every main water supply. Every ocean, river, mountain and stream became undrinkable."

"That's not true," I said. "I remember a river that was fresh and healthy."

"Are you sure about that?"

"Quite sure."

"Did anyone ever drink from it?"

"No," I said, a bit defeated. "We drank from our well."

"Did anyone ever swim in it?"

"It was forbidden for fear of rapid tides sweeping a child into the current."

"My point exactly. But you do bring up a good point. A lot of people had wells on their properties. But everyone was so scared of being killed for it, they were more than willing to pay any and all termites for the right to use it. Money was extinct by then, so the payment came from the well itself. I remember because I used to have one. If we didn't give the tyrants free access to as much water as they wanted, we'd be killed. That well dried up faster than you can say scrumdiddlyumptious. When that happened, you were basically shit out of luck. Convert, become a slave or die a slow death."

"I'm sorry to hear that."

"Not as sorry as I am for everyone who died when the water was first contaminated."

"Was it because they drank the water?"

"For some, others because of dehydration and still others because of the widespread violence that erupted. It wasn't until word spread that you could acquire water through other means that things started to calm, but for a couple of years, it was as if a second war had been started."

"What happened when your well ran out?"

"Ryker chose to barter with the scum rags. He never spoke about what he did to get it, but my mom and I knew they had to be pretty terrible."

"Is it the trade agreements he made for water that got him killed?"

Danielle turned her head down. "After I left him, I found out pretty quick what it was he was involved in. The cruelty of it all made me so sick, I couldn't sleep or eat for days. I would have killed myself over it if it hadn't been for Lila. She said something I'll never forget.

" 'Don't let it beat you. If you find it that reprehensible, fight to make it right.'

"So I made it my mission to take back the water supply. The first thing I did was track down a water courier to find out how I could become one. Turns out, a woman working in that capacity was unthinkable, and just mentioning it was blasphemous. I was taken into custody and jailed for even considering it. Over the next couple of days, I was starved and brandished with this scar."

Danielle lifted her sleeve. A long thick scar ran down the side of her arm.

"How did you get out?"

"Lila talked me out of the charges and secured my release."

"How did she do that?"

"She never told me and it really didn't matter. The objective was never to become a courier. It was to gain Intel on the compound that housed the mine."

"You wanted to be arrested," I said with pride.

Danielle smiled coyly. "It gave us everything we needed to know. Then it was just a matter of gathering enough people willing to fight for the cause."

"So if you had what you needed, why spend years digging a giant hole? Why not infiltrate the compound?"

"Because snipers were posted strategically along the outskirts of the compounds and the only way in or out were guarded by dozens of soldiers, with another hundred or so keeping watch inside, just itching for a reason to shoot someone's head off. There was no way a band of rebels was ever going to take the compound in a straight-up firefight. If we wanted to take the compound, we had to be smart about it and find a way to take them by surprise. What better way to do that then to slip in the back door through the very thing they were trying to protect?"

"The mine," I said. "You're going to try and steal the source from them?"

"Unfortunately, no," Rockwell said. "If that were even possible, stealing the water without wiping out the Muslims would just get us all killed."

"The only way we can guarantee that we can mine this water without fear," Danielle added, "is to wipe them out completely and plant our flag in victory."

"Are you sure this will be enough to do that? You just said there are hundreds of soldiers inside. What makes you think this group can beat them, even with the element of surprise?"

"You don't think I thought about that?" Danielle said.

"What do you mean?" Rockwell said. He was as genuinely confused as I was.

"You don't honestly believe I would have put this plan into action without a plan B, do you? I have a dozen people inside the compound as we speak, waiting for us to make our move."

"Why didn't I know about this?" Rockwell said.

"This was way before I met you, Rock. By that time, we had already acquired enough weapons that I didn't think I was going to need to bring them in on this."

"You should have told me. What if they had been found out?"

"It's possible at least one already has," Danielle said. Her voice cracked and was much lower than was normal. She knew more than she was letting on.

"That's how they found us," Rockwell said.

Danielle turned away.

"You had no right to keep this a secret."

"I did it to protect us," Danielle bit back. "If everyone knew we had people inside that compound, there's no telling what might have happened. The less people who knew about them, the better."

"You had no right," Rockwell repeated. "How am I supposed to trust you now?" He brushed past Danielle with a step of indignation and swept down the tunnel. I stayed close to Penelope, my eye strongly fixed on Danielle.

"He's right you know," I said. "It's because of your people being found out that this all happened."

"As far as I know, they only know about one of them."

"Who?"

"Her name was Safiya," Danielle said and my body chilled. "She was sent in to get close to the Imam, earn his trust. The last report I got from inside was that she was stoned to death."

Memories flooded my mind and I felt the rock hit my body in punishment for my forged insolence. My stomach churned and my head contracted.

"What's wrong?" Danielle said.

"Abdullah," I said. "The man who runs the mine. His name is Abdullah."

"Abdullah Shareef Mohammad. Yeah. How did you know that?"

I looked to Penelope and closed my eyes, needing to hide myself from the answer. "He hurt me once," I said.

"He's hurt a lot of people," Danielle said.

"So have I."

"What do you mean?"

I stroked Penelope's cheeks. They felt colder than before. "I killed her," I said.

"Killed who?"

"Safiya," I said, finding courage enough to look Danielle in the eye.

"You killed Safiya?"

"She was helping me. Grayland had been sent into the mine to work, and I was to become Abdullah's next wife. Safiya helped me to see him."

"That's not why she died. My report said she was accused of adultery and sentenced to death."

"Who do you think threw the first stone?" My head fell to Penelope's chest.

I felt Danielle's hand brush my back. Her silence was the perfect apology. Suddenly, I had a realization and a fresh surge of energy flowed through my veins. I turned up and looked directly into Danielle's eyes.

"I can lead you through," I said.

"Lead us through what?"

"The mine. I've been in them. I know where everything is. I can help you."

Danielle stood and took a step back, as if I had suddenly been infected with a virus. I stood to follow.

"What's wrong?"

"I can't have you going with us."

"Why not? It makes complete sense. Having someone to help guide you through those mines is an advantage. And, it would allow me the chance to pay that bastard back for all he's done."

"Exactly why it can't happen."

"What do you mean? That rag hurt me, hurt my father. Killed my mother and nearly killed my sister. I want to see him pay."

"That's right. All you can see is blood-red revenge. There's no doubt you're the perfect asset to have on this, but once this becomes about revenge, we're all lost. That's when innocent people die."

"But I owe it to you to help," I said. "I owe it to Penelope."

"You owe it to Penelope to keep her safe. Stay here. Keep her company in case she wakes up. Let us take care of Abdullah."

Danielle turned and called out for Rockwell. I wanted to follow, but she had a point. The only thing I could think about was seeing Abdullah's eyes when I put the barrel of my gun between them and pulled the trigger. But Penelope could die if I left her alone, and I couldn't have that on my conscience. Enough people had died because of decisions I had made. It was time to end all of that. I needed to listen to those who knew better than I did and let them take care of the problems that were out of my control.

I sat back down next to Penelope and sang her a song until the last brother had left. Rockwell came to me before leaving. He handed me his pistol.

"Just in case something unwanted finds its way down here," he said.

"Be careful," I said, setting the gun by my side.

"I will." He kissed me gently, lingered for several long seconds, and then was gone.

CHAPTER 39

I sang to Penelope for most of our time together. It was nice to believe that she could hear me as she rested, though that may have been simply an impossible hope. In reality, it was more a nervous reaction to my own apprehensions and my uncomfortable loneliness, which had noticeably depressed my senses. I wanted to sleep, but my eyes were too heavy; I wanted to eat, but my stomach turned with the thought; I wanted to move around, but my appendages were a trembling mess. Hearing the melody of my voice helped keep me calm and hide me from the thoughts of my mind, which whenever I listened, furthered the well of anger I had for Danielle.

It wasn't so much that I believed Penelope's accident was her fault, but that she didn't convey any sympathy or guilt for the consequences of her actions. She was supposed to keep Penelope safe, yet there was no remorse over her failure. But then, who really failed her? I chose to become Penelope's guardian upon Lila's death. It was I who took on the role of protector, and it was I who trusted Danielle. The blame for any mistakes had to ultimately fall on me, though Danielle wasn't completely blameless in what had happened. She placed those spies in the compound, and she forced me to work on the tunnel, events which led to Penelope being in that room when the attack happened. Then again, my thoughts were so focused on Rockwell and our companionship over the past few days, I couldn't remember the last time I had thought about Penelope up until I heard she was hurt. My first reaction when we arrived back to find the destruction was relief that Rockwell and I hadn't been there when it happened. That may have been my biggest remorse and the real reason I agreed to stay with Penelope when all I wanted was to be holding Rockwell's hand and leading the attack against Abdullah and his tyranny. It had all started in that mine, in that compound, and I had just as much right to fight against him as anyone. But Lila would have wanted me to be there when Penelope woke, to provide her with a hug and a sense of relief and comfort, something I couldn't remember ever receiving after such a traumatic event. My obligation to her and to Penelope's safety far outweighed my sense of retribution. When Penelope opened those pretty eyes once again—if it ever were to happen—I needed to be the first thing she saw. I just wish Danielle had stayed as well, to show that she did, in fact, care about Penelope the way she claimed she did. The confusion of it all left me tense and drained.

I had all but lost hope when I heard the first sign of Penelope's revitalization. I fell forward to brush her hair and whispered her name repeatedly, waiting anxiously for her eyes to open. When they finally did, they were followed with a sincere and loving smile. I tasted the tears on my lips as I pulled her into my arms and kissed her. Penelope chirped as I squeezed her hard against me. I apologized, and she forgave me with her bright smile. Suddenly, she grabbed her arm and vomited. I tried to relax her but nothing I did could stop the constant shed of tears, interrupted only by the gags on her own lack of breath. It was only when she passed out that it all finally stopped.

It was I who was now crying without end. By the time I had gained my composure, my eyes burned and kept everything blurred beyond recognition. Despite that, I watched Penelope closely, unable to take my eyes off her. The rise and fall of her chest had become less frequent and far less noticeable, and her lips had turned a rich purple. I felt so helpless and unworthy that my entire body shook with joy when she coughed and opened her eyes again. This time, I showed my comfort and affection through the gentle touch of my hand rather than with my full embrace. Once her eyes had fully focused, her dimples appeared gently against the dirt on her face and she took hold of my hand with her own proof of love.

"Mommy," she said. Her voice was so soft and full of innocence. I knew then she was an angel. She was my little angel, and I was happy to be here with her.

"I'm here," I said just as gently. "I'm here."

"I love you." Her voice drifted when her body suddenly tightened and shook dramatically.

I screamed out for help. I knew no one would hear me, but I was desperate to do all I could to help her, regardless of its viability. The loneliness was heavier now than it had already been.

"Don't do this, Penelope," I screamed. "Please."

When her body finally stopped shaking, it went cold. I tried to find any sign of consciousness, but her eyes were as dead as her body appeared to be. The only sign I had that life still coursed her body was the soft air that blew upon my cheek every few seconds as I held her tightly against me.

"I love you," I heard Penelope say again without warning. I laid her back on the ground quickly. She found the strength to produce one last smile before her last breath was taken.

I watched her a long while afterward, praying her life would return. When it was evident I was only dreaming for a miracle I wasn't worthy enough to receive, I kissed her one last time, holding my lips against hers for as long as I could bear.

"I love you, too, my child."

Screaming my outrage at the walls of the tunnel, I scratched and pulled on the rocks and dirt that sat above Penelope's body until I had dug enough of it away to completely cover her. I then sat and cried over her burial, washing my tears over her grave.

After a time, I realized it wasn't only Penelope's grave that I mourned over. It was that of my mother, my father, Miss Safiya and the shadow that covered the innocence of my past. They had all been stolen from me and no matter how much I wanted to blame it all on Danielle, there was only one person that was responsible for it all. His name was Abdullah Shareef Mohammad, and his death had to be at my hand.

I kissed the grave before rising with a newfound sense of determination and sprinted away from the last love he would ever take from me.

CHAPTER 40

Taking as little rest as I was able, I caught up with the group a few hours after leaving Penelope's grave. Everyone was taking their own rest along the wall of the tunnel, some chatting wildly while others attempted to sleep. The atmosphere of their collective spirit sparked my own wave of calming delight. It had been a while since it was this joyous among the family, yet I couldn't relish in it. My focus had to remain finding my way to Abdullah.

"Where's Danielle?" I said in rushed breaths. It was hardly audible, but my sister pointed me to the front of the group. I skirted through the crowd, stepping on some, kneeing others and pushing each of them from the path I traversed with nimble steps. My apologies came quick and vibrant, but insincere, as they were more a collective generality than a personal consideration. I was in far too much of a hurry to worry about that.

I found Danielle standing with Rockwell a few feet from the group. The disparity between them and the rest of the family was evident in their solitude. The mood was quite inert—focused.

I watched them carefully as I fought the burn in my lungs. "Danielle," I said clearly.

They both turned, Rockwell quicker than Danielle. His reaction was of pleasure and surprise; Danielle's was of confusion and abhorrence.

"What the hell are you doing here?" she barked.

Rockwell's excitement dropped into annoyance. He fell away, unwilling to lend his hand of support. I was on my own.

"I'm coming with you," I said.

"To hell you are. You're supposed to be watching Penelope."

My silence said more than any words could convey.

Danielle was suddenly laden with guilt. She leaned up against the wall and held her forehead. "Damn it," she said, hitting the wall.

Rockwell, with a saddened posture and a compassionate expression, hugged me for as long as he could bear. When he let go, his hand remained gentle upon my shoulder blade. "I'm sorry."

"Thank you," I said and kissed him. "I'll be okay." It was easier to say than to believe.

"It doesn't change anything," Danielle said. "I still can't let you come."

"Why not?" I said. Rockwell's touch no longer helped my tension.

"You're still a liability."

"That's not true. Not anymore."

"Then tell me. If you had to let the rag escape to save someone's life, you'd do it without hesitation?"

"There's no question I want to see that man dead. Does it matter if it's at my hand? Not if it means more good people must die. It's obvious that Lila, Penelope, Safiya and anyone else he had a hand in murdering deserve justice. But there are dozens of people here who believe in something more, just as they once did, and if I allowed any one of them to die because of detestable bloodlust, I could never forgive myself. This family conveys a great amount of devotion to you and to the cause you have implored on them. They are loyal, determined and righteous. None of them deserves the fate that has befallen those closest to me. I owe it to them, and to you, to fight for the future of the people who can't fight, to help give them freedom they once lost. If I didn't, then every death I've witnessed over the past year will have been in vain. I can't allow that. I fight for their souls. I fight for this family's protection. I fight for you. Abdullah be damned."

Danielle rubbed her foot against the wall. She didn't look directly at me to say what she had to say next.

"How long did it take you to come up with that bullshit?"

The shock stunned me cold.

"You cold-hearted bitch," I said vehemently under a light breath.

That got her attention. "I might be," she said just as intensely. "It's only because I'm honest. You should try it sometime."

I couldn't find words to convey what I truly felt. "My god, you are something else."

"What makes you think she isn't sincere?" Rockwell said.

"What makes you think she is?" Danielle bit back.

"I don't know, but from what I've seen over the last couple of weeks, I have to believe her."

"Thank you," I said.

"This coming from the nigger who wanted to leave her to die at the safe house."

Rockwell was painted with restrained rage. "I only saw a deceitful termite back then, Danielle. I didn't know the truth."

"And what would that be?"

"This woman has more integrity than anyone I've ever met."

Danielle seemed awkwardly betrayed.

"I'm not going to do anything that would cost anyone their life," I said, hoping to ease the hostility. "You trusted me once, Danielle. I will be forever grateful for that. All I ask is you trust me again."

Danielle's eyes were locked to Rockwell. "You've had a black cloud following you ever since we met you. I don't know if it's coincidence or something more, but I can't let my guard down, not when we're this close."

"You think something bad will happen if I go?"

Danielle finally looked at me. She didn't need to say anything.

"Then I won't go," I said.

Rockwell lowered his head, disappointed.

"If Danielle thinks someone will get hurt because I'm some sort of bad luck charm, then I'm going to respect that."

"You're not," Rockwell said.

"It doesn't matter. If she feels I am, it'll hinder her concentration, and for this, she needs to stay focused."

"Get them up," Danielle said to Rockwell shortly after. "We have to move." Danielle left us without another word.

Rockwell watched her, even after she disappeared into the darkness. I walked up to him and rubbed his back soothingly.

"You understand, don't you?"

"Yeah," he said. "It's bullshit, but I get it." He kissed me with just the slightest touch of his lips. "Come on."

He took my hand, and we rallied the family to their feet. It took us several hours to reach the wall at the end of the tunnel, where Danielle stood waiting. She had her back to us and didn't acknowledge our arrival with movement.

"How well do you know this mine?" she said.

"It's been a while," I said after a little bit of thought.

"Can you guide us through or not?" Her annoyance was uncontrollable.

"That was a dark time for me. I don't think I'll ever forget it."

Danielle pressed her hand to her forehead and then finally turned to us.

"Congratulations. You got your wish." She averted her eyes as she brushed past me, but I could still see a deep red waxed across her eyes. It didn't matter; the confusion and joy overwhelmed my senses.

"What changed your mind?" Rockwell said for me.

"If we're going to keep our advantage, we can't be wandering around blind with a bunch of torches. She knows where she's going and is the only one I know that's been trained to see in the dark."

I smiled slightly, unsure as to whether it was a compliment or not. I accepted it nonetheless and smiled graciously in recognition.

Danielle nodded her head ever so slightly and raised her arms to her family.

"Listen up," she called out. Her commanding voice silenced the group within seconds. "I know the last couple of weeks have been hard on everyone here. We have all lost friends and loved ones, and I hate to have to ask any of you to sacrifice even more. Unfortunately, it's a necessary evil. We lost almost all of our firepower in the cave-in and there's no guarantee we'll find much more than the pistols Rockwell and I have. Which leaves us in a very precarious position. We're so close to completing our mission, but to do so might mean suicide. At this point, I understand if anyone isn't up to fighting with me, and I can't ask any of you to risk your lives if you're even the slightest bit hesitant. For those of you who are hurt, or feel in their heart that they can't give me their life, you have my blessing to remain here. Head back down the tunnel and make camp no less than a half a mile from here. We will come and find you should we survive. If we're not back within a day's time, assume we have failed and do what you must. For those of you who are ready to see this thing through to the end, I will do my best to protect you, but that's the most I can offer.

"I'm very sorry I've had to put you in this position, but if we succeed, it will mean the end of Abdullah Shareef Mohammad's tyranny and bring freedom to a lot of deserving people. That alone is worth the risk. I respect each and every one of you and thank you all for your help and your sacrifice."

Danielle folded her hands together and rested her head upon them for several seconds. She then sat at the wall and waited for decisions to be made. Rockwell and I joined her, but remained standing, flanking her with protection.

The family took in her words with silence for some time before a wave of whispers floated about. The first to head back down the tunnel were the wounded, followed tentatively by several others, who kept looking back to us as if they would suddenly find the courage to change their mind. In the wake of it all, it seemed at first that no one was ready, but when all was said and done, sixteen brothers took their positions beside us.

"Thank you," Danielle said, giving each her gratification.

"The way I figure, we only have a short window of time to do what we need to do once this wall comes down before things go to hell. We'll need to move quick and quiet. We can't afford getting trapped in a firefight before we're ready. With Madeline guiding us through, and the allies we have inside, we hold the element of surprise."

"If our allies haven't all been killed," Rockwell said.

"I need to believe they haven't."

"That's a risk you're willing to take?" I said.

"I have to."

I accepted, resting my chin on Rockwell's shoulder. I scratched his back with the tips of my fingernails.

"What's the plan," one of the brothers said.

"How many guards are assigned to the mine?" Danielle asked me.

"It depends," I said. "During the day when everyone is working, there could be nearly a dozen patrols at any given time, while at night, sometimes no more than two guards were ever used to protect the cells."

"Okay, good. If I'm right, it's currently the middle of the night, so there shouldn't be any problems."

"And if you're wrong?" I said.

"Then I failed," she said. She took a moment to reflect on what she had said and then continued. "Once we get inside, Madeline will guide us to the main entrance and to where the slaves are being held. I'll take half of you to secure the mine, while Rockwell takes the rest to secure us our weapons."

"How do I do that?"

"If I'm correct, there should be a concealed shed to the north of the mine. That is where they keep their entire stockpile of weapons."

"At least it was," I said.

"We have to assume it still is," she said.

"That's a lot of assumptions."

"Right now, assumptions are all we have."

"Okay, then. Assuming you're right," Rockwell said, "how many guards will be on this shed?"

"That I don't know. What we do know is they will be protecting it, so it shouldn't be hard to find."

Rockwell looked to me with concern but didn't interject any other doubts. He knew she was right; we all did.

"Are we ready then?" Danielle said.

When no one said anything in return, Danielle grabbed an ax and rested it on her shoulder.

"If that's the case," she said with a sharp grin. "Let's take this bitch down."

CHAPTER 41

Danielle took the ax to the wall with tremendous force. Rockwell took up his own and joined her, each taking turns striking the wall until it had been eradicated. A cool mist with the scent of moistened rock brushed past us. It was a smell I wish I could remember fondly.

"Take this," Danielle said, handing one of our brothers her ax. "Back me up best you can." Rockwell did the same with his.

"You're up, pup." She gave my shoulder a strong grip.

My nerves shot into overdrive. I controlled my breathing but couldn't stop my hands from shaking. Rockwell took them in his and massaged them. I closed my eyes and found his calm sweetness overwhelm me.

"Find your way," I said softly.

I rested my hand on the wall of the mine and read its shape and its texture. I allowed it to take me inside and lead me. For a moment, I was unsure as to where I might be, afraid we had entered into a part of the mine I had never been. Then I felt something soft and cold on my feet. I picked it up and took in its odor, which brought painful tears to my eyes.

"What is it?" Rockwell asked, taking the shroud from me.

I wiped my mouth clean of the cloth's filth and lowered my head in prayer. "My past." Suddenly, I wasn't afraid. I tightened my grip around Rockwell's hand and confidently led them through the mine. Keeping the pace slow, yet steady, I was able to allow the walls to speak to me with clear resonance while keeping my ears sharp for footsteps of any approaching guard. As I regained the flavor of my senses, I was seduced by each crevice and protrusion of the mine, every moist lick on my fingertips and change in temperature on my palm.

That's when I felt the fire light the backs of my eyelids and returned to the reality that nothing lasts forever. Opening my eyes, I could see a row of torches lighting the fork I knew would come to split us up.

"Which way?" Danielle said immediately. Her voice was soft but commanding.

I pointed down the smaller path. "That'll take you to the cells. There are a couple of paths that branch off, but those are smaller than the main path."

Danielle checked her pistol. "Four of you with me. The rest, stay with Rock. Stay sharp, and get us our weapons. We'll catch up as soon as we can."

"Good luck," Rockwell said.

"You too." Danielle kissed him just off the corner of his mouth. "I'm sorry for what I said," she whispered.

Rockwell nodded and returned her kiss. I couldn't help but feel a hint of bitter resentment, which was hard to ignore, no matter how hard I tried.

Danielle held her hand to Rockwell's neck in appreciation and then was gone. Half a dozen brothers remained, each of who looked more frightened than I had ever seen them.

"What are we waiting for?" Rockwell said. It was hard to accept his hand, but I did and was soon free from my taste of jealousy. We navigated the mine together as one unit, our brothers holding back a few feet, keeping an eye out for anyone coming up behind us.

As we drew closer to the mouth of the mine, Rockwell and I took notice of a patrol stationed just outside. Two men paced across the opening and then stood at either edge for several minutes before trading places once again. A third held ground a few feet in front of them. All of them were equipped with large guns.

Rockwell pushed us all into hiding behind a small array of rocks. I tightened my grip around Rockwell's hand, revealing my sudden trepidation through my touch. Comfort and reassurance revealed itself through his. I kissed him and nodded with assertive trust.

He signaled the brothers to remain hidden and swapped his gun for the ax. He pulled the blade off and balanced it in his palm, familiarizing himself with its size and weight, and then handed me a small knife he had hidden around his ankle.

"We have to do this together," he said, rectifying my trepidation. "Wait here for my signal. You guys watch our backs."

Rockwell waited for the men to transition and then scurried across to the opposite side of the cave. He held his finger up and counted the time between crossovers. Once the men fixed their position again, Rockwell waved his hand forward, initiating our move. We both found our way to the entrance, where we fell against the wall. My grip was so tight on the knife as I counted the seconds away I nearly cut my palm. But it was of no matter. Just as the men turned to move, Rockwell signaled and we both swiveled around the edge. I grabbed the man around his mouth and pushed his head up, allowing the knife to slide across his neck.

Then I heard a shot.

I turned to Rockwell, who tore the gun from the guard's hand and fired it into the guard's chest, just above the wound that still held the pick. Before my kill had hit the ground, Rockwell was firing across at the third guard to silence the steady alarm.

"Damn it," Rockwell said through clenched teeth.

I dropped the knife and caressed the blood through my fingers as Rockwell grabbed the guns from the other two men. Without realizing it, our brothers joined us.

"What now?" one of them asked.

"Which way is it," Rockwell asked me. He grabbed my arm when I didn't respond. "Hey, Madeline."

I finally acknowledged him.

"We need to get to those weapons. Which way to the shed?"

"North," I said, still unclear. After a moment, I realized what was happening. "That way," I said.

Rockwell handed the weapons to our brothers and took his own pistol back. I was ready to follow them, but Rockwell stopped me and stared into my eyes.

"You still with me?" he said.

"Yeah," I said, a bit annoyed. "I'm fine."

It took a moment for him to believe me, but when he did, he gave me a swift kiss and grabbed my hand, the blood of our respective targets mixing into one another.

Suddenly, shots rang out, and we could see several rags running toward us. We ducked quickly back into the mine and found our refuge behind the rock.

"I'm sorry," I said.

"Let's just hope our guys get to that shed."

Several heartbeats later, the men were inside the mine. I couldn't pinpoint how many, but knew Rockwell needed to know.

"Six, maybe seven," I said as quietly as I could. "Flanked evenly on each side."

"They find us, we're dead," he said.

"I know."

Rockwell kissed me for what felt like the last time. It was full of passion and fear, love and bereavement. But it was the most honest kiss I had ever felt, and I took it in with the light of serenity.

When his lips fell away, the gunfire began. My heart thundered as I felt the bite of Grayland's wound and his call for my protection. I couldn't be sure as to how many men Rockwell had shot at any given time, but he would take cover after every few shots to regain his composure. One rag found his way past our cover, but Rockwell was quick to end his attack. I grabbed his gun away and gave it to Rockwell when his own gun ran out of ammunition. He used it with precision to continue our defense, though at times it felt as if the rags were multiplying with each shot.

It didn't take long after the rag's weapon fired its final round that the men cautiously stormed in after us.

"I love you," I said, resting my head to his chest.

"We're not done yet," he said. He squeezed my arm tightly. "Stay down."

Before I could object, Rockwell screamed out his surrender and raised his arms high. I shook my head, failing to remain strong for him, or for myself. He just smiled apologetically and slowly stood, resting his hands to the back of his head.

"I surrender," he said again and left me.

I remained curled up next to the rock, trusting Rockwell in his attempt to sacrifice himself to protect me. But when I heard the butt of a gun strike Rockwell to his knees, followed by a round of celebratory chants, I knew they had no intention of giving Rockwell any type of reprieve, and my goal would be lost in his death. So I gathered my courage and called out for my personal immortality.

"Spare his life. I beg of you. He was only protecting my own."

"Show yourself," one of the rags called out.

After a long relaxing breath filled my resolve, I stood. "My name is Madeline, wife of Abdullah Shareef Mohammad, and I demand you set this man free in accordance with his word through the love of Allah."

Rockwell lowered his head in what seemed absolute disappointment. I couldn't dwell on it, though. I wrapped my fingers together behind my head and walked slowly to his side.

"I wish you to take us to my husband."

"The wife of Abdullah is a traitor," one of the rags said and bloodied my jaw with his gun.

"No," I said, staggering to remain on my feet. I spit out some blood and stood erect.

"I was taken against my will. That man used me as leverage to escape. Once he was far enough away, he beat me and left me to die. This man was my refuge. Take us to him so that I may prove to you my allegiance to our lord and our God."

The rag grabbed my tender jaw and examined the scars on my face. Blood dripped from my lips, and I felt the pinch of excruciating pain, but I didn't fight him. The moment he sought the truth from my eyes, I made sure to reveal only the honesty of my convictions.

"Take her to the lord," he said and tossed me to the men behind him. They grabbed my arms, turning them red under their grip.

"Wait," I said "What of him? He is to come with me."

"His fate has already been written," the rag said.

"No," I cried, breaking my vigor. "I demand you spare his life, as he spared mine."

"Get her out of here," the rag said.

I let out another scream of defiance. I don't remember much after that.

(CHAPTER 42

By the time I became cognizant, I was lying in bed. The back of my head pounded and I could still taste the blood oozing from my gums. I quickly realized that my wrists were locked to the headboard, but I didn't attempt to break free of them. Sitting next to me, resting a knife to my throat was Abdullah. His robes were heavy with different materials and jewels, which contrasted with the humble, sparse surroundings.

"Welcome back, dear," he said. "You can imagine my surprise."

"My lord," I said, forcing a smile. "Why have you restrained me? I'm not here to harm you."

Abdullah wrapped his finger across my face. "Why do you lie to me?"

"I lie not," I said. The cold steel pressed more firmly against my skin. "I prayed each day for Allah to return me to you. Praise him for answering my call. Please allow me to prove my love." I licked my lips with just the very tip of my tongue.

Abdullah accepted my invitation, and I consented to his kiss with a generous tongue.

The knife was lowered from my neck and held near my breast. I followed the rise of his head as far as my locks would allow before breaking from the grip of his lips.

"My husband, I admit I was cruel to you once, but I was young and I feared a love I didn't understand. Being taken helped teach me what it meant to love, and how I could not survive without your touch and your protection. I have been waiting for this moment for a very long time. You must forgive my transgressions and welcome me back into our bed as the woman I was always meant to be—your wife."

Abdullah took my head in his hands and kissed me again. "I have thought of nothing but your betrayal over the past months."

"I am sorry," I said, my voice soft, tempting,

"When I saw you lying there, dressed as one of them, I was prepared to kill you."

"The infidels forced me to shed the cloth of our Lord, but it was a necessary sacrifice. I needed to gain their trust so that I could bring you their leader."

"And did you succeed?"

"She is defenseless, and her misguided love for her family will be her demise. I know where the cowards keep camp. We can wipe them all out. Together."

Abdullah smiled in devilment. He touched my body with the seduction for a mistress, and I was intent on enveloping it all with great pleasure.

"Before I bring you back into my bed, you will prove your loyalty."

He left my side and pounded the door three times. Soon after, two men dragged Rockwell's weathered, beaten body into the room.

I wanted to tear the locks from my hands and beat them all, but I kept my feelings subdued. "What have you done?" I said.

"He is one of them," Abdullah said. "I delivered justice."

"He wasn't one of them. He saved my life. He came with me to pledge his allegiance to Allah."

"He protected you, for that I am grateful. That does not forgive the atrocities he has committed upon my people. For these sins, he has been found a traitor and will die at your hand."

"Please, my lord. Spare him. He seeks not your head, but your heart."

"Prove to me that you do not also deserve his fate." Abdullah unlocked my chains and helped me from the bed. I rubbed the redness from my wrists as he walked me to Rockwell. "Kill the one you thought a friend, and I will accept you back into my bed, under the gracious hand of our Lord."

He handed me one of the guard's pistols. "His blood is your life."

"Yes, my lord." Without further hesitation, I buried the gun into Rockwell's shoulder blade and rested my hand on his neck. I lowered my head and whispered a prayer.

And then pulled the trigger.

Blood immediately poured from the wound, soaking into his clothes.

"Now we become one," I said, "under the blood and soul of our God." I tucked the pistol into my belt and kissed Abdullah with intense devotion and lust.

He grabbed a hold of me and threw me to the bed. The heat from the pistol seared my skin gently as a reminder of my sin. I sat up and curled my legs under my body seductively. He came to me, and we kissed with heated passion. I quickly forced him down onto the bed and straddled his waist. Settling, I stroked his neck with my nose, leaving behind a trail of warm breath in its wake, and cupped his hand in mine.

"I finally understand the meaning of true devotion," I said. "Now I wish to present to you my soul, as I should have given to you so long ago."

I swiped the restraint from the bed and locked Abdullah's wrist within. At the same instant, I pulled the gun from my belt and shot both guards with such precision, neither knew what hit them. I then shoved the barrel into the center of Abdullah's forehead, burning him in screams of rage.

"Devotion is sacrifice," I said. I pulled the gun from his head and pushed it into his hand. "And I'm devoted to the one who saved my life." I then put a hole into his palm.

"You bitch," he screamed. "You fucking flag."

"I'm not a flag," I said. "I'm not a termite, or a Muslim, or anything of the sort. I am Madeline of the Ark, and I am free."

I swung the pistol behind me and pushed it up against his penis.

"Fuck this."

I felt the burn of the shot between my legs. Abdullah screamed in rage and relentless pain as I rolled from the bed and over to Rockwell. I picked him up in my arms and checked his breaths. They were short and far between, but were present, and that's what mattered. It frightened me when Rockwell remained unresponsive as I pushed my fingers into the wound to retrieve the bullet. It took me longer than I had hoped, but I finally found it and tossed it aside. I quickly tore the robes from one of the guards and shoved it into the wound, tying the excess around his body the best I could. Rocking him in my arms, I couldn't help but believe Danielle was right. My sins had cost many people their lives that otherwise would still be alive. I didn't want to face her with that truth out in the open, but I couldn't let Rockwell die. With each breath, my soul cracked just a little, and I knew that only Danielle would be able to save him now. I had to sacrifice my pride for the one I loved.

"Devotion is sacrifice," I whispered and kissed Rockwell.

I stood with cold determination and a steel heart. A couple of guards were shot dead the instant they stepped into the room and it didn't stop there. Roving my way through the temple, I executed anyone who came before me as a loyal servant to Abdullah and his God.

A full war raged on the grounds of the compound. Each side traded volleys of gunfire in an unrelenting stalemate. I couldn't see Danielle, but the brothers had found the weapons hold and used its might to survive. But they couldn't hope for victory unless their opposition was diminished. The rags were all positioned at the temple side of the compound, which gave me the opportunity to swing the tide of this war, and I wasn't going to let it slip away.

I aimed and fired several shots before anyone realized my existence. By the time they had, I had killed almost a dozen rags and slipped back into the temple for my own cover. Hidden behind a corner of the main hall with a vantage of the main hall door, I made sure that every rag that tried to hunt me down found his death at my hand. After my ammunition had run out, I held my ground and waited for them to creep up upon me. When it was right, I kicked out the lead rag's knee, dropping him to the ground and whipped his gun into my hands, using it to take out those that followed him. What I didn't expect was for the wounded rag to sweep my leg and use the advantage to pull my arms to my back and pound my head to the floor.

He swiped the gun from me and shoved it into the base of my neck. I thought I had died when the shot rang out. But the rag fell off of me instead, and I saw his darkened, blood-soaked eye. I turned up and Danielle was standing over me, her hand held out. Though I didn't deserve it, I took it.

"Where's Rock?" she said.

Searching for the words broke the wall of my emotions. I didn't cry, but Danielle could see the turmoil and regret.

"Madeline. Tell me."

I took Danielle's hand and ran her to Abdullah's quarters, where Rockwell laid in a pool of his own drying blood.

"God damn it, Madeline." Danielle ran to him and immediately checked his vitals.

I fell to my knees and could no longer hold back. I cried hard and saw no end in sight to those tears.

"How could you let this happen?" Danielle said, not expecting an answer. She picked Rockwell into her arms and left the room.

I covered my eyes and just allowed everything to fall from me. I don't know how long I sat there, or for how long it took for our band of brothers to take control of the compound, but when it had all finished, I felt more alone than I ever had. I wanted to find Danielle, apologize for what I had done, but I had no strength to face her. And though I wanted desperately to know that Rockwell was okay, I knew now that it was better for everyone if I had never existed.

I walked from the temple. The family had found their way out of the tunnel and was helping to clean up the area. I was happy for their victory, and prayed for their continued survival. But I said nothing to anyone as I fled the compound, following the land as far as it would take me before I collapsed in exhaustion. It was then that I cried out to the sky above to take me before I found rest upon the bed of my sin and remorse.

CHAPTER 43

I'm still unsure as to how many days passed before finding the strength to move. My skin had been scorched redder than the painted petals on my arm, and my body ached in thirst and hunger. Where I would find food or water was beyond me, and I wasn't even sure I would even want it if and when I found it. Simply thinking about it made my stomach turn. Part of me felt I deserved to shake the hand of death and should do so with grace and dignity; yet it was impossible for me to give up now. The angel of mercy came to me when I had all but given up after Grayland's death, and it was in her breath that set in motion the events that would lead to so many unnecessary deaths, yet at the same time, a future that would see the liberation of many more. My purpose, it seemed, had ultimately been fulfilled, but how could I ever look my angel in the eye if I were to allow the sacrifice of so many to live in vain? There was much more I was meant to do, and if mercy returned to my side, I would allow their spirits to speak through me and guide my hand in benevolent charity.

My fate then chose to give its hand and offer me the shelter of a young, vibrant couple. They caught sight of me traipsing along the land they had recently been gifted, and felt it only right to pass their blessing onto another. Without pause, Katie and Thomas invited me in and supplied me with food, water, clothes and, most importantly, shelter. I returned the favor with my own generous hand, working the fields and harvesting the crops they chose to grow. At times, I grew extremely weary and sick, and still others would be as hungry as could be. Thomas thought that the heat stroke I endured hadn't been treated properly, while Katie, always with an amused grin, kept her own thoughts of what it might be to herself.

The next four months slipped by with grateful companionship. We enjoyed one another's company and never spoke ill of each other, not even when an argument broke out, because we were all very fortunate to have each other. Our love blended us into a solid familial unit, and none of us wanted to see that foundation break. But I had made a promise to help all of those less fortunate than I, and it was time for me to fulfill that promise.

I don't know why but I was surprised by how sympathetic Katie and Thomas were toward my desires. They prayed that night for my safety and the next morning bid me farewell with the invitation to return when I had completed what I set out to do. I kissed them both for their affection and understanding, and left them with a blessing of hope and renewal.

Executing my good intentions turned out to be harder than I had expected. The first few people I encountered were hypocrites and liars, claiming they were in need, only to reveal their greed through the wealth of envy they possessed, mostly for control of the new water supply that was being circulated throughout the various towns for free. Some were sadists wanting nothing more than to force me into their beds, and still others wished only for the hand of vengeance be laid upon their most insufferable enemies. I would have given up if it weren't for the very few causes I found worthwhile that littered my otherwise dire experiences. After a while, I learned how to distinguish between the wicked and the noble, which allowed me to choose my cases more wisely, leading to a greater number of people who deserved a helping hand.

About this same time, I noticed my stomach beginning to grow ever so slightly every day. It was odd to me, since my diet had not changed, and for a while I believed I may have caught a virus or had been infected by a parasite. It wasn't until I helped a woman gain access to several medicinal pills for her son that I found out what I assumed Katie had suspected all along but didn't want to jinx by saying it out loud.

"How far along are you?" the woman asked after helping to administer the pills. We sat next to her son, waiting to see if they would have any effect on him.

"Pardon me?" I said.

"It looks about six months."

"I'm sorry. I'm not sure what you're referring to."

"Your pregnancy." The woman pointed to my stomach.

I rubbed it gently and flashed a smile. "I'm not really sure."

"Don't worry. The first is always hard to gauge."

Her boy coughed, and I gently wiped some sweat from his forehead, calming him with my whispers.

"I have no doubt you'll be a great mother," the woman said.

I didn't say much else, and it was almost a day before I came to the full realization that I was carrying a child. I wasn't sure what to think, but as I was picking fruit from a flourishing brush, I felt a small kick and chills raced my skin. I placed my hand against my stomach and waited. When I felt the child kick again, it was clear to me that I could no longer sustain my current endeavors. All of my time and energy must be focused on protecting the child and giving her my best. I couldn't do that knowing that at any moment, I could be attacked or injured in some way. The absolute best thing I could do for her would be to return to the open arms of comfort and stability, a place I trusted and felt safe—a life I could happily call home.

My friends were overjoyed with the news of my pregnancy, especially Katie, who cried out, "I knew it," several times while smothering me in her arms. Only once did she ask who the father was.

"A good man who gave his life for me," I told her, which satisfied her curiosity. She did everything she could to help me over the weeks that followed. Thomas, at times, would appear jealous of the attention Katie gave to me, leading to the occasional argument. It was nice to know, though, that reconciliation always followed, usually in bed while expressing their love.

Two months later, as my stomach was now the size of a kickball I enjoyed playing with when I was young, and it became harder to move around, I asked Thomas and Katie if they would be willing to help me raise the child. Katie was more boisterous with her answer than Thomas, but he was nonetheless very excited to be part of my child's life, as I had become a sister to him and he a brother to me. I could not wish for a more honorable or virtuous couple to help raise this child, and it warmed my spirit to know that they would forever be an integral part of what I now considered to be our child's life.

That is when the unexpected twist of fate, as it will always be, presented me, for better or for worse, a new path to follow.

As I finished my usual afternoon walk along the fields of our home, a time I used to reflect and sing my graces for the child of my womb, I saw Danielle. She seemed humble and cast a shadow of regret as she walked toward me. Neither of us spoke a word before I took her in my arms and shared our forgiveness. We spoke very little as we ate dinner with Thomas and Katie, who found Danielle to be nice, yet reticent. That night, after they skirted off to bed, Danielle and I sat at the fire.

"They're nice," Danielle said. She took a sip from her cup of tea.

"I am blessed," I said, massaging the tip of my belly.

"I saw that. Congratulations."

"Thank you." I took a sip of tea. "And congratulations to you as well, I suppose."

Danielle flashed a smile. "It's been rewarding," she said. "But not as much as what I've heard about you."

"Me?"

"From what I hear, you've been quite the busy bee."

"Are you talking about my charitable work? How did you know that was me?"

"I pieced it together. They call you Ramiel."

"Ramiel?"

"The angel of hope."

I lowered my head and smiled.

"As the story goes, Ramiel is an angel who appears to those who cry out in need. If she believes them to be worthy of her praise, she helps them without any need of payment or gratitude, vanishing as mysteriously as she appears. If she deems their intentions to be less than honest, she will not appear and allow the wicked to squalor in their sin."

I had no words to express my wonder.

"At first I thought it was me they were talking about, but as time went on, more and more people were left waiting for Ramiel's help. Rumors began flying around that Ramiel was just a legend, that she never really existed. Ramiel was a fairytale someone made up to fool everyone. I took it as such and didn't think anything of it.

"That's when I talked to a woman who claimed she had received Ramiel's help. When I asked about her, she told me that Ramiel wasn't an angel at all, but a young woman looking to fill a void in her life. I asked why she thought that, and she told me it was because she was pregnant and didn't realize it. She said she looked distraught and confused. I asked if she said anything about where she might be going and the woman said, 'Home.'"

"Then how did you find me?"

"I followed the trail of bread crumbs. I asked around about you, to see who might have gotten your help in any way. From what I could tell, as I traveled away from the more populated areas, there were only a few isolated instances that matched what I was looking for. Eventually, those incidents led me in this direction, and when I figured out where I was headed, I just knew."

"You knew of this place?"

"This was one of the first lands we liberated from Abdullah's control. I never met them personally, but from what I had heard, they were good people. I hoped I'd find you here."

"Why have you been looking for me?" The question felt cold.

"I was angry with you, Madeline. But I never wanted you to leave."

I took a sip from my tea and tried to understand what she meant. "How could I stay when there was no way you could trust me anymore?"

This time, Danielle lacked for words. She set her tea down and moved next to me. "It wasn't you I didn't trust, it was what might happen if you were with us I didn't trust."

"I don't understand."

Danielle took my hand. "If what was going on between you and Rock was real, I knew that if you were with us and were in any sort of danger, Rock would do anything to keep you safe. I was trying to protect both of you by keeping you away."

I gave Danielle my affection.

"I was hoping that once we took the compound, you would be there to help Rock and I deliver the supplies and earn your place in our family. But judging from what you've done over the past few months, I think that qualifies."

We enjoyed a small laugh. "Thank you," I said. "I appreciate your candor and I do love you all, but I have a new family, one who has cared for me and given me more than I've ever needed. I can't leave them."

"Not even for Rockwell?"

It was the first time I had ever heard Danielle speak his full name and it fluttered my heart to think he was still alive. "What do you mean?"

"I understand what you have here is special, but I also know Rock holds a unique place in your heart. I believe that is enough to help him once and for all."

"What do you mean help him?" I said.

"Madeline. Rockwell is still alive."

I stole my hand away from Danielle and almost dropped my tea. "How is that possible? He was dying."

"He lost a lot of blood, that's for sure, but that tourniquet you provided him kept him alive long enough for us to help him."

"How?"

"There was a hospital I knew about some ten miles from the compound. It had been eradicated for the most part, but it's where I always went to gather supplies and knew it had what I needed. We got him on an IV and patched him up best we could, but he's never fully recovered from the shock and blood loss. He's been in a coma ever since."

"But he's alive?" I still couldn't believe it.

"And I thought that if you were able to talk to him, to let him know you were there waiting for him, that he has a child on the way that needs him, he might find his way back to us."

"Is that even possible?"

"Love is a powerful drug," Danielle said.

I set my cup down and looked at my stomach.

"All I ask is you sleep on it." Danielle kissed me goodnight.

I watched her sleep until the red light of morning broke through the window. The conflict over whether to stay with the family I needed, or return to the family I belonged to, raged within me even after Danielle had risen. I asked my heart to guide me and continued to pray on the matter through breakfast. By mid-day, as Thomas and Katie toiled in the fields, the choice my heart kept calling out for was clear.

"I will go back with you," I said to Danielle.

Danielle hugged me with gratitude. That night, I sat down with Thomas and Katie and took their hands in mine.

"I'm sorry to have to say this," I said, holding back my sadness, "but this will be my last night I spend with you. I thought the father of my child had died, but it turns out, he's still alive, and he needs my help."

"You can't go," Katie said through tears.

"I have to."

"Why?"

"I know how it feels to have lost a father before I ever knew him. If there's a chance that he can be a part of her life with me, I have to take it. You are a wonderful, young couple, and I love you both dearly, but you have to let me go."

"But I was so looking forward to taking care of her," Katie said.

"I have no doubt you will be blessed with many children of your own to care for, and know that any child you may have will be blessed to have you as parents. Because of that, I hope you can understand why I must give my child hers before it's too late."

Katie didn't want to let go, but Thomas convinced her that it was the right thing to do. She hugged me tenderly and wished me the best of luck.

"You are welcome back here any time," she said.

"I love you," I said and kissed her. "You will always be my sister."

The next morning, Thomas and Katie graciously took Danielle into their arms and asked her to protect me and my child before collecting me for one last grace of affection.

As I watched them shrink into the distance, I blew them one last kiss and whispered to the wind.

"God bless."

CHAPTER 44

Danielle had designated all of the vehicles at her disposal as delivery units for supplying the communities with water, so she packed what she needed for a week's time and departed on foot. Alone, it would have taken Danielle about a day and a half, with minimal breaks to return to the hospital. But because of my condition, she was forced to take longer and more frequent breaks than she had expected. When I attempted to push myself, my back and legs grew wearier and the sides of my stomach cramped, sometimes excruciatingly so, making it hard for me to breathe. Danielle was mindful of these issues and did her best to keep her temperament in check. We spoke very little other than to communicate when and how long I could walk. When we did speak at length, mostly to pass the time during longer meal breaks, we told stories of our time apart. It was when Danielle talked about Rockwell that gave me the strength I needed to keep going, thinking of once again accepting his touch.

It took us over three days to reach the hospital, which at the distance it first came into view looked to have been completely incinerated. But as we inched closer, I could make out deeper wells within the structure that still stood strong against the weakened steel bearings.

"What happened here?" I said as we reached the outer wall.

Because of the way the hospital had been built, there weren't any points of entry that hadn't been destroyed or completely sealed shut. Climbing through the rubble was the only way to get inside.

"This is nothing compared to most. Hospitals and medical practices alike were a main target of the termites long before the war even started. Several policies the government passed in the early part of the century slowly wore down the capability of hospitals to operate effectively. By the time the war struck, half of them had been closed down due to lack of funds or the inability to sufficiently execute the new laws. The rest were systematically targeted for destruction during the war."

"That seems odd. Why destroy the hospitals?"

"What better way to defeat your enemy than to take away their only means of medical help? Hundreds of thousands of people died by infection alone, you can imagine how many died because they lost access to adequate care or the means to treat wounds or extreme illnesses. The idea was to weaken by stripping away the ability to heal."

"If that's the case, how did anyone survive?"

"When news broke that hospitals were being destroyed, some facilities took necessary steps to protect as many as they could. Rumor has it only about a dozen remain standing. This is one of them."

"Have they all been abandoned?"

"I can't speak for all of them, though I can't see how they could be, what with the production of medicine as extinct as officially licensed doctors. This hospital was plagued by a viral outbreak sometime near the end of the war. It was sealed off, and anyone caught in the quarantine died within days. No one wanted to come close for fear of being infected and it was considered lost."

"How did you know you wouldn't be infected?"

"I didn't. Before I met Rock, I didn't even think twice about it. All I wanted were medical supplies, and I hoped to God it was still stocked. You can imagine my surprise when I found the remnants of all the people who died here. It wasn't until I met Rock that I learned about what actually happened."

"Rockwell was here when it was infected?"

"Rock wasn't. But his mother was. She was a surgeon here when the outbreak happened. He couldn't have been more then four years old."

"My god."

"Yeah." Danielle and I stepped from the debris, and I sat down on the bench nearby.

"He told me his mother died when he was young, but I never knew how."

"He never liked talking about it, but she was his inspiration to do something meaningful once he sobered up. He worked hard with Lila to learn all he could about medicine, and for a while was a leader in black market care."

"Why did he stop?"

"Because our cause became more important."

"It's a shame he couldn't do more," I said.

"Maybe he still can," Danielle said, taking my hand. "Come on."

Danielle helped me to my feet and we walked to Rockwell's room. I was reluctant to follow her inside. He appeared at peace, and I didn't want to disrupt the tranquility.

"Don't be afraid," she said and waited patiently for me to find my courage. She stood at the foot of the bed as I sat beside him.

Tears flooded my eyes as I kissed his hand and watched his chest rise and fall. The stillness of its motion was so intoxicating that I had not noticed Danielle's departure. It finally occurred to me that I was alone with Rockwell for the first time since we conceived our child, and it felt wonderful to do nothing but explore the silence of our world together.

"My beloved," I finally said after a long while. I held my hand on his face and caressed his beautiful, rugged features. "I'm sorry I left you in such a fragile state. I was scared. I didn't know what else I could do. Danielle was right; I tried to protect you by focusing on a personal vendetta, and it cost us both our lives. I couldn't bear to look Danielle in the eye with the guilt I felt over what I had done. Never once did I think you would survive the wound I inflicted with my own hand. I spent the next few months seeking reparation for spilling your blood to earn the trust of a man who deserved less than death. But the more I sought it, the more I did to rectify my feelings, the more I knew nothing I did could change what I had done.

"Then I learned that your seed had flowered within me a new life. And suddenly, your soul was with me once again, and a fresh light infected my heart.

I rested his hand on my stomach. The child kicked, and I couldn't help but laugh. "Did you feel that? It's our child, Rockwell; our bodies combined as one. A life we must lead, a heart we must guide and support.

"I had always been taught through the tales of the fruit that when the earth felt it time for the treasure of a child be gifted upon the land, that the flower of life would bow and bear its fruit to the purest and most humble. It is only most recently that I learned a child was not born of the flower, but of the mother, and though I encouraged the legend of the fruit to flourish as the truth behind the lie, I knew deep down that it was just that. There was no reason behind the birth of a child other than that of a mistaken act of attrition. It was never only the most pure or the most humble who received the gift, so how could a child ever be considered anything but a product of sin?

"But as I have become more aware, I can see there is a much deeper meaning behind the legend. The flower that produces life is the woman, and it is only when she is ready to accept the gift that only her body can provide that she bear her fruit to the one she deems the most pure and humble, allowing him to plant the seed of new life upon the earth.

"You are my chosen life, and I cannot raise this child without your hand to help guide me. Please, Rockwell. Feel our fruit and come back to me. I need you more than ever. I love you."

I kissed him and laid my head on his chest.

For the next two weeks, I remained by his bedside, singing to him and praying for his awakening. Danielle would join us on occasion to check up on him or bring us food. She would sometimes lie next to me and hold my hand as I slept, if only to help give me comfort in knowing that Rockwell was with us through her hand.

It was one of those nights, after Danielle held me when I couldn't sleep, that I woke suddenly with a painful cramp. It didn't last long, and I thought perhaps it was the byproduct of a dream or a minor illness. Adrenaline kept my heart beat rapid for another minute or so after the pain had gone away, but it was difficult to return to sleep, especially now that Danielle had gone. I walked around the room a bit, hoping this might calm my nerves, but the more I did, the more awake I felt. I sat down at the window and took in the night, wondering if that was where Rockwell had been all these months, or if dreams were allowing him life as he healed. I rested my head across my arms and could feel myself begin to drift away when another cramp woke me up. This one felt longer, but there was no telling how long it had taken me to fully realize the pain from the first cramp. When it had subsided, I lied back down next to Rockwell and took his hand. The cramps continued to attack my body more frequently, as did the need to urinate, which kept me awake for the remainder of the night.

As day broke, I rose to head for the bathroom once again when I felt fluid pour down my leg. This was followed by a much longer and more intense cramp that forced me to drop to my knee and let out a soft yell. Courtney must have heard me because she was next to my side before the cramps had stopped, frantically asking if I was all right.

"Get Danielle," I said when the pain subsided and I was able to breathe normally again.

Courtney was quick to acquiesce and returned with Danielle just before another cramp tore at my body.

"Breathe," Danielle said, calm and collected. She held my hand as she examined the musty colored fluid on the floor, waiting for me to relax once more.

"What's happening," I said, my eyes red with panic.

"By the looks of it, I'd say you're about ready to calf."

I looked at her quizzically and she couldn't help but laugh.

"You're in labor, Madeline."

My joy in hearing those words was overshadowed by another wave of cramps.

"Help me get her up," Danielle said, pulling my arm around her neck as Courtney grabbed the other.

"No," I said through clenched teeth.

"Madeline, we need to get you to a proper room."

"I don't care. I'm not leaving him. This is his child, and he deserves to be with me for this."

Danielle was sympathetic. "Fine," she said, lowering my arm. "Courtney, I need you to get some blankets, water, surgical scissors, clamps and some gauze."

Once Courtney had left, Danielle grabbed a couple of pillows from the chair for me to lie on and then pulled away my pants. It felt rather uncomfortable, but I allowed her to spread my legs apart and check what was needed.

"Hang in there," she said. "It looks like it might be a couple more hours."

When Courtney returned, she brought with her several curious brothers and sisters. Danielle was quick to send them away, but I could still feel them lingering just outside. Courtney was the only one to stay and sat with her arm around my head, dabbing the sweat from my brow while feeding me water whenever my body relaxed. Every so often, Danielle would check to see if I was ready to deliver the child and always responded in the negative. I wasn't quite sure how she could tell, but I trusted her and continued to bear through what Courtney began to refer to as contractions, even though their intensity became almost unbearable.

Finally, after what seemed like a day, Danielle smiled bright and positioned herself on her knees as close to my body as she could. "I think we're ready. Madeline, on the next contraction, I want you to push."

"How," I said naively.

"Just do what you would if you were taking a shit," Danielle said rather vulgarly.

I did as she asked. When the next contraction hit, I tensed my body and pushed as hard as I could. The pain was excruciating, and it didn't feel as if anything had happened.

"She's crowning," Danielle called out and I could feel the tips of her fingers resting on the tips of my inner thighs.

Courtney smiled brightly, anxious and excited. She poured a little water over my head and took my hand. "You're doing good," she said.

"I want Rockwell," I said. I reached out for Rockwell's hand and Courtney was more than eager to help me. She cupped her hands around ours as the next contraction bit me.

"Push," Danielle called out, and this time I felt something break through. "You're doing great," she called out.

Just then, I felt Rockwell's hand tighten around mine. At first, I thought perhaps he had woken from his coma, but as we all looked up to the bed, we could see his body floundering about, seizing uncontrollably.

"I need help in here," Danielle cried out.

All of the brothers and sisters waiting anxiously outside came rushing in, frantic. Our sisters came to Danielle's aid as the brothers flashed toward Rockwell. They administered several shots before I could no longer concentrate on him. After my next push, I felt Rockwell's grip fall dead at my touch, but I didn't let go.

"Just one more good, hard push," Danielle said, and I obliged. Within seconds, the tension in my body eased and I felt a surge of blissful emotions course my body.

Then I heard the light cough and the first cry of my child.

"How is she?" I said.

"He's fine," Danielle said just as joyfully.

Courtney brushed the wet bangs from my face. She kissed me with a sweet congratulatory smile as Danielle worked on completing the delivery.

"Can I see him?" I said.

Danielle didn't say anything for a few minutes, but finally, lifted my child up off the floor, wrapped in a thick array of blankets, and handed him to me. As my sisters and I took our first look at the precious features of my little boy, Danielle slid up to help our brothers at Rockwell's side.

"What are you going to name him?" Courtney asked vigorously.

Without pause I whispered, "Ryker Trevor Rockwell," and kissed him.

But through all of the admiration came the cold touch of demise. Danielle urged Courtney to step away and knelt down to my side. "He's lovely," she said, flashing a saddened smile. I knew then of Rockwell's fate, and though Danielle's sympathetic kiss couldn't quell my sadness, the breath of my child kept me strong. In Rockwell's death came a new soul that he could live through in all eternity.

"May I have a minute alone?" I said.

Danielle insisted everyone leave and then sat down between my legs again to check on any bleeding. "Don't move," she said, explaining what was still to come to complete the birth. She then left me alone to cry my love through my song.

(CHAPTER 45

Rockwell's funeral was lovely, with many reminiscing about the joys he brought to the family and what his presence meant to each of them. Danielle and I were the most soft-spoken, unable to express our individual love for him. At the time, we both needed to keep our most beloved sentiments and memories closely guarded. I remained with him long after everyone else had gone to enjoy a meal in his honor and sang him his final lullaby. It was only until Ryker woke that I chose to retreat indoors and escape the onset of nightfall.

Though encouraged to eat, I apologized and found a quiet room to explore the thoughts that had been festering for the last few days and allow Ryker to suckle my breast. As I shifted Ryker to begin feeding from the opposite breast, Danielle knocked and asked to come in.

"Please," I said politely.

Danielle blushed lightly and hid her eyes from us as she entered.

"Don't be embarrassed," I laughed. "It's a biological honesty."

Though she was extremely uncomfortable, she sat next to me and watched Ryker eat. "You're good with him," she said.

"I never thought I could be," I said.

"Why not? I saw how you were with Penelope. You're a natural mother."

"Thank you."

"What's wrong?" Danielle could clearly see my disquiet.

"Nothing," I said softly.

"Don't lie to me. Something's got you in a funk. Talk to me."

I felt Danielle's sincerity. Her hand rested on my knee with the touch I remembered as a kid when being solaced or taught a lesson of acceptance and patience, and for the first time, completely trusted her without constraint.

"It's been hard for me to remember them," I said finally, looking her directly in the eye.

"Remember who?"

"The family who raised me. I have great memories of them and can feel them within me, but I'm having trouble remembering their faces, their names. Even my experiences seem to be fading."

"You've been away a long time," Danielle said. "It's only natural that new experiences would overwrite the old ones."

"But they were my family. How could I forget them so easily?"

"You haven't forgotten them, Madeline. You just don't need them anymore."

"But I do."

"You don't. Look, before you showed up, Grayland was more of an afterthought than anything else. I'm not even sure the memories I still have of him are real, or just what I want to remember. The same thing will happen to you. In a few years you won't be able to remember Rock as clearly as you do now. It's just how it is."

"But I don't want to lose who I am."

"You'll never lose who you are, Madeline. Just because names and faces fade doesn't mean your experiences do. Everyone in our lives shapes us, for better or worse. We just need to accept that sometimes you just have to let go. It's how we grow."

"I guess." I pulled Ryker from my breast and lifted him over my shoulder. "It scares me to believe that such an integral part of my past could vanish like smoke in the wind." I tapped Ryker gently on the back.

"What can I say? That's life."

Ryker burped, and Danielle and I both laughed lightly. I wrapped him across my chest and rocked him to sleep. My posture suddenly became languorous, which caused Danielle's to follow.

"You want to go back, don't you?" she said.

"I don't know," I said, half lying. "Maybe."

"Why? You have a family, Madeline. Here, with us."

"And I love you all very much. I just feel that going back may be better for Ryker."

"Why's that? You don't trust us?"

"No, please don't think that. It's just…" I trailed off, trying hard to find words of honesty that wouldn't hurt Danielle.

One of our brothers knocked and shied away suddenly upon seeing my breast. I covered up and he spoke in a blushed flurry.

"Danielle, we got word from the mine."

"Thank you," Danielle said. He was gone before she finished.

"You have to go," I said.

"We have to keep fighting if we expect to get back what we lost. This is our chance to get a foothold in another major water supply."

"When will it ever end?"

"I don't think it ever will."

"And that's why I can't stay," I said. "It may be hard for me to remember precise details, but my previous family had a peaceful, nurturing atmosphere. Their love was pure and unconditional, without regret, without jealousy."

"He can have that here." Danielle's voice was incensed.

"I wish that were true, but this world will never be at peace. You just said so yourself."

"Yeah, but you can't protect him from the evil in this world. The most you can do is teach him right from wrong and hope for the best."

"You're wrong. When something doesn't exist, how can a child ever learn of it?"

Danielle turned her back to me.

"He deserves a life free of sin," I said. "I can't give him that while fighting for our freedom from it."

"You're making a mistake."

"I'm only doing for my son what my mother did for me."

Danielle turned, enraged. "Lila thought you were dead. No matter what she might have told you, she never looked for you because, for her, it would've been in vain."

"I don't believe that." I stood to match Danielle's authority.

"Why do you think she replaced you?"

I wanted desperately to hit Danielle, but Ryker weighed down my arms. "Lila was a good mother and an even better woman."

"I agree."

"Whether she thought I was dead is irrelevant. She chose fate over her own selfishness, and that's the lesson I'm choosing to follow."

"So you've made up your mind."

"I guess I have."

"Tell me, then, what makes you think you'll find this place again? Or if it's even still there?"

"I don't. But I have to take that chance."

"Why?"

"They're my family."

"I'm your family."

"And I love you dearly. But no matter how much you want to change the world, I'm afraid that can't happen without first changing the views of the child. The only way to do that is to raise them in the absence of bigotry, corruption and vice, which is impossible when so much of it exists, ready and eager to envelop the soul."

"It's a fucking dream, Madeline."

"It was my life."

"Exactly. *Was* your life. This world may not be perfect, but that's how humanity works. Nothing can ever change the human spirit. You can raise your kid with whatever barriers you want, but eventually, all the walls you've built up will come crumbling down. With everything you've learned, what makes you think it will be any different for him?"

I was silenced.

"Whether you like it or not," Danielle continued, "you've been corrupted. There's no going back."

"I have to try."

"You're fucking hopeless, you know that?"

"Why can't you just respect my decision?"

"Because you're letting your emotions dictate your actions. Think a minute and take stock in what you're trying to find and what you'd be leaving behind."

"I already have."

"No, you haven't. You're kidding yourself if you actually believe that."

"Why? What makes you think I haven't thought this through?"

"Because..."

Danielle pulled me close and kissed me, not as a friend or as a sister. She kissed me as she would a lover. Once the initial shock wore off, I found the tender passion within it and didn't want to let it go.

We looked into one another after. *Stay with me*, she said with the burn in her eyes.

"I'm sorry," I said and kissed her again. I lingered next to her with my cheek tickling her own and my hand rested gently across her neck. I caressed her lower ear with the tip of my finger. "I'm sorry," I said again and retreated from the room.

I left the following morning without seeking her farewell. If I had, I wouldn't have had the courage to leave, and it was imperative that I give Ryker what he truly needed—the fruit of blindness to the chaos of our hearts.

CHAPTER 46

Danielle's kiss resonated more intensely with each passing day. Whenever I grew cold or felt alone with doubt, the taste of her lips and smell of her skin warmed my body to the point of laughter and the need to please myself through the ghost of her touch. Her aura seduced me even in my dreams, touching her as I once did Rockwell and swimming in the comfort of her eyes.

Whenever Ryker would wake with cries of loneliness and hunger, the seal between reality and fantasy would break, causing the world to waft into the fog of night and leave me saddened with the realization that it was just a dream. The uncontrollable urge to return would never quite fade as I fed him, or as I rocked him to sleep, and it took every ounce of my will to keep from turning back. It wasn't until the third night, when I almost cried after Ryker pulled me from the dream, that I knew if I truly wanted to escape the sins of the world, I had to do as I once did with her father, as I once did with my lover, and stop holding on to her with such vigor. It was going to be painful because it meant breaking my own heart, but for the health of Ryker, and for my own sanity, I needed to sever Danielle from my consciousness and my soul.

After Ryker fell back to sleep, I walked several yards from our camp and took to breaking the magnetic hold Danielle had on me. I turned my thoughts against her, focusing on the attributes that made her the cold, vile woman who would have killed me without regret if had it suited her own arrogant interests. I cursed her name and screamed out for her death, blaming her for those that had been taken from me. I flushed any and all doubts from my mind, which turned to fierce tears of remorse, a feeling of stupidity forever trusting her. I didn't like it, but I forced myself to believe everything I said and eventually cried myself to sleep. I fell into a dream that brought her kiss back to me, but which forced me awake when her skin began to scale and she licked my scars with a split tongue that crawled from the mouth of her father.

Sweat covered my body, and I couldn't find sleep again. With Ryker in clear view, I chose to take a walk around the camp to clear my mind. Whenever thoughts of Danielle tried to poach my mind, I suppressed them, leaving me a bit shallow and empty. As I incurred the depression that filled the hole I had created, I dropped to my knees and watched Ryker sleep. His stillness and peaceful innocence helped me remember why I did what I did and gave me the spark of hope I needed to continue. He was the beginning of a new life, and I yearned for his warmth in my arms.

As I crawled toward him, the butt of my hand hit what I thought at first was a rock. But upon further examination, it looked like the bind of a book. Curious, I dug the dirt away and pulled it from the earth. The jacket was worn and the edges of its pages were torn and weathered. There was an imprint on the cover that I didn't recognize at first but which stunned my senses the moment I set my hand upon it. I closed my eyes and wept as I took in the memory of my fathers, my teachers and my family. But what I remembered most prominently was the vague touch and sweet whisper of a sister who I had long forgotten; a girl, now a woman, who urged me to rise and live my future at a time when I was lost and incapable of strength; a friend who only wished me the best even when my choices hindered our partnership.

"Cleo," I whispered at the same time her smile washed across mine.

I opened the book, hoping it would continue to pull my memories from the depths of my mind, but all I found were blank, yellowed and crumbling pages. I was about to give up when a leaflet fell from the center of the book. I picked it up and read the words imprinted upon it.

** ** **

The Traveler and His Guide

Before our time there once lived a traveler. He was meek and young, and trusted without fear. Those that met him all admired his honesty and his integrity, including a young lady with eyes of water and hair of gold, who fell in love with the traveler with a simple glance. She asked for him to marry her, but he could not, for he was on a quest that he could not deter. When asked of his quest, the traveler spoke of the legendary point of purity, the only place in the world for which was absolutely perfect, with nary a flaw. The lady fought to make him reconsider, but the traveler had his eye set on his prize and would not end his journey until he could drink from its water.

"Do not go," the lady cried upon his final day in her arms.

"I must," the traveler replied. "I promise I will return to you upon the conclusion of my quest with a cup of its water, so that we may drink upon it as one."

"I do not wish for a cup of water from this place," the lady said. "I only wish for you and I, as we were meant to be."

"I cannot stop," the traveler said, "else I may never know the truth of its legend."

"Take this," the lady said, presenting the traveler with a medallion from around her neck. "And remember me."

The traveler presented the lady with a farewell kiss and with that, continued on his quest, spending the next twenty years of his life searching for that place of pure perfection. He rested only when he was hungry or tired, traveled until his feet were blistered and his heart was heavy and never allowed himself to be deterred from his quest. Even when he was told that no such place existed, he sought it. Through it all, he never forgot his promise to the lady.

One searing morning, as the traveler rested in the shade of a lone palm in the middle of the sunken desert near a small, but delightfully cool stream, an older man, masked and feeble, appeared upon the traveler with a dry tongue.

"May I drink of your water, kind sir?" the feeble man asked.

"Help yourself, my friend. It is not my water to give."

"Thank you, thank you, sir," the feeble man said. He walked quickly to the small stream and took sustenance upon the water. Before long, all of the water had been quelled, and the feeble man had become young and *vigorous. But he was regretful, as he did not share his gift with the man that had been so generous.*

"I am sorry," he said. "I fear I have taken all of your water."

"It is all right, dear friend. I am in no need of water. I carry all that I need with me around my neck."

"Please, I must repay you for my selfishness. If you would allow me to help, I give you my hand."

"I have my feet to walk upon and my hands to eat," the traveler said. "I am sure that I have all that I need."

"I am but a lonely migrant without any possessions but my thoughts. Surely I have some knowledge that you may be in need of."

"And I am but meek, and am in no need of knowledge."

"Where is it that you travel? Perhaps I may be of assistance?"

"I seek only that which is of honest purity."

"Yes, yes. I know of the place that you seek," the vigorous man said. "Please, allow me to be your guide and lead you to your destination."

With a joyous heart, the traveler accepted the guide's assistance and followed him through the desert, traveling without end for two days and two nights. On the third day, the traveler grew weary and asked his guide, "Are you sure you know of the place I seek?"

"Yes, of course," the guide happily replied. "It is just over this hill."

Upon reaching the top of the hill, the guide pointed downward at the mountain.

"The place you seek resides there, within the mouth of the mountain."

"You will not come with me?" the traveler said.

"I am afraid the place you seek can only be found by the one who searches. I can no longer help you in your quest."

"I thank you, kind sir. I appreciate your gracious help."

"There is one last hint of knowledge that I must convey before I depart. Within the mountain, you will be confronted with three unenviable tasks.

The first is a test of your body; the second, a test of your mind; the third, a test of your heart. You must accomplish these tasks before you are allowed to walk among the purity for which you seek. But beware, for your destination will continue to elude you should you ever stray from your chosen path."

"Thank you," the traveler said again, but the guide had gone.

The traveler did not dwell on the mystery of the guide, as his lifelong quest was nearing its end, and he would soon be reunited with his lady. He walked down to the mouth of the mountain and entered without delay. Taking no rest or sustenance, the traveler walked to the mouth of the mountain and entered. For a day the traveler trekked through the darkening mountain until he reached a dead end at the base of a massive cliff. He tried to climb the cliff, but he was not strong enough.

"Oh, why must this be so difficult?" the traveler moaned.

Just then, a gollum, nearing only eight inches high with large ears that hugged his entire body, appeared through one of the small crevices in the cliff.

"Who dare disturb my rest with his moaning and whining?" the gollum asked.

"I am a traveler," the traveler spoke. "And I am seeking the great treasure that can only be found in this mountain. But I am too weak to climb the cliff and continue my journey."

"Too weak to climb?" the gollum repeated. "Then you should find another path to complete your journey."

"That might take a lifetime," the traveler said.

"And it most certainly will."

"I cannot wait that long, when I am so close already. Can you help me?"

"I can give you the strength to climb this cliff," the gollum said. "But you must do me a favor in return."

"Anything," the traveler replied back.

"You must leave everything you now carry behind and forget about it, as if you had never before owned it."

"I will do as you ask," the traveler said. And with not another word, he stripped his entire body of all of his belongings, including his lady's medallion, leaving him bare-skinned and free.

"Now climb," the gollum said.

The traveler did as he was told, and climb he did. The gollum watched as the traveler made his way to the top of the cliff and then disappeared within the crevice to resume his napping.

The traveler, having now forgotten about all of his possessions, continued walking for another day, when he came upon a door. There was writing along the edge that read as a riddle. It said, "You can only know the past when you seek the future. You can only know the future when you seek the past. One will always bring you truth, one will always lie in jest, and hidden within is the key to your quest."

The traveler puzzled over this riddle for two days, attempting to find the key. When he could not, he cried out, "Oh, why must this be so difficult?"

With those words, a dragon appeared from atop the highest cave and lowered its head to the traveler.

"Who dare disturb my rest with his moaning and whining?"

"I am a traveler," the traveler began. "And I am seeking the great treasure that can only be found in this mountain. But I cannot translate the riddle to continue my journey."

"Cannot translate the riddle?" the dragon uttered. "Then you should return to whence you came until you have mastered the art of thinking."

"That might take a lifetime," the traveler said.

"And it most certainly will."

"I cannot wait that long, when I am so close already. Can you help me?"

"I can give you the answer to this riddle," the dragon said. "But you must do me a favor in return."

"Anything," the traveler answered.

"You must trust that my word is true, and cast off all others as frauds."

"I will do as you ask," the traveler said. And with that, the dragon gave the traveler the answer to what he was seeking and the door opened.

"Thank you, kind dragon," the traveler said.

"Do not thank me," the dragon murmured. "I did you no service."

The dragon lifted its mighty head and disappeared into the darkness of the cave. The traveler hesitated no more and walked through the door. He journeyed for one final day until he reached a lake where two women sat. One woman was beautiful and lush, with vibrant eyes and a smile of warmth. The other was old and cripple, with weak eyes and a frown of sorrow.

"Do you know of the great treasure that can only be found in this mountain?" the traveler asked.

"I know of this place," the young woman said. "And only I can help you complete your journey."

"It is I who knows of this place," the old woman muttered. "And only I can help you complete your journey."

"Only one can be believed," the young woman said.

"Only one can be trusted," the old woman concluded.

"Who am I to choose?" the traveler moaned. "The young and quick, or the old and wise. Oh, why must this be so difficult? Can you help me?"

"Choose me and make me your love," the young woman said, "and we will travel to your heart's desire. For my word is true, and all other is fraud."

"Choose me, and return me to my home," the old woman said, "and I will reveal to you the truth. For I am protection, and all other is harm."

"I must think long and hard about this choice," the traveler said, and made himself a home in the far corner of the cave to think over this quandary. After three days, and with a decision in hand, he approached the women once again.

"To help the old woman might take a lifetime," the traveler said.

"And it most certainly would," the old woman said.

"But I cannot wait that long when I am so close already." And with that, the traveler went to the young woman and made love to her. When it was over, the man stood and looked upon the young woman.

"Now show me what I seek."

"I cannot," the young woman replied. "For the place you seek is only for the blind of heart." And with that, the young woman transformed into a giant snake and devoured the traveler in one bite.

"What a shame," the snake hissed.

"Indeed," the old woman replied. She then transformed into the young lady with her medallion lying upon the bosom of her broken heart.

(CHAPTER 47

I cried as the prayer concluded, but I now understood the path I was fated to travel, one that would hurt me greatly, but which would allow me to protect the ones I loved most dear and allow me my own peace in the darkness I would never escape.

Over the next several days, I sang to Ryker as much as my voice would allow and built the strength I needed to do what had to be done. By the time I reached the edge of the river, and found solace in the gloss of life bestowed upon the trees and brush around us, my soliloquies of the home and family I sought to provide him were no longer laced with tears, but of hope. The river itself wasn't as tainted in the mucky brown hue as I had been led to believe, but hinted at the glory of its youth with a highlight of soft blue and crystal white. How long it had been like this I was unsure, but it didn't matter; the earth was healing.

I laid Ryker down and took to building a bassinet out of malleable twigs, tree branches and grass while listening to the birds whistle beautifully in tune with the song of the winds. I would test its buoyancy with each stage of its construction until I was confident that it would protect my young from the dangers of the river. I spent the night carving sharp edges into the tips of several twigs and then mixed the juices from the berries that grew ripe around us with mud from the banks of the river. By the time the sky burned with its morning mist of light, I had a sufficiently workable ink and writing utensils that I used to write a letter on the back of the parchment provided to me by my Father. My thoughts poured from the tips of my fingers onto the parchment with a graceful fluidity.

When I had finished, I fed Ryker from my bosom one final time and kissed him gently with a lasting tear. After tying the parchment to the bassinet, I layered the bed with the petals of the flower and rested Ryker inside. With a kiss and a final tear, I gave him to the river.

"Goodbye my child," I prayed. "Bless ye to the bosom of our earth so that she may love you as much as I. Let the hand of fate guide you and accept the nurture of the family who will always accept you as you are."

I folded my chin to my chest and blew my son a kiss, touched with the air of my everlasting affection. I then lowered my forehead to the ground and whispered a final plea that he be found as I once had been found.

"For the love of my life eternal, Amen." When I raised my head, the bassinet had gone. I rose slowly, accepting the calm of my heart, and took the first step away from the past I could never return to. There wasn't any rest in my return to the compound, for which I was welcomed with sincere happiness. I appreciated each and every blessing, but there was only one I truly sought—only one I needed unconditionally.

I entered Danielle's room, believing for a moment that all I would find would be the serenity of absence. To my surprise—and immense pleasure—I found Danielle watching the brisk dance of the fire upon the hearth. The moment she turned to me, her tears matched the joyous emotion that liberated my own eyes. Words were unnecessary as we accepted each other's souls with a nod and the touch of our smiles. Danielle immediately took me into her arms with an apologetic embrace, but there was only one thing I needed to solidify our eternal bond.

I cradled her head in my hands, brushed my thumb across her lips and kissed her as the last lover I would ever embrace.

EPILOGUE

Cleo walked along the edge of the river watching her charge, Delilah, chase after a butterfly nearby. It seemed an ordinary day for her, assuming responsibility over Delilah after having spent the morning tending the crops. Though she spent most days in the ecclesia teaching Delilah about patience and kindness, Cleo always rewarded her with a day of simple pleasures. For Delilah, that usually meant a day under the sun, running and playing among the tall grass of the fields near the river. But unlike any other day prior, Cleo could feel something different in the air about her. As she sat at the river's edge for prayer and allowed the river to lick her toes, she caught sight of an object sailing upon the current. As it neared, the wind carried with it the small cry of an infant. Cleo quickly brought her legs up underneath her and stretched out to swipe the bassinet from the water. Within its cradle was a terrified child shaking in fear and frost.

"Lemme," Delilah said, pulling upon Cleo's arm to find a glimpse of her gift.

"Please, Delilah," Cleo said. "Remember…"

"Paythents." Delilah stepped back and stood erect with her hands cupped behind her back.

Cleo nodded after a minute's time and set the basket down between them. Upon seeing the child, Delilah lit up with glee and fell to grab him from the bassinet.

"Not yet," Cleo said, firm but pleasant. She took Delilah's hand and sat her down upon her lap. "He seems to carry a message."

Cleo untied the parchment from the side of the bassinet and read aloud to Delilah. "The traveler and his guide." She smiled in fond reminiscence.

"Read me," Delilah said emphatically.

Cleo read the prayer as a gentle song. Delilah listened thoughtfully with her head rested upon Cleo's bosom and her thumb nestled between her own tiny lips. Although she didn't understand much of it, when Cleo had finished, Delilah sat to life with the snap of applause. Cleo kissed her gently and handed her the parchment. As she ran off to sing the nonsense of what she remembered from the prayer, Cleo looked upon the child, who had found his quiet slumber, and kissed him as soft as her lips would allow. "Blissful dreams," she said.

"Cleo, Cleo," Delilah said, running up to her. "Whasts-is?" She handed the parchment back to Cleo. On the back of the prayer was another, this written in a hand quite different from that of the previous author. The ink was thick and pale, and had pealed away in several places. Nonetheless, Cleo did not have trouble reading its contents.

** ** **

Cleo, loving sister and dear friend, if you are reading this you have found the only life I am able to return to the land. As my journey comes to a close, I have been washed with many a sin, leaving only remnants of my soul untouched. Those remnants lie within the seed of my fruit. His name is Ryker Trevor Rockwell. I pray that you find it in your heart to love him as you once did me and bring him to your bosom as his own mother, teacher, sister and friend. I do wish I could do these very things of my own will, but I cannot allow my world to taint him as it has done me since my departure from the sanctity of our home. I find, as I grow into my eighteenth annual and the year of the songbird ends, that it has been a long while since I was first devoured by the snake. I fear that should I step foot among my sisters and brothers once again, I would only bring to them my fears, my biases and my indulgences, which would only hinder the development of a world I know is possible through the hand of man, and that of our Father. Give your child what he needs, what he deserves, and never forget the love I embrace upon him and the love I deign for you.

Sing sweet the lullaby of my song,

When I was given the opportunity of sight, I wasn't afraid of what I would see; I was afraid of what I would feel. And what I felt was a burning need to return to the fruit of my blindness, for only in the dark was I truly able to see.

The truest of hearts abound forever in our souls,

Madeline of the Ark

Year of the Tigress, R.H. 28

**   **   **

Cleo cleaned away her tears and kissed Ryker. "I promise," she said.

"Promisch," Delilah said in echo, repeating Cleo's kiss upon the babe.

Cleo smiled. "Come with me, sweetheart. Miss Jezebel awaits us."

Delilah took hold of Cleo's hand, the other of which took hold of the bassinet, and they walked from the river with the sun falling behind them, leaving the wind to return the prayers to the river where they belonged.

ABOUT THE AUTHOR

BRYAN CARON is a multi-talented, award-winning artist with works in several mediums, including print, film and design. After acquiring a bachelor's degree in creative writing and an associate's degree in computer graphic design, Bryan studied filmmaking and film editing while working at a performing arts studio in San Diego, California. He took this knowledge to write, direct and edit films under his banner, Divine Trinity Films. Soon after, he would team up with the Fallbrook Film Factory, a non-profit film consortium, to continue his growth in the areas of writing, directing and editing, all the while fleshing out his talents in fiction writing and working as a graphic designer.

His works as writer and director include the short films *My Necklace, Myself* (Best Screenplay, Short Film, 2009 Treasure Coast International Film Festival) and *12*, the feature film *Secrets of the Desert Nymph*, and the commercial *Charlie's Ticket,* which ran on dozens of television stations and in movie theaters in San Diego County to advertise the Fallbrook International Film Festival. Works as editor include the short film *Puzzle Box* and *No Books*, the first of several episodes he has edited for the online sketch-series, *Treelore Theatre*.

Bryan currently resides in Riverside County.

www.divinetrinityfilms.com